SOLOMON'S TEARS

A Pale Woods Suspense

Courtnee Turner Hoyle

Pale Woods

To my children,
may you never see shadows where there are none

To the ghosts in my mind,
please don't talk all at once

To my daddy and pap-paw,
keep watching over me, and let me know you're there

Solomon's Tears

A Pale Woods Suspense

Copyright © August 2, 2022

Erwin, TN

by Courtnee Turner Hoyle

Library of Congress Control Number: 2022907482

Print IBSN 979-8-9855408-5-7

E-book IBSN: 979-8-9855408-6-4

This book is a work of fiction. Names, characters, businesses, places, events, and incidents are the product of the author's imagination or used in a fictitious manner. Any similarities or resemblance to actual persons, living or dead, events, or places is entirely coincidental.

Cover Design: Taylor Dawn, Sweet15 Designs, LLC

Author Photo: Tosha Cannon

Solomon's Tears Playlist

1. "Lullaby" Shaun Mullins

2. "Paint It Black" Rolling Stones

3. "Iris" Goo Goo Dolls

4. "Walking On Broken Glass" Annie Lennox

5. "Zombie" Cranberries

6. "Freak" Sub Urban

7. "Sweet Dreams" Eurythmics

8. "Hotel California" The Eagles

9. "When the Levee Breaks" Led Zeppelin

10. "Only Happy When It Rains" Garbage

11. "One" Metallica

12. "(Don't Fear) The Reaper" Blue Oyster Cult

13. "Iron Man" Black Sabbath

14. "Sonny Came Home" Shawn Colvin

15. "In the Air Tonight" Phil Collins

A Letter to My Readers

Dear Reader,

Thank you for plucking my book from the forest of titles available! I'll do my best not to disappoint you.

Solomon's Tears is a stand-alone novel, but readers of my previous books may recognize several of the characters from my other works. Don't worry! You won't ruin any of my other novels by reading this one first. If you like this story, you may want to read My Brother's Keeper. Two of the characters in this book are in the pages of that award-winning novel.

My stories are set in my hometown area, Unicoi County, Tennessee. I enjoy the Appalachian Mountains and valleys, and I know them well enough to capture the traditions and lovely scenery. There are books in which my county is not specifically mentioned, but the people who know the area can recognize it in my work.

The story that follows this letter can be somewhat dark at times, but I ask you to remember the only thing left in the box Pandora was given after she opened it. I *hope* you enjoy Solomon's Tears!

Your friend in the written world,
Courtnee

Prologue

My baby lay motionless. No matter how much I willed the eyes to open, or begged to see a breath inflate the small, rounded belly, my little darling stayed still. Tiny fingers wound into a palm, heavily indented with lifelines of unrealized lifetimes. Had the hand been reaching for me? How long did the fingers stretch before the attempt was futile?

I had so much hope for the future of my children. Each life held a promise and potential, golden and shining, but my baby would never hold a diploma high in celebration or call me with the news of a treasured partner.

Where had I been when my baby had needed me? What was I doing when my precious child had looked to me as a safeguard against the swirling abyss of death? Was I even aware, or was this just another consequence of the illness that had been genetically bequeathed to me? I was my mother's daughter. I knew that the occasional blackouts were a symptom of the same disease that had taken over my mother's mind. I had always condemned her for letting it possess her, but now I was guilty of the same inaction. I had heard the voices. I had seen the signs.

I hadn't wanted to be taken away from my children. I feared sitting passively in a numb room with medicated zombies as I was slowly erased from the memories of my children. The victim of my denial and subsequent neglect was my own treasured child.

I was supposed to be the protector, but I hadn't even heard a cry. I was right there, and I never heard a sound. Had there been pain or screams for me while I was in that other state, that place my mind went when the disease invaded my consciousness? I was the one who was meant to keep the shadows away, but my child, my sweet baby, had been swallowed by the darkness.

I was there, and I didn't even remember how it happened.

Chapter One

Present

At first, Ketron thought she had forgotten one of her children at home. A quick check confirmed that they were all there. Bonnie was with her father, but she would return in a couple of days. The nagging feeling that her "kid count" was one short wouldn't leave her alone, though, and it had nothing to do with Bonnie's absence. She had several little people to keep up with, so she continued to walk, her brain still nagging her about checking for one more than the four children with her.

The white clouds cupped the sky on the muggy July evening. The sun dipped behind the mountains in the middle of their walk but left behind the remnants of its light in orange and red hues. She moved a strand of her blonde hair behind her ear, and it dragged across the perspiration on her forehead.

Ketron shifted the baby to face outward as she walked holding her. Amelia was happy to remain free to yell at the birds and watch her siblings.

"No! Sonny!" Ketron yelled. She stared in disbelief as her four-year-old jiggled the chain on the fence that surrounded the baseball field. Winslow and Nora ran to catch their little brother before he stretched the chain far enough to wriggle his body onto the field. When he saw them, he ran down the length of the fence. Winslow broke away from Nora, cutting off his brother before he made it out of sight. Sonny swung his arms defiantly between them, but he allowed himself to be herded back to his mother.

"You can't run off like that," Ketron scolded him, wishing her husband had been there to help. She didn't like to rely on her children to babysit each other.

"I want to play," Sonny pouted. He crossed his arms and refused to move.

"I can wait here all day." It was an empty threat, but Ketron raised her eyebrows and stood silently, waiting for his next move.

"Okay!" Sonny dropped his posture and sulked down the side of the road.

A car pulled up and slowed behind them. The baby turned and waved frantically, making noises that sounded simultaneously like "hi" and "hey."

"Is that Amelia?"

Amelia opened and closed her hands in greeting until the action became her primary focus.

"Hey, Mrs. Franks! Are you back from your trip?" Ketron asked.

Her neighbor shook her head, her silver hair bouncing lightly against her shoulders. She pushed her glasses back up her nose. "You know me. I'll be back to the city before long." She made a show of looking around. "Where's Marvin?"

Ketron envied Mrs. Franks's long metropolitan trips. She wondered what it was like to live in two totally separate worlds. "He's at the house." She didn't add that her husband was probably finishing a six pack.

Mrs. Franks flicked a mosquito off her steering wheel. "Well, he works all week, so he probably just wants to relax."

And drink himself into a stupor, Ketron thought, but she said, "I'm sure you're right."

"When are you going to let me hold that baby? Is she walking yet?"

Ketron was used to those questions. Since the birth of her fourth child, she had kept her children closer to her. Everyone thought it was post-partum depression, but Ketron hid her true reasons, even from those who knew her best. She chose to answer the latter question. "She takes a couple of steps here and there. I'm in no hurry for her to grow up."

Mrs. Franks nodded like a seasoned mother. "It was like that with my last child, too."

Ketron hadn't said that Amelia was her last child, but a lot of people in her community believed she'd had enough children, and they were happy to push their feelings onto her. Ketron extended a tight-lipped smile.

A car halted behind her, and Mrs. Franks waved as she pulled away.

Amelia doubled over, and Ketron worried that she was putting too much pressure on her infant's stomach. She struggled to pull the baby upright and hold Sonny's hand.

"Hey, Sonny! Hold my hand and you can look at my rock," Winslow offered.

Ketron was thankful for her son's help. She smiled at his effort, and he gave her the self-sacrificing look that all older siblings wear at one point or another.

The children bolted up the hill that led to their small, ranch-styled brick home, and Ketron moved as swiftly as Amelia would let her go. The baby had been finished with their walk before they had gotten into town, and she tried to free herself from her mother's hold by walking up her ribs and bending backwards.

Sonny banged on the door, but he moved aside for Ketron to open it with her key. Cooler air rushed out and started to dry the perspiration from their two-mile excursion. The refrigerator was thrown open and Winslow divided the freezer pops, offering the first of his popsicle to Amelia. The baby put her whole mouth over it, leaving a large portion of her saliva. Winslow ate it anyway, undisturbed by his sibling's excessive bodily fluids.

"Can my friend have one, too?" Sonny asked.

Ketron smoothed his wavy blonde hair, pulling her fingers through some of the looser knots. He had a perfect button nose that reminded most people of her husband, but his eyes were a light blue-green he shared with his mother. "Who's your friend?"

"You know, my friend." Sonny stared at her as if the answer were obvious.

Thinking he was attempting to exploit another popsicle from her, Ketron replied, "Well, tell your friend that he has to eat more dinner if he wants a popsicle."

Sonny rolled his eyes. "He doesn't like broccoli."

Ketron laughed, letting Amelia down and hugging her son. "How do you know that your friend doesn't like broccoli?"

"No one likes broccoli," he said seriously.

"I like broccoli," Nora piped up. "But not with cheese."

Ketron smiled at her daughter. Nora was a people-pleaser. She and Winslow were so different physically and socially, even though they were twins. Nora had chocolate brown hair and honey-brown eyes, and Winslow sported a strawberry blonde fade and cerulean eyes. Nora was shy and easy going, but despite his occasional kindnesses, Winslow ruled the house with his steady stream of demands and the pouts that followed if his requests were not met instantaneously.

"Broccoli is gross," Winslow commented. "I hate it."

"We don't use the h-word in the house," Ketron reminded him. He rolled his eyes and stormed off to his room, stomping louder with every step.

Ketron took a deep breath. It would have been nice to have had someone to back her up on her rules, but her husband hardly spent time with his family. He would occasionally surface from his room to say a few words and sneak a beer into the pocket of his basketball shorts, but Ketron was expected to handle the household by herself. Her husband believed that the money he brought in from his forty-hour job every week was the only contribution he needed to make. At first, Ketron had tried to encourage his involvement, but as the tension grew between them, she found herself relishing the time she had without him.

Ketron busied herself with her nightly chores as the children played. She washed the dishes and folded the never-ending pile of laundry. She was on her hands and knees under the table when she heard wood scraping against Marvin's door frame.

"Daddy!" Sonny cried, running to his father. His father bent down and rubbed his head. "Will you watch dinosaurs on television with me?"

"Maybe in a minute, buddy."

Sonny ran back to the couch to watch the same movie for the tenth time that week, and Marvin asked Ketron, "Why do you clean the floors like that? You have a mop and a broom."

Ketron willed herself to have the patience to answer him evenly. "It puts me on the same level as Amelia. That way I can see anything that might be on the floor before she puts it in her mouth."

He closed the refrigerator door and faced her, a cylindrical bulge protruding from his pocket. Ketron preferred for him to hide the beer from the children, but she sometimes wished that he'd hide it from her, too.

Sweat dotted Marvin's forehead below a marginally receding hairline, and he was too short to hide the extra weight his favorite beverage was giving him. His clean-shaven face already showed evidence of broken blood vessels, but when he looked in the mirror, he couldn't see the ways his habit had changed him.

"You love that baby, don't you?" he stated placidly, weaving ever so slightly.

"I love them all," Ketron returned, turning back to her task.

"I know. I just mean that you ain't in another room readin' or playin' with the kids, so cleanin' the floor must be important to you."

Ketron winced at his speech. For the most part, they had both been raised in Northeast Tennessee, but Ketron had chosen to be more precise with her language. She tried to model better speech patterns for her children, but Marvin had abandoned his efforts to speak more clearly a few weeks after they moved into their new home.

Amelia toddled into the room and climbed onto Ketron's back. She eased out from under the table to prevent the baby from hitting it.

Most of the time, Marvin ignored Amelia, because he said that she was too clingy and whiny, but he took advantage of Amelia's good mood. "There's Daddy's girl!"

The baby responded to his happy face and shimmied off Ketron's back. She clapped her hands, and Marvin joined her. She reached for him, and Ketron swooped her up. "I bet you need a diaper change," she told the baby.

"Why do you always do that?" Marvin demanded. "You take her away from me when I'm playing with her."

Because you're always drinking when you're here, and I don't want you to accidently hurt her, Ketron thought, but she didn't say it.

Marvin followed her into the next room. Winslow breezed past him to fill a glass of water. Marvin patted his shoulder, but Winslow barely acknowledged him. Marvin didn't fool the boy. He was eight years old, and his father's drinking had forced him to mature early in many ways.

"She likes me," Marvin insisted, continuing their argument. "You can let me hold her once in a while."

So you can drop her.

"You know, I want to play with her, too."

Is that so? You didn't show interest in her for ten months because she cried every time I handed her to you.

"I'd like to rock her, and tell her stories, like you do. I could tell her how she got her name."

Ketron scoffed, finally irritated enough to speak. "You won that fight and then you didn't acknowledge her for months."

"I just let you do what you do." He motioned over Sonny's and Amelia's heads. "You know how you get after you have a baby. You're territorial."

Some of that was true, but Ketron felt a pull to keep her children safe from their father's newly developed habit. He'd always leaned toward one addiction or another, and even though beer was legal, she didn't want the children to think it was acceptable for their father to drink around them.

"Why do you get that look on your face when we talk about her name? The delivery nurses all loved it."

"I'm sure they did," Ketron snapped. "I'll bet they hear it all the time."

"And Bonnie is so original." He drew out the o until Ketron was almost embarrassed for him.

Ketron hated it when Marvin brought her teenager into an argument. Bonnie and Marvin were barely on speaking terms, and Bonnie wasn't even at home. "I made the mistake of letting the father of my child pick that name, too."

"And I guess we know what happened there," he shot back.

Ketron didn't like to disagree with her husband in front of the children. Before they'd moved, Ketron and Marvin had argued in the basement of their home so the children wouldn't be privy to their harsh words. She hoped to end the argument by holding her tongue and it paid off. Marvin lost interest in pushing her buttons and stalked to his room. She let out a breath she hadn't known she was holding when she heard his video game resume.

Ketron finished her housework as quickly as the children allowed. Winslow needed help with his shower, Sonny enlisted her for a quick dinosaur battle, and Amelia wanted her to stop and clap every time she toddled a couple of steps.

She threw Sonny and Amelia into the shower with her, much later than she would admit to another mom, and they bathed quickly. Ketron balanced the baby in her arms while she twisted in the awkward angles that helped her shave her legs. It was summer, and she couldn't skip it if she wanted to wear shorts.

She was rinsing the soap from her face when she heard Sonny say, "Stop it!"

"Stop what?" She rubbed the water out of her eyes.

He shifted irritably into a crouched position. *He must be really tired,* she thought. *I wonder if he dozed off.*

The baby was having a hard time holding her head on her neck, and the steady hum of the shower was lulling Ketron into a relaxed state. She stepped out of the shower with the baby and let Sonny play while she and Amelia dressed. He jolted back to life, bouncing a triceratops through the jets of water.

After their shower, Ketron played a card game with the older children while Amelia dozed in her arms. She threw a sheet down for Sonny, Amelia, and herself on the chaise lounge of their sectional couch and added two pillows for Sonny and her. She had only told one other person that she hadn't slept in the same bed with Marvin since before Amelia was born. When she and Marvin had talked about it, Ketron had used the excuse that she needed to get up with the children at night without disturbing him, and Marvin had relished the freedom it gave him to play video games as long as he wished.

Sonny cuddled against Ketron's back, and she cradled Amelia. The distant clicking of the game controller and the steady hum of the air conditioning unit were the only sounds that accompanied the gentle puffs of baby breath. It was a mixture of sounds that always sent her into an easy slumber.

Chapter Two

Present

Ketron was startled awake. At first, she didn't know what had pulled her from her heavy sleep.

"Go away!" Sonny mumbled.

Ketron turned over, cradling her son. "What's wrong, Sonny?"

"Nothing," he spoke irritably, and she wondered if his dream was an extension of the one he had experienced in the shower. She kissed him and moved to her back.

She couldn't drift back into a doze, so she went over the list of things she had to do for the day, week, and month. Anxiety over her upcoming appointment with Dr. Richards consumed her thoughts. *How could she tell him that she was thinking about leaving her husband?* They had talked about it over a series of appointments after Marvin and Ketron had moved into their new house, but the psychiatrist had dismissed her concerns. He questioned her reasons for leaving a strong male provider and alluded to her inability to maintain an intimate connection with a partner. She had decided to exclude the topic in their future sessions, but she needed to revisit it.

Marvin's drinking had gotten out of control. He went to work sober, but he'd pop the tab on his first beer within moments of getting home. He put it in the garage while he mowed or slid it into a drawer or under the bed when he played video games in his bedroom. Every time Ketron mentioned alcoholism, Marvin would turn her words into a joke, and she would laugh along, nervous about upsetting him while he was in an altered state.

The children noticed his slurred speech and erratic behavior. Winslow and Nora skirted him, trying to avoid his notice. When he paid attention to them, they hurriedly agreed with him and found an excuse to go back to their room.

Ketron slipped out of Amelia's and Sonny's holds and tip-toed down the hall to check on the twins. The streetlight just outside their window negated the need for a nightlight in their room. Nora slept peacefully on the bottom bunk with her arm wrapped around a baby doll in her old purple tutu. Winslow had his foot dangling off the railing of his top bunk and his action figures were positioned in a battle at the edge above his head. He breathed in soft, rhythmic sounds, and Ketron envied his ease. She hoped she would be able to fall asleep again soon.

She rubbed a sore spot on her calf and felt a new bruise forming. She didn't remember hitting anything with that part of her leg recently, but it wasn't uncommon for her to forget bumps with the counter or brief encounters with sharp toys, so she dismissed it.

Muffled sounds came from Marvin's room. A string of curses and a rattling controller told her that he hadn't drunk enough beer to pass out yet. She decided she needed to talk about his insatiable appetite for alcohol with another person again, and in case Dr. Richards was no help, she concluded that she'd ask for the opinion of someone else.

Chapter Three

Present

"I could have told you that," Shauna said, picking the cuticles on her unpainted fingernails. "He's an addict."

Ketron had just finished explaining the situation to her friend. "But it's only beer."

"Sell it to someone who's buying. You don't think I notice when you suddenly drop a play date, or when I see Marvin red-faced and hardly able to hold up his head." She stared at Ketron. "Give me more credit than that. You know my history."

Shauna's father had been addicted to drugs, and after her mother's death, she'd ran away with a girlfriend to the west coast. They spent years repeating the same patterns as their fathers until Shauna's girlfriend was shot in front of her. She only loosely referenced that part of her life, so Ketron drew conclusions from an online newspaper write up about the incident and the rumors about a bad drug deal.

Shauna broke from the seriousness of the conversation to scold her son. "Stop it, Matty! No one will want to play with you if you hit them over the head with your truck." Matty dropped the truck and glared at his mother. Shauna stood up and put her hands on her hips. Ketron stifled a giggle as her best friend had a standoff with her toddler. Finally, Matty turned around and jumped into the pool, his splash indicating his last word in the argument.

Shauna grabbed her towel, tried to smooth it over her lawn chair, and slung it on the ground. "He's lucky I'm a changed person," she laughed, letting her anger drop with the towel.

"You've really come a long way," Ketron agreed.

"Who knew I would have a kid. Especially five years ago."

Ketron remembered when she met Shauna. Her friend was addicted to heroin, dehydrated, and sleeping in the basement of a local church. Against Marvin's reservations, Ketron took Shauna into their home, drove her to addiction counseling, and was a reference for her first legal job at a local distribution center. Ketron had graduated with a degree in psychology, and she used everything she learned in her classes, and every ounce of her compassion, to pull Shauna out of the depths of her disease and into a healthy, sustainable environment. Her friend sped through recovery, a success she attributed to Ketron's unwavering faith in her, and in six months she leased her own apartment. She met Luke, her neighbor, after she moved in, and a year later, Ketron was Shauna's maid-of-honor in a small wedding by the river.

"I brought you ladies some homemade lemonade." Luke placed a pitcher and two cups between them.

Shauna kissed her husband when he bent down. "You can join us."

"It sounded like the two of you were having a serious discussion." Ketron saw the wink that was only meant for Shauna. He had heard more than he wanted to hear. "I think I'll go play with the kids." He ran to the edge of the pool and jumped, landing in the water as a cannon ball. Nora shrieked when she was sprayed in the face but recovered quickly when she realized the offender was Matty's father.

"How did you do it?" Ketron asked. Shauna raised her eyebrows over her sunglasses.

"Luke. You found someone who loved you, and he keeps loving you."

"Well, I didn't try to save him." She set her glass back on the table. "Instead of trying to have a relationship with someone who was emotionally wounded, I opted for a man who was ready for commitment."

Ketron shifted uncomfortably. "I didn't know what I was getting into."

"Yeah, you did." Shauna sighed, stretching and placing her hands behind her head.

Ketron envied her friend's coffee-colored skin and voluptuous curves. She took off her sunglasses, and even without makeup, Shauna's long eyelashes nearly rested on her eyebrows. Shauna had bragged about her friend's height, and she loved Ketron's naturally blonde hair, but Ketron had to keep reapplying sunscreen to her ivory skin and her freckles couldn't be counted.

Shauna picked up her towel and cleaned her sunglasses with it. "Marvin had just lost his brother to drugs, and there you were, ready to take care of him."

"I was a good friend."

"Sure, a good friend that overlooked the rigs she found in the bathroom."

"I thought he was diabetic."

Shauna turned the smile that sprang to her lips into a forced frown. "You were pregnant, and you wanted a father for your children. You thought you could take the scraps that were left of him and mold him into a family man."

"We've been married a long time. He's changed."

Shauna chuckled without mirth. "Yeah, he's changed. He's changed his habit. He's gone from meth to Suboxone, and now he's drinking on top of the Suboxone. How did he even get it anyway? He never used opioids."

Ketron assumed that her husband lied to get Suboxone. She had been fully against any drug, but her husband had gotten a prescription anyway. When she spoke out about it, he told her that she could 'deal with it or leave his house.' That had been six months ago.

"I stayed on it for a year," Shauna admitted. "I was jumpy, and the nerve pills the doctors prescribed with it made me a zombie."

"You were a little out of it for a while." Ketron had worried that Shauna would lose her job because of the frequency with which she nodded out. Thankfully, the business was fast-paced, and Shauna stayed in motion. She stopped taking the nerve pills within weeks of receiving them, opting to distract herself from her drug cravings with her job and a couple of college classes each semester. She was able to quit her job after marrying Luke, but she continued taking classes.

"How is the world of storytelling?"

Shauna drew in a breath. "It's boring and completely unoriginal. The old biddies in my classes think that they're doing me a favor by passing down stories about knitting and cats."

"It sounds unimaginative."

"It is." She took another sip of lemonade and prompted Ketron to try hers. Ketron drank most of the glass. She hadn't realized she was so thirsty. "They don't enjoy my murder mysteries or true crime stories."

"They're old, Shauna. They want to go to sleep at night without one eye open."

Shauna waved her hand at Ketron. "You're getting me off the subject. We were discussing your thoughts on leaving your husband."

"I never said I would leave him."

"You didn't have to. You're finally talking to me about Marvin's habits." Her eyebrows peaked over her glasses again. "Even though I would have been a fool not to have known about them."

"I wanted someone to tell me..." Ketron trailed off, unclear about what she really needed.

"You wouldn't have come to me if you expected me to tell you to stand by and put up with him. Especially after hearing about how he acts now."

"He doesn't hit me," Ketron defended, "And the children like him."

"What message does that send to the kids?" Shauna asked. "What kind of relationships will Bonnie, Nora, and Amelia have if they watch their mother placate a drug- or alcohol-addicted father." Ketron's gaze settled on Nora as she pulled Amelia in her pool floaty. She couldn't look at her friend. "You have to tell him that he needs a serious recovery program, or you need to leave him."

"He'll get joint custody, and I can't trust him with the children." Ketron didn't realize that she had put so much thought into the idea until she'd said it.

"I think we both know that he'll only want Sonny."

Ketron cringed at her friend's words. The children were still in the pool, safely out of earshot. "He still loves them."

"Sonny is his favorite child. He'll only want him. In fact, if he hangs around that crowd he and his brother sold drugs with, then he may just take Sonny and run off one day."

"Sonny would hate him for it."

"Maybe," she said, twirling a piece of her raven hair around her finger. "But he could tell Sonny a story that he would believe after years of hearing it." Shauna flipped on her side. "Look, why don't you just mention a recovery program to him. Maybe he'll agree to it."

"You don't think he will, though, do you?"

"I doubt it. He has everything the way he likes it. Why would he change?"

Before she could ask Shauna to elaborate, Winslow carried a slippery Amelia to Ketron and dropped the baby in her lap. "She's tired of swimming," he announced, and padded back to the pool.

Amelia burrowed her head into Ketron's chest until she found a nipple. Ketron leaned back with the baby, positioning the umbrella on her chair to cast a shadow over them. The baby fell asleep almost immediately, and her head rolled onto Ketron's stomach.

"She is such a pretty baby," Shauna remarked. "I wish you would have named her instead of letting Marvin do it." She brushed Amelia's curly blond locks behind her ear. "She doesn't deserve to have to carry around his mother's name."

"Her name is okay," Ketron tried to argue, but her words fell flat.

"Your heart was set on a name, but his mother died—if you can even call her a mother—and you caved."

"I didn't cave. We had a conversation, and he swayed my opinion."

"You caved," Shauna repeated. She lowered her voice. "He wanted another boy, and you thought you had to make it up to him when you had a girl." Shauna grabbed her suntan oil and smoothed it over her legs. "It's just another reason that the two of you aren't good for each other anymore."

Ketron recalled a time when she and Marvin had been a functional couple. "You remember when things were good, though, don't you?"

Shauna stopped rubbing oil on her body. "I remember that he listened to you. He respected you." She smoothed the rest of the liquid over her arms. "I also remember that you did everything for him. He went to work, but you called about insurance for him, you paid for the specialist when he was convinced that he had gall bladder issues, and you warmed his slippers for him to wear as soon as he got home."

"I have kind of slacked off on my wifely duties," Ketron laughed.

"Yeah, okay," Shauna returned. "You have five children. You cook, clean, and make sure that their needs are met. He thought everything could stay the same, even with a bunch of little kids running around. He only has himself to blame if he wanted a mother instead of a wife."

Sonny stalked out of the pool, carrying one of his "long neck" dinosaurs. He nudged Amelia to the side and claimed a place on his mother. Soft snores escaped his pouted lips within moments.

Once it was clear that he was asleep, Shauna motioned to Sonny. "You're going to have to watch that one. Part of him realizes that he's his father's favorite child, and if you aren't careful, he'll think he's entitled to more than you give him."

Ketron stared at her sleeping son and believed that he deserved the best of everything.

Shauna read into the loving look she gave Sonny. "It's our job to make sure they're healthy, safe, and well-adjusted. We don't have to give in to *everything* they want."

"I don't."

Shauna placed her hand on Ketron's arm. "I saw the way he pushed his sister over to make room for himself. He sees the way Marvin acts around the baby and you. Sonny treats you like a glorified servant, and I have never seen him respond to Amelia with more than casual indifference. Does he tell her that he loves her?"

The conversation had taken an uncomfortable turn. "He's four."

"And Matty's three. He tells us he loves us all the time."

Nora erupted in wails. "I didn't do anything!" Winslow cried out.

Ketron took a deep breath and closed her eyes. "I'm sorry. I think that's my cue to go home."

Shauna helped her balance Amelia, and Luke carried Sonny to the van. On the way, Nora spilled a long and detailed story about every offense Winslow had made in the pool.

Shauna stood and waited until the children were loaded while Matty swung around one of her legs. "I'll be here no matter what you decide. I have the cottage out back if you need it. It only has one bedroom, but it may help if you need somewhere to stay while you look for your own place."

Ketron slid into the van and embraced the cool air streaming out of the vents. Sonny and Amelia stayed asleep, and Nora and Winslow soon joined them. Ketron drove around town, taking in the new Independence Day banners and the improved store fronts. She needed the drive, and she hoped to clear her head before her children demanded her attention. Her mind rolled around so many questions, and she didn't know the answers to any of them.

Chapter Four

Present

Ketron was making doughnuts in the kitchen when Sonny asked if he could help. He brought the plant butter and yogurt to her, and he stirred the milk and cinnamon into the batter. He was too impatient to wait until the mixture was cooked, so she gave him a large spoonful in a bowl. She asked him to eat it at the dining room table, but he detoured to his father's room. Realizing she had lost the battle, she spooned more of the batter into the doughnut maker, careful to keep Amelia away from it.

Another batch of dough was in the maker, and she was feeding small bites of doughnut to the baby when she saw a small figure crawl under the dining room table. He was dressed in yellow and about the same size as Sonny, so she thought it was him. But Sonny wasn't wearing yellow that day, and Winslow and Nora were singing church hymns in their room.

Ketron shifted Amelia on her hip and peered over the counter. No one was under the table. She was unable to completely dismiss it, though, so she turned off the doughnut maker and looked fully under the table. No one was there.

She almost called for Sonny to come out of hiding, but she checked her husband's room for him first. Sonny was licking a spoon, and he was wearing a blue superhero pajama suit.

Marvin was pasted to his television, completely absorbed in his zombie game. "Are the doughnuts ready?" Sonny asked.

"Not yet, but maybe we can go check on them."

"He's fine," Marvin said, realizing the reason for Ketron's suggestion.

"He shouldn't be in here with the blood and violence."

"It's a *video game*."

"Let's go, Sonny." Ketron added a bright note to his name when she spoke it.

"Just go with her, son," Marvin huffed, without looking away from the digital blood and gore. "I'm tired of hearing her mouth." Ketron led Sonny out of the room and pulled the door shut. "My son won't be a sissy," he mumbled as she shut the door. Thankfully, Sonny was too far away to hear him.

Ketron pushed in the doughnut maker's plug and waited for the light. She told Sonny to count until the light went off. He could only count to forty-nine, so he'd start back at one each time he ran out of numbers.

Ketron's mind drifted to the child she thought she saw crawl under the table. *Had it been a trick of the sunlight? Had she heard the child as well as seen him?*

"Mommy?"

Ketron jerked out of daze. Sonny was staring at her with doughnut batter crusting over his mouth. "The light's on."

Ketron tried to put it out of her mind, but the image revisited her throughout the day. She was convinced that she had seen a child Sonny's size crawl under the table, and the more she thought about it, the more she believed it hadn't been Sonny.

Chapter Five

Present

"You're certain that you saw the child," Dr. Richards asked.

As she put it down, Ketron's plastic cup wobbled on the wooden coffee table before it settled, and she leaned back on the couch. It was stiff, with an intricate blue and gold diamond pattern. She believed a couch in a psychiatrist's office should be more welcoming and relaxing. Four fluffy pillows filled out the sides of the sofa, but the cushion was thin and unforgiving.

"Yes, I saw him crawl under the dining room table."

"Him?" His silver eyebrows shot up over his simple black frames.

Ketron squirmed. She couldn't explain to the doctor how she knew the child was a boy.

Dr. Richards wrote on his notepad. She watched his spray-tanned face, but he didn't commit to a smile or frown, so she was unsure what he had deduced. "Are you certain that it wasn't Sonny?"

"He was in his father's bedroom."

"He could have played a trick on you. Children like to play games of hide-and-go-seek."

Ketron had thought about that, too. "I didn't see him sneak back, and he wouldn't have had enough time to change out of the yellow pajamas. Sonny doesn't even have yellow pajamas."

Dr. Richards scribbled something else. It made her nervous when he recorded his observations during their meetings. She wondered what he wrote. *Could he be listing the ways she was unfit for her children?*

"Well?" she prompted. "What do you think?"

Dr. Richards sucked in a breath and held his hands out benevolently. "It doesn't really matter what I think, but since you asked, I believe it was nothing more than a trick of the eyes."

Ketron exhaled the breath she had been holding. "I don't need to be worried?"

He tapped his pen against the yellow notepad absent-mindedly. "Certainly not yet." The pen stopped tapping. "Wait. Did the little boy tell you to do anything?"

"No. I barely caught him crawling under the table."

Dr. Richards reached out for her hands. He meant well, but she still felt uncomfortable touching him in the silent room. "Your mother's disease may not affect you."

Ketron took his hand. "I know, but I don't want to end up like her."

He released her and pulled his appointment book from under the table. "It can skip a generation, but I understand your concern. No one really knew how sick she was, except you, until..." He trailed off, choosing not to start another topic when their session was ending.

Ketron planned an appointment for the following week, continuing the promise she'd made to her husband when she had been at the lowest point of her life. She saw Dr. Richards for fifty hours a year, and sometimes she felt like she talked to him more than she spoke to Marvin. She hadn't even brought up her thoughts about divorce. She was too nervous that he would dismiss it. The moments that the conversation had veered to her mother had been uncomfortable enough.

She ran across the street to the small skate park. Winslow and Nora took turns going down a small ramp on a Tinker Bell skateboard, and Sonny rotated his scooter on its front wheels. Matty kept bumping into him with his tricycle, but Sonny stared straight ahead, willing himself not to yell at a child younger than him. Shauna sat on one of the white wooden benches, bouncing Amelia on her leg.

"What did Dr. Crackpot wiggle loose in your brain today?"

Ketron liked her friend's sense of humor. It was Shauna's way of opening a conversation without pushing her into details.

"I told him about the little boy I saw. He thinks the lights were playing tricks on me."

Shauna rolled it around in her mind. "Yeah. Maybe. You haven't been living there long, so you're not used to the way the reflections from the windows catch your eyes."

"He didn't think I was hallucinating."

Shauna put her arm around her, and she could smell sweat and tea tree oil. "Oh, Ketron, you didn't tell me you were thinking about your mom's sickness."

"She saw people who weren't there."

"Yeah, but you told me that she talked to them, too."

Amelia reached for her mother, and Shauna passed the baby to Ketron. "I guess I'll just have to watch myself."

"You have more people around you." Shauna patted her hand. "He may be cooped up in his room a lot now, but Marvin stays in the same house, and Winslow and Nora haven't told me that you're acting weird. You've got a good friend" —she wiggled her eyebrows to emphasize the point— "who looks out for you, and a lot of moms at the twins' dance studio seem to really like you. Any one of us would notice if something was off."

Ketron shook her head. She hadn't really been aware of her mother's decent from managing her illness to allowing it to fully consume her. She had been too worried about making everything appear normal that she couldn't remember the true onset of her mother's most alarming symptoms. She thought her mother might have stopped taking her medication around the time Ketron was ten, but it could have been even earlier than she remembered.

"And if none of us saw the signs, your father's good buddy would notice." Shauna nodded her head at Dr. Richard's practice. "Why do you see him anyway? You realize he's biased."

Ketron agreed with her friend, but her hands were tied. After the incident four years ago, she had promised Marvin that she would return to regular therapy sessions, and her father would only finance it if she saw his old fraternity brother.

"My father won't pay for me to go anywhere else."

"That's a load of—" Shauna stopped herself and smiled at Sonny who had briefly cycled into their range of conversation. She lowered her voice. "Why won't Marvin pay for it? Doesn't his work insurance cover therapy?"

"His work insurance has too many hoops to jump through for a good psychiatrist because of my pre-existing condition."

Shauna pursed her lips. She prepared herself to broach a subject Ketron always avoided. "Why did you tell them about it?"

"It's in my medical history. I can't hide it." Ketron busied herself with the baby, fusing over buttons that were already securely fastened.

Shauna sensed her friend's discomfort and changed the subject quickly. "All I'm saying is that it was a long time ago, and it shouldn't have to follow you the rest of your life.

"Did you talk to him about leaving Marvin?"

Ketron looked up and scanned the skate park. All the children were playing well together, but they'd need to get out of the July sun soon. "No. We didn't get to it today."

Shauna recognized the excuse and got up. She adjusted a perfectly fitting helmet on Matty's head. Ketron took the chance to prepare for a subject that would be less upsetting.

"I saw Mrs. Franks," she said when Shauna rejoined her. "She's back from Paris, but I think she's leaving to go back to New York soon."

"Great. Maybe you can go with her."

Ketron closed her mouth with a pop.

Shauna shook her head and sat back down. "Look, I'm not sorry about what I said. You're a good person, and you deserve better."

"I'm okay, Shauna. He doesn't hit me and he's a good father."

"How is he a father?" Shauna lowered her voice to a hissing whisper so the children wouldn't hear, but Winslow had picked up on her body language. He stayed on the ramp, watching Shauna, as his siblings and Matty played around him. "He goes to work, and pays the bills, but does he know Winslow has a new loose tooth or what cereal Nora likes to eat? Has he ever changed Amelia's diaper?"

"I thought you liked him?"

"I liked him five years ago." She threw up her hands. "I even liked him a year ago, but that was when he listened to you, and he respected your decisions. He's changed, and you're to blame for some of it."

Ketron stood up with Amelia on her hip. "What?"

"You did everything for him, and when you had Sonny and Amelia you had to give them most of the attention you were giving to him."

"Can we go home now?" Winslow asked. He looked from Shauna to Ketron, aware that there was tension. Ketron had been so involved in their argument that she hadn't noticed her son was within earshot of their discussion until he spoke.

"We were just packing up," Shauna responded brightly, handing Ketron the diaper bag. As they walked to their vehicles, Ketron let go of her anger, but she could feel Shauna's indignation rolling off her in waves hotter than summer heat, and she knew the conversation was far from over.

Chapter Six

Present

The noise blared through the house. The first couple of beats woke Ketron, but she was too disoriented to recognize the source until Amelia cried in her arms.

Marvin stomped out of his room, his dark form hanging accusingly over his wife. He blamed her for his interrupted sleep.

"WHAT THE—" he bellowed, unconcerned about the baby's terrified cries.

"It's not me," Ketron defended. "It's Nora's tablet!"

Marvin stormed through the house, found the offending object, and powered it off. "What were you doing?" he yelled at Nora.

"Nothing," came Nora's hazy reply. She wasn't faking; she had been asleep.

"Someone had to turn on the tablet," he accused.

"It wasn't me!" Winslow shouted at him from the top bunk. "I was asleep!"

After some spirited comments, Ketron was able to intervene. "Is the tablet completely off?"

"I turned it off," Marvin huffed.

"I'll put it up for the rest of the night." Ketron took it from him. "We should all go back to sleep."

"Some of us have to work to pay the bills," Marvin grumbled. "My daddy doesn't send me checks every month."

Ketron was hurt that he'd used her father against her. She had never met the man who sired her, and his idea of involvement had always been to throw money at Ketron. He sent her enough money each month to cover her mental health expenses and a small portion of their bills.

"I don't get to sleep all day like everyone else," Marvin added when Ketron didn't respond to his taunt.

Ketron let him mumble all the way to his room, while she turned off the lights and settled back onto the couch. Amelia found her mother's breast and snuggled back to sleep.

"Mommy," Sonny spoke.

"Yes, sweetheart." Ketron didn't know he was awake, but the shouting hadn't helped.

"I'm sorry."

"For what? You didn't do anything." She kept her voice just above a whisper so Marvin wouldn't be disturbed again.

"I didn't know he was going to do that."

"Who was going to do what?"

"That boy. He turned on Nora's tablet."

He must have been dreaming, Ketron thought. "That's okay, honey. We worked it out. You can go back to sleep."

"He doesn't like to be alone while everyone is sleeping."

Ketron wondered what type of dream her son had been having before the tablet had sounded through the house. "How can he be alone in a house this full?" Ketron replied, rubbing his back to ease him into sleep.

Even though she knew his words were the product of a mind jerked from a dream, his next statement chilled her.

"He doesn't like the dark because he's been there too long."

Chapter Seven

Ketron's mother used to tell her ghost stories. Gwynevieve Renfro would stare out the window for hours, and suddenly, she would ease into a narrative about a ghost who lived in the house where she grew up. Ketron had a clear memory of the times she spoke about her interactions with spirits because they simultaneously excited and scared her.

"Gwynnie and I played hide-and-go-seek," she told Ketron one day. Ketron had been eleven years old, and she was making cupcakes for her school's parent involvement night. The teacher had asked her mother to bake them, but Ketron's mom was in no shape to operate appliances. Ketron remembered almost every detail of her youth. After Gwynevieve Renfro stopped taking her medication, Ketron burned each memory into her mind for fear that her mother would be taken away from her at any moment.

"I like to play hide-and-go-seek," Ketron had replied. "Maybe we could play after I finish the cupcakes."

As she often did, Ketron's mother ignored her and continued with the story from her youth. She may or may not have realized her daughter was listening. In her head, she always had a full audience of phantom voices.

"We lived on a beautiful farm with gardens of every variety, chickens, two cows, and a horse. Our father worked in the fields, and we tended to the cattle and chickens. Our mother taught us academic lessons, cleaned the house, cooked, and planted sunflowers. It was a pretty place, and we were self-sufficient, so we hardly ever went to town. Father usually went to town by himself, and he always brought us something back when he did."

"What did he bring you, Mama?"

"Oh, just sewing kits, and bits of cloth for making dresses," she answered.

"The people from town asked Father about his family. Preachers came up to our house to encourage us to visit their churches. Gwynnie and I had read the Bible several times, and we liked to surprise those men with our knowledge about it. One of them must have told a police officer that he'd seen my sister and me because an officer of the law brought up a school official. He told Mother that she needed to send us to public school. Mother showed him two of her diplomas from college, and he left after he talked to Gwynnie and me about math and reading." She laughed, and the action lit up the far-away look in her eyes. "I guess he changed his mind about our parents sending us to public school when Gwynnie recited the preamble to the American Constitution at seven years old!"

Ketron placed the cupcakes in the oven and set the timer. She sat down at their white and red checked kitchen table with her mother. She tried to see what held her mother's eyes as she stared out the window, but all she saw were the cars lined up in neat rows in front of the apartment building.

Ketron's mother took a long sip of sweet tea, the only luxury she insisted upon. Ketron watched her mother's lips when she spoke, attempting to immerse herself in a time when her mother was happy and sane.

"When we were twelve," she continued, "Father took Gwynnie, Mother, and me with him into town. It had been a good season, and we had more than enough food. He decided to sell our surplus to buy some things we didn't have on the farm.

"Gwynnie and I had never seen buildings so close together, and girls our age ran down the sidewalks in what my sister and I wore to bed on hot July nights. Mother seemed nervous, and Gwynnie and I felt out of place when people asked us our religion, or if we were in a cult. We didn't have their talking boxes in our house, and they didn't collect eggs from hens for their breakfast. Later, I learned that the boxes were called televisions, and everyone who lived in the town went to the grocery store for their food. It was clear that my family and the people in the town were from two separate worlds. Before, I had been upset with my father for not taking us on his trips, but I wasn't mad at him anymore. I was apprehensive about the people we saw and glad my sister was with me.

"Father sold all the fruits and vegetables that he had loaded into the trunk of our car, and he was excited when he counted the money. He told us that there would be plenty to fall back on for the winter and an extra special Christmas.

"He stopped at a store before he left town. I remember thinking that it was a big place, and I wondered how many people were inside selling food.

Mother laughed at me and told me that food was on shelves, and people picked it out of aisles and brought it to the front of the market to cashiers.

"Father came back to the car with a couple of bags of food and gifts for us. He bought Mother a bouquet of flowers, and Gwynnie and I had to be told not to swallow the chewing gum in the bright, silver wrappers. He selected brown bottles with an amber liquid in them for himself, and cans, boxes of oatmeal, and cereal poked out of the other bags.

"'That will help us through the month,' he told us.

"Gwynnie and I looked over every can. There were pictures of corn, peaches, peas, and beans wrapped around aluminum cans. My sister and I had never seen food packaged that way. Our mother always stored it in clear glass jars with lids."

Ketron wondered what it would have been like to eat food from a garden her family had grown. Contrary to the way her mother was raised, Genevieve always bought food pre-packaged or in cans. Most of Ketron's meals were simple things she could microwave or macaroni and mashed potatoes from a box.

The timer dinged, but Ketron didn't move. She had no reason to wish for it, but Ketron hoped her mother would jump up and get the cupcakes out of the oven. Her mother didn't budge. A casual observer might think Ketron's mother was willfully ignoring the dinging timer, but she didn't hear it. Ketron silenced the timer as her mother picked the story up again.

"Gwynnie and I made our chewing gum last for a month, but our father finished his drinks in one night. He went back and got more the next day. That's when my mother told me it was called beer, and my sister and I couldn't drink it. I didn't want to try it anyway. Father's breath always smelled like rotting fruit when he drank it."

She sighed, and the weight of her childhood was in the breath she exhaled. "My sister and I hid our chewing gum behind our bedposts and vanity, and our father hid his beer in the barn and in the hole in the old oak tree. We chewed our gum in front of everyone, but he took sips when no one was looking.

"That's when we started our hide-and-seek games. Gwynnie would hide, and I would find her. Her mind was always so loud, and I could feel her brain buzzing whenever I got close to her hiding spot. Sometimes, we hid together, and Gail would find us."

Ketron already knew that her mother and her twin had a special way of communicating without speaking. "Who's Gail, Mama?"

"She was the woman who lived in the house before us," Ketron's mother said matter-of-factly. "She died in our room, so her spirit was always clearest there."

Ketron worried when her mother talked about ghosts. It felt like her mother carried the spirits with her, and they were listening to their words.

"Gail told us about father's hiding places, and she knew when he started carrying pounds of sugar into the woods that he had switched to a stronger drink. Since he made liquor, he didn't go into town anymore, but he hardly came out of the woods. When he was in the house, he would lash out at Mother, Gwynnie, and me, so Gwynnie and I would hide when we heard his voice. Gail would pretend to play the game with us, drifting through the rooms, but really, she stayed to watch over our well-being. Not that she could have done anything," Ketron's mother scoffed.

"What did she look like?" Ketron chanced.

Her mother slid her hands around her glass of tea, rubbing the condensation away. "Gwynnie saw her, but I could only hear her," she confessed.

Her mother didn't continue, so Ketron got up and iced the cupcakes. She wanted it to look like little flowers, but it turned out like dots of icing had been dropped on the cupcakes. She held one up to show her mother, but her mother's mind was back in the past. Ketron was used to the silence, but she was happy when her mother returned to her story. Without her mother's reflections, the apartment would be silent.

"It was a Tuesday," she said. It had been so long since her mother had spoken that it startled Ketron. "Mother finished our lessons early, and she sent Gwynnie and me to the creek for crawdads. She was going to fry them for dinner. We didn't have any luck at the creek, and we carried the empty pail between us with our fingers intertwined.

"I felt Gail rush out to us. She swirled Gwynnie's hair, and I broke out in gooseflesh on my arms. She told us to hide, and she'd find us, but Gwynnie was worried about Mother, so she ran inside. Mother was in bed with a dish rag pressed to her ear. Her lips were purple and swollen, and she instructed us to get a few of our things and come back to the room. I noticed a suitcase by her bedroom door, and I remembered that she had told Father she would leave him if he didn't stop drinking. We ran to our room and grabbed all six of our dresses and our matching rabbits, Pansy and Marigold, that our mother had sewed for us. We were ready to go back to Mother's room, but Gail shouted for us to hide. We dropped our clothes and dove under the bed. We peered out from our place on the floor until our father's heavy boots came into view."

Ketron had been apathetic as she listened to the story of physical abuse. Her grandmother had died before she was born, and she'd never heard what had happened to her grandfather. Even though she didn't have siblings, the next part rattled her.

"He found us and grabbed under the bed. I don't think he cared about which daughter he snatched, and he caught me under my arm and pulled me from under the bed." She shivered and wrapped her arms around herself. "Gwynnie grabbed for my hand, but our fingers wouldn't lace together in time. I don't know what he planned to do to me once he saw the pile of our belongings in the floor, but Gwynnie snaked out from under the bed with lightning speed and kicked his leg until he took notice of her.

"He slung me against the wall and shouted at her, 'You want to kick somebody! I'll show you what it feels like!'"

She whispered, "He started with her legs. He swung his foot into them and knocked her down. She fell into a fetal position and covered her head. I pulled his arms. I tried to hold his legs. At some point, I ended up against the wall. I think he broke one of my ribs, because it was hard to breathe. I tried to crawl to Gwynnie, but he kept shoving me away while he kicked her. He stomped his boots into her ribs and her back and her head until she stopped moving."

Tears poured down Gwynevieve's face from reliving the experience. Ketron reached for her mother's hand, but she wiped her eyes and stood, stretching to her full height.

Suddenly, her eyes narrowed. "Who is that woman?" She pointed at a smartly dressed female who had just gotten out of a white SUV. Her brown hair spilled over her shoulders, and she fumbled with an umbrella until she gave up on it, having gotten more rain on her while trying to open the umbrella than if she had come to the front door without it.

"It's Mrs. Collins," Ketron sighed. "She's my teacher."

"What is she doing here?" her mother's eyes bore into her, searching Ketron for lies before she spoke.

"I don't know," Ketron answered. "Maybe it's because you never come to the school or sign my folders."

The latter part probably wasn't true. Ketron had been signing her folders for the last three weeks, but Mrs. Collins had been concerned when Ketron's mother hadn't made an appearance during any of the parent involvement nights. Out of all the third-grade parents, Gwynevive had been the only one who had never attended.

A knock interrupted them. Ketron's mother put her finger to her lips. She pointed to the bedroom and indicated that they should hide under the bed.

Ketron's mouth formed a thin line. She stalked to the door and opened it before her mother could stop her.

"Hello, Ketron," Mrs. Collins said. "Is your mother home?"

"I am always home," Ketron's mother announced from behind the door. She stepped around Ketron and extended her hand. "I'm Gwynevieve Renfro."

"Mrs. Renfro, I am Mrs. Collins, Ketron's teacher." They shook hands loosely.

"You may call me Gwynevieve."

"Okay, Gwynevieve it is." She didn't offer her first name. "I came here today because I haven't seen you on parent nights. In fact, no one at the school remembers having met you."

"I was there during registration."

"That was several years ago."

Mrs. Collins peered inside like she was expecting Ketron's mother to invite her inside. There was an awning over their porch, but it was raining, and the wind whipped through the trees.

"Will you come inside?" Ketron offered, dipping her body in a grand gesture she had seen butlers do on television.

"Thank you, Ketron." Mrs. Collins stepped sideways into the house, brushing past Gwynevieve. She looked over the house fully and seemed satisfied with the cleanliness.

"You have a nice home, Genevieve." Thankfully, Ketron's mother didn't correct the mispronunciation of her name.

Ketron pulled out a chair at the kitchen table. "Please sit down." The ladies took their places, and Ketron poured tea into a glass. She brought it to Mrs. Collins and refilled her mother's glass. They spoke of Ketron's excellent grades, and her mother told Mrs. Collins that she would have been a valedictorian if she had graduated from public school. Mrs. Collins had expected her mother to compliment Ketron, so her hubris seemed to surprise her.

Struck by inspiration, Ketron ran back to the kitchen and gathered some flour in her hand. She brought each woman a cupcake, and she covered the hand her mother had under the table with flour.

"Are these the cupcakes for tomorrow night?" Mrs. Collins asked.

"Yes," Ketron answered. "I thought you could have yours now, and my mom can have mine."

Touched by the gesture, Mrs. Collins placed a hand on Ketron's back, while her mother eyed them cautiously. Ketron jumped away when she noticed her mother's stare. "My mom just finished the cupcakes," she said, and stood beside her mother. She lifted Gwynevieve's hand and showed the flour in it. "See? She's worked all day on these delicious cupcakes for the class." The flour poured onto the table.

Mrs. Collins looked at the pile of white powder. "I didn't know when I shook your hand that you had flour on it."

Ketron realized her mistake and dropped her mother's hand. There was an uncomfortable silence that doubled in length in Ketron's mind.

"You made the cupcakes, didn't you, Ketron?" Mrs. Collins spoke. There was disappointment in her tone, like when she caught one of the children cheating in class, so Ketron hung her head. "Mrs. Renfro," she addressed Ketron's mother formally, "I hope you come to the next parent involvement night. School takes up a large portion of a child's life and it would be a shame to miss their accomplishments there. Since you were homeschooled, maybe you remember how you felt when you made your mother proud during a lesson." Ketron raised her head and looked at her mother, but she remained perfectly composed. "Perhaps you want Ketron to experience the same feeling."

"We appreciate your time," her mother replied, rising from her chair. Mrs. Collins walked to the door, stopping only to regurgitate the necessary formalities. Ketron's mother watched Mrs. Collins pull out of the parking space allotted for them.

Her mother's silence was worse than a shouting match. The quietness meant that Ketron would have to pay for every inconvenience brought about by Mrs. Collins's visit. Even though she hadn't invited her teacher to their home, Ketron's failure to prevent it was all that mattered.

"I'm sorry, Mother." She hoped her humility would weaken her punishment.

Her mother continued to stare out the window. She didn't speak until Ketron was almost in the kitchen. "Everyone is mad. Especially Gwynnie."

Ketron was used to her mother's casual references to the voices in her head. She understood that more than two people lived in their tiny one-bedroom apartment.

Ketron took the plates with uneaten cupcakes back to the sink. She thought about putting the cupcakes back with the others but ended up tossing them into the trash.

A plate rattled on the counter and startled her. She wondered if a train had suddenly jerked to a stop on a nearby track. She hadn't heard a train horn, but they were so common in her small town that the sound could have blended into the background.

Ketron washed the plates and Mrs. Collins's cup. When she turned around, a sharp pain hit the back of her knee and her feet were knocked out from under her. She sat on the floor for almost a full minute, wondering how she had slipped. She hadn't gotten water on the floor or tripped herself with her own feet.

Ketron's mother didn't move to help her. She sat at the kitchen table and sipped her sweet tea, never taking her eyes off the still scenery through the window. "We don't like visitors," her mother spoke flatly from her place at the table. As if in agreement, her hair moved from an invisible force and the plate rattled against the cup in the drainer.

Chapter Eight

Present

"I didn't do it," Nora asserted. She was close to a melt-down.

"Then who did?" Marvin asked her.

"Pass the carrots," Winslow asked, in hopes of steering the conversation away from his sister. He didn't like carrots, so he hoped to surprise his parents into changing the subject.

Sonny was unusually quiet. He had hardly touched his dinosaur nuggets, only moving them around his plate with his fingers.

"I think your mother should keep the tablet until I find out who woke me up with it."

Ketron paused the spoon that had been on its way to Amelia's mouth. "I gave it back to her this morning." Ketron felt his stare, but she avoided it by wiping the creamed potatoes off the baby's chin.

"So, the kids can just do whatever they want? When I was their age, my butt was spanked, and my privileges were taken if I stepped one little toe out of line."

"She said she didn't do it, so I gave the tablet back to her." Ketron clinched her jaw and released it. "Your parents weren't the type of people I want to model my parenting after."

He shoved the table hard enough to rattle it. "And your mother's such a gem?"

"I don't do things like my mother either. I don't spank the children."

"It's the only way to get them to behave!" Marvin yelled, standing up from the table.

"I did it," Winslow spoke up, desperately trying to keep his parents from fighting. Sonny jerked his head in his brother's direction and raised his eyebrows. Ketron didn't believe Winslow had turned on the device in the night, but she was surprised that Sonny seemed so convinced that he was innocent, too.

Marvin focused his anger on Ketron, oblivious to Winslow's admission. "These kids are wild, Ket, and I'll have to do something about it if you don't!"

Marvin had drawn a line in the sand. Usually, Ketron let him mumble about the imaginary slights done to him, but she didn't let him have his way when her children were involved. "You will not touch my children. Especially not in your shape!"

Ketron was careful about making references to her husband's drinking, so Marvin was thrown off balance by her remark. He fumbled for an answer, pushed his chair under the table a little harder than he intended, and stomped to his room.

"You raise them then!" The slamming door ended their discussion.

"I really didn't do it," Nora spoke softly.

"I don't think you did it intentionally, honey, but you may have set an alarm or something."

Nora accepted her explanation and finished her dinner. Winslow picked at his food.

Sensing leftover tension in the room, Ketron grasped for anything to lighten the atmosphere. "Can I still get you to eat carrots?" Ketron teased her son.

Winslow smiled over his plate. "Not a chance."

Ketron folded the towels first. It made her feel like she had less laundry when their bulk was missing from the basket. Sonny sat nearby, watching his favorite dinosaur movie.

"I want to be like the Solo Dinosaur," he told her. "He's really cool."

"He *is* cool, sweetie, but he will never be as cool as you."

Sonny rolled his eyes and tuned back to his show. She realized how tall he had grown in the last six months and scolded herself for not starting a height chart on one of the doorframes of their new home. She pushed her laundry away and pulled him to her. "I love you so much." He moved his hair out of his eyes and stared at the television.

"Jeremy likes the Solo Dinosaur, too."

"Who's Jeremy?"

"He's the one who turned on Nora's tablet last night." The lines on his forehead creased. "Don't tell him I told you. He says you'll send him back to the darkness."

Ketron tried not to show her amusement. It was odd for Sonny to have made up an imaginary friend when he had so many siblings to play with him.

Amelia grabbed Ketron's hair and put herself between Ketron and Sonny. "I'm Sonny's mommy, too," Ketron told her, holding the baby at her side.

"Jeremy doesn't like her," Sonny commented. "He says he's going to put her in the darkness."

Ketron's eyebrows drew together. It sounded like Sonny was experiencing some sibling rivalry. Amelia wasn't brand new to the family, but she required more of Ketron's attention as she got older. "Do *you* want your sister to be put into the darkness?"

Sonny shrugged his shoulders. "I like her, but Jeremy thinks she gets in the way."

Ketron worried that Sonny was expressing his true feelings about his sister by communicating them through a fictional third party. "You know that you're still my very special boy, right?" Sonny tuned her out, engrossed in his show. "I hope you know that there's no one who can replace you," she told him, hoping that he heard her while watching the powerful stand-off between a tyrannosaurus rex and a triceratops. He pulled away from her arms, intently watching the scene.

Ketron went back to folding laundry, and Amelia climbed in and out of the basket. "You are a silly baby!" Ketron cooed. Amelia gave her a full smile of sporadic teeth and dived back out of the clothes. Moving to her knees, Amelia crawled, slapping the floor from the living room to the dining room. Ketron stood up to retrieve the baby and an ear-splitting wail resounded through the house. It was seconds before Ketron got to the baby, but no other cry came forth. In those moments, Ketron didn't know if Amelia had been hurt so badly that she'd lost consciousness.

She turned on the dining room light and saw Amelia pinned under one of the heavy wooden dining chairs. She was face down on the floor with her nose pressed against the parquet floor. Ketron slung the chair off her baby and Amelia issued another cry. Each cry extended until it was almost soundless before another soul-crushing wail followed, rattling Amelia's body. Ketron scanned the baby for injuries. A purple mark stood out on her cheek.

"What did you do?" Marvin asked between the baby's shrieks. Ketron had been so focused on Amelia that she hadn't heard him come out of his room.

His question put Ketron on the defensive. "I didn't do anything! Why don't you go back to your room so I can take care of her?"

He grabbed his door like he was going to rip it off its hinges and sling it at her. "I can't spank the kids, but you can let them get hurt. What were you doing? Talking on the phone?"

"I was doing laundry," Ketron defended. "I was on my way to get her when—"

He slammed the door on her explanation.

With Marvin back in his room, Ketron was able to soothe the baby. She walked Amelia around the house, allowing her to touch each picture and window.

"You'll have baby prints everywhere."

Ketron jumped. She hadn't heard Marvin open the door to his room again. "I don't mind her fingerprints."

Marvin sat on a recliner in the living room. He smiled at Sonny on the carpet while he played with a stegosaurus. "I shouldn't have yelled at you."

Ketron stayed quiet. She didn't want to interrupt the only apology she'd heard from her husband in weeks.

"You're a good mother, so I know you didn't mean for her to get hurt." Unfortunately, that was all he was going to say to his wife about his behavior. "Did you pull the chair on yourself?" he asked Amelia. The baby smiled at him and then hid her face. She played the game several times, looking at her father and then shying away into Ketron's neck.

"Jeremy threw the chair on her," Sonny said. He didn't look up from his stegosaurus as it rampaged through a village of blocks.

"Who's Jeremy?" Marvin asked Sonny.

"He's Sonny's new friend," Ketron answered.

"Is he Sonny's friend or your friend?" Marvin implication.

Heat flashed across Ketron's face. "Really, Marvin? You're here. Why would I have another man in the house?"

"What does Jeremy look like?" Marvin pressed, tapping Sonny on the shoulder.

Sonny gave Marvin his attention. Ketron found herself jealous of their connection. No matter how hard she tried, Sonny never looked at her the way he looked at Marvin. "He has hair like Winso, and brown eyes." Sonny couldn't say Winslow's name yet, but no one seemed to mind the way he shortened it.

"Is he tall?" Marvin asked, standing to his full height. "Like Daddy?"

Ketron felt red hot anger rise from her chest to her face. *Why was it okay for him to question her fidelity when he was one beer short of a six pack?*

Sonny shook his head. "He's like Winso."

Ketron finally felt comfortable with the turn of the conversation. "He idolizes his brother."

Marvin nodded, hugged Sonny, and went back to his room. He didn't apologize to Ketron about his insinuation, and Ketron didn't visit his room after the children fell asleep.

Chapter Nine

Present

Bonnie trudged through the house, mumbled a greeting to her mother, and closed the door to her room. She came out for dinner, but she stayed in her room for most of the evening.

It was the way of the teenager. Ketron had been told that by her own mother as she had recalled her experiences with older siblings in foster care. Ketron tried to tempt Bonnie with treats and activities, but Bonnie would disappear after the incentives were eaten or over, and she hardly participated in family card games or watched television with them.

The shift between her parents was always hard for Bonnie. At her father's house, she was the only child. She was free to roam the house while he was at work, she received his full attention when he was at home, and he allowed her to do things Ketron didn't feel Bonnie was ready for yet. Ketron was home all the time, but her attention was divided. She slipped away to a different part of the house to participate in special activities with Bonnie, but Amelia's cries or Sonny's temper tantrums could cut their time together short. Bonnie was usually sullen for the first day after a switch, and sometimes it took most of the week for her to acclimate to the difference in households.

The door to Bonnie's room popped open, and she showed Ketron a funny video that was popular on the internet. Ketron wouldn't know any of the trends if it weren't for her oldest daughter. She had tried some of the dances, but she couldn't keep up with the famous personalities and grown men dressed like British boys.

Marvin stomped through the living room on his way to the bathroom. He didn't speak to either of them.

Bonnie slung her shimmery, blonde hair over her shoulder. "I straightened it," she told Ketron.

At thirteen, Bonnie could be caking makeup on her bright green eyes and going boy crazy, but she preferred a more natural look. She was athletically built, didn't count calories, and valued comfy shorts and big tee shirts over jeans and stylish dresses. Ketron remembered the way she dressed and acted at Bonnie's age, and she counted her blessings when she thought of their differences. "It looks nice but be certain you aren't frying your hair."

"Ahh, Mom. Can't you just say you like it? Dad does."

"I said that it looked nice, but your father doesn't understand how hard it can be to repair damaged hair."

Bonnie lifted off the couch, tossed Amelia a toy, and stalked to her room. The familiar and resolute seal of her door closing sounded through the house.

Ketron crept behind the baby as she crawled around the corner into the twins' room. She held her phone up to catch the baby's steps, but Amelia only stood, caressed a dent in the wall, and dropped onto her bottom.

Amelia raced down the short hallway on her hands and knees, pausing once to look back and smile at her mother. She gave chase again, slapping across the floor almost faster than Ketron could keep up.

"What are you doing?" Winslow asked her.

"I haven't gotten a video of your sister walking yet, and I thought I could get one while she was in a good mood."

He nodded and rejoined his twin in their room. Berry Batch Buddies was almost over, so it would be his turn to pick the next show they watched. Ketron was glad they had established that system without her guidance.

Sonny finished coloring a picture in his prehistoric coloring book. "Look, Mommy! I colored a long neck!"

Amelia had just gotten to her feet again. Ketron positioned the phone's camera on her daughter. "Just a minute, sweetie. I need to get this video of your sister." She thought she heard him say something else, but she was too focused on the baby to concentrate on it.

Amelia lifted her foot, hovered it over the ground, and stepped down. She followed it with another step before she grabbed onto her learning tree and moved into a sitting position.

Ketron erupted in celebration. "I got it!"

She had recorded her first four children's first steps, but she hadn't been able to capture Amelia's first toddling attempt. She had been at Shauna's house, and when Amelia had lunged for the cat, she had taken a few steps. Ketron was glad she had witnessed it, but she wished she had recorded the experience.

Ketron ran across the house to her daughter's bedroom door. "Bonnie! Come look at this!"

The teen initially protested, but her mother finally coaxed her into the living room. They sat next to each other and watched the toddler take two steps, giggling over her deliberate movements, but as Amelia moved her foot the first time, a voice could be heard that caused the hair on Ketron's neck to stand up.

"Was Matty here?" Bonnie asked. "I thought he'd been sick?"

It was difficult for Ketron to form words. "That wasn't Matty."

Bonnie tilted her head, studying Ketron's expression. "Who was it then?"

"I don't know."

Ketron grabbed Amelia and rushed into Marvin's room. "Marvin, you have to hear this!"

Bonnie followed her and stood just outside the door. Ketron had him watch the video three times as Amelia struggled to get down. He was unaffected by its contents.

"It's just the TV," he told Ketron, resuming his game, and apologizing to his online teammates.

Ketron shifted the baby's weight and pulled the headphones off his head. "We were in the dining room. The TV is in the living room, and it was off!"

He tore the headphones out of her hands and fumbled them onto his head while trying to maneuver his avatar out of the kill zone. "It was the twins' TV."

"That didn't sound like anything the Berry Batch Buddies would say," Bonnie commented.

Marvin slid his beer out from under his chair and took a long drink. Unwilling to subject her teenager to Marvin's alcoholism, Ketron left the room, quickly shutting the door behind her.

Sonny was still at the table coloring another picture. "Can you see my picture now, Mommy?"

Ketron approached him cautiously. "Sure, honey." She put on an extra-large smile and complimented the purple volcano and green and pink apatosaurus.

"Hey, Sonny," Bonnie tried. "Was there anyone here a minute ago?"

Sonny stopped coloring, but he didn't look at his sister. "Mommy and Melia were here."

Usually, Ketron's heart would melt when he said his younger sister's name, but her nerves were frayed. "Was there anyone else in the room with us, sweetheart?"

Sonny resumed coloring a triceratops with a gold crayon, and Ketron thought he was going to ignore their question. He paused, selecting a bright green for the frill. "Jeremy was here, but he's gone now."

"Who's Jeremy?" Bonnie asked.

Ketron ignored her question. "You wouldn't do what he told you to do, would you?'

Sonny shook his head, his expression unchanged. "I told you. Jeremy doesn't like Melia."

Ketron felt weak and out of control. She started pacing, but that kept her in the house, and she really wanted to get away. She couldn't fight an unseen presence, so she bolted outside, with Bonnie close behind her.

"Who is Jeremy?" Bonnie repeated.

They were lucky enough to live in a county with a low crime rate, so they rarely locked their vehicles. Ketron jumped into her van. The heat from the day was stifling, but Ketron resisted rolling down the windows. Bonnie climbed into the passenger seat, and her mother motioned for her to shut the door. Somehow, Ketron felt safer in her van, even though she believed spirits weren't bound by earthly limitations.

"I thought Jeremy was Sonny's imaginary friend, but now..." Ketron shook her head as if disagreeing with herself. "I think he might be a ghost."

Bonnie's eyes widened and she exhibited the same exhilaration as most teens when they think they have witnessed something supernatural. "That's so cool!"

"Not if he's knocking chairs over on my baby and talking about taking her into the darkness!"

"Do you think we'll be on TV?"

Ketron glared at her. "Just go back inside."

Bonnie calmed her features and tried to act seriously. "Okay, Mom. Do you know who lived here before you?"

Amelia bounced up and down as she tried to turn the steering wheel. Ketron fumbled for a pack of yogurt melts in the glove box. "We bought it from the Sheltons, but they only remodeled it a little. They never lived here."

"Maybe you could call them about the people they bought it from?"

Ketron shook her head. Her breaths had been clipped, but she was beginning to relax. "I doubt they would take my call. I haggled ten thousand dollars off the asking price of the house because the roof was damaged, and the driveway hadn't been resurfaced. We're not on speaking terms."

Bonnie put her hand on her mother's arm. "It's going to be okay. And if it's not, then maybe they can teach us señora's dance." She mocked well-known moves from a ghostly comedy. "Jump in the line!"

Ketron laughed despite herself, and Bonnie curled her fingers around her mother's hand. Ketron wished that Marvin had moderated his reaction through the incident, but she was glad Bonnie had helped cast some humor on a tense situation.

Later, when everyone was sleeping peacefully, Ketron's senses were on high alert. Every crack and pop in the house made her jump or caused her eyes to fly open. It was hard to sleep when she couldn't get the words Jeremy spoke about Amelia out of her mind.

She held her baby close and tried not to hear his voice, but it echoed through the almost silent chambers that pulled her both toward and away from sleep. *"Let me take her into the darkness with me."*

Chapter Ten

Past

"Why did you tell them?" Ketron's mother yelled. She held a ceramic bookend Ketron had painted for her during a school field trip. She unmercifully threw the multicolored bookend to the ground. Some of the shards slid and scattered at Ketron's feet. Ketron's heart dropped into her stomach. Her mother had never been sentimental with her, but that trinket had meant a great deal to Ketron when she had painted it.

"What did I do?" Ketron ran through her mind in search of any slip.

"Your teacher! Why did you tell her I had a mental condition?"

Ketron's blood ran cold. She had gone to school earlier in the week with bruises on her wrists. She had worn a long-sleeved shirt to school, even though the temperature was near ninety degrees that day, and the teacher didn't notice the marks until she handed in her spelling test.

"Ketron," she had spoken softly. "What happened, honey?"

Ketron had been stuck between trying to keep her life with her mother secret and the need to finally talk about the daily abuse she endured. She sputtered a couple of practiced excuses, but Mrs. Collins wouldn't accept any of them. Waving at her assistant to take over the classroom, she led Ketron out of the room and into the hallway. They walked into the teacher's workroom.

It took twenty minutes of smooth words and promises before Ketron finally broke down. She couldn't remember everything she'd said to Mrs. Collins, but she had felt safe and validated for the first time in her life.

"Do you promise you won't tell anyone?" Ketron had asked her teacher.

"I promise," Mrs. Collins had told her as she hugged her. Mrs. Collins had cried with Ketron, and she had to wait until her teacher cleaned the running mascara from her face before they returned to class.

When they walked back through the door, some of the boys had sung, "Eww! Ketron's in trouble!"

"She most certainly is not!" Mrs. Collins had snapped, and her tone kept the boys from making any other comments. Sadly, however, they had been right. Ketron was in trouble, but not with her teacher.

"What am I going to do?" Ketron's mother paced back and forth in the kitchen. A broken piece of the bookend nicked her foot, and blossoms of blood laid bright red petals on the linoleum.

Ketron ran to the bathroom to get the peroxide, a bandage, and a wad of toilet paper. She knelt at her mother's foot.

"What are you doing?" her mother yelled, kicking her with her injured foot.

"I just wanted to help you," Ketron cried. "You're bleeding." She showed her the blood she had left on her shirt when she'd kicked her.

"What does it matter if I'm bleeding? How am I going to get past this?" She picked up a piece of paper from the kitchen table and pushed it in Ketron's face. Her mother held the paper inches from her face, so Ketron couldn't focus on the words.

"They'll be here tomorrow!" her mother screamed at her. She tapped the paper, her long, red fingernails marking the creamy stationery each time she touched it. *"Tomorrow!"*

"I can help you clean up?" Ketron offered.

"Clean up?" Her mother dramatically swept in a circle. "The place is clean, Ketron. They aren't looking at the apartment. They're coming here to evaluate me because of the lies you told the brunette hooker at school!"

Ketron was certain that her teacher wasn't the word her mother called her, but Mrs. Collins *was* a liar. She had promised Ketron that she wouldn't tell anyone about their conversation in the teacher's lounge. "She said she wouldn't tell," Ketron squeaked out.

Ketron realized her mistake when her mother landed a slap across her face. "You just told on yourself, missy," she shouted. "I didn't know that you had worked with that woman at the school to put me away, but you just said it. Is she going to take you in when they lock me in a padded room?"

Her mother's eyes lost focus and she chewed her thumbnail. She resumed pacing, but the blood petals from her foot were smaller. "I won't go back. I can't go back," she cried into the air, focusing on something only she could see.

She's hearing voices again, Ketron thought. Ketron hadn't had a moment of peace the last time her mother had talked back to the voices. There was no rest in the house as her mother had shouted, sung, and laughed with her imaginary companions.

Her mother sat down, and Ketron took the opportunity to dress her wound. After she secured the bandage to her mother's heel, Ketron set to work cleaning the blood off the floor. When the rainbow shards of ceramic were dumped in the trash, and the pattern of blood from her mother's foot had been cleaned, Ketron made sure that her mother was safely locked in wherever her mind traveled when the world was too much for her to handle. She was hungry, but she skipped dinner and went to bed. Her mother usually didn't bother her if she was asleep. It was almost like Ketron didn't exist when she lost consciousness. If her mother went through another tirade, she could just yell at the people in her mind.

Something kept flicking her in the night. It started with her toes, but she couldn't ignore it anymore when a phantasmal hand wrapped around her throat. She gasped for air, and tried to get her mother's attention, but her mother was asleep on the bed across from her with her back to Ketron. A puff of air circled her face, picking up her hair and caressing her cheeks. Ketron faded into darkness, but awoke the next morning, wondering if it had all been a dream.

At school, Ketron couldn't look at her teacher. Mrs. Collins must have known something was wrong because she didn't ask Ketron to do her classroom job.

At recess, she told Ketron to remain in the classroom. "You're mad at me," she observed.

Ketron didn't answer her.

"I have to tell the things I hear if someone is being harmed or if that person is going to cause harm to himself or herself." She reached for Ketron's hands, but Ketron shoved them into the pockets of her jeans. "You are being harmed, Ketron."

"You promised." Ketron narrowed her eyes and focused all her hate on Mrs. Collins, as if it would knock the offending woman out of her seat and onto the floor.

"I'm not going to apologize for helping you." She crossed her legs and bit the end of a pen cap. "You wouldn't have told me if I would have explained it to you."

Ketron couldn't think of words strong enough to convey the way she felt about her teacher's betrayal. Her emotions bubbled up and frothed over, spewing out of her mouth like burning lava. "You're a hooker!" she shouted and stormed out of the room.

Surprisingly, she wasn't punished for her outburst. Ketron reasoned that it was because part of Mrs. Collins felt badly over the broken trust. Ketron doubted she could get away with calling her teacher that word again, though.

During math class, an announcement on her computer caught Mrs. Collins's attention. "You need to go to the office for check out, Ketron." Ketron must have seemed noticeably surprised, because her teacher asked, "Do you have a dentist or doctor appointment?" Ketron shrugged her shoulders, genuinely bewildered.

Ketron trudged down the hall with a weighted backpack of books. Her mother was waiting for her in the office, talking to the receptionist. If Ketron hadn't known her mother, she would have thought it was a regular conversation between two adults, but her mother didn't possess social skills. She never spoke to other people unless it was necessary, but there she was, carrying on a perfectly acceptable conversation about the unseasonable amount of rain they had been having. "Are you ready?" she asked Ketron with a bright smile. Since Gwynevieve had stopped taking her medication, Ketron had wanted her mother to look at her that way, but it felt wrong. She returned her smile, and they walked to the vehicle hand-in-hand.

Ketron didn't fully understand until she got into the car. Bags and suitcases were thrown into the backseat. Food was in a cooler at Ketron's feet. Two stuffed rabbits, Pansy and Marigold, reclined against the back windshield.

"What's going on?" Ketron asked carefully.

Her mother continued to smile while they were under the surveillance cameras in the school parking lot. "I didn't know what to do when I received the letter," her mother responded. "But someone reminded me that I didn't have to stay in one place."

Ketron knew the person her mother referenced was only in her mind.

"Do you remember how you've always wanted to meet my sister?"

Ketron didn't remember saying anything about her mother's sister, but she nodded. The school passed out of view and her mother dropped her smile. "Well, you're finally going to meet her," she said without inflection.

The wind picked up Ketron's hair and swirled it. She laid her head against the car window and a tear slid down her cheek.

Chapter Eleven

Present

Thoughts about her past mingled with the challenges of her current situation, and Ketron decided she was glad that part of her life was over. Most people wanted to return to the simplistic days of their childhood, but she was content to leave it behind her.

She shuddered under her blanket. Something hit her foot and she startled. Had she forgotten to put away a toy?

Ketron switched on the flashlight feature on her phone and looked around the room. Silent darkness surrounded her. She turned off the flashlight and tried to think about the future instead of the past. Amelia had a checkup scheduled, and she worried about the nurse pricking her finger. Amelia's blood would need to be tested for lead, now that they lived in an old house with ongoing renovations.

Flick

Her eyes instantly watered and her nose ran. It was like someone had knocked their fingernail against her nose. The pain was real. She couldn't have imagined it.

Ketron lifted herself up on the couch, trying not to rouse Sonny and Amelia. She spoke aloud, but softly. "Who's there?"

There was a cackle, but it wasn't a sound that could be heard with her ears. It echoed in her head. She ducked between her two youngest children and cried. "Please don't let it happen to me, too," she begged, but she wondered if it was too late for her pleas to be answered.

Chapter Twelve

Present

Bonnie ran the ball across the soccer field, dodging defenders. She easily passed it to a mid-field player, and the ball made it back to her. She scored effortlessly, kicking it through the goalie's outstretched hands. The sideline erupted; it had been the only point scored during the game, so Bonnie's team was in the lead.

Ketron struggled to keep Sonny interested in a pile of rocks she had gathered for him. For her, the hour passed quickly as she watched her daughter, but Sonny grew tired of seeing young girls chase a ball up and down a field. Amelia screamed at Bonnie. She was testing her voice, trying to mock the sounds of the crowd around her. A girl waved at the baby as she lined up for a side kick.

Five more minutes. If the Yellow Jackets could keep the other team from scoring a point, they would win. This was only a scrimmage, and Ketron knew that it would be hard to beat the team during a regular season game. Several members of the opposing team were traveling with their families, so some of their players were stationed at alternate positions.

The rival team lined up for a shot directly down the middle. At this skill level, those shots were hardly missed, and Ketron worried about keeping Sonny entertained during a possible overtime. The player moved her leg back for a more forceful kick, and the point seemed to be theirs. A red-headed defender ran out from the side of the field and kicked the ball away from the goal. Seconds later, the buzzer echoed off the mountains, announcing the end of the game.

The Yellow Jackets ran to each other with their arms out, hugging and yelling about their victory. Afterward, Bonnie gathered with her teammates to celebrate and listen to the coach's after-game talk. Ketron couldn't keep Sonny busy any longer, so she edged her way over to the assembled team.

Winslow and Nora walked behind her, keeping their noses buried in a cartoon on Nora's tablet.

"Way to go, Mandi!" Ketron heard the coach say to a player as they approached. "That was a great block!"

Mandi blushed. "Bonnie scored the goal, though," she squeaked out.

The attention shifted to Bonnie. "Yes! Good job, Bon-Bon!"

Ketron cringed at her child's nickname, but she was powerless to stop its spread. Bella, her best friend, had called her Bon-Bon on the first day of kindergarten and Bonnie's father, Kyle, had laughed. It had stuck after he referred to them as "Bon-Bon" and "Bell-Bell."

Bonnie soaked in her accolades before she walked with them to the van. Amelia pulled at Ketron's shirt, wanting compensation for her delayed dinner. "We'll be home in a minute," she told the baby.

The soccer field was only a short drive from their home. In fact, they could have walked there if Sonny wouldn't have stopped for every small rock and sparkling piece of sand along the way.

Ketron turned onto the one-lane road that led to their house and eight other homes, and stopped for a large, black dog. It sniffed the air in front of them before she blew the horn, causing it to run into the woods that lined the other side of the road. As she pulled into the driveway, Ketron spotted Mrs. Franks in her yard and waved.

"Oh, no," Bonnie moaned. "She's coming over here."

"Be nice," Ketron cautioned, and pulled her mouth into a wide grin for her neighbor.

Mrs. Franks jogged across her lawn. Each step was high, since it was mowed on an elevated setting, but it looked like a lush, green carpet. She was still spritely for her age. Her calves were toned and tanned, and she had retained some of her natural curves. She had been working in her garden, and her white hair clung to her forehead. She wiped the sweat away with the back of one of her gloves and it left a streak of dirt just over her eyebrows. Ketron called her attention to it, and she dismissed it. "I'm filthy. I'll be taking a shower soon." She pushed her head around Ketron and stared into the van. Nora, Winslow, and Sonny threw up their hands in an uncertain greeting. "Where's Marvin?"

Marvin's truck was in the driveway, so she wondered why Mrs. Franks had asked about him. Was she curious why he wasn't with them, or was she insinuating that Ketron should be more available to him while he was home? Ketron believed the latter explanation was most likely. "I guess he's inside playing video games."

"Well, he's worked all week, so he needs a little time to himself." When Ketron said nothing in return, she added, "It has to be hard on him to work all day and come home to a house full of kids."

"Yeah, that must be hard on him," she repeated flatly. Ketron didn't bother to remind her neighbor that Marvin was partially responsible for the number of the children in the house.

"He's done a great job with the lawn," Mrs. Franks commented. She appraised the property. "Have you had any time to clean up the house?"

Some statements were truly innocuous. That was not one of them. Mrs. Franks had come over to bring the family a casserole a couple of months ago and the house had been in a disarray. They had just returned from almost two hours of dance classes, and they were preparing to leave for the last game of Bonnie's spring soccer tournament. Ketron had thrown peanut sandwiches together, and Sonny had run around the house, burning pent-up energy. Mrs. Franks had looked at the unwashed lunch dishes and the toys that had littered the floor and pronounced her judgement on Ketron's housekeeping abilities.

It bothered Ketron that her neighbor thought she was an unclean person. She wanted to tell Mrs. Franks that the dishes were washed and the floors were scrubbed each night before she laid down for bed, but she doubted the lady would believe her. Mrs. Franks's opinion of her was deeper than the state of the house during that visit. She didn't value Ketron's contributions because she stayed home with her children. In her eyes, Marvin was the more valuable parent because he was employed. To Mrs. Franks, who had focused on her career and hardly interacted with her grandchildren and adult children, it was inconceivable that the house was messy when Ketron was there all day, even if there were four or five messy children living there with her.

Ketron tried to defend herself; she couldn't help it. "It's clean before I go to bed at night."

Mrs. Franks closed her eyes and smiled in a gesture meant to show her unspoken disbelief. Thankfully, she changed the subject.

"Will you watch my place while I'm gone?" Ketron nodded like she did every time Mrs. Franks asked her that question. "I heard there were break ins on the other side of the creek."

Ketron hadn't heard reports about robbers, but she had avoided the town's online news for a couple of weeks. She wondered if some of the noises she had heard at night were burglars assessing the house. Before she could say so, Bonnie spoke.

"Mom and I were talking about the house. Who lived in it before us?"

Mrs. Franks placed her hand on Ketron's car door. Dirt from her gloves brushed the leather, leaving a long, brown line across it. "That nice couple that fixed it up owned the house before your family. The Sheltons had it for a decade or more. You guys bought the house from them," she reminded Ketron.

"Yeah, but who lived here before them," Bonnie pressed.

Mrs. Franks weighed her question. "I honestly don't know. I didn't live here long before the Sheltons started fixing up the place.

Bonnie opened her door and started to unbuckle Sonny. Once he was free, Ketron would have to run after him or wrestle him into the house. Either way, she had come to the uncomfortable part of the conversation where she was supposed to invite her neighbor inside.

A truck chugged up the road, causing both women to turn. Mrs. Franks waved happily, but she dropped her smile as soon as the vehicle passed. "Who was that?" Ketron asked.

"Lisa Paul." She took a coated hair band from the pocket of her shorts and pulled her hair through it. "If there's a crazy lady in town then it's her." She chuckled. "She's nuts, but she has the memory of an elephant. She might know the answer to your question about the house."

An awkward silence followed. Ketron busied herself with unfastening Amelia from her car seat, but the pause in the conversation weighed on her.

"I guess you need to get in there and make your hard-working husband some dinner," Mrs. Franks said. "Are you having peanut butter sandwiches tonight?"

Ketron tried to stay cordial. "I think I'm going to fix chicken."

"Well, that's nice." Ketron was happy with her neighbor's response until she added, "The children will like chicken nuggets. Let Marvin know that I baked some coconut pie. I'll bring him over a slice. He deserves a treat after working all week."

Ketron's face burned. She had planned to make homemade chicken and dumplings, but Mrs. Franks assumed she was preparing a quick freezer meal. And why was Marvin the only one who deserved coconut pie? Ketron had cleaned the house, washed the laundry, and chauffeured the children to their appointments and activities.

"Coconut pie will go great with my mom's homemade ice cream!" Bonnie volunteered.

God bless that child, Ketron thought. Thankfully, none of the other children contradicted her.

"You make homemade ice cream?" Mrs. Franks was awestruck, and Ketron enjoyed the feeling.

"I have a lot of children," she replied simply. "And children love ice cream."

Ketron's chicken and dumplings melted in her mouth. The satisfaction of Bonnie's unexpected lie had trickled into her meal, and she savored the feeling of vindication.

Marvin picked at his food. He sighed heavily every time he put his spoon into a dumpling. "Are they done?" he asked, immediately deflating Ketron's mood.

"I didn't want them to be dry."

"Mine are fine," Bonnie voiced.

Marvin usually didn't address Bonnie directly. "I have a doughy mess in my bowl. Maybe everyone else got the good dumplings."

"You can have my bowl," Ketron offered, and placed her dumplings in front of him. "I'm not hungry anymore."

Marvin continued to huff and didn't eat the dumplings out of her bowl. Ketron fed Amelia small bites along with her baby food. The baby smiled and waved at her father, and he waved back. "There's Daddy's girl."

Ketron rarely argued, especially in front of the children, but her temper flared. It was as if someone else were speaking the words for her, even though she meant them. "Daddy's girl? You hardly see her, and you haven't really been involved with her since you made sure that she had your mother's name."

Marvin stood up so fast that he pushed his chair over behind him. The light above them flickered. Ketron reasoned that a wire may have pulled loose when his chair hit the floor. "What's wrong with you? I'm her father. I have rights."

Ketron should have waited until the children were out of range of their argument to say something to him, but she couldn't keep her mouth closed. "Sure, you have rights, but how is she suddenly a Daddy's girl? When she was a newborn, I let you hold her, but you'd give her right back because she cried."

"I don't have food for her." He cupped his hands under his chest.

Amelia sensed the tension and stretched her hands out to her mother. Ketron unbuckled the straps on the highchair and sat the baby in her lap. "That may be so, but she's not been hungry every second for the last eleven months! She smiles at you now, so you pay attention to her, but when she cries, you only check on her long enough to assign blame. You don't comfort her."

Sonny stopped eating and stared at his parents. Nora and Winslow were unaffected.

Marvin threw his hands up as the light flickered again. "All you do is nag at me. Why are you even here?"

"Why *am* I here?" Ketron returned, raising her voice. "You stay in your room with your video games and beer. You don't come out anymore."

Marvin picked up his chair and slammed it against the table. "Oh, poor Ketron. Maybe you could talk about it with your psychiatrist. But when you do, be sure to tell him you're keeping my daughter from me!"

Two things happened almost simultaneously. Sonny slung his spoon on the floor and the light over their heads popped. Everyone shielded their eyes, and Ketron covered Amelia when they heard the light blow, so no one was hurt. The sun hadn't set, and the dusky light allowed them to pick up the pieces of the broken bulb and change it.

"I've never seen a bulb shatter like that," Ketron commented.

"Me neither," Marvin agreed.

Nora picked up her spoon, but Ketron stopped her. "No, sweetie. There could be glass particles in your food."

"He hit the light so you would stop fighting," Sonny said. He bounced a dinosaur on his dumplings before Ketron could move his plate.

"Who, buddy?" Marvin asked him.

Sonny squirmed in his seat and then ran into the living room.

"Jeremy again?" he asked Ketron.

Ketron shrugged her shoulders. Now that the crisis had been resolved, she was still angry with Marvin. He stopped collecting the glass and left her to finish. Bonnie took Amelia in the living room and watched a show with Sonny and the baby. Nora and Winslow tried to help, but Ketron sent them to another room after Nora was cut by a piece of the glass. She bandaged her daughter's wound and finally finished cleaning the mess.

"Are you going to that woman's house?" Bonnie asked when she joined her.

"What woman?"

"Lisa Paul. Mrs. Franks said she'd know about the history of this house."

"You're really curious," Ketron marveled. "You don't seem to get excited about anything."

Bonnie rolled her eyes. "There could be a ghost living here. Of course I want to know. Can I go with you when you talk to her?

Ketron considered her daughter's suggestion. "I have no business going to her house. What am I going to do? Should I knock on her door and hope for the best?"

"We could ask her to buy Girl Scout cookies," Bonnie grinned, exposing a slight overbite she was trying to correct with an overnight retainer.

"Sure, but the cookie sale ended in March."

"We still have some boxes left over. Do you think she likes the chocolate coconut ones?"

Ketron shook her head. "Everyone likes those, but that's not the point. She's going to know that we're using an excuse to talk to her."

"But that's what we're doing, so..."

Ketron sighed. "Only you would be so arrogant to assume that everyone wants to talk to you. We live on the side of a mountain, and she lives farther up than us. She probably likes the privacy."

"What does that have to do with us?"

Ketron narrowed her eyes. "Lisa Paul may not like visitors. Mrs. Franks believes she's crazy, so I bet she stays to herself."

Bonnie hoisted Amelia into her arms and then passed her to Ketron. "I think we should go."

Ketron was unconvinced. What could Lisa Paul know about her house anyway?

Chapter Thirteen

Present

"Why do you do this to yourself?" Shauna asked her as they pulled Sonny and Matty up a hill on their tricycles. "It's hot and sticky, and there are so many other things we could do, like drink wine."

Ketron laughed. "I like to walk, and I like the company."

"Why don't you get Marvin to walk with you? He could stand to lose some of that beer belly."

Ketron eyed her friend, and Shauna put her hand over her mouth. She looked at Sonny and back at Ketron. "I'm sorry. I wasn't thinking about little ears."

"That's okay. To be honest, I think he knows his father is not doing well."

They walked up the rest of the hill in silence. Bonnie stayed behind them, staring at her phone, and imitating jerky movements from a new dance trend. Amelia kicked her legs against her mother's sides and Nora and Winslow padded along, choosing to push their bikes up the hill at a comfortable distance from the adults.

"They have the same highlights," Shauna marveled. She had been fascinated with the twins since she'd met them, always finding small similarities.

"They *are* siblings," Ketron replied. "They share DNA like any other set of siblings from the same parents."

"Have you told them yet?"

Ketron shook her head fiercely. She put her finger to her lips and hoped that Nora and Winslow had not heard her.

Shauna took the hint. "I wish I had been a twin. Could you imagine having someone to share almost every memory with you?"

Both women had been their parents' only child. Ketron's mother had not wanted more children and Shauna's father was a drug addict. He had left her mom before Shauna could remember him. Her mom devoted her life to her, but she died when Shauna was a teenager. Shauna took her death hard, turning to drugs for comfort.

After going downhill, the rest of the walk passed quickly with both women pausing their conversations to call to one or all of their children to watch for cars or stay out of a neighbor's yard. Ketron enjoyed the shared experience with another mother, even if Shauna was not as devoted to Matty as Ketron was to her children.

The cool air enveloped them when they walked into the house and the children ran to the freezer for popsicles. Ketron grabbed two water bottles and handed one to Shauna. Marvin pushed his door open and barely uttered a word on his way to get another beer.

He waved at Shauna half-heartedly, but she didn't return the gesture. "It's not a good idea to normalize beer consumption in front of the children."

"This is *my* house." He turned his face, showing his profile. "Don't you drink wine?" he pointed out.

"I drink it when my son is tucked into bed for the night," she returned.

"This is my house. I'll do whatever I want." He shuffled back to his room.

Before Marvin was out of earshot, Shauna called after him, "Hitler called. He said he wants his friendship bracelet back."

Bonnie laughed so hard that the juice from her popsicle came out of her nose. The comment wasn't heard by the rest of the children who were playing at the other end of the house.

Marvin shut his door a little harder than necessary.

Ketron muffled her laughter so her husband wouldn't hear her. "I thought you liked him."

Shauna took a long pull from her water bottle and set it down between them. "I did, but he's changed, and it's not for the better."

Shauna placed her hand on Ketron's arm. She could feel her friend's concern in her touch. Shauna had been through the same cycles as Marvin, but she had recovered. She had confessed to Ketron that she was sometimes triggered or tempted, but she could keep her urges from consuming her new life. Marvin was different. He had every reason to stay sober, but he didn't think he had a problem.

"If it doesn't get better soon, what are you going to do?" Shauna asked her.

Two sets of eyes stared at Ketron. She didn't have an answer.

Chapter Fourteen

Present

Sometimes Ketron was alone in her thoughts. It didn't happen often, but there were stolen moments where she'd sneak into the bathroom or open her eyes into the night while everyone slept. The air was still, and the people in the house seemed far away, even though she hadn't left. She couldn't plan for the brief reprieves, and she never knew their length. She just absorbed them fully, allowing the quiet to surround her and either relax or inspire her.

It was well after midnight when she finally laid down, so she could only guess that she had awakened around four o'clock in the morning. At first, she welcomed the hour, thinking that she could rest more before she prepared Marvin for work, but then she realized her mind had leaped out of sleep and was searching for the anxieties that plagued her daily thoughts.

The air unit turned off and Ketron was thankful that her husband had remembered to turn off his television. He needed the noise in the background to drift into a comfortable doze, but it kept her from achieving her best sleep. Pops and cracks announced the wood's expansion from the heating and cooling temperatures, and the refrigerator hummed steadily.

The tapping was the only sound Ketron didn't recognize. At first, she thought it came from the kitchen. The sound made her think of a metal object tapping on the kitchen tile. She imagined that it was like the clicking of a bug. Somehow, the noise shifted, and Ketron sensed a presence move into the dining room where it would have a clear view of her. The tapping stopped for a moment. She had seconds to tell herself that she had imagined it, but then it resumed. With it, the feeling of being watched consumed her. She was overwhelmed with anger so venomous that it almost took her breath. There was no shadow or form. There was only the feeling that something was staring at her through the darkness. It knew she was awake...and it hated her.

Chapter Fifteen

Past

Ketron's mother pulled over to the side of the road. Ketron heard the rapid clicking of the signal and opened one eye. The last time it had ticked so fast, her mother had said it was because the light was about to stop working.

Gwynevive was talking to herself, or whoever she thought was in the car with them. She had been crying, and her voice was pregnant with emotion.

"It is not the only way!" she whisper-shouted. "We can move and live a normal life. We were normal once, when you let me take my medicine. Don't you remember?"

Her mother cowered as if someone had shouted, but Ketron could only hear the cars passing on the road and the insistent clicking of the taillight. She didn't want her mother to be upset, so she let out a low groan and stretched. "Why are we stopped, Mom?"

Her mother wiped her eyes quickly with her thumbs. "I had to pull over for a minute, but we'll be on our way again soon." She looked at the passenger seat, and fear replaced the smile she had put on for Ketron's sake. She shook her head violently, and then ignored whatever presence she had conjured in her mind.

They pulled back onto the road, and a loud horn sounded. Her mother jumped and threw up her hand. "I think I've been driving too long."

Ketron didn't know if she was talking to her, so she remained quiet. Within minutes, her mother's hand slid off the steering wheel, and they headed toward an embankment. "Mom!"

She popped back to life and jerked the steering wheel. They veered safely back onto the road. Luckily, no one else had been in either lane when her mother had fallen asleep.

"Can we stop somewhere?" Ketron suggested. A cold chill swept over her.

"No," her mother said resolutely.

"We almost wrecked," Ketron pressed. "Can't you just pull over for a few hours?"

"NO!"

Ketron didn't try to argue. For the next hour she watched her mother do little things to keep herself awake. She sang with the music on the radio until she slurred the words together. She moved around erratically, sometimes uttering nonsense. She dug her fingernails into the palms of her hands, drawing blood.

Ketron was afraid to incite any more of her mother's anger, so she didn't mention when the car started to slow. She watched as her mother's body slumped. Without a foot on the accelerator, the car drifted to the middle of the road and stopped. On the radio, Chumbawumba was singing about emotional stamina.

Ketron sat in the vehicle while it idled, wondering what she should do. In the still night, her hair floated around her face as if it were held up by strong static electricity.

"Mom?"

Her hair dropped, and Ketron wondered if she had imagined it. She tapped her mother's shoulder.

Ketron's mom shot up and gasped for air like she had been held underwater. She glanced back at Ketron and then stared at the road, slowly remembering what she had been doing before she fell asleep.

Headlights washed over them, and a truck pulled up beside their car. It had to move to the shoulder of the road to get around the vehicle, but it gave Ketron a good view of the occupant. The driver was a robust middle-aged man with a copper beard and sweaty red cheeks. He nodded at Ketron and smiled. "Are you ladies okay?"

Ketron's mother flicked the automatic window down and responded, "We had some car trouble, but a nice young man helped us. We were just getting ready to move out of the middle of the road." She added a smile.

The man looked down the road, possibly in search of the young man Ketron's mother had mentioned. He seemed unconvinced when he addressed her mother again. "If you don't mind me sayin' so, you look really tired. Are you goin' somewhere far?"

"No," Ketron's mother answered. "And yes," she corrected. "We're moving to Erwin, but we're stopping in Nashville for the night."

"Erwin!" The man's full face glowed. "Northeast Tennessee is pretty this time of year. I take my mother and her sister to the Apple Festival there almost every October." His mouth formed a thin line that was just visible under his recently groomed facial hair. "Nashville is still an hour out from here. Can I follow you there and make sure that you make it to your hotel?"

"That's not necessary," Ketron's mother said sweetly. "My daughter's awake now, so she can help keep me from falling asleep."

Ketron's heart soared at her mother's mention of her. She was going to trust Ketron to keep her awake, and that would mean an hour of uninterrupted talking with her mom!

The man rummaged in his car and produced an envelope and a pen. He wrote something down quickly. "Will you call me when you get to your hotel? I won't be able to sleep tonight if I think you're off the road somewhere with that little girl."

Ketron's mother accepted the envelope he tossed into the passenger seat and looked at it. "John Winslow?"

The man nodded. "Most people call me Big John or Big Red." He stroked his beard to illustrate the reason for the latter nickname. "I had 'Big Red' painted on my truck until some gum company made me take it down."

Ketron couldn't see where the name had been painted over on his pickup truck, so she assumed he was talking about an eighteen-wheeler. She thought he looked like a truck driver, even though she had never met one.

"I'll call you when we get there," her mother promised.

"I keep the phone with me." He held up a black phone that looked like a cordless phone with a long antenna. "It's my work phone. They use some sort of satellite to bounce a signal in places you wouldn't think it'd reach!"

"Fascinating," her mother said flatly.

Big Red chuckled. "I'm sorry for just goin' on. I don't have many people to talk to since my wife passed. It's just me and my mom, and she's got a tad of dementia." He put his truck back in gear. "You ladies be safe."

He stopped before he was out of shouting distance. "I didn't catch your names."

"Gwynevieve," her mother called back. "This is Chelsea." She jabbed her thumb in Ketron's direction. Big Red threw up his hand and his truck glided up the road.

Ketron waved at him as he left. His jolly mood was infectious, and she would have loved for him to have followed them to their hotel.

A hotel! Ketron had never stayed in a hotel. She wondered if it would have a swimming pool and a balcony. She hoped it would have little soaps and soft, fluffy towels. She hadn't taken a shower since the day she left school and she was starting to stink.

The conversation with Big Red had revived her mother, and it was almost an hour before her posture began to droop again. Sensing that they had been traveling for some time, Ketron asked, "When will we get to the hotel?"

The dreams she had of swimming pools and trial-sized soaps were dashed when her mother laughed. "Do you think I'm made of money? I only told that dope we had a hotel so he would leave us alone." She took the envelope off the dashboard, wadded it up, and tossed it into the passenger seat. "He must be some sort of pervert."

Ketron crossed her arms. "He was nice. I don't know why you lied to him about my name."

"Wake up Ketron! He asked me if he could follow us to the hotel. I gave him your middle name to protect you."

"He was just being a good person."

Her mother snorted. "You actually think there are good people in this world?"

"I have lots of friends at school. They're good."

"Yeah, right. Your friends will forget about you after the end of next week." She glanced back with a cruel smile playing on her lips. "It won't matter, though. You won't be going back there."

Ketron had already guessed that she would never see the home she had known her whole life again, but it still hurt her. She looked down at her feet.

Her mother continued to lecture her. "I've done you a favor. You don't need to get close to people and have them wreck your life."

Ketron was quiet for a few minutes before she remarked, "We're going to Erwin. Where is that?"

For once, her mother didn't have a brisk reply. "It's a small town in Northeast Tennessee. I grew up there."

"Are the kids nice?" Ketron imagined making new friends and exploring the mountains.

"No," her mother chuckled. "Not at all."

Ketron shrugged her shoulders; she didn't believe her, but she refrained from arguing. She was determined that something good would come out of their move. She would find a friend if she had to search for years to find the right person.

Ketron grew concerned about her mother's promise to Big Red. She had told him that she would call him when they reached their hotel, but it was clear that they weren't going to stop. Loose change jiggled in the cup holder opposite of her mother's styrofoam cup of sweet tea. She wished she could call Big Red without her mother's notice, but she had very little experience with phones, so she doubted she could call him quickly. She imagined him sitting at his house in front of a large stone fireplace, worried that the woman and girl he had met were stranded on the road. She thought of him getting in his truck and searching for them until his eyes wouldn't stay open. Would he run off an embankment, like Ketron and her mother almost did? Ketron couldn't stand the idea of the sweet man getting into an accident because of her mother's false promise.

After another hour, her mother pulled into a gas station. "Don't move," she ordered, and went inside. A breeze stirred around her mother, but Ketron only felt oppressive heat.

Ketron spied a pay phone in front of the car. She snatched the wadded envelope off the passenger seat and grabbed a couple of quarters from the cupholder. She dialed the number and deposited the required amount to place the call. She was connected quickly, and Big Red answered on the first ring.

"Hello, Big Red," she said. "This is Ketron. My mother told you my name was Chelsea because she thought you were a pervert."

Big Red let out a hearty laugh. "I suspect your mama's only tryin' to protect you. Wait! She doesn't know you're callin' me?"

"No, sir," Ketron replied. "She wasn't going to call you, and I didn't want you to worry. You were so nice to us."

"That was sweet of you, but you shouldn't call strangers without your mama's permission. You need to respect her decisions."

"You're not a stranger. You're John Winslow. Your friends call you Big Red. I want to call you Big Red."

Ketron could feel the huge grin in his voice when he spoke. "If that means you want to be my friend, then I'll be happy if you call me Big Red. You'll need a nickname, too. I'll call you Ketty-Kat."

Ketron giggled. Her mother was skeptical of everyone, but Ketron was convinced Big Red was a good person.

"Now, I better let you go before you get into trouble. Did you make it to the hotel?"

"Yes, sir. My mom is checking us in right now." She felt badly for lying to him, but the purpose of the call was to keep him from worrying, so she pushed the guilt away.

"Okay, good. Now, listen. I want you to keep my number in case you need it."

"I will." Ketron looked up and noticed her mother was at the counter paying for her items and gas for their car.

"Call me if you ever need anything. It may take me three or four hours to make it to Erwin, depending on where my company has me in my truck, but

I'll get to you as fast as I can." Ketron realized that Big Red had probably guessed more about her situation than he had let on.

"Have a good night, Ketty-Kat," he told her. "Maybe I'll see you when I'm back in Erwin."

"Goodnight," Ketron echoed and hung up the receiver. She hadn't wanted to conclude the call so abruptly, but she had to get back to the car before her mother got back in the car.

When she looked back up, her body froze. Her mother was walking to the car!

Ketron's mother opened the car door and replaced her empty can of sweet tea with a new can. She picked up a few pieces of trash before she stepped back outside. She hadn't noticed Ketron was out of the car.

Ketron waited until her mother fully faced the gas pumps before she dove into her open window. She settled in her seat in time for her mother to dip her head into the window.

"Stop shaking the car!"

Ketron gave an audible sigh of relief. She felt confident until her mother climbed back into the car.

"Where's that envelope?"

Ketron's heart skipped a beat. She hadn't put the envelope back in the seat!

Her mind worked fast. "Did you throw it away?"

Her mother appeared genuinely thoughtful. "You're probably right."

Gwynevieve pulled out of the gas station and popped the tab on her sweet tea. Ketron smiled, slipping the envelope into the pocket of her jeans.

Chapter Sixteen

Present

Ketron was exhausted. She was usually the last to go to sleep and the first to rise, but her body only allowed her to rest until Marvin's door broke the silence. His heavy footfalls vibrated through the couch, and he managed a considerable yawn before he made it to the bathroom.

Amelia rolled over and smiled. Ketron put her nipple in the baby's mouth and hoped that she'd be able to read or relax before she was expected to cook and run behind each child with a vacuum and an antibacterial wipe, but Marvin exited the bathroom, saw that he had jolted Amelia from her sleep, and spoke.

"I want eggs and bacon for breakfast."

Ketron put her index finger to her lips, but the damage was done. Amelia rolled over and scooted into a standing position, holding Ketron's arm for support and jumping against the back rest of the couch. "I'll go make it," Ketron said. Her plans to relax were defeated.

He shrugged. "I meant later. I'm going back to sleep."

Ketron could have cried. Her chance for a little quiet time to herself was gone. "Then why did you wake the baby?"

"She was already awake," he insisted. "You were feeding her, and she was moving around."

"But she would have gone back to sleep! I was going to rest a few minutes before the kids woke up."

"What? So you can play around on your phone?"

"I don't 'play around on my phone.'" She put air quotes arounds his words. "I read my electronic books."

"Call it what you want. It's just another excuse." He walked to his bedroom.

"What's that supposed to mean?" Ketron called after him.

He mumbled something from inside the confines of his walls that sounded like 'for you not to do your job,' but he wouldn't repeat it when she pressed him. Sonny had overheard his father's breakfast request, and he hounded Ketron until she baked an entire pack of turkey bacon in the oven.

"Why do you bake it?" Bonnie asked when she joined them. "Dad just puts it in the frying pan."

"I don't want the grease to pop onto Amelia or Sonny while I'm cooking."

Bonnie nodded. It was rare for her to peek out of her blankets before noon, so Ketron tried to take advantage of the extra time she had with her before Winslow and Nora woke up.

"Are you excited about school this year?"

Bonnie leaned against the counter, propping her head on her hands. "I guess. I hope Bell-Bell and I are in the same classes."

Ketron cracked the last of the eggs over her glass mixing bowl and added a little milk. "If not, you can see her at soccer. And it looks like the coach has scheduled fourteen games this month."

Bonnie put her face in her hands. "Ahh! We'll have to play the Cyclones twice!"

"Three times if you win the first game of the tournament."

The cyclones were the only team that beat them in their sixth and seventh grade years. The Cyclones coach placed defenders on Bonnie and Bella who kept them from working their combined magic on the field.

Ketron paused, debating if she would ask the question on her mind. "Did you hear anything last night?"

"I hear everything," Bonnie replied. "This place is haunted." She wiggled her fingers in front of Ketron's face.

Ketron playfully swatted her hand away. "I'm serious. I thought I heard something last night."

"Where?"

"In the dining room," Ketron replied, taking out the bread.

The house had once been a wooden, one-bedroom shack. Through the years, various owners had added on to it until it had three bedrooms. The back door was most accessible to the driveway, and it emptied into the dining room. From there, the open floor plan allowed easy access to the kitchen and living room. Marvin's room was on one side of the house, and he often complained about the noise from the television when he went to bed early for work, as his room was next to the living room. A small hallway ran along the other side of the house, and Bonnie's room, the twins' room and the only bathroom in the house could be accessed from it. The single bathroom was a sore spot with Bonnie, as her showers were limited to fifteen minutes.

Bonnie glanced over at the fireplace. It was the focal point of the dining room, with rocks from the river stacked upon one another. Winslow and Sonny climbed it when Ketron wasn't looking, and she feared a broken arm or leg was in their future.

"Maybe it came from there," Bonnie suggested.

It had been converted into a gas fireplace, but Marvin had cleaned it out when they moved in, and he had found evidence of bird and squirrel nests. There was a decent-sized hole at the bottom corner of the fireplace, and Marvin was uncertain if it led all the way to the basement. Ketron had hoped he would patch the hole, but it was just another project that didn't get done when he started drinking.

"I doubt it," Ketron replied. "It came from inside the house." She didn't tell her daughter about the presence she had felt. "I suppose it could have been a rat." If Bonnie hadn't heard the noise, she didn't want her to worry in case it was her overactive imagination.

"Then maybe it was your husband," she giggled. "He's kind of like a rat."

Ketron shook her head and checked the bacon. She scrambled the eggs and buttered the toast. The smell of bacon woke the twins, and Nora and Winslow filtered into the kitchen, rubbing their eyes. They plopped down in their chairs unceremoniously.

"I heard there was bacon," Winslow barked.

He was usually the last child to wake up, sometimes outsleeping Bonnie. Ketron usually let him rest. When she woke him before he was ready, Winslow's days were harder, and he found offense in the smallest things.

Ketron scooped a couple of slices onto each plate and added eggs and bacon. They all enjoyed the meal, keeping their voices low, so that they didn't disturb Marvin. Ketron had made an entire package of bacon, but little hands kept grabbing for more, and she didn't have the heart to stop them. *Marvin will get over it if he doesn't have bacon this morning*, she thought and hoped there wouldn't be an argument over it. Their growing children needed a good meal to start the day, and he wouldn't be able to refuse their extra portions either if he could see their happy faces around the breakfast table.

Bonnie looked around thoughtfully. "Do you know anything else about the house?"

Ketron didn't want to discuss the sound she'd heard with little ears listening, but she decided that talking about the history of the house was innocuous. She had been through the documents in their mortgage, and she made some assumptions based on the information in the listing the realtor had posted. She had glanced over it when they had made the appointment to view the house, but she hadn't considered the house as a real option until Marvin told her he had made an offer. She had thought they were going to live in a bright yellow two-story house in town, but they were outbid. "It was built a little over a hundred years ago," she explained. "I'd say it's been through a couple of owners, but the Shelton's had it for ten years before they sold it to us. They put in a lot of updates, like the shower."

The Sheltons had made several major renovations. The husband-and-wife team knocked down a wall and moved the laundry room to the basement. They cleared out a portion of the basement, but they never made it past the gaping hole that led to a crawl space under the dining room and kitchen. Ketron couldn't look at the opening without envisioning a yawning mouth, ready to swallow anyone who crawled inside it.

Bonnie wrinkled her nose. "Yeah, they just had to put in a shower and take the bath out."

Ketron agreed. It made oatmeal baths impossible, and she was worried that Sonny was going to need them, since he loved to roll in weeds. "I think the husband was fixing this place for his wife's mother, but she died before he finished the project."

"That explains the weird handles everywhere," Bonnie commented.

"Yep. It was a safety feature for her to pull herself up if she fell."

"I guess that big, long bar in their room was supposed to be by the old lady's bed." She jerked her thumb at the twins.

Ketron cringed at the way her daughter referenced an elder. "That was going to be her bedroom, since it was right next to the bathroom, so he put the rod there in case she fell out of bed."

Bonnie shook her head. "Why didn't your husband take it down?"

Ketron didn't want to say that Marvin had concentrated on very little indoors before he started falling asleep with a beer in his hand. Fortunately, Nora piped up. "I like the bar. I use it to practice my ballet positions."

Marvin's door popped open, and Sonny ran to him. "Can you play a dinosaur battle with me, Daddy?"

Marvin rubbed his eyes and stumbled around his son. "Not right now, buddy. Let Daddy get some coffee and breakfast. The bacon smells good."

"We're fresh out of bacon," Bonnie said casually, popping a bite into her mouth.

Marvin stopped and stood with his back to them. "I told you I wanted bacon," he directed at Ketron.

"The children were hungry," Ketron defended. "I didn't eat any."

He resumed his trek to the coffee pot and mumbled, "I don't know why I work all week if I can't get anything to eat."

Ketron stared at his rounding belly. It was mostly from his late-night alcohol binges, but he never missed a meal.

"I'll make you sausage biscuits," Ketron offered.

"Don't bother," he spat and took his coffee back to his room.

Bonnie raised her eyebrows and chuckled. Sonny glared at her. "Don't laugh at my daddy," he scolded. Bonnie raised her hands in defeat and took her plate to the sink.

The children watched a dinosaur movie together and Ketron washed the breakfast dishes. She took Marvin sausage biscuits and eggs after she had given him enough time to grieve over the bacon.

"After you finish eating, will you take the laundry basket to the basement?"

He nodded. Marvin complained about the heavy load in the basket, and he fussed about the amount of water and electricity that it took to wash laundry for seven people. However, he realized the necessity of actually doing the laundry. Ketron could have shoved the basket down the narrow stairs, but she'd rather keep it all in the basket.

Amelia always traveled to the basement with her. Marvin wasn't usually sober enough to keep an eye on her, and Ketron didn't like to ask any of her children to watch their baby sister. It didn't seem fair.

Marvin knocked on Bonnie's door. The entry to the basement was in her room. She flicked the door open and plopped back down on her bed. Ketron wandered into the room and Bonnie made faces at Amelia.

"Is that Daddy's girl?" Marvin called as he climbed the steps.

Bonnie rolled her eyes. Marvin didn't acknowledge his stepdaughter's response.

How sad, Ketron thought. *They used to at least pretend to get along before he started drinking.*

Marvin had left the basement door open, so she turned around to inch her way down the steps. The door had once opened into a closet, but someone had opened the floor of the closet up to allow access to the basement. It was exceptionally narrow, so Ketron had to hold the baby facing out and go down the steps backward until the last three steps. Then she could turn around without playing limbo with the ceiling.

For some reason, she looked behind her when she was halfway down. What she saw caused her body to turn cold and her hands to sweat. She tightened her hold on Amelia and bolted up the stairs.

Bonnie jumped up from her bed and grabbed her mother's shoulders. "What's wrong?" Nora and Winslow ran in to investigate, and they started screaming, "Snake!" Sonny wandered into the room, looked at the serpent winding its way up the steps, and shrugged his shoulders. "My daddy will kill it," he said dismissively.

"MARVIN!" Ketron yelled. It took several calls, but he finally appeared in Bonnie's doorway.

"What?" he asked. "My team was one point away. Somebody better be dead."

Ketron was having a hard time regulating her breathing. Her legs felt like gelatin, and she could almost feel the snake slithering across her feet. It had been inches away from her!

"There is a snake in the basement," Ketron managed to say.

"It's ten feet long!" Winslow exaggerated, hugging his twin. Nora nodded with her mouth open.

"Great! There's a snake, and you send the only one in the house who's working after it," he said. "If I get bitten, I'll be laid up in the hospital, and who's gonna pay the bills?"

Ketron's fear turned to anger. "Well, maybe I should have picked it up in my other hand and tossed it outside while I was holding our infant daughter!" Ketron wouldn't kill any living thing unless it directly threatened her family. She had been startled by the snake, but she realized that it had probably slithered through the drainpipe that ran along the basement floor.

"Bonnie's here," he countered. "You could have given the baby to her and killed it with the shovel at the bottom of the stairs."

"Those are strong words, coming from a man who's afraid to get bitten by it!"

"I'm not afraid of a bite. I just can't pave roads from a hospital bed." Ketron didn't move, and he finally gave in. "Fine! I'll go catch the snake." He carefully inched his way through the door and down the steps. The metal from the shovel grated against the concrete floor. Ketron grabbed Bonnie's elbow, preparing for a sudden bang.

Several minutes passed, and Ketron became nervous. "Are you okay?"

"Yeah," he yelled back. "I can't find it."

"What? It was right at the foot of the steps."

"It must have gone down the drainpipe."

"Or into a corner to hide," Bonnie muttered.

Marvin stomped up the steps. "I don't see it. Are you sure it was there?"

"Yes, Marvin," Ketron said, irritated. "The kids saw it, too."

"Did you see the snake?" he asked Sonny. Sonny simply smiled and walked out of the room like he was playing a game.

"How about you two?"

The twins nodded their heads vigorously. "It was ten feet long," Winslow repeated.

Marvin sized them up like he was having trouble believing them. Ketron couldn't contain her anger.

"Really, Marvin!" she shouted. "I saw a snake and it scared me to death!"

"Okay, okay," he conceded. "But I have to check, given your mom's history."

"Stop it!" Ketron hissed. "What happened to my mother might not happen to me. You've spoken to my doctor."

"It's genetic," he insisted. "You could just start seeing things one day."

Ketron stormed out of the room. She needed a place to cool off, but she didn't have an area of her own in the house. The children were in their rooms, she couldn't sit in their only bathroom, and Marvin would follow her to any other room. She grabbed her keys and stalked to her van.

She was not like Gwynevieve Renfro! She would recognize if schizophrenia took hold of her because it had swallowed her mother. She had seen a snake, and Marvin was turning her mother's mental illness around on her just because he couldn't find it. Ketron was so angry, and she had nowhere to direct her emotions. She finally broke down and cried, but she stopped quickly, angry with herself for allowing the tears, and worried that one of the neighbors would see her.

Amelia babbled contentedly in the passenger seat, playing with a closed tub of wipes from her diaper bag. She noticed Ketron staring at her and smiled.

"Why can't it be easy?" she asked her baby. She looked out the windshield. Seeing no one, she continued to talk to her infant. "We used to love each other so much. I confided my fears to him, and he seemed to understand. He used to be compassionate."

The infant arched an eyebrow as if she were skeptical.

"Okay," Ketron backpedaled. "He seemed to really care for me, though. And now, here I am, crying in a car over a snake."

Ten minutes later, she carried Amelia back into the house. She went straight to the kitchen and pulled the spices down for spring rolls.

Marvin ventured into the room a few minutes later. Ketron waited for an apology that didn't come. Finally, she put aside her anger and told him, "I hope you enjoy doing laundry from now on. I'll fold it and put it away, but I won't go back into the basement until I'm sure the snake is gone."

His jaw clinched and unclenched. "So, I work all week, and you want me to come home and do *your* job. That's—"

Ketron's expression stopped whatever argument he was going to raise. He dipped his head into the refrigerator, grabbed a beer, and went back into his room.

Chapter Seventeen

Present

Ketron didn't know why she was standing in front of Lisa Paul's house. The house itself wasn't exactly welcoming, but the 'No Trespassing' signs made her think twice before she opened the mossy gate. The cracker box house rarely received sun, and the dark curtains kept the little bit of light outside from reaching inside.

She climbed the steps without allowing her feet to rest her entire weight on the wood. The stairs announced her presence anyway, and the curtain to her left rustled as two eyes peeked out at her. They stared at each other with the glass between them. Ketron remembered her purpose and knocked on the door. The person on the other side was clearly nearby, but she made Ketron wait almost a full minute before she opened the door.

Ketron had seen Lisa Paul when she rode up and down the one-lane road past her house, so she didn't realize that the woman was only about Bonnie's height. Her hair was almost the color of carrots, and it frizzed out of her low ponytail. Skin hung around her mouth as if it were used to wearing a permanent frown and icy blue eyes calculated Ketron's next move.

"I—" Ketron started, but Lisa held up her hand.

"I know why yer here."

Ketron couldn't think of anything to say. Luckily, Lisa saved her from reaching for an explanation for her visit.

"You want to know about yer house, don't cha?"

Ketron wanted Lisa to respect her, so that she could glean as much information as possible, but she could only nod.

"Stay right there. I'll be out in a minute."

Ketron had imagined that she would have been brought inside, but Lisa closed the door. Ketron glanced around the porch and settled on an old black metal chair. It shouted its disapproval when she leaned back on it, so she inched into the middle of the seat.

"Nursing back," Lisa spoke when she rounded her house. Ketron had thought the lady would go through her front door, but she had walked around the house via her back door. "I had it when I nursed my boy," she continued as she climbed the steps. Each one seemed to bother her, and she grimaced from the pressure it put on her hip. A small, black and tan Yorkie ran around her legs.

Ketron hadn't noticed her posture and she sat up straight. The muscles in her lower back cried against it, but she didn't want to seem too casual in Lisa's presence.

Lisa stood on the porch, looking down at Ketron. She carried an aluminum can that Ketron thought was a beer but turned out to be an off-brand cola. Ketron felt uncomfortable, so she strung some words together. "I was in my garden, and I realized that I had never spoken to you, so I thought—"

"You thought you'd wander up here and see what the crazy old lady had to say about your house."

Ketron recognized defeat. "No one will tell me about the house."

The lady let out a chuckle. "Of course not."

"Why?" Ketron asked innocently. "Why do people pretend that they don't know about it?"

"I'd imagine it's 'cause they don't want to be sad."

"Is it that bad?'

"Well, only you can judge the way you feel about it, but I wasn't happy when I heard what happened."

"Were they nice people?" Ketron asked. She needed to move their conversation in the right direction, and she hoped her question would help.

"The boy's father was no good," Lisa spat. She dragged a metal chair closer to Ketron and relaxed against its rusted flecks of paint. The Yorkie glanced up for an invitation to sit in her owner's lap, and receiving none, the dog settled across her feet. Lisa stared into the woods that covered the area in front of her house, looking out into trees that obscured any view aside from the one in her mind. "He drank all the time. The boy's mother was a saint, and she loved Christmas. I'd see her out every year, no matter the weather, stringing up lights around the house and pullin' an inflatable Jesus into the yard."

The women sat in silence for a moment when the rare sound of a train horn blared in the distance. "The mother was mute. I don't know if she was born that way, or if it happened during her life, but I never heard the woman say a word."

Lisa looked at the break in the trees that began the subdivided neighborhood as if she were looking at an opening into the past. "She used to walk with the boy as he rode his bicycle up the hill." Lisa glanced at Ketron before turning her attention to the closed forest again. "A lot like you with your young uns. Anyway, the tyke fell off his bicycle into the ditch once. She didn't get upset or make a sound. She walked over to him, picked him up, and stared into his eyes. She caressed his face, right down his jawline." Lisa mimicked the gesture in the air in front of her. "She showed more compassion with her eyes than anyone could have put into words. And that's the thing," she went on, "The two of 'em didn't seem to need words. He nodded and got back on his bicycle. Another little kid would have been wailin' for much longer."

Ketron thought of Sonny. She loved him dearly, but he would have screamed until she got him home if he had fallen into a ditch.

After another sip of her cola, Lisa continued, "That poor woman became sickly, though. When she couldn't preform household duties anymore, the boy's father left her for another woman. The child couldn't have seen more than a decade of life before he started cookin', cleanin', and takin' care of his mother. He was such a good boy, but he was silent. His mother couldn't speak to him, and he'd suffered under his father's hand, so there was a permanent bitterness on his face.

Without warning, she shook a cigarette out of a pack and lit it. Ketron opened her mouth to protest, but she was on the woman's property, and she didn't want to offend Lisa before she had told her more about the boy and his family. Lisa noticed her discomfort and said, "You don't smoke, do ya?" She let out a knowing chuckle. Instead of extinguishing it, she added, "That's okay. I can smoke enough of 'em fer you too." Lisa smiled, revealing four sporadic teeth, the color of cornbread.

Ketron was relieved when Lisa revisited the story, more somber than she had been previously. "I didn't see 'em for a couple of weeks. It was gettin' close to winter, so I didn't pay it any mind. I had a glancin' thought that the boy's mother had died, but I was busy with my dogs. Annie'd had a new litter of pups," she mentioned, as if Ketron was familiar with her dog. "After a while, a neighbor reported the smell."

Ketron let out a small breath that she hadn't known she was holding. *So, the boy's mother* had *died.* She swallowed hard, and briefly wondered what her children would do if something happened to her. She hoped Marvin would stop drinking and become a better father, but she honestly doubted he was strong enough to seek the help he needed.

"When the authorities finally burst through the door," Lisa said, "they found his mother in the hallway and Jeremy was at the bottom of the basement steps."

Ketron gasped, and Lisa nodded at her realization. "What? The little boy died."

Lisa took two quick puffs from her cigarette and held the smoke before releasing it in one long streaming cloud. "There was a chair in front of the fireplace and Christmas decorations around it, so the best they could guess is that he was on his way to hang a wreath on the mantle for Christmas. Poor soul lost his balance on the basement stairs and broke his neck."

"What about his mother?"

"Turns out that sweet lady had probably sensed the commotion. They found her in the hallway. Seems to me like she had heard the ruckus and she was trying to get to her son. I suppose it took too much out of her."

"She died on the same day," Ketron said miserably. Although, truth be known, she would wish for the same fate if she were in that position.

"I think it took a couple of days," Lisa informed her. "The coroner's a good friend of mine. He told me about it."

Ketron couldn't imagine lying in a hallway, without the ability to speak, and know that her son was most likely dead. She was still putting herself in the place of the woman who had died in the hallway of her house when Lisa spoke again.

"That good-for-nothing man, Joseph was his name, came back after the house was cleaned up and the funerals were over. He brought his floozie with him too!"

She shoved her cigarette against the chair's arm rest and let the embers on the end die out. The orange butt stuck up in a zig-zagged angle. Lisa chuckled, and Ketron snapped back, realizing that she had been staring at the cigarette. "It must be a real shock to you to come up here and see how the other half lives."

Ketron was mildly offended. "I live on the same road," she defended. "My house is maybe a block and a half away."

"Just like a city girl. You measure your distance from me in blocks, but we're in the country, missy. I would tell someone that your house is two up from the creek or the one with the bikes in the yard."

"You and my husband would get along," Ketron found herself saying. "He doesn't like the way I talk either."

Lisa grew serious. "Now, just because I pointed out that you're different doesn't mean I'd condone a husband speakin' against his wife."

Ketron was aghast. She thought Lisa had been making fun of her, but it was only her way of joking with a guest.

"A husband takes a wife for better or worse," Lisa continued. "You are one in the sight of the Lord, so both people need to treat the other like they are talkin' to the mirror."

Ketron pondered her statement. She was certainly guilty of some ill thoughts about her husband.

"I've seen your husband out tendin' your yard," she said, arching one copper and white eyebrow. "He's either a bit clumsy or strong in the drink."

Remembering that she had just heard the woman speak against talking badly about her spouse, Ketron only nodded.

Lisa returned her nod and shook out another cigarette. She paused with it in her hand. "He doesn't hit you, does he?"

"No," Ketron answered quickly.

Lisa sized her up, uncertain if her rushed answer was to cover up abuse. She took a deep breath and set her jaw.

"I'd better get back home," Ketron said, not wanting to outstay her welcome.

"I imagine the kiddies are missin' their mama."

"It's almost dinner time," Ketron explained, motioning to a summer sun that had fallen from its zenith but was still high in the sky.

"Yeah, you'll want to get that after supper walk in before dark."

Ketron was a little unnerved at the ease with which Lisa spoke about her family's routine. "Are we that predictable?"

Lisa jumped, but quickly recovered. "I see you out enough. You stop just outside my land."

"I don't want Sonny to run into the woods," Ketron said, hoping that Lisa didn't think that she had intentionally avoided her property.

"He's a wild one," Lisa commented. "He'll grow out of it soon enough."

"I don't know," Ketron countered. "This is the second year he's acted this way."

"Your baby's about a year old, right? I suspect yer boy is just after some attention."

Ketron gave her an uncertain smile and waved a farewell as she hurried home. Lisa had given her a lot to think about, and it wasn't only about the mysterious happenings at her house.

Chapter Eighteen

Present

"Did you make nice with the crazy lady?" Shauna asked.

She fed freeze-dried yogurt bites to Amelia while Sonny tried to crush his carrot sticks with a play hammer. "They were hungry," she explained when she noticed Ketron looking at the snacks.

"It's fine. I'll start dinner." She put a pot of water on the stove and added, "Lisa's not crazy."

"Oh, it's *Lisa* now." Shauna nodded her head knowingly. "Did she tell you what you wanted to know about the house?"

Ketron had confided her interest in the house to her friend, but she had omitted her paranormal experiences. If she had mentioned the presence she had felt, Shauna would have reluctantly sided with Marvin and told Ketron to seek psychiatric treatment. Shauna was pragmatic, and the voice in the video wouldn't have been enough proof to back up Ketron's claim.

"Yeah," Ketron answered. "There was a family that lived here before the Sheltons started remodeling it. A mother, father, and a boy who was a little older than the twins. The mother was sick, and the father left—"

Shauna scoffed. "Sounds about right."

Ketron was used to her friend's interruptions when it came to the perceived differences between genders, or the abandonment of spouses and children. "Anyway, the mother loved Christmas, and the boy was decorating the house for her, when he fell down the basement steps and died."

"That must have been some fall!"

"You've been down my basement steps. You know how tricky it is." Ketron hadn't allowed the children to enter the basement, other than Amelia when she carried the baby with her to do the laundry, but she could picture Winslow turning with difficulty on the staircase and padding down it while using the stairs for balance. "It would be hard for anyone to manage, especially a little boy with decorations in his hands."

"So, a child died in your house. That's disconcerting." She folded her hands in her lap and looked at them. To an outside observer, Shauna might appear to be praying, but she wasn't religious.

The water had reached a rolling boil, so Ketron poured the noodles out of the box. "His mother crawled after him and died in the hallway."

Shauna's head shot up. "What? Why didn't I hear about it?"

"You may have been in California at the time." Ketron stopped stirring the macaroni and shook her head. "Or maybe it wasn't an incident that happened in the last couple of decades. I didn't hear about it either, so they may have died a while ago."

"Two people died here. Isn't the realtor supposed to tell you about that?"

Ketron laughed. "I don't think there's a paranormal clause in the paperwork."

"I didn't say anything about paranormal activity." Her comment was brisk. "I meant that two people died here. You don't even know why the mother was sick to begin with. What if something in the house made her sick?"

Ketron pushed her wounded feelings down and remembered that she needed to maintain a rational approach to their conversation. "We had the radon levels tested before we moved in, but I got the feeling that the mother had cancer."

Shauna glanced outside and froze. She blinked rapidly and grabbed her keys. "I need to get back. Luke probably has dinner ready." Her composure slipped, and her last words were shaky.

Ketron had witnessed her friend's change. "What's wrong?"

Shauna hurried to the door, calling goodbyes to the children within earshot. "Nothing. I-I thought I saw someone in the window, but I didn't." She forced a laugh. "We were talking about ghosts, so my mind made one up for me."

Ketron watched her friend leave. Shauna dropped her keys in the grass, and she had a harder time than usual backing out of the driveway.

Ketron wondered why her friend was so rattled if she didn't believe in ghosts. She reasoned that it took experiences to spark the belief and fan it into a fire. Had Shauna witnessed something that had caused her feelings about the supernatural to change, burning through her doubt?

Ketron drained the noodles into a colander. When she looked up to see if Shauna had negotiated her way out of the driveway, a reflection stared back at her that was not her own. She almost would have mistaken it for Sonny, but he and Amelia had migrated to the twins' room.

Ketron startled, dropping the pot onto the colander. The reflection moved in dark grays and blacks over the wall behind her until she couldn't see it anymore.

Shauna might have called it a trick of the light, but Ketron knew that there had been something in the kitchen with her. And it had been almost close enough to touch her.

"Is this like a séance?" Bonnie sat down and crossed one leg over the other.

"No. I just want to see if you feel anything." Ketron looked behind her, but Nora and Sonny were zoned out watching the Berry Batch Buddies. Winslow had selected a superhero show on the television in the living room. Amelia drooled on Ketron's shoulder, and she laid the napping toddler across her legs.

"Are we trying to channel his mother's spirit?"

Ketron narrowed her eyes. She had been glad to share the information she had gleaned from Lisa with Bonnie, but she wished her teenager would have taken the deaths more seriously. For someone who believed in ghosts, Bonnie was rather flippant when she was confronted with possible proof of their existence. *Maybe it's her way of dealing with the fear that something creepy could be in the house,* Ketron thought.

Bonnie put her hands up. "Okay, okay. Do we just sit here?"

"Yeah, I think so." Ketron glanced around the narrow hallway. The bulb above them was off, but artificial light leaked in from the living room and the twins' room.

Ketron closed her eyes and tried to feel something. She was aware of her breathing and Bonnie flicking her fingernails against the floor. "Stop that."

"Stop what? I'm just sitting here."

Bonnie seemed genuinely surprised by Ketron's admonishment. Both of her hands were in her lap.

"Never mind. It must have been Winslow clicking a pen in the living room."

Bonnie stared at her skeptically. When Ketron didn't say anything else, she spoke. "My butt hurts. Can I have some ice cream?"

Ketron pulled a sigh from deep inside her chest. "I'll make you a sundae if you sit here for another few minutes."

"How many?"

Ketron tried to keep her voice level, as not to disturb Amelia, but she conveyed her thinly veiled frustration in the misplaced lilt of her voice. "I don't know, *dear*. Maybe five more minutes."

"Uhh!" Bonnie flopped onto her legs, but when she lifted her upper body, she had her eyes closed.

Ketron regulated her breathing and tried to feel the house around her. The air conditioner hummed through the floorboards, and the eucalyptus scent from Marvin's last shower found its way to her. Ketron was so relaxed that she almost fell asleep.

"Hey, Mom?" Winslow had appeared in the doorway that led to the living room. At first, Ketron only saw his shadow, but then he moved into view.

"What is it sweetie?"

"My show is over. Can I watch something else?"

"Yeah. I'll be in there in a minute." One of the children had lost the remote to the television before they moved. Ketron had thought it would turn up in one of the boxes when they unpacked, but it was gone. It was possible that Sonny had slid it down one of heating and air vents in the house where they had lived previously. Ketron had downloaded an app that allowed her to control the television with a remote on her phone.

She decided that she wasn't going to feel a ghost in the hallway. "I need to go get my phone so I can turn something on for your brother."

Bonnie looked at her mother with tired eyes. "I think I heard something."

Ketron jumped to attention. "What?"

"Well, there was a voice," Bonnie told her sheepishly, "and it said for you to make me a sundae."

Ketron smiled weakly. "Not funny."

"It's hilarious." Bonnie moved to her feet. "I'll wait for you in the kitchen." She started to leave and stopped, pushing herself back and forth on the frame that led out of the hallway. "I didn't feel anything, though."

"Me either," Ketron admitted.

Bonnie tapped the frame twice with her knuckles and left.

Ketron lifted Amelia back onto her shoulder. She could still see the outline from Winslow's shadow on the wall. She was a little irritated by his impatience. "I'll be right there," she told him.

"Okay."

Ketron's breath caught in her throat, and her body shuddered. Everything seemed to vibrate around her as blood marched in her ears.

Winslow had yelled back to her from the living room, but his shadow remained on the wall in the hallway. At her notice, the shadow's hand traced a wave on the wall and the head tilted. The hand crumbled into a fist. The shadow didn't disappear, but it jumped up the wall, thinned into a whisper of a line, and wiggled through the crack at the top of Bonnie's door.

Ketron didn't move until Amelia lifted her head and smiled. Whatever expression she saw on her mother's face caused her to draw up her features in concern and issue a soft, "Who?"

The baby could only make a few sounds, so the word she formed was merely a coincidence, but Ketron answered her daughter as if she had voiced a question. "It was Jeremy. And I wonder how long he's been watching us."

Chapter Nineteen

Past

Ketron didn't like the creepy white house. It smelled like dust and mold, and it was right next to the woods. The branches scraped across the windows at night as they blew in the wind, like someone was dragging their nails across the glass, and she would suddenly feel heat blaring around her, even though cool breezes blew through the rooms. She almost stepped on a snake when she went to the bathroom one morning, and squirrels woke her up at daybreak, running across the attic floor. Her mother kept a fire in the fireplace, but the nights were still cold. There were electric lights and appliances, but the bulbs flickered, and only one eye on the stove worked. Television was absent from the living room, and an ancient radio only popped when she tried to plug it in.

The house rested next to a mountain. Trees surrounded them on three sides, and a sizable creek ran in front of the house. The road was distant, but it could be seen from the front porch. Ketron couldn't see other houses, and it made her feel more isolated.

Ketron spent most of her days finding bugs by the creek or looking for something to play with under the beds, in the closets, or in the attic. Her mother locked the attic after she caught Ketron rummaging through an old tote. She claimed that rats and squirrels were in the attic, and they could be rabid.

They were there for two days before Ketron's mother drove into town for supplies. She had never left Ketron alone before, and when Ketron asked her the reason, her mother simply told her that the people in the town would take Ketron away if they saw her.

Ketron found freedom in her mother's absence. She danced around to the music of the birds in the trees and the sun that streamed through the windows. She explored the forest and found a wooden playhouse that belonged to some area children, but they weren't playing inside it when Ketron peeked in the dusty window.

Ketron edged close to a road, marking her way by following it. Across the road, she spotted a small house that sat uncomfortably close to two maple trees. Identical blond boys around her age played catch with a man she presumed was their father. The boys stood on one side, and he was across from them, scratching his face and arms and darting paranoid glances at the woods around him. Even though she wanted to make new friends her own age, Ketron decided she didn't want to be around the man. With his shifty nature, he might be one of the townspeople her mother feared would take her.

She hiked up a hill and the forest ended abruptly. Cows grazed and chickens ran between their feet. A proud white farmhouse with a dark green metal roof and a wrap-around porch stood in the middle of the property. Yellow and white flowers dotted the walkway, and purple blooms peeked over the planters that lined the steps.

Without thinking about it, Ketron made her way to the farmhouse. She wanted to get a closer look, so she stepped out of the trees and pushed past tall sunflowers that seemed to smile down at her. She stood staring at the house for some time before the door opened and a middle-aged woman with silver-blonde hair jogged down the steps. She pressed on with the air of someone with a rigid routine. The woman stopped short when she noticed Ketron staring at her.

"Are you lost, sweetie?" the woman asked. She edged over to Ketron and offered her hand. Ketron stared at it. "My name is Nora Miller. What's your name?"

Ketron liked the kind lady with pale skin and blue eyes, but she remembered her mother's warning. "I'm Katie," she lied, using the name people said in place of her name because of its uniqueness.

Realizing that Ketron wasn't going to shake her hand, Nora withdrew it. "Are you new to Erwin?"

Ketron pointed to the high hill behind her. "I live over there."

Nora's eyebrows drew together. "Nothing's over there except the old Renfro place."

Ketron nodded. "We live in the white house with the blue mailbox."

Nora nodded. "That's definitely the one. I thought they were all dead, especially after what happened to that little girl."

Ketron didn't want to answer any more questions, especially since her mother seemed to want their location to remain a secret. "I'm going to go home before my mother comes back." She backed up a little and smiled.

"It was nice to meet you." Nora waved and Ketron turned and ran back into the forest. She had just burst through the back door when she heard her mother's car crunch the gravel in the driveway.

When she unloaded the supplies, Ketron's mother unpacked a cordless phone. She explained that she had paid for service on it, but that Ketron was only to use it if an emergency arose when she was visiting the town for necessities.

At their apartment, a phone with a rotary dial had sat in the corner of their living room. It had stayed mostly silent, but when it rang, Ketron had been tasked with answering it. She was confused when her mother hid the new phone, muttering something about her lack of trust in her daughter.

Her mother didn't suspect that Ketron had ventured so far from their new home. Ketron was happy that she had met Nora, but she was a little nervous about the woman repeating the whereabouts of her mother and her to the townspeople. She decided to trust the kind lady in the same way she had trusted John Winslow.

Several days later, Ketron was rolling some marbles across the porch when Nora walked out of the woods. She spotted Ketron and waved. Ketron waved back uncertainly, fearful about what her mother would do when she learned that Ketron had gone beyond the borders of their property.

Ketron's mother was standing over her by the time Nora reached the top of the steps. The friendly lady smiled warmly down at Ketron, but before she could speak, Ketron blurted out, "Hi, I'm Katie!"

Nora's smile faltered, but she pulled it back up quickly. "It's nice to meet you, Katie. Is this your mother?"

Ketron's mother extended her hand. "I'm Gwynevieve Renfro."

Nora appeared stupefied. Her mouth hung open for a moment before she spoke again. "You're the other one."

Her mother straightened to her full height. "I beg your pardon?" Her tone was clipped and cold.

Nora startled at the change in her temperament. "I'm sorry. I was just a girl when—" Gwynevieve's posture tightened, and Nora shifted her conversational path. "I live just over the hill, and I wanted to welcome you—" she paused and searched for the right word, "—back to the area."

Ketron's mother relaxed. "We've only just arrived, and I don't know if we'll be staying long."

It was the first time Ketron had heard her mother talk about her plans since she had moved them into the house, so she hung on every word. "Of course, I may be the only one here in a couple of weeks. Katie may return to her father."

Ketron tried to mask her shock by resuming her place in front of the marbles. She drifted one lazily down a crack in the wood, imagining what it would be like to meet her father for the first time.

Her mother invited Nora inside, and they drank sweet tea. They didn't talk about anything of importance, but Ketron stayed near the window to catch bits of their conversation that filtered through the screen.

On the way out the door, Nora patted Ketron's shoulder. The simple gesture let Ketron know that Nora had really been there to see her. It made her feel better to know that she had a friend.

The day her mother decided to go back into town, it was raining. The rain fell in heavy sheets across their lawn, and the sky was dark and oppressive.

"Why don't you wait until it's sunny outside?" Ketron had a dual purpose for suggesting a day with better weather. She wanted to explore the forest some more, and she didn't want to be alone in the eerie house on a dark day.

Her mother believed she was only interested in her safety. "I'll be fine," she assured her daughter. "I will only be gone for a couple of hours, and the storm will clear soon."

Ketron wondered how her mother was able to predict the weather. She'd always had that uncanny ability.

Ketron was rolling her marbles in the groves of her bedroom floor when her mother dropped a phone receiver into her lap. "Remember, I told you that it is only to be used in emergencies, okay?" Ketron nodded. "Do you understand what I mean?"

"Yes, ma'am," Ketron answered, outwardly bored, but excited on the inside about having a phone at her disposal.

"So, if the house is on fire, who do you call?"

Ketron narrowed her eyes. "Ghostbusters."

Her mother shook her head. "Wrong answer." She snatched up the phone and was halfway to the door before Ketron called after her. She stopped, but only turned slightly, raising one perfectly arched brow.

"I would call the fire department."

Her mother motioned her over, and Ketron rose. Her mother patted her on the arm, her idea of a hug, and dropped the phone into her waiting hand.

"Who do you call if someone is trying to break into the house?"

Inwardly, Ketron rolled her eyes. "The police department."

Satisfied, her mother left, throwing up a hand at Ketron as she watched her pull out of the driveway from the window. When the car was comfortably out of sight, Ketron returned to her room to pick up the marbles, but when she got there, they were gone. She didn't remember gathering them. She usually kept them in a Blue Ridge Pottery dish by her bed, but that was missing too.

Ketron threw up the tattered bedspread, but she only saw an old hair dryer in its case, and the underside of a musty and buckling box spring mattress. She was certain that she had been playing with the marbles when her mother had walked into the room, and she had no recollection of putting them away. She walked through the house with doubt eating at her. Where were the marbles?

She still had the phone in her hand. She rushed to the kitchen and pulled up the loose flap of linoleum next to the refrigerator. It was her job to clean the kitchen floor, and her mother rarely cooked, so the kitchen was the perfect place to hide anything Ketron wanted to keep from her mother.

She pulled out the envelope and opened it. She had a little trouble dialing the number because her hands were shaking, but soon she heard the unmistakable voice of the kind man who had offered to help a woman and her child on a dark night.

"This is Big Red."

"It's Ketron," she spoke quickly, "My mother got a phone for me to use when she's away, but I'm only supposed to use it to make emergency calls."

"Ketty-Kat!" His jovial tone eased Ketron's frayed nerves.

"How are you?" She felt awkward, but she had heard enough grown-up conversations to know how to begin one.

"Well, my back's been botherin' me a bit. It put me on my butt fer a couple o'days. That's somethin' you young people don't have to worry about." He chuckled. "Enjoy your health, Ketty-Kat."

Ketron didn't know what to say, so she stayed quiet.

"How have you been gettin' along?"

Ketron started to pace as she talked, keeping her eyes out for her missing marbles. "I've been okay, I guess. I met a sweet lady named Nora Miller. She lives across the hill, and she visited us."

"That musta been nice."

"Yeah." Ketron wanted to tell him about her mother's deteriorating mental health, but she didn't know how to begin. She didn't want him to tell her mother, or worse, stop talking to her.

"Are you sure you're okay?" he asked, reading her silence.

"My mom talks to herself more now." The words were out before she could think about them.

Big Red laughed. "We've all been known to talk to ourselves."

"I guess," Ketron replied, tracing her fingers across a lace doily. "But my mom believes the voices that answer her in her head are real." She took a deep breath and added, "Sometimes the voices tell her to do things and she listens to them."

The line was silent for almost a minute. When Big Red spoke again, his voice was grave. "Well, that's a different matter."

Ketron waited for some sage advice, but every time it sounded like Big Red was going to speak, he'd only take a deep breath and seem to change his mind about it.

"You said you could only use the phone for emergencies when your mama's gone. Can you make it to the phone if you're scared while your mama's there?"

"I don't know. She keeps it unplugged and hides it when she's here."

"I want you to watch her and see where she puts it. If you need anything, you can call me. I'm a couple hours out, but I'll get there as fast as I can."

"You don't even know where I am." Ketron peeked out the window. A heavy fog had settled just over the house.

"Do you know your address?" Ice clinked when he took a sip of whatever he was drinking.

"No."

"Try to find out. Erwin's not a big place." When he spoke again his voice was brighter. "You'll be in town for the Apple Festival this year!"

"Sure. If she lets me go." She resumed pacing from the living room to the kitchen, taking giant steps, and avoiding the cracks in the linoleum. "She says the townspeople will take me if they see me."

He cleared his throat. "Are you back in school?"

"No."

"Is your mama givin' you lessons at home?"

"No. I had some books in my backpack from my last school. I've been looking through them."

"You know you can call me any time." He tried to sound cheerful, but there was a hard edge to his voice that wasn't directed at her.

"Can I call you the next time my mother leaves the house?" She hoped he wouldn't be bothered by her enthusiasm to speak with him.

"You bet! It makes these old ears happy to hear a young voice."

"Can I ask you a question?" She waited for his answer and hoped her request wouldn't be too much. "Will you be my friend?"

The line was silent, and her heart tumbled into her stomach. Had she upset the kind man? When he spoke, his voice was laced with emotion. "Ketty-Kat, I have been your friend since I saw you in your mama's backseat. You can count on me if you need anything."

Ketron kicked her foot back and forth on the carpet before she hopped across the most worn area in the blue and white pattern. "I probably need to go before my mother gets back."

Before he ended the call, Big Red made her promise to secretly find out where her mother put the phone when she was at home.

Three hours later, Ketron's mother ran into the house with only two bags on her arms. When Ketron asked her about the other supplies, she waved away her question and told her that she'd left them in the trunk of the car. Ketron thought it was odd for her mother to leave them there, but it was raining, so she assumed her mother didn't want to get soaked carrying them inside.

She tried to watch her mother, to discreetly find out where she put the phone when she took it from Ketron, but her mother smartly slipped away when Ketron was distracted with preparing dinner. Ketron had no idea when she moved it into her secret hiding place.

Chapter Twenty

Present

Ketron pulled open the heavy wooden door. Usually, visitors almost plowed over her to get inside, but the woman stood with her hip holding the screen door open.

"I have these maters." Lisa lifted a shopping bag of bright red tomatoes. "They'll make good samiches for the kiddoes."

Ketron accepted the bag and surveyed the beautifully ripe fruit. "We can have tomato and cheese sandwiches and soup tonight."

Lisa chuckled, sticking her hand in the pocket of her stone-washed jeans. "You may be a country girl after all."

Ketron held the door a little wider. "Do you want to come inside?"

Lisa turned and looked down the road like she had a pressing engagement, but she accepted Ketron's offer. She settled at the dining room table while Ketron lined the fruit along the windowsill. Amelia was playing with her learning tree. The disembodied voice responded to Amelia's merciless slaps by shouting "red bird" and "Do you want to play?"

"Do you like your toy?" Lisa asked her. Amelia dipped her head shyly onto the top of her tree. She shot back up smiling and then lay her head on her arm. Even though she could see them, it was her version of a peek-a-boo game. Lisa caught on and hid her eyes behind her hands. Amelia toddled in her direction, curious about their visitor.

"She's a little timid, but she likes smiling faces," Ketron explained.

"It's her age." Lisa continued their game, revealing her eyes to Amelia.

It was the second time Lisa had expressed inside knowledge about children. Ketron thought she remembered Lisa saying something about a son. "Does your son live around here?"

Nora wondered into the room holding a book. She marked her place, ready to be part of an adult conversation.

Lisa picked up Amelia and placed her in her lap. "I suppose he's around somewhere."

Ketron thought she had stumbled onto a raw subject, and she quickly backpedaled. "I didn't mean to bring up something that upsets you."

Lisa gave Amelia her stretchy pink keyring to entertain her. "Oh, don't worry about that. My son knows his mama's strong and full of pride. He finds me on holidays and a handful of Sundays."

Ketron changed the conversation into something more upbeat. "He goes to church with you?"

"We watch it on that thing he has," she replied, waving her hand in the air. "You know. That thing you can watch TV on?"

Ketron wondered if her neighbor was up to date on modern technology. "You mean a cell phone?"

Lisa fished one out of her pocket and held it up, laughing. "I have Wi-fi and indoor plumbing, too," she joked.

"A tablet?" Nora squeaked. There had always been a raspy quality to her voice, but her words were barely audible.

"That's it!" Lisa pointed to Nora and the child blushed.

Nora hiked her shoulders. "Mommy and Daddy got one for Winslow and one for me for Christmas."

"Nifty little gadgets," Lisa commented, bouncing Amelia on her legs. "I don't really see the need for them for older people, though, unless you can't see small stuff on your phone."

"Would you like something to drink?" Ketron asked.

"I'll take some sweet tea."

Ketron fumbled for a reply. "W-We have juice, water, and milk, and I think my husband has some soft drinks in the crisper."

Lisa stopped bouncing Amelia and lifted her eyebrows. "No sweet tea, huh? I take back what I said earlier. You're a city girl."

Nora laughed and Amelia joined in. Winslow peeked his head into the room to see what he was missing. "Are you the crazy lady?"

Ketron could have beat her head on the counter repeatedly. *Why was Winslow so brazen?*

"I am," responded Lisa, not skipping a beat. "But you can call me Lisa."

"*Miss* Lisa," Ketron corrected. She was embarrassed that Lisa thought she had referred to her in a negative way. Winslow had regurgitated Shauna's comment, but it made Ketron seem like she was talking about her neighbor behind her back.

Lisa put a hand on his shoulder. "Okay, you can call me Miss Lisa, for now, but only until you get your first job. Then we're equals."

"Mom pays me to clean the windows."

"She means your first job with a company," Ketron told him.

Sonny ran into the room with a dinosaur in each hand, but he stopped when he saw Lisa. He widened his eyes and ran behind his mother.

"Can you say 'hi' to Miss Lisa?" Ketron prompted. Sonny wouldn't budge.

"He must be shy, or something," Ketron apologized.

"Or something," Lisa repeated. Her attention shifted to the fireplace, and she darted her eyes without moving her head.

"I think it's time for me to go." Her words were crisp, and Ketron wondered if they were directed at whatever she had noticed around the fireplace. She stood up, still holding Amelia and handed her to Ketron.

"Come back when you can stay longer," Ketron told her. "I'll try to have sweet tea next time."

"You really shouldn't deprive these children of it," she responded, but the mirth was gone from her eyes.

"Did I do or say something?" Ketron asked her children when Lisa left.

Winslow shrugged. "Maybe she's mad because you don't like sweat tea."

"I doubt it."

"Jeremy doesn't like her," Sonny mumbled.

"What?" Ketron asked, trying to pull him away so she could look into his eyes. Sonny wouldn't say anything more when he was pressed, and Ketron finally sent him into the living room to play.

"What do you think Sonny meant?" Ketron voiced more to herself than to the children standing around her.

Nora glanced up from her tablet. "Jeremy doesn't like Miss Lisa." Her reply was swift and simple. "When he doesn't like someone then they go into the darkness."

Ketron's heart dropped, and she grabbed the counter for support. "You can see Jeremy too?"

Chapter Twenty-One

Present

"Mom, I need you to come in here and look at this."

Ketron had a pot of potatoes boiling on the stove, Sonny whining while he held onto her leg, and Amelia pulling her hair as she balanced her away from the stove. "Can it wait until after dinner?" She begged Bonnie with her eyes.

"No, Mom," Bonnie insisted. "You need to see this now."

Ketron turned down the temperature on the stove and hobbled behind Bonnie. Sonny let go of her leg in the living room and threw himself onto the sofa. "I don't like mashed tatoes! I won't eat them!"

Ketron left him to pout about the dinner she was making. She had already planned to microwave dinosaur nuggets for him if he wouldn't eat the food on his plate, but she didn't want to tell him. One day, she hoped he would consistently sit down and eat the same meal as everyone at the table.

Bonnie pointed at the door to the basement. Small beads of liquid bubbled over the wood.

Ketron arrived at an explanation immediately. "It's just condensation."

"What?" Bonnie's forehead wrinkled. She had gone over the subject in school, but that information had been flushed when she had to memorize the moves to various trends or the quotes from her favorite vampire saga.

Ketron explained it quickly. "It's hot outside today, and your door leads to the basement. The basement is really cold, and the door is hot. It creates condensation from the moisture in the air."

"It's not hot in here, though," Bonnie argued. "The air conditioner is on."

Ketron stared at the door thoughtfully while Amelia poked her ear. "Maybe it's just colder in the basement."

"Like much colder."

Ketron pondered just how cold the basement had to be in order to produce the effect she was witnessing. She was still trying to come up with a reasonable answer when Nora let out a scream. Ketron and Bonnie followed the sound to the living room. Nora stood with a handful of waded brown hair. "He pulled my hair!"

"I did not!" Sonny shot back defiantly.

Bonnie determined that there wasn't a loss of limb or a celebrity at the door, so she migrated back to her room.

"Okay, let's sort this out guys." Ketron guided Sonny and Nora to the couch. She always started with the victim, so she waited while Nora told her side of the story.

"I was just playing with my baby dolls, and he pulled my hair."

"I did not," Sonny spoke up again.

Ketron surveyed her four-year-old. He didn't have on the smug expression he usually wore whenever he denied his participation in something he had done. He seemed genuinely upset over Nora's accusation.

"Nora, we've heard your side. Now, Sonny, can you tell me what happened?"

His eyes dropped and he toed an imaginary line. "I don't know."

"Tell me what happened." Ketron hoped her voice was firm enough.

"I didn't do it."

"You've told me that." Ketron took his hand. He looked up for a moment but dropped his eyes quickly. "I want to know what happened."

"See? He pulled my hair!" Nora pushed the wad of hair under her mother's nose.

Sonny glared at her. "I didn't pull your yucky hair!"

"No name-calling," Ketron admonished.

She addressed Sonny, "Why does your sister have a wad of hair in her hand?"

"*I* didn't do it," Sonny repeated.

"Then who did it?"

Sonny tried to walk away, but Ketron gently pulled him back.

"No," Ketron scolded. "This discussion is not finished until you admit that you pulled your sister's hair, or you tell me who did it."

Sonny eyed Ketron in stony silence. She pretended like she had all the time in the world to hold his eyes, while there was still dinner to cook and evening chores to complete.

Winslow came out of the hallway. "Just so you know, I was in my room."

"It wasn't Winslow," Nora confirmed. "I went out of our room and sat down in here. Sonny was behind me, and he pulled my hair."

Tears filled Sonny's eyes. "IT WASN'T ME!" he screamed.

Ketron wanted to believe him, but the evidence was there. Nora wouldn't pull her own hair, and Sonny had been the only one behind her when it had happened.

The door to Marvin's room burst open. "Is dinner ready yet?" he slurred.

Ketron could tell from the sway in his steps that he hadn't eaten enough to come close to balancing the alcohol in his system. "It will be ready soon. I was dealing with something."

He guessed that his favorite child was the subject of discipline. "Daddy's boy!" he called.

Sonny didn't miss the opportunity to break away. "Daddy's boy!" he returned, running to his father and wrapping his arms around his legs.

There was nothing she could do now to punish her son, so Ketron hugged Nora. Nora sobbed a little, but she cleared her emotions quickly. "I'm sorry that I wasn't able to punish him for what he did to you," Ketron told her.

"It's okay, Mommy," Nora returned, and added a sad smile.

Sonny had coerced Marvin into turning on a show for him, and he locked onto the program immediately.

She put Amelia on the living room floor to play and headed back to the kitchen. Marvin caught her at his room door.

"When did you say dinner would be ready?" Marvin asked.

Ketron didn't camouflage her feelings. "It will be ready when it's ready.

He had the nerve to laugh. "Yeah, but how much longer?"

"Why don't you make it yourself!" Ketron yelled.

He took an angry step forward and his eyes narrowed. "Because it's not *my* job!"

Ketron felt cornered. She didn't mind making meals. In fact, she preferred preparing the food as opposed to worrying about her alcoholic husband burning the house down, but she was angered by his insinuation that every meal was her responsibility. Ketron decided to swallow her pride. "I will have dinner on the table in fifteen minutes."

Marvin's eyes searched her for another spirited outburst, and he turned around when she dropped her head. Ketron lifted her eyes and focused her unspoken words at his back. He tripped over a toy and caught himself against the wall. "They need to keep their toys picked up," he barked before he slammed the door to his room.

Ketron didn't want her children to get into trouble, so she elected to move the toy before Marvin came out again. Ketron thought she knew every toy in the house, since she constantly picked them up, but she didn't recognize this one. It was a well-loved stuffed dog. She took it to Nora's and Winslow's room.

"It's not mine," Winslow said, jumping from the ladder on his bunk.

Ketron was going to scold him, but she let it slide. In the month that the twins had slept in the bunk beds, she had already told him numerous times not to jump off the ladder or the top bunk. It was exhausting to repeat herself.

Nora crawled out from her bottom bunk where she had been nursing her damaged feelings over her pulled hair. "It's not mine either. Did Bonnie bring it from her dad's house?"

A quick check with Bonnie didn't reveal the toy's origin. "I don't have a lot of stuffed animals anymore," she said, snarling her upper lip. "And I've never seen it before. Maybe it's Sonny's."

Ketron was certain that she knew all of Sonny's toys, but maybe Mavin had slipped one by her. She took it in the living room and paused Sonny's show. "Hey!"

"Is this your doggie?" Ketron asked him.

He shook his head, still angry with her for interrupting his show. "I never seen it in my entire life."

Ketron started Sonny's cartoon again. She didn't know how the dog had ended up in the house, but it was cute. It almost reminded her of a German Shepard her friend had rescued from the pound and brought to show her class in kindergarten. She put the stuffed animal next to Sonny and hurried back to the kitchen before Marvin yelled at her over his dinner again.

Chapter Twenty-Two

Past

The next time her mother left to get supplies, Ketron flew out of the house the moment she couldn't see the gray outline of her car anymore. She turned cartwheels through the yard and dived into the forest. It was a warm day, but the forest had a chill. It seemed to go through her skin, permeating the bones in her body.

She traced her footsteps from her last outing, leading her past the house with the maple trees. The boys weren't out, but their father smoked a rolled cigarette on the porch. He seemed to be speaking to the trees, but then a woman came around the side of the house, and Ketron wondered if he had been talking to her.

Her feet led her to the clearing, and she stepped around a garden of herbs that ran in a line next to the woods. She heard voices, and she found Nora in the garden behind her house. The two blond boys were with her.

"Hello, Katie." She stood and dusted the dirt from her gloves before she slipped them off. "These are my nephews, Ky and Ly."

Ketron said an awkward "hi" and busied herself by drawing in the dirt with her toe. The boys were identical, and she didn't know how she was going to assign a name to one if she had to address them individually.

Nora explained that she was gathering the last of the corn in the field, so Ketron helped them pull a few ears from the stalks. Nora wiped her forehead with the back of her hand before she announced that they should find some shade.

It was early autumn, but the noon sun bore down on them fiercely as they carried in bushels of the corn in baskets. They set them down on the covered porch, and Nora brought each of them a tall glass of lemonade.

"I'd invite you inside," she told Ketron, "but I'm afraid it's hotter in there than it is out here."

They each had a rocker to sit in while they tore the shucks from the corn. Nora encouraged her nephews to talk to Ketron, and soon they were friends.

"Do you live in that house with the maple trees against it?"

"Yeah," they said in unison. It was a little off-putting, but Ketron reminded herself that they were brothers, so they probably did things like that all the time.

"Where do you live?" The boy who sat closest to his aunt had asked the question, and Ketron was glad she didn't have to know his name to answer it.

"I'm staying in the house over that hill." Ketron pointed in a south-westerly direction.

The twins exchanged a glance. The boy who had spoken to her, clearly the most vocal of the two, asked if it was the old Renfro place and she nodded.

"That place is haunted," he said matter-of-factly.

"Hand me that brush, Ky," Nora requested. Ketron wondered if she had called him by name to help her.

While Nora used the wire brush to scrape away the silky thread left on the corn she had pulled from its shuck, Ketron selected two ears and passed them down to Ky and Ly. "I haven't seen any ghosts."

The twins laughed and Nora smiled. "Then you haven't been paying attention," she said.

"That's why we're not playing in the woods today," Ly piped up.

Ketron's forehead crinkled. "Because of the ghosts in my house?"

Ly rolled his eyes. "No. Because of the ghosts in the woods." He went back to ripping the husk off the corn. "Didn't you feel it?"

"It was cold in there, but it's fall."

He looked at his brother and they shook their heads. "You can go to any other mountain, and it won't be as cold as Pale Woods when the spirits are moving," Ky informed her.

Ketron glanced at Nora to see if she believed what her nephews were saying. She raised her eyebrows without looking up. "My brother, Lyle, and I never played in the woods on those days. Sometimes it was so cold that you could see your breath." She looked up at Ketron and added, "In July."

Ketron had wondered if the boy's father was their aunt's brother and Nora had confirmed it. They had the same almost silver hair, but the woman Ketron had seen at the house had been blonde, too.

"They're twins like us," Ky volunteered when he noticed Ketron staring at his aunt.

Everything Ketron knew about twins could be summed up in her knowledge about her mother and her mother's sister. "Boys and girls can't be twins."

Nora pressed her lips into a line. "Lyle and I were born at the same time—well, within ten minutes of one another— so we're twins. I'm afraid you're going to have to ask your mother if you want more clarification than that."

Ky and Ly turned a deep shade of red, and Ly excused himself to use the facilities.

Ketron didn't need a further explanation. She hadn't really wanted to know as much as Nora had told her.

"What's that smell?" Ketron asked. Both boys lifted their arms and sniffed the air beneath them. "It's like sweet grass with lemon juice."

The twin shared a glance and chuckled. "It's not us," they said.

Nora motioned over Ketron's shoulder. "It's the dill in my wreath."

While learning to cook, Ketron had put dill in her tuna salad, but she hadn't heard of placing it in a wreath. "Why do you put it in your wreath?"

Bright dots of pink colored Nora's prominent cheekbones.

"It's to ward off spirits," Ky told her.

"Evil spirits," his aunt corrected. "I have a garden of herbs by the woods. You had to pass it to get to the house." Ketron nodded. "I planted it because I could feel the spirits of the woods and their cold breath on me when I walked outside. It was like constantly having wolves at my door."

Ketron took another ear of corn out of the basket. "What do you do in the winter?"

"I let the last few herbs hang around until they die out. I was surprised when it was almost December before the winter held a different coldness to it." Her mouth moved into a line, and Ketron realized that Nora had to be strong, knowledgeable, and resilient to live on the mountain alone. "When winter comes, I lay bundles of sage at the property line every week until my herbs grow back."

Ketron wanted to ask Nora about her experience with ghosts but kept her eyes on her task. It was Nora's story, and she'd tell it when she was ready.

"Do you want to hang out in our fort sometime?" Ky asked.

Ketron welcomed the change of subject. "Sure. But I don't know when..." She was going to say, 'I don't know when my mother will leave again,' but she trailed off.

"Her mother doesn't know she wonders away from home," Nora offered.

Ketron nodded. "I can only go past the creek around the house when she goes into town." She quickly added, "But I'd like to play in the fort. I think I saw it on my way here the first time. Is it that wooden playhouse?"

Ky shook his head. "You don't *play* in the fort; you have battles in the fort. But, yeah, it was the wooden building up from our house."

Ketron smiled as his distinction. "She goes to town on Fridays." Once she said it, she was worried that she had revealed too much. What if her mother was right to mistrust people?

It was easier for Ketron to tell Ky and Ly apart, now that she had spent some time with them. Ky was extroverted and had a brush of freckles on the left side of his neck. Ly was quiet, almost withdrawn, and a dimple on one side of his mouth flashed when he smiled. Ketron watched Nora labor over the corn, concentrating on each stroke of the wire brush. When one of the boys said something playfully, or tucked husks into the back of her shirt, she laughed and joined in their games.

These people are good, Ketron thought.

"Hey, Katie, maybe we could come over to your house one day," Ky suggested.

Ketron had a twinge of sadness when she realized that she would never see the twins run up the steps of her porch to ask if she could play with them. She couldn't catch bugs with them in her creek or roll marbles with them on the porch on rainy days.

"I don't want you boys to visit Katie, okay?" Nora had spoken when Ketron couldn't answer Ky. "Her mother is less than receptive to visitors." She glanced over at Ketron and winked. "I hope you don't mind me saying so about your mother."

Ketron shook her head. "My mother doesn't want me to talk to anyone. She thinks someone from town will take me away or something."

"That's crazy!" A quick look from his aunt caused Ky to close his mouth with a snap.

"I'm happy to have you visit me any time," Nora told her.

Once the sun fell from its zenith, Ketron told them she had to go home. Nora offered to give her some corn, but she didn't press the issue when Ketron declined.

"It was nice to meet you, Katie!" Ky and Ly echoed each other.

"Wait a minute." Nora stood and brushed silken threads off her lap. "You boys should walk Katie back home."

"Oh, I'm fine."

Nora held up her hand. "The forest is chilly today, and it never hurts to have an extra pair of eyes when there might be danger."

"In this case, two extra pairs of eyes." Ky put his arm around his brother.

Nora disappeared briefly and came back with three large, peanut butter cookies. She told her nephews to be careful and to come back for a bushel of corn before they went home. The trio left with full mouths, waving and skipping into the woods.

Fear unhinged Ly's jaw, and he talked almost nonstop through the woods. Every time he bounced from one subject to another, Ky's eyebrows climbed a little higher on his forehead.

They took Ketron on a more linear route, so they didn't pass the twins' house, but they stopped at the fort. Ky took over the conversation, allowing her to climb into the area where he and his brother had empty chip bags, open comic books, and crushed soda cans. She slipped on a comic book when she examined the Star Wars curtains in the only window. Ky caught her and blushed when she grabbed onto him for balance. "Well, uh, that's the fort," he announced.

Ketron was happy to spend time with her new friends, but she was worried that her mother would already be there when she got home. "I really need to get back before my mother gets there."

The woods had grown darker and colder while they were in the fort. Ketron voiced her concern, and Ky and Ly looked at each other. Ly moved his head toward their house almost imperceptibly.

"What did you just say to each other?" Ketron demanded.

Kyle shrugged. "We didn't say anything."

"Yes, you did. You motioned to your house, and you said something to Ly."

"It's just body language," Ly said defensively. "Don't be crazy." He softened his tone when he noticed the reaction Ketron had when he said 'crazy.' He grabbed a tree for support before he jumped onto a path Ketron didn't recognize. "Our mother tells people we talk to each other with our body language."

"We can hear each other in our heads," Ky cut in.

Ly was outraged. "Why did you tell her! We don't even know her."

Ky waved him off. "She lives on the old Renfro property." He appraised Ketron. "I don't think she's going to tell anyone about our secrets."

Ketron suddenly felt badly for lying about her name. "My name is really Ketron," she blurted out.

Ky chuckled. "I figured you were using a different name. You said your mom doesn't want people to know you're here. It makes sense that she would change your name." He ruffled her hair. "You don't even look like a Katie."

Ketron tried to brush her hair into place and her irritation away. "She didn't change *her* name, though."

Ly stroked his chin thoughtfully. "I don't think she could do it and still claim that she belonged on the Renfro property." Ketron wondered if part of his silent nature was due to his intelligence. Maybe he was quietly observing, instead of filling his head full of what he was expected to say next.

"What were you guys talking about in your head," Ketron asked, picking up an oddly shaped rock and sticking it into her pocket.

The boys stopped and stared.

"What?"

"We don't take anything out of the woods," Ky explained. "We don't want whatever's here to follow us out."

Ketron rolled her eyes, but she dug into her pocket and tossed the rock onto the ground. "Are we good now?"

"Yes," Ky answered. Another moment passed before he addressed her previous question. "We can tell it's going to be a rough night when we go back home." He winced. "Our father is a little meaner when the woods are cold."

Ly scoffed. "If he's even there when we get home."

Ky looked at Ketron apologetically.

She held up her hands. "Look, I don't even have a father, so I'm not judging."

Ky kicked up some dry leaves. "Did he die?"

"I don't think so." Ketron didn't want to tell them that she was pretty sure he was alive and had abandoned her mother while she was pregnant.

Ly sighed. "It's better to have no dad than to have ours." He meant it to make her feel better, but all she could offer in return was a sideways smile.

Ky shook his head at his twin. "It's not a contest. We come from a messed-up family, but at least we have Aunt Nora and our mom. Do you have anyone you can count on?"

Ketron couldn't think of a single family member. She didn't want to be pitied, though. "I have my Uncle Red." The lie was worth the relief she saw wash over their faces. She was one of them again.

"So, can all twins talk to each other inside their heads?"

Ky answered her after he jumped up to touch a low-hanging branch. "I don't think so."

Lyle playfully punched his brother on the arm. "Mama says all the twins born around here can talk that way."

Ketron wondered if her mother had spoken to her twin in her mind. After all, they had been born in the same area as Ky and Ly.

"Does your dad talk to your Aunt Nora in his head?"

Ky smiled, but he didn't answer her.

"They won't admit it, but Aunt Nora always knows when our dad gets really bad. She comes to get us, and we stay with her for a couple of days," Ly told her.

Ketron made out the blue mailbox in the distance and soon the white house came into view. "Thanks for walking me back."

After they had exchanged goodbyes in the form of some strange handshake, Ketron ran to the front door. She was relieved to see her mother's car was not in the driveway.

Her mother's rabbits stared at her from their place on the mantle. She turned them around to stop the feeling that they were silently judging her.

She congratulated herself on barely making it back when she heard the gravel in the driveway crunch less than ten minutes later. She smiled to herself as she peeled a corn husk off the side of her shoe. Her mother had no idea that she finally had friends. Real friends.

Ketron woke up frequently at night. Sometimes, her mother was battling with herself over a bottle of amber liquid, but most of the time, it was because of the creaks in the house. Her mother had explained that houses settled, and sometimes wood expands when it's hot during the day, but the house had probably settled long ago, and the days were much cooler than they had been when she and her mother had first arrived.

She lay awake at night, counting the sounds. They formed a pattern as they seemed to echo through the kitchen, into the living room, and ended in Ketron's room, at which time they would circle around and repeat. It wasn't so different than the path she had taken when she paced during her phone calls with Big Red.

Ketron wondered if whatever made the sounds was protecting her in some way. Could a spirit be standing sentinel as she slept?

One morning, after a long night of listening to what she had convinced herself was a pacing spirit, Ketron was awakened by a startling sound above her head. A silvery drop popped and rolled down the ceiling as the sound seemed to glide along a groove above her head. It was almost like a ball at a bowling alley that had landed in the gutter.

Her mother was asleep in the room that joined hers. Soft snores blew into the air and retreated. Ketron spotted the car keys and noticed a key without groves. Her mother had called it a bump key, and she had used it to open the doors inside the house. She grabbed the keys in her fist and bolted into the dining room. The attic door was loose, so it moved freely on its hinges when Ketron opened it.

Ketron ran up the stairs on the tips of her toes, but the steps still cried out against her weight. When she got to the top, she stopped. Despite a film of dust on their surfaces, daylight streamed through two open windows, providing her with enough light to scan every corner of the room.

She looked under stacks of cloth, and moved magazines that outdated her mother, but she couldn't find the source of the noise. She plopped onto the floor. "What was it?" she asked herself.

As if in answer, a marble rolled to her from an unseen source. She followed the path it had taken. At first, she was uncertain about what she saw, so she crawled over to get a closer look. When her eyes settled on the object, she heard scratching. It was soft, but distinct. "Who's there?"

She dipped her head low and ducked under the coats hanging on an ancient rack. She could see something shift its weight just beyond her reach. She focused on it, willing her eyes to see details in the shadow and give form to an undefined shape. Dark eyes moved into her view only a moment before the creature lunged, scratching her.

Ketron backed away quickly, knocking the coat rack onto the floor. She remained motionless, on her feet and palms. The squirrel surveyed her, twitched its nose, and released two marbles from its tiny paws. They traced a path to Ketron, and she picked them up. Disinterested in the human who perpetrated its home, the squirrel darted to another corner.

Ketron didn't notice it. She was captivated by the marbles she held. They were unlike the ones she had found under the downstairs bed. Sunset oranges and golds traced a swirling path over a white base. Ketron wasn't certain how long she held them before she noticed the Blue Ridge Pottery dish resting on a tote.

She rose and walked cautiously over to the storage container. A white dish with a lovely blue flower pattern rested on the plastic lid and her marbles were inside it. She knew if she counted them, there would be eleven identical marbles. The additional marbles rested in her palm. She grabbed the dish and turned, eager to return the keys to her mother's nightstand, but a bump vibrated the boards beneath her bare feet.

Ketron knelt in front of the tote. It wasn't as old as the other items in the attic. It looked like any other storage container. It was made of blue plastic with two gray handles on the sides. She flipped them up and pulled off the lid. A musty smell swelled.

"What are you doing up here?"

Ketron jumped up and faced her mother, putting the hand that held the unique marbles behind her back. "I heard a sound."

"Yes, Ketron. Of course you heard something. There are disease infested animals running through this room at all hours."

Ketron glanced at the scratch on her wrist. Her mother followed her stare.

"You've already been infected!" she screeched.

Ketron startled and instinctively covered the wound.

"There's no sense in hiding it now." Her mother started to pace. "I can't take you to the doctor. What would they say? What would they do with me?"

"I'm okay, Mother. I won't need to go to the doctor."

Her mother covered her eyes. "What am I going to do?"

"I'll use the first aid kit."

Her mother looked up. "Yes. We should definitely disinfect it."

She followed her mother downstairs, handing her the keys when they reached the bottom. She'd had the presence of mind to grab the dish with the marbles. She added the marbles she had found to her collection.

In the bathroom, her mother held Ketron's wrist over the sink as she poured peroxide over the wound. It bubbled, but it hardly stung. Ketron was left with the supplies and instructed to apply a disinfectant cream and secure a bandage over it.

Gwynevieve Renfro held mini conversations with herself all day. She would make an abrupt announcement and sometimes her thoughts would trail off in the middle of a thought.

After almost a full day of listening to her mother's sporadic conversations with no one she could see, Ketron went outside and sat on the porch. The sun hadn't warmed the cool boards from the chilly air, but Ketron didn't mind. She looked at the mountains that rose and fell like dinosaurs that had bent their backs to the sun. The only sound was the whisper of the wind through the crackling leaves and the chatter of the squirrels running past the creek. "I am alone."

She sensed the sincerity of the words as she spoke them, but bringing them to life by uttering them made it real. "I am alone," she repeated. Then she thought about Big Red, Nora, Ky, and Ly, and a smile tickled the corners of her mouth until it made it to her eyes. She felt the same stillness and solitude, but it was edged by a flutter of hope. "I am alone. But it won't always be that way."

Chapter Twenty-Three

Present

"You're surprised?' Lisa asked her.

"Well, yes," Ketron responded. She had told Lisa about Nora's startling comment about Jeremy.

They sat at a small wooden table with piles of newspapers and mail on one side. Lisa was seated in the kitchen, and Ketron's feet brushed the living room carpet. It was an odd place to put a table, but there wasn't another reasonable alternative in the small house.

Lisa had offered her sweet tea or water, but Ketron had declined. The smell of dampness, old grease, and stale smoke was too strong for her to eat or drink anything.

"You must be blind as a bat." Lisa laughed, fingering an unlit cigarette. "The girl's a twin! She already has a heightened sense of being, but living in a house with spirits—"

Ketron held up her hand. "Hold on. I have to catch up. You think my daughter can see spirits just because she's a twin?"

"Well, yeah," Lisa answered. "I can recognize an intuit or an empath at ninety yards."

"Why?" Ketron asked. It was a reflexive question that she hadn't planned to ask.

She dangled the cigarette from her lips, but to Ketron's relief, she didn't light it. "It takes one to know one."

"What? A twin or an intuit?"

"Both, actually."

Ketron didn't try to hide her surprise. "I didn't realize you were a twin."

Lisa glanced away and her mouth turned down in the corners, making the hanging skin on her chin and neck more noticeable. "I don't talk about it much. My sweet sister passed before her seventeenth birthday."

Ketron's hand darted across the table and covered Lisa's wrist. Her skin was thin and moved easily when Ketron squeezed her hand to comfort her. "I'm so sorry. That must have been hard."

Lisa gave her a half-hearted smile and patted her hand with her other hand. "She was my best friend. We did everything together." She stared at her dusty orange curtains like they were the gateway to a treasured memory. "We even loved the same man."

Ketron tried to think of something to say. "I didn't think there were so many twins around here. I read about a village in Africa with a lot of twins. I think the young women ate a lot of yams."

Lisa smiled knowingly. "Certain families in this town have been producin' twins pretty regular for three generations now." She stood and slapped the wrinkles from her jeans. "But that's a different story."

Ketron took it as her cue to leave. "I'm sorry I mentioned your sister."

Lisa took the cigarette out of her mouth and rested it on the lip of an overloaded ashtray. "Don't worry about it. I had almost seventeen glorious years with the best person to walk the Earth. Now she's my guardian angel." She pulled a trinket off the shelf and showed it to Ketron. "Dusty got me this one when he was a teenager. He mowed three lawns for it." She beamed with pride for a moment before she shook herself out of her reverie. "I shouldn't be so upset. After all, I got to spend my childhood with my twin, but your son never met his."

"Nora is Winslow's twin," she corrected.

Lisa folded her arms across her chest. "I meant the little one." She shook her head slowly. "That poor little baby's wandering around this world without his other half. I knew it as soon as I saw him."

Unexpected tears touched Ketron's eyes. "I'm sorry. I have to go."

"Oh, now I've danced on a hard subject." Lisa reached out to her, but Ketron pulled away.

"It's fine." Ketron stood and shakily raked the chair back under the table. She threw Lisa an obligatory smile as she bolted to the door. "Thank you for your hospitality. I just need to go."

Her feet flew across the lawn, but she didn't let the tears fall until she reached the edge of Lisa's property. She thought she heard Lisa call for her, but she couldn't be sure.

Ketron allowed herself to cry until she saw the brick outline of her house. Then she stuffed the memories of the most traumatic experience of her life into the back of her mind.

Sonny waved at her through the glass in the dining room, and his eyes lit up when he saw her wave back. She was overtaken by her love for him, and she wondered what it would have been like to have seen two of him at the window, welcoming her home.

Chapter Twenty-Four

Past

Ketron woke with the sunrise and prepared a pancake breakfast for her mother. She was too excited to eat, and she counted the number of bites her mother took until she placed her dish in the sink and announced her plans for the day.

"Is there anything you need from town?"

Ketron shook her head. "I can't think of anything. We still have plenty of oats and cornmeal."

Her mother nodded as if the news was expected. She never concerned herself with the quantity of products in the house until it was time to buy more. Without Ketron, her mother would likely run out of many items before she knew she needed them.

Her mother disappeared. Ketron didn't follow her because she understood that her mother was retrieving the phone from wherever she concealed it when she was home. Ketron had tried to follow her when she hid or retrieved it, but her mother was acutely aware of her presence, and busied herself with inessential tasks until Ketron abandoned her surreptitious attempts.

When Gwynevieve Renfro appeared again, she had her hair loose on her shoulders. It was uncommon to see it out of its characteristic schoolmarm bun, unless she was preparing for bed. Ketron didn't want to make her mother self-conscious, so she refrained from inquiring about her changed appearance.

A crisp apple scent drifted to Ketron when her mother tossed the phone onto the table in front of her. Was that body spray?

"I'll be back in a couple of hours." She stared at Ketron, as if challenging her daughter to make a remark about her changes. "If the house is on fire, what do you do?"

Ketron willed her eyes to remain fixed, but her voice betrayed the irritation she felt. "I call the fire department."

Ketron's mother's mouth drooped from an uncommitted thin line into a frown. "I may ask you every time, but I must know that you will follow directions."

"Yes, ma'am," Ketron replied, dropping her eyes. She hoped she had made herself insignificant so that she could have a few hours to herself.

Her happiness returned when she heard her mother's keys rattle, but her stomach plummeted when her mother yelled, "Ketron! Why did you open the attic door?"

"I didn't." Ketron left the receiver on the table when she ran to the dining room.

The door to the attic had opened, and her mother was standing beside it with her eyes narrowed. She made a production of locking it on the inside and shutting it. She checked her keyring and bobbed her head when she saw the bump key was still attached.

She spoke through gritted teeth. "Don't open that door again."

Ketron only stared back in response.

Her mother marched out of the house as if she were on a timetable. Ketron hovered just beyond the dining room window and watched her mother back down the driveway.

The silence was loud around her. It was almost like the house was holding its breath. Behind her, there was a scratch, like someone had ripped a piece of paper, and whatever had made that sound edged the attic door open until it yawned into the dining room.

Ketron was afraid to turn around. Perhaps Pansy and Marigold were creeping across the floor, bearing down on her with their beady eyes and shapeless mouths. The silent pacer could be behind her, materialized from a string of shadows.

She focused on the glass in front of her, hoping the panes would provide insight. No form, ethereal or otherwise reflected on the glass. Comforted by the absence of a figure, Ketron whirled around. The space around the door and the attic steps was empty.

Ketron let out a breath she hadn't known she was holding. "The jam must be broken." She spoke aloud to bring life to the still house, but her emotions shook her voice.

The front door rattled and startled her. She grabbed her chest and cried out.

Peals of laughter echoed from the other side. "Don't be such a scaredy cat!" the twins joked from the other side. "It's just us."

Ketron threw open the door. "What are you guys doing here! My mother will kill me if she sees you!"

"That's why we waited in the woods over there" —Ky pointed to the thickest coniferous trees around their property— "until she left."

Without invitation the two boys filtered into the house, taking in its high ceilings and outdated look. "It's a lot like our house," Ly commented.

"Yeah," Ky agreed. "The rooms are in the same places, but we only have two bedrooms."

"Do you have an attic?"

"We have an attic," Ky volunteered. "But our dad is the only one who goes in it."

"Does it open up at random times?"

The boys looked at each other. "No, but our house isn't haunted." As soon as he had spoken the words, Ky toed a line with his foot.

Ly smiled at his brother. "I'll race ya." They bolted up the steps as Ketron called after them. After it was clear that they weren't coming back down the steps, she followed them.

Ky had already found the old magazines, and he sat on the floor fanning them out. Ly was busy peeking around every corner. He grabbed a pork pie hat from the coat rack and donned an Irish accent. "Ye don wanna mess with the likes of me, lass."

Ketron laughed, and ran over to the rack, choosing a purple silk gown that she draped over her front. She walked with the air of royalty, her chin held high, and her hand held out as if it were meant to be kissed.

Ky jumped up from the floor. "Look at these magazines, Ketron. They must be over fifty years old!"

"Simple math will tell you how old those magazines are. A baby could do it." Ly was irritated that his brother had interrupted their play. It was the first show of sibling rivalry Ketron had seen between the twins.

Ky was stung, but he didn't take long to recover. "The lady in this magazine said that she can cure any man from drinking. Her husband drank for twenty years, but she made a tonic and cured him. How long has our dad been drinking?"

"I don't know." Ly shrugged his shoulders. He picked up one of the magazines. "What's a tonic anyway?"

"It's a mixture of medicines," Ketron replied knowingly. She returned the dress to the hook on the coat rack. The smell of jasmine on the fabric was starting to hurt her head.

Ky held up another ad. He studied it closely, turning it as if to get a better view. "What's a mimsy?" He gave the ad to his brother, and Ly handed it to

Ketron. The advertisement showed a woman against a yellow background. After reading the description that included the words *flaps* and *women only*, Ketron felt heat rise from her chest to her face.

"You can't see your freckles when you turn red," Ly joked, elbowing her gently in the ribs.

"Hey, I've wanted to look in this tub for a while." Ketron grabbed a hand from each twin and guided them to the blue tote where she had found her marbles and the dish that held them. She thought she saw Ly roll his eyes, but the boys allowed themselves to be led to the farthest corner of the attic.

She unlatched the lid and tossed it behind her. She knelt, and Ky and Ly sat down on either side of her, flanking the tote. "It smells like old lady perfume," Ly complained.

"It's jasmine." Ketron thought the scent was a little strong, but it didn't have the penetration of perfume. It dangled in the air like fresh flowers.

She pulled out a long, tattered dress. It was silk with a lace overlay, and the buttons were opalescent. The lace extended to the neck, and it was lengthy enough to drag the floor if it were worn by a woman of average height.

"It's a wedding dress," Ky remarked.

"I don't know," Ketron spoke up. She didn't want to disagree outright, but the object she pulled out next shed some doubt on Ky's comment.

The boys helped her unravel a plain white dress. It was no longer than her arm, and Ketron was certain that it was meant for an infant. The newspaper clipping pinned to the garment confirmed it.

Ketron read aloud. "Mr. and Mrs. Able Renfro request your attendance for the christening of their son, Solomon David Renfro." She read the date and venue, but the rest of the information had been rubbed away with age.

"Wow! That was a long time ago," Ky remarked.

"Um, guys," Ly interrupted. "Look at this." He read from a smaller article. "Mrs. Able Renfro and her infant son perished in a fire."

There was more, but Ketron tuned it out. She handled the christening gown with more reverence, folding it, and placing it back in the tote. She wondered why someone hadn't put the memories in a cedar chest. She doubted storage containers like the one in front of her were available when the woman and her baby died. She didn't want to voice her thoughts to the boys, so she said, "Back in those days, when women died, they didn't have an identity. They were still only known by their husband's name."

Ly patted her back awkwardly. "I think that was only around here at that time. It was different after World War Two."

"Things have really changed," Ky spoke. "You could look through the genealogy records at the library and find her first name."

"I doubt my mother would let me go."

The boys looked at each other with wide eyes. Ky said, "It's the only place our mama will let us go every time we ask."

"There and Aunt Nora's house," Ly added.

Ketron considered their offer, but she worried that the trip to and from the library would take too much time. "I'll do it next Friday. My mother could be home soon."

Ly's eyes settled on a model Ford and he crossed the distance to it in long strides. He rambled on about it, and Ketron was glad that he didn't expect her to listen. Ky was noticeably bored, but he feigned interest in his twin's obsession.

Ky and Ly went around the room while Ketron explored the rest of the tote's contents. She was intrigued by a certain item, and she thought about calling Big Red about it. She stuffed it under the white dress and christening gown.

When she pulled herself away from scavenging in the tote, the boys were looking out of one of the long windows. "Come here," they whispered.

It always freaked her out a little when they said something at the same time, and it added to her uneasiness when she noticed Ly biting his right thumbnail and Ky biting his left. She drew closer to them, using their proximity as protection. The light streamed into the other window on the opposite wall and Ketron could see the room behind her in the window's reflection. Peering out, she noticed nothing, and she relayed it to the twins.

"Over there," they intoned, each taking their thumb from their mouth to point to the creek just beyond the house.

At first, Ketron only saw water rushing over rocks, and wind tracing its way through empty branches, but then a flash of white caught her eye. "It's a body," she gasped.

Ky and Ly raced down the steps, and Ketron flew behind them. Once they broke out the front door, she kept her eyes trained to the spot where she had seen a white bloated mass bobbing in the swollen creek. They rushed to the bank, but they saw nothing. The trio traced the length of the property, searching for the corpse they had seen only moments before.

"Where did it go?" Ky stomped and broke a twig over his knee. "It was just there."

"It may have washed downstream," Ketron offered.

Ky's eyebrows drew together. "In the twelve seconds it took us to get down here?"

His brother threw up his hands. "The water's moving pretty fast."

Ky glared at him.

Ketron's blood turned to ice in her veins as she heard a car crunch the gravel behind them. It was too late to keep the boys from her mother's trained eyes, but she told them to run anyway. Ly started to jog down the creek, but he stopped when he realized that his brother hadn't moved.

"It's too late now," Ky told him. "Ketron's in trouble, so we should stay here and try to make her mom like us."

"My mother won't like you."

Ky cocked his head to the side and smiled cockily. "Everyone likes Ly and me."

Ly ran back and put his arm over Ky's shoulder. "Yeah. We're delightful."

She was reassured by their confidence, but the scowl on her mother's face and the tight fists at her sides as she marched down the hill from the driveway to the creek, caused her to prepare for the worst. Ketron braced herself for a verbal assault and she hoped her new friends were truly ready for an encounter with Gwynevieve Renfro.

"Good afternoon, Ms. Renfro," Ky volunteered, stepping in her path and extending his hand. "It's so nice to meet you. I'm—"

"I don't care who you are." She spoke slowly and deliberately, carefully keeping her rage from overflowing. "You are trespassing on private property."

"They were just passing through," Ketron told her mother. "Their family lives just over the hill."

"How do you know that?" she snapped.

For three full, agonizing seconds, Ketron thought she was caught. Her mother would take her phone privileges away, and Ketron would be required to lie down in the back seat while her mother went on errands every Friday.

"We told her," Ly interjected.

Her mother was satisfied with the answer, but she wasn't happy about the young visitors on her property. "You boys aren't welcome here."

"Why?" Ketron pulled her mother's arm commanding her attention. "I need to have friends, Mother, and they live close by."

Her mother glared at her. "I know exactly who they are and where they live. Their mother is a saint"—she glanced at the twins, and they nodded—"but their father is a drunkard and a deadbeat."

Ky advanced a step, but Ly held him back. "He just has bad luck," Ky defended.

Ketron's mother stared at him. "Is that what he tells you? Is it bad luck when he walks away from job sites after only a couple of days? Is it bad luck when he plants his seed in any woman who is willing to let him tend her garden?"

Ky struggled against his brother's hold, but Ly used all his strength to keep his brother in place. "You're a hateful old bat!" he spat at her.

Gwynevieve smiled at the affect she was having on the boys. "Tell me, do the trees still talk to him?"

Ky had settled against his brother, tired of fighting. "Yeah," Ly responded. "They tell him you're nothing but a—"

"Do you still talk to your dead sister?" Ky shouted at her.

Ketron sucked in an audible breath before she could close her mouth. Her mother's eyes widened as she realized that she had been the subject of enough rumors to make her disease known to the general public. She pointed a finger in the direction from which Ky and Ly had arrived. "LEAVE NOW!"

The boys jumped as if they had been slapped. Ly bolted for the woods, and Ky followed him after he threw a sympathetic look at Ketron. "See ya later, Katie!" they called from the protection of the trees.

Ketron's mother's anger was now focused solely upon her. "What do you think you were doing!" she grabbed Ketron under her arm and almost dragged her to the house. Ketron tried to keep up with her mother's long strides, but her legs were too short to match her pace. "I trusted you to mind my rules." She jerked on Ketron's arm, pushing her up the stairs and causing Ketron to wince. She smirked when she noticed her daughter's pain.

Ketron had one alarming thought: She hadn't closed the attic door. What was her mother going to say when she saw it? Ketron prepared herself for another wave of her mother's anger.

Gwynevieve threw open the door and slung Ketron onto the worn carpet. Ketron skinned her hands catching herself, but she didn't land on her face. She hung her head as her mother quickly bolted the door.

"Phone!" Her mother's one-word demand was clear, and Ketron pointed to the kitchen. Her mother marched to the kitchen to hide the only outlet Ketron had to the outside world. She folded her legs to her chest and rested her head on her knees as she waited for her mother to return from wherever she had hidden her phone.

Ketron debated on locking the attic door before her mother returned, but she decided it might creak and give her away. It was much better to fake ignorance when she was asked for the reason it was open. Her mother might accuse her of finding a key to the attic and Ketron would invite her to search her room for it.

Her mother breezed by her on her way back from hiding the phone. She rattled pots and pans and Ketron rose. Her mother could only cook tacos and macaroni and cheese, so she recognized the signal. It was time for her to prepare the evening meal. As expected, her mother left the room as soon as Ketron placed a pot of water on the stove.

Ketron pulled the cornmeal out of the cabinet and measured it, but when she opened the refrigerator, she realized that there were less than a half dozen eggs. Where were the groceries?

She didn't want to ask, but she was afraid that the fruits and milk wouldn't last long in the car if her mother had forgotten about them.

"Did you bring in the supplies?"

"I didn't have time to go to the store since you were up here with a bunch of little boys!" An angry puff of wind accompanied her words.

"There were two boys." Ketron felt the need to defend herself. "I deserve to have friends."

Her mother flew into the room so fast that her hair seemed to float above her head. "Deserve? What do you think you deserve? I gave you life. I brought you into this world, and when I ask you to do something, I expect for my orders to be obeyed to the letter!"

Ketron cowered under her mother's glowering stare. The measuring cup that held the cornmeal fell to the floor. After watching her mother's intensity bear down on her, Ketron felt a sound. The vibration did not reach her ears but pulsated somewhere in her upper back. Her mother's posture relaxed and the eyes that had darted left to right, as if reading her daughter for signs of rebellion, moved around the room. "Someone's here."

Ketron followed her mother at a distance as she scanned the house. She breezed through each room, without finding a tangible clue. She moved from the kitchen to the living room, and then explored Ketron's room, her room, and the unoccupied room. As she padded after her mother, Ketron wondered if she could blame the open attic door on the unseen presence.

"Ah-ha!" her mother cried.

Ketron went into the dining room. Her mother was standing in the middle of the room, holding a leather belt. Ketron hesitated when she saw it folded in her mother's hands. Was she going to punish her with it?

The attic door was closed and the dish with her marbles had been placed in front of it. Who had closed the door?

Her mother's smile stretched menacingly across her features. It gave an unsheltered view of her teeth in a grin that exposed most of her gums. She snapped the belt. "I knew if we stayed here long enough that he'd come out."

She addressed Ketron without looking at her. Her mother's words were meant as an invitation to embody the entity that had attached itself to the foundation and boards of the house. He had been drifting through darkness, but he rose from cold earth and stone to cause the same pain he had known in life.

A young girl stood in his house. She was the same age as his daughters were when they sought to leave and take his wife away, but she wasn't *his* daughter. He decided she looked enough like them to satisfy his need to punish the ones who had wronged him.

He felt a pull to his daughter's body. He allowed the gentle tug to guide him, and he slipped into her form. Once he had control of Gwynevieve's flesh, he leered down at the girl and said, "Your granddaddy's come out to play!"

Chapter Twenty-Five

Present

Shauna knocked over her soda. She picked up the bottle and flicked it. Tiny bubbles bounced off the plastic.

"It's going to be flat when you drink it," Ketron warned.

Shauna shrugged. "It's my soda. You don't have to drink it."

"Suit yourself," Ketron chuckled. "There's enough sugar in one of those to kill you, so if it were me, I would want to drink it with the fizz."

Ketron had just picked up Nora, Winslow, and Sonny from school and she was prepping vegetables for dinner. Matty and Sonny chased each other through the house, and Sonny grabbed his mother.

"Ezekiel Thomas!" Ketron scolded. "I have a knife in my hand. Don't grab me!"

The boys rushed off without registering her words. Shauna put her feet in another chair and leaned back in her seat. "Why don't you drop his nickname? It was cute when you were pregnant, but the kid should know his name. If he has to have a nickname, why can't you call him Zeke?"

"He doesn't need a nickname, but I like calling him Sonny.

"Why?"

Most of the time, Ketron enjoyed the way her friend challenged her to be better by pointing out things Ketron had naturally accepted, but she didn't appreciate it when Shauna was invasive. Her question sounded more like a challenge than an innocent inquiry.

"He is my son, and right now, he is the center of this family's galaxy, so it fits."

Shauna raised her eyebrows. "Okay." She pronounced the o a little longer before following it with the rest of the word. "I'm glad I only had one kid. I wouldn't want Matty's younger brother or sister to know he was the favorite."

Ketron knew what Shauna was insinuating. "Sonny is not my favorite. I love each of my children equally."

"Then why aren't they all the center of your galaxy?"

"They are." Ketron nicked her finger as she cut into a tomato. "Ow!"

Shauna jumped out of her chair and studied Ketron's hand. "Your cut won't need stitches, but you should put a bandage on it." Shauna followed her to the bathroom and poured peroxide over the wound. "I'm sorry that I said something about his name. I just don't want you to keep calling him 'Sonny' because his father came up with it. He wouldn't let you name Amelia, so you should be able to call your son by the name you gave him."

Ketron agreed with Shauna, but she didn't want to add fuel to her friend's fire. "Amelia is a nice name."

"No, it's not," Shauna countered, drying the excess peroxide from around the cut. "It was his mother's name, and she hated you."

"What would you have me do?" Ketron asked, not liking the whiny quality of her voice. "The baby is almost a year old, and Sonny is four. They're used to their names."

Shauna leaned in conspiratorially and whispered, "Change it."

"What? Change her name? Are you kidding me?"

Shauna held up her hands. "Hear me out. In this state, you can change a child's name for free until they're a year old. Just change it and tell him after her birthday. He won't want to go through the hassle of changing it back."

Ketron tried, but she couldn't dismiss the idea. "What would I have to do?"

Shauna smiled and wrapped the bandage firmly around her finger. "You fill out a request online and send it to the same place that handles birth certificates."

"I'm surprised you don't have the papers with you," Ketron joked. "Seriously, though. You used to like Marvin. Why does it seem like you don't like him anymore?'

"I liked him when he was good to you and the kids," Shauna responded, dropping Ketron's hand. "Now, he just hurts you and picks favorites with them." Sonny ran past her, with Matty close behind. "Or *a* favorite."

Ketron took out the antibacterial wipes to clean up the blood, but the area around the tomato was clean. The only red spot was on the floor, and it belonged to some of the tomato juice that had splattered when she had cut into the juicy fruit. "Where's the blood?"

"Did you clean it up?" she asked Shauna.

"I went to the bathroom with you." Shauna shrugged her shoulders. "Maybe you only bled on yourself."

Ketron thought she had bled on the counter and the floor, but she must have been wrong. She didn't see evidence of blood anywhere.

Ketron weighed the look Shauna was giving Sonny. "But you like *Sonny*, right?"

Shauna snapped at her words. "I love little Zeke," she responded, drawing on his birth-given name. "He's a kid. He can't help that his father's an—"

"What about daddy?" Sonny asked. "Is he home?"

"Not yet," Ketron told him, casting a pointed look in Shauna's direction.

Sonny stared at the ground until Matty tagged him again. They were running out of the room when Shauna stopped them. "Hey, come here a minute."

Realizing that she had spoken to him, Sonny took the chair that Shauna pulled out for him. Matty sat down on the floor and grabbed two dinosaurs. Little roars accompanied the clicks of the dinos as they fought.

"Do you like your name?"

Sonny stared at her with his mouth open and nodded.

"I mean, do you like the name Ezekiel?"

Sonny recognized his name from hearing it at doctor's offices or from people who weren't familiar with the family. He nodded again. "I guess so."

Ketron wanted to interfere, but part of her wondered if Shauna had a point. He was called by his first name at school, and it might be easier if he had a nickname linked to it.

"Do you like the name Zeke?" Shauna asked.

"I guess it's okay," Sonny replied, watching himself loop one finger over another.

Shauna lifted his chin so he could meet her eyes. "What if I started calling you Zeke? Would that be okay?"

"Maybe I could ask my dad." He wiggled in his seat and looked over at Matty.

"Your dad can still call you Sonny," Shauna clarified. "Matty and I will call you Zeke." She tugged the side of his hair like she'd done since he was barely a toddler, and Sonny smiled. "Mommy can start calling you that, too," she added.

Sonny looked at Ketron and she tried to keep her face expressionless.

"Good, then. It's settled." She called for Matty's attention. "From now on, this fine young gentleman is Zeke, okay?"

"Okay," Matty said, grabbing his hand. "Hey, Zeke, do you want to play dinos with me?"

"Sure."

Ketron and Shauna watched them for a few minutes, smiling at their creative play. Amelia woke from her nap, and Nora carried the baby to Ketron. She fed Amelia small bites of tomato as she acclimated to consciousness.

"What's that sound?" Shauna asked.

The boys continued to play, but Ketron could hear the scratching noises. "I think it's coming from the fireplace."

The women approached the mantle and Ketron carefully slid open the glass enclosure. Chirping echoed in the chimney.

"Marvin is going to love this." Ketron closed the grate. "He is not going to like cleaning up the mess when the birds leave the nest."

"Hire someone to do it."

"Sure. I'll do that with the cash I have stuffed in the mattresses," Ketron quipped. Sometimes she forgot about the economic differences between Shauna and herself.

"If it's important you'll find a way."

"That's easy for you to say." Ketron's temper flared. "You can go soak in your pool or have fancy vacations."

Shauna was unaffected. "You could do that, too, if you market your psychology degree."

Fighting with Shauna wouldn't bring the result she wanted. She didn't know if she was really upset about the birds in the chimney or the forced change to her son's nickname. She decided to drop it.

Shauna saved her from awkward exchanges by leaving. "I'll see you later, Zeke!" she called as she went out the door.

"Zeke?" Winslow questioned. He had resurfaced after finishing his homework.

"Shauna thinks it's a good idea to start calling him something closer to his name," Ketron told him.

"Dad's not going to like it."

Marvin's truck rumbled up the one-lane road beside their house. Marvin had a new muffler and knew a guy who would attach it for practically nothing, but he never seemed to have the time to get it fixed.

"Daddy's boy!" Marvin called when he saw Sonny in the window.

"Daddy's boy!" Sonny echoed.

Marvin stomped into his room, leaving a trail of dried mud behind him. Ketron didn't want to start a fight, so she grabbed the broom and dustpan.

Marvin sat down in front of the hearth and started removing his boots. He shook little chunks of dirt out onto the floor. "We had to stand in the mud this morning and flag traffic," he complained.

Ketron waited until he had finished dumping dirt onto the floor before she swept around him. The broom touched his toe, and he jumped away from it, spitting on the broom.

"Gross," Winslow said.

"Your mother bumped my feet with a broom."

"You're superstitious," Ketron admonished. "You won't go to jail because I hit your foot with the broom."

"Whatever. I've seen it happen before."

Like so many other things, Ketron let it drop. She almost enjoyed watching him dance around the broom as she swept.

"Can't you wait until I'm in the shower to sweep?"

"I could," Ketron answered, "but the baby would crawl through it."

"God made dirt—"

"Yes, but I don't think He meant for my infant to eat it."

Marvin rolled his eyes. Sonny plowed into him, ready to play.

"Your boots are off," he commented. "That means you can play dinosaurs with me."

Marvin and Ketron shared a chuckle. When Sonny was three, he started bombarding Marvin the moment he came in from work, begging for attention. Marvin had told him that he had to wait until his boots were off before he asked him questions. "I will in a minute, buddy."

"Let Dad take a shower first, *Zeke*," Winslow said.

Marvin shot a look at Winslow, and Ketron felt her heart drop into her stomach. "Why're you callin' him that?"

"Shauna thinks his nickname should sound more like his real name." Winslow shrugged and smiled at Ketron. He knew that he'd caused a ripple between his father and mother.

"It's none of her business," Marvin snapped, and Ketron immediately defended her friend.

"Shauna loves the children. She's not going to do or say anything to hurt them."

"But she's not his parent," he barked, pointing at Sonny.

"Then maybe you should be." Ketron dropped the broom and dustpan on the floor, and the dust puffed up around the fireplace. She stomped into the bathroom, carrying Amelia with her. She glanced around the room for a toy, and finding none, she obliged Amelia with a hairbrush when she reached for it.

She was tired of honoring Marvin's feelings when he didn't appreciate or respect hers. She hadn't felt love from him in almost a year, and she could no longer tell if his words were laced with true sentiment or alcohol.

Marvin didn't want to stray from the nickname he had given his son because Ketron had named him. Fine. Ketron would change her baby's name, and Amelia would be a nickname that only her father called her. Instead of sticking together, Marvin and Ketron had started a war against each other.

"So, sweet baby, what's your name?"

The infant smiled and gurgled, biting the end of the hairbrush. Something flashed in her eyes, and the child's name became clear to Ketron in that moment. She hugged her daughter and wondered if her marriage would survive the battle.

Chapter Twenty-Six

Present

"What's that noise?" Marvin asked after a spoon full of oatmeal.

Ketron paused and listened. "It's the birds in the chimney."

He dropped his spoon in his bowl. "They'll make us all sick!"

Ketron shrugged. "We have a glass enclosure and a damper door that shuts off the firebox from the rest of the house, and I don't see bird droppings on the hearth. I think we're okay. When the birds aren't in their nest, you could get some copper mesh, and put it over the entry to the chimney."

"But the birds won't have a home," Nora cried.

"They can build a new one," Ketron assured her. "We can make it easy for them by putting out the hair from the hairbrushes and gathering a pile of grass and twigs."

"How will the little birds see it?" Nora asked.

"We can put it outside, beside the chimney."

"Great!" Marvin laughed. "Then we can have birds in the attic and on the porch!"

Ketron didn't acknowledge her husband's sarcasm. "We'll gather some twigs after breakfast."

Nora rushed through her breakfast, eager to help the birds. Visions of benign, animated creatures danced through her thoughts, instead of the feathered worm-eaters in their chimney. Ketron hoped it would bring Nora closer to animals. She had feared them since she was a baby, afraid of their unpredictable movements.

Ketron scooped Amelia up from the floor. She had secretly been whispering her new name to her, just to see if the baby responded to it. So far, she hadn't answered to the different name, but she had hugged her mother, as if she were worried that Ketron had forgotten what to call her.

"Can I be your friend?" Amelia's learning tree voiced.

Ketron reminded herself to change the batteries. The baby had only played with the toy a couple of times since Christmas, but Sonny may have used it to set the scene in his dinosaur battles. He could have flipped the *on* switch and weakened the batteries.

The day was unseasonably humid. The sky had a few dark clouds, but nothing particularly ominous. Ketron slowed her movements, but she was sweating after only a few minutes of gently rocking with Amelia on the swing.

Winslow burst out the back door with Nora right behind him. They gathered a few twigs and placed them by the outside of the fireplace. Nora kept inching the pile closer to the exterior of the house each time she returned with a pile. She noticed Ketron watching her. "I want to make sure the birdies can see it," she said with her gap-toothed grin.

Sonny punched the door open and stalked to his bicycle. He brooded over his siblings' fun.

"You can sit with me on the swing," Ketron offered.

"Daddy won't come outside with me," he pouted, and crossed his arms. Ketron rose from the saucer swing. Sonny turned around when she approached him, his arms still crossed. "Can I play with you instead?" Ketron asked him.

"No."

Ketron ran a hand through his hair. It was growing past his shoulders in loose, golden curls. "Do you want to help Nora and Winslow gather twigs and grass for the birds?"

"No." He kept his arms crossed but allowed her to see his profile. "Daddy says the birds will die when he covers the chimney."

"I hope not," Ketron replied honestly. "Wild birds tend to be pretty hardy. They can rebuild a nest." She hoped her words were true.

Sonny stared in the opposite direction, committing to his pout. Ketron gave up on consoling him and inched down the slope in the yard to the swing set. "I'll be over here if you need me."

After a few minutes, Sonny's posture relaxed, and he climbed onto his bicycle. He rode circles in the driveway with the wind wiping through his hair. "You can watch me, Mommy?" he called to her.

Ketron rose from the swing set and stood by the driveway. She loved the way younger children formed questions. It was almost like they were giving you permission to watch them or help them.

"I get to watch you?" she responded.

Sonny's smile lit up all his features. "Yes! Watch this!" He rode down the driveway, lifting his legs off the pedals. After he came to a stop, he looked back at her, waiting for praise.

"Fantastic!" Ketron clapped one hand against the arm that was holding Amelia. The baby stared at her action and imitated it.

Ketron heard an old truck turn onto the road. "Come back this way," she told her son, and Sonny pedaled away from the road. The truck stalled just before her driveway, and Lisa killed the motor and jumped out. She didn't bother to park in the driveway, leaving no room for anyone to get past her vehicle.

"Hey, little mister," she said to Sonny.

"You can call me Zeke now."

Lisa looked at Ketron for confirmation, and Ketron nodded. "The kids at school don't know about the nickname his father gave him, so they might make fun of him if they found out." At least that was one of the reasons Ketron had given Marvin for the switch when he had yelled against Shauna's motives.

Lisa pressed her mouth into a line. "I suppose so, but the best people are born out of trials and suffering."

Sonny nodded solemnly. "Just don't call me that around my dad. He doesn't like my real name."

Lisa patted his back. "I wouldn't dream of making your daddy mad."

The screen door flung open, and Marvin stepped onto the porch. His face was slack, until he noticed Lisa. He smiled, showing all his teeth and threw up his arm to wave. He glanced at Nora and Winslow, like he was a proud father, looking over his children while they played, but Ketron knew better. He wanted something, and he came out of his bedroom to ask her for it.

He jogged up to the two women with a considerable effort, holding the weight his newest addiction had given him. He stumbled slightly, and Lisa noticed the slip. "It's a bit early for a nip."

Ketron wasn't familiar with the feeling that washed over her, but she thought it was validation. She worked hard to hide Marvin's illness from certain people, more for her reputation than his, but she was tired of covering for him with friends and neighbors. Lisa's understanding was more comforting to Ketron than if she had held her while she cried.

Marvin ignored her comment. "What are you ladies up to?"

"I was just about to ask your wife if she wanted to help me with my flower garden."

It was the wrong time of year to plant flowers, but Ketron remained silent. Lisa would reveal the real reason she stopped at their house when she was ready.

"Ket can't grow anything," Marvin laughed. "Everything she plants dies."

Ketron dropped her eyes and stepped back. "I did well with the marigolds."

"You had them growing in patchy handfuls along the driveway." He chuckled. "There's a bunch of flowers," he mocked, pointing to the ground. He moved his finger a few feet. "Oh, there's another bunch."

The sides of Lisa's mouth dropped into a low frown. "Just the same. I'd like her help." Ketron hadn't heard Lisa's voice sound so cold, even when she'd visited her house unannounced.

"I guess it's your business if you want dead flowers." Marvin shrugged and stuck his hands in his pockets.

"Will you make me a pot of cheesy butter noodles?" he asked Ketron.

Ketron nodded, and Marvin went back inside. He hadn't bothered to introduce himself or ask Lisa for her name.

"Do you really want me to help with your garden?" Ketron asked after her husband shut the door.

"No. I just want you to have an excuse to get away when you need it." Her eyes had followed Marvin into the house. "Sometimes, a woman needs to escape."

Ketron's heart swelled when she realized that Lisa wanted to protect her. She wondered if Lisa had experienced something similar with her husband.

"I guess you better go make your husband the cheesy doodles."

"Cheesy butter noodles," Ketron corrected.

"It sounds interesting." Her smirk suggested otherwise.

"Oh, they're a favorite in the house."

"If you say so," Lisa conceded. "Maybe I'll try them sometime." She gave Ketron her phone number and threw up her hand as she walked out of the driveway. An impatient car full of teenagers slowed to a stop behind her truck. They looked for a way around it, and the driver hit his steering wheel when he realized there was a ditch on either side of the road.

Ketron wondered why Lisa had gotten out of her truck to talk to her. It certainly wasn't about a flower garden. "Hey, Lisa," Ketron called. "Why did you stop?"

"I just wanted to check on you." She didn't turn around when she spoke, and Ketron could hardly hear her words.

The teenager behind her blew his horn and threw up his hands. Lisa stopped and stared at him for almost a full minute before she slowly climbed into her truck. She made a production of checking her mirrors and adjusting the radio before she put the truck into drive.

Ketron was curious about Lisa's words. *Why was Lisa concerned for her?*

Finally, she shrugged and called the children to go into the house. One thing was certain, Lisa was her friend.

Chapter Twenty-Seven

Present

"I found the website," Shauna whispered conspiratorially.

"You don't have to lower your voice," Ketron told her. "It's just the four of us."

The children were at school and Marvin was at work. Matty played with Amelia on the rug in front of the television.

Shauna sipped her cola and gulped hard. "You don't have a lot of time to do this before she turns a year old."

"I think it will process a couple of days before her birthday," Ketron assured her. "Now that we've come this far, I have to try."

Shauna nodded while she typed. She filled out the form until it asked for Amelia's social security number.

"You know my address?"

"Yeah." Shauna handed the laptop to Ketron.

"I didn't realize you had memorized it."

"I wrote it down when I realized—" she glanced over at the children to make sure they couldn't hear her, "—that I might need to tell it to the police one day."

"He doesn't hit me." Ketron's voice was cold.

"But do you think he never will?" Shauna stood up. "Could you have guessed a couple of months ago that he'd be a full-blown alcoholic?"

Ketron couldn't say anything. She had often wondered how her husband had fallen so far so fast.

"He'll come out of it. He just needs me to be understanding—"

"What is there to understand?" Shauna broke in. "What is going on in his life that's so hard that he needs to escape? Isn't his dinner the right temperature? Isn't his house clean enough? Are the kids he never plays with too loud?"

Ketron could hear the emotion building in Shauna's tone. She was reminded of all the terrible events that had led to her friend's drug abuse. Ketron had never met her father, but Shauna had a few memories of her father before he abandoned his family, and they weren't great.

"Forget it." Shauna took a deep breath and attempted to reset her feelings.

"No." Ketron grabbed her hand. "Thank you for being concerned. You know where Marvin's addiction leads, and you don't want the children and me to suffer."

Relief in the form of a half-smile flitted across Shauna's face. She glanced at the computer. "It looks like you have everything except her new name. What are you changing it to?"

In answer, Ketron tapped the keys. She showed Shauna the name she had been calling her daughter for weeks. Shauna glanced over at the baby as she played with Matty. She chewed on a pink plastic block and giggled at the funny faces the three-year-old made at her. Shauna leaned back in her chair and put her hands behind her head, soaking in the beautiful moment. "I think it's perfect."

Chapter Twenty-Eight

Present

A shiver of sound escaped the kitchen, and Ketron was sure that the bread had fallen. *I must have had it on the edge of the counter*, she thought, but it didn't seem right. She had placed it on the coffee maker, a foot away from the edge.

Ketron pushed herself up, inching away from Amelia and slinking out of Sonny's arms. She hardly touched the floor as she stepped across it, barely putting her weight on each foot. She thought the baby moved, but she settled quickly.

The kitchen was quiet except for the gentle hum of the refrigerator. Ketron looked at the floor, but she couldn't see anything on it. The bread and all the other things on the counter were in their places. Ketron made her way back to the couch and slid between her youngest children. The baby nuzzled her chest and Ketron offered her nipple to soothe her back to sleep.

Ketron was drifting into a doze, when she heard another shuffling sound in the kitchen. *We have a mouse*, she realized, and worried about the bread. She would have to send the children with enough money to buy school lunches because she was almost certain that the bread had been compromised.

"Will you be my friend?"

Ketron recognized the disembodied voice of Amelia's learning tree. She thought she had turned it off, but Sonny had demanded more of her attention at bedtime so she couldn't remember if she had flipped the off switch on all the talking toys.

"Will you be my friend?" the toy repeated.

Not if you wake up my toddler, Ketron thought.

She dislodged her nipple from Amelia's mouth and slid off the couch. The lights on the toy weren't active, but it could have been because the batteries were low.

"Friend! Friend!" the toy called out.

Finally, Ketron ran her fingers underneath the tree and flipped the switch. She was ready to slide between her children again, when she heard, "Will you be my friend?"

All the warmth drained from her body. No one else in the house stirred, and it sounded like the learning tree was in the same room. She had put the toy down in the den, hadn't she?

"Friend?" It spoke again, and Ketron was almost certain it was a question directed at her.

She focused on the source of the sound, trying to make out the shadows against the wall. She inched toward the shape she thought looked the most like the baby's toy. Sure enough, the tree was against the wall. *I guess I could have brought it with me*, she thought. She knew it wasn't true, though, as she carried the tree to the kitchen. She turned on the dim light above the stove, and her breath caught. The flap under the tree was open, exposing the empty battery compartment.

"Friend?"

Ketron dropped the toy. The sound startled Amelia and she wailed. Sonny stood up and wondered around the living room, completely disoriented. Marvin threw open his bedroom door. "What's going on?" he yelled.

"It doesn't have batteries," Ketron squeaked out.

"What?" he asked, rubbing his eyes with his thumb and forefinger. "Oh, yeah. I took the batteries out after breakfast the other day. You were outside talking to that crazy lady."

Ketron was too shocked to address his slight against Lisa. "*You* took them out?"

Marvin stumbled into the kitchen, squinting in the low light. "It kept repeating itself. Kinda freaked me out, so I took out the batteries. Why do you want to put batteries in it at two in the morning?"

Ketron stared at the toy as if it were alive and baring its teeth at her. "I don't. It was talking without the batteries in it."

Marvin picked up the tree and looked at the battery compartment. "It must be faulty wiring." His eyebrows met. "Wait. Did you say it *talked* to you?"

Even though she was still frightened, Ketron understood his inference. She laughed, a very unconvincing sound. "You're right. What am I even doing in the kitchen? I had a dream about the baby playing with the learning tree, and I must have gotten up and thought that I was putting batteries in it for her." She didn't look to see if he believed her.

Ketron picked up Amelia and ushered Sonny back to his place on the couch. The door to Marvin's room rubbed loudly against the doorframe as he shut them out.

"Is it still dark?" Sonny asked.

"Yes, it is still very dark," Ketron replied, running her fingers through his hair. "Go back to sleep."

Sonny popped up and pointed into the kitchen. Ketron thought he saw something until he asked her about the kitchen light. "I'm going to leave it on tonight," she told him.

Amelia nursed herself back to sleep and Sonny snored in mere moments. Ketron's eyes and ears searched for sounds, upset when the air conditioning unit muffled the creaks and groans the old house made at night. She didn't want its vibrations to camouflage an ethereal presence.

Ketron's mind kept returning to the learning tree. Although it was silent, she kept expecting it to speak again. Finally, she got up and grabbed the tree. She placed the toy just outside the door, decided it wasn't far away enough, and walked it to the driveway.

Chapter Twenty-Nine

Present

Ketron loved the still mornings when sunlight streamed through the space between the curtains, offering a new day. On those mornings, Sonny would hug himself closer to her, and they would cuddle before Amelia woke up.

"How is my little dinosaur?"

"I am a T-Rex," Sonny informed her.

"How do you know you are a T-Rex?" Ketron asked playfully.

"The dinosaurs told me."

"Oh, you can talk to dinosaurs. Can I talk to them, too?"

"No," he answered decisively. "You can't see them."

Sonny held the worn stuffed dog loosely in his hand. He swung it up and down.

"You like that doggie, don't you?"

"Yep."

"What's its name?"

"Buddy."

"Oh! Like how your father sometimes calls you his buddy?"

"No, that was its name before."

"Before when?"

"Before." He squirmed and turned over.

Ketron tried to get Sonny to play with her some more, but he appeared irritated. She decided it was the best time to ask him the question that had plagued her. "Do you still talk to Jeremy?"

No answer.

Ketron waited for a minute before she tried another approach. "Does Jeremy like your dog?"

He showed her his profile and narrowed his eyes. "He's right. You don't pay attention."

Ketron sucked in a breath, and she decided to address the accusation. "Honey, I give you a lot of my attention." She rubbed his shoulder.

He shrugged her hand away. "Humph! You play with the baby, feed the baby, and change the baby. You don't have time to play with me anymore."

She could have argued with her four-year-old. She could have reminded him that she carried him to the bathroom in the mornings, participated in his epic dinosaur battles, and used his metal trucks to build dirt roads with him, but she understood the truth behind his words: He wanted attention. "Can I play a game with you now? I'll play whatever you want to play."

At first, she thought he was going to ignore her, but he inched off the couch and brought back two plastic dinosaurs. "You get to be the long-neck," he told her, handing over a green Apatosaurus. "I'll be the T-Rex."

Ketron and Sonny played for a few minutes before she chanced another question. "Does Jeremy like dinosaurs?"

"Yeah, but he didn't have any to play with. He plays with mine."

Ketron tried to keep up their conversation. "It's nice that you share with him. Does he share anything with you?"

Sonny shrugged. "Sometimes."

Marvin's door popped open, rattling against the frame. Sonny's eyes lit up, and he ran to his father. "Let me go to the bathroom," Marvin spoke gruffly, prying Sonny's fingers off his legs. Sonny trailed after him, talking about his morning while Marvin ignored him. His father trudged back through the living room with Sonny wrapped around his leg. He shook him off and rubbed his eyes. Ketron could smell last night's alcohol on him.

"Will you play dinosaurs with me, Daddy?" he asked hopefully.

"Maybe in a little while, buddy."

Ketron watched her son's posture deflate. "I can play with you," she offered. "I thought we were having a good time."

"I don't want to play with dinosaurs anymore." He dropped his head and poked out his lip. Ketron tried to hug him, but he pulled away and grabbed Buddy.

Reading her son's cue to be left alone, she picked up Amelia who had stirred when her father's footsteps had vibrated the floor next to her. She took the baby to the kitchen with her.

Ketron was deciding what she would fix for breakfast, when something hit her foot. A yellow truck had rolled into her heel. She looked around for someone who could have sent the toy in her direction. Everyone else was in their bedrooms, except Sonny, but he was playing in the far corner of the living room. She recognized the truck as a toy that was often around Sonny while he played, but she seldom saw it in his hand.

She put the truck on the dining room table and continued her assessment of the breakfast options. A gentle tapping, almost like a nudge, startled her. She looked down at the yellow truck and her breath stopped. She walked in a circle around it, unwilling to pick up the truck a second time. Finally, she kicked it into the dining room, and tried to convince herself it had not moved.

Ketron and Amelia were happily stirring pancake batter and spooning it onto the hot griddle when Sonny joined them. He hugged his mother, but he put excessive force around her waist. It was too much for her, and Ketron almost lost her breath from the sudden pressure.

"Stop, Sonny. You're hurting me." She tried to pull his hands away, but he squeezed tighter. She had to put Amelia down to dislodge his grip. At first, he hung his head, and Ketron thought he was remorseful, but then he lifted his face. His eyes met hers and she realized that he was not her son. Sonny's features were the same, but they were being used by someone else. A snarl lifted his mouth in a peculiar way.

Sonny saw his mother's reaction to his differentness and was fueled by it. He smiled with a maliciousness that was much older than his years. Ketron backed away from him, unsure of what to do or say. "Sonny?"

Sonny held her gaze and lifted his hand. He splayed his small fingers out, and Ketron braced herself for a slap. She couldn't say anything to stop his actions. She was too frightened of the thing that was not her son. She closed her eyes, and a piercing scream shattered her ears.

When she opened her eyes, Sonny was holding his hand on the griddle. His flesh sizzled alongside the burning pancake. Marvin's door burst open, and he ran into the kitchen. Sonny took his hand off the griddle and fell onto the floor.

"What's going on?" Marvin yelled and glared at her. "Why aren't you helping him?" He knelt onto the floor in front of Sonny and jerked his hand into view. "What happened, son?" He sucked in a breath when he saw the damage. Bright blisters were already forming on the angry red palm. "Do something!" he demanded.

Nora and Winslow ran into the room. Nora screamed when she saw Sonny's hand, and Winslow shouted something Ketron couldn't hear. Marvin barked at them to go to their room, and they unwillingly complied. Winslow put his arm around Nora and guided her out of the kitchen while she cried for her younger brother.

Amelia wailed in Ketron's arms. The baby took a breath and screamed with all the force in her body, vibrating her mother's arms as she shook in fear. She clung to Ketron, but she wouldn't take her eyes off Sonny.

Usually, Ketron would have flown into action, but she moved to the refrigerator like she was walking through water. She took the chilled aloe vera to Marvin, and he shouted commands she couldn't make out over Amelia's screams. After he repeated himself, she understood that he wanted her to put the ointment on the hand he held. Ketron didn't want to touch the impostor, so she stood, dazed, until Marvin grabbed the tube from her and applied it.

"What's wrong with you?" he roared. He blew on the hand, trying to cool the inflamed fingers. After a moment, he was a little calmer when he asked, "Do you think he needs to go to the hospital?"

"I'm okay, Daddy." The voice coughed and sputtered, and Ketron would have believed it was her son if she hadn't witnessed him burn his hand purposely.

Marvin rubbed his hair away from his forehead. "Are you sure, Sonny? We can take you to the hospital."

The fraud shook his head. "Mommy will take care of me."

Normally, Ketron would have covered Sonny in a flurry of kisses and held him in her arms, but she stood back, scared to move or to turn away. Marvin glanced at her expectantly, and in those few seconds, an evil smile danced across the impostor's face.

Ketron wanted to shake him and demand that he release his control over her son, but she could see calculating movements under the guise of a helpless child. He had created a situation where he had complete control. Ketron was powerless.

"I will take care of him," she promised.

Marvin read her trepidation as shock over what he believed was an accident, and he released Sonny. The child's small arms reach up for her and she had to accept the hug he gave her.

Marvin turned off the griddle and put the burned pancakes in the trash. Before he went back to his room, he opened the windows, as the smoke and smell of burnt flesh was overpowering.

Ketron sat on the floor, cradled Amelia, and offered her a breast. She took it gratefully, but she kept her eyes wide, as if looking for the impostor in her peripheral vision.

Ketron decided to go through the motions of a mother. Her son could return to her at any moment, and she wanted to reduce any pain he might feel. She silently blew on the blistered hand, trying not to look at his face.

"Are you okay, Mommy?" he spoke.

Ketron nodded her head. "I just want my son back."

"What do you mean?" Even though any other four-year-old would be writhing in pain from the injured hand, he chuckled. "I *am* your son."

Ketron's frustration rose to the surface. "Let's get this straight," she whispered, "you may be in my son's body, but you are not my son. You didn't even try to *act* like you were Sonny. You wanted me to know you had taken him over. Now bring him back!"

"What's going on?" Marvin demanded. He had resurfaced when he heard Ketron raise her voice. "Why are you holding his wrist?"

Ketron had lightly held her son's arm when she had blown on the inflamed hand, but she had tightened her grip in her anger. The impostor winced, and Ketron waited to see if he would accuse her of abuse.

"Mommy held my wrist too tight, but she didn't mean to."

There was a flicker of misrecognition that crossed Marvin's face, but it was only there for a moment. He dismissed it quickly, possibly attributing his doubts to the stress of the situation or the amount of alcohol he had ingested.

"Daddy's boy," he called sweetly.

Marvin echoed the words and smiled. Any doubt he had was cleared, and he drifted to his room to play a game.

"See, *Daddy* knows that I'm his son." He laughed, using Sonny's vocal cords, but making a sound Ketron had never heard from her son.

"*Please* bring Sonny back," Ketron begged. "What do you want? I'll do it if you give him back to me."

Amelia whimpered, and the thing controlling Sonny's body tried to comfort her. She let out a shriek when he touched her. Ketron pulled her away quickly. She tried to offer Amelia more milk, but the baby was too upset. She shook in her mother's arms and pointed, uttering sounds only known to her.

Ketron glared at him. "Amelia knows something isn't right."

"She's just a dumb baby."

Ketron stood with Amelia and looked down at him. "Sonny would never say that about his sister."

The thing mocked her son's voice. "You play with the baby, feed the baby, and change the baby. You never play with me anymore." They stared at each other before Ketron stormed off into the living room. She had cared for Sonny's hand, but she wasn't going to mother the impostor in his body.

In less than a minute, a piercing scream echoed through the house. It was followed by cries for her. Ketron ran to the source of the sound and found

Sonny in the same place with a familiar look on his face. She scooped him into her arms. She held Amelia with him, and the baby didn't protest, even though Sonny was screaming in her ear.

Marvin resurfaced. "Why is he crying again? I thought you took care of it." Marvin didn't know that it was the first time Sonny had experienced the pain from the burn.

"He's just a child," Ketron covered. "It hurts to have a burn like that."

Marvin squatted in front of Sonny and put a hand on his shoulder. "Are you sure you don't want us to take you to the doctor?"

Sonny responded by screaming his cries into his father's face, and Marvin gave up on trying to help him. Ketron scooted Sonny and Amelia with her to the freezer and opened it, thankful that she asked Marvin to purchase a side-by-side model. The frozen peas were just within her reach once she put Amelia across her legs. She placed the frozen bag over Sonny's hand. He cried for several more minutes, but he finally soothed into erratic sobs. Ketron hugged him closely and stroked his hair.

Sonny didn't ask what had happened to his hand, so Ketron believed he had still been there in some way. She didn't let him out of her sight for the rest of the day, convinced that he would change if she left him alone in a room. She was relieved by each recognizable expression that graced his features, even though most of the time he was in pain.

"It will get better," she promised him. "Each day your hand will hurt a little less."

Just before he drifted off to sleep, Sonny asked, "Why did my hand burn?"

Ketron asked what he remembered.

He didn't answer for so long that she thought he had fallen asleep. "I went into the kitchen to help you with pancakes and then my hand got hot."

"You burned it sweetheart," was all she could say. How could she tell him the truth?

Chapter Thirty

Past

Ketron's mother had always spoken in an unbroken way, and her sentences were mostly grammatical. In fact, Ketron answered her practice sentences in language arts by thinking about the way her mother would speak if she had read the examples. After a month in her childhood home, Gwynevieve Renfro started to lose touch with her speech formalities. At first, she spoke in blended contractions, like "shouldn't've" in place of "should not have", but when she told Ketron that her "granddaddy" had resurfaced, Ketron's spine tingled.

She had thought the rush to get to Erwin was only to go into hiding, but her mother's frequent trips into town weren't indicative of a woman who was trying to conceal her whereabouts. More than once, Ketron had heard her mother in late-night debates with herself. She must have thought that she was talking to someone else, as she didn't realize that she had spoken both ends of the conversation.

After her announcement, it was clear that her mother's homecoming was an attempt to battle the spirits from her past. Ketron didn't think the ghosts from Gwynevieve's mind liked her.

Ketron bolted out of the dining room and flew to her bedroom. She thought of anywhere she could hide from the terrible force that had taken over her mother's features. Her mother had always carried an *other* with her. That alter-ego only showed itself to Ketron when her mother was frustrated or scared. Whatever had taken possession of her mother had slipped through the wooden floorboards from its shadowy place beneath the ground, and now it was ready to show itself.

The quiet house throbbed around her as the room shrank and expanded. Ketron searched for a place to hide. Finally, she dove under the bed. She didn't question the presence of the marbles under her bed, even after she had seen them in front of the attic door. She pulled the dish to her soundlessly, happy to feel its weight in her palms.

Footfalls echoed down the hall. They didn't belong to her mother, even though he was using her mother to find her. Pounding steps vibrated the boards beneath her, as if her mother were wearing boats instead of thrift store flats.

The reverberations stopped and her mother's feet came into view. Ketron held her breath while the room breathed.

She didn't want to imagine the look on her mother's face. She held the marbles tighter, and they rattled in the dish. His ears picked up the sound and the shoes pointed to her. He was listening for her breath, so she took tiny bits of air into her lungs. Ketron froze, and she didn't see her mother's legs cross the distance between them, but she recalled the cruelty in the voice that said, "Get out. We have work to do."

Ketron left the marbles under the bed. She didn't know why, but she didn't want him to see them.

He stood in her mother's body. His presence in her form denied all the natural laws, but there was no other explanation for the difference in her mother's appearance. The belly that she sucked in with her abdominal muscles bloated out, and the spine was straight, but the chin was tucked in instead of carried in a proud lift. He walked hard on the ground, as if he were punishing it for an unknown offense, and before she knew it, they were stabbing the soil outside with their shovels.

Ketron remembered the path they had taken, but she couldn't see the house. The sun had set, and the trees had grown quiet. She felt like she had been swallowed by the woods and they were ready to digest her. She wondered if the cold would creep silently onto them and consume them before her mother pushed her grandfather out of her body.

The pair worked without words. He shoveled each spade full of dirt into a pile that grew larger each hour. It was well into the night before Ketron spoke. "Why are we digging a hole?"

He stood to her mother's full height. The grin that reminded her of a rat's face pulled her features wide. "It's for you. Without you, she'll stay with us forever."

Chapter Thirty-One

Present

The dog barked before Ketron walked onto Lisa's property. She edged up the steps, holding Amelia with one arm and guiding Sonny. Winslow nudged Nora out of the way so that he could go up the stairs first.

"That's no way to treat your sister," Lisa scolded him. She had opened the door while Ketron had been busy negotiating the stairs.

Winslow shrugged. He appeared apathetic, but he was chastised by the older woman's words.

"You will never find a better friend than your siblin'," she said. "'Especially your twin."

Winslow crossed his arms and looked away. "She does stuff to me, too," was his half-hearted defense.

"I don't condone *any* hurt between two people, but I *saw* what you did on my steps. You need to tell your sister you're sorry."

"Yeah, like *that's* gonna happen."

Ketron was deeply embarrassed. "Winslow Nehemiah, you will apologize to Nora, and then you will tell Mrs. Paul that you're sorry."

"But what did I do to *her*?" he yelled, pointing at Lisa. Several birds squawked their displeasure over his elevated voice.

Ketron took a deep breath and forced a grin. "You will tell Mrs. Paul that you are sorry for being rude to her on her own property." She pushed the words through gritted teeth and didn't flinch from her son's narrowed eyes.

"Fine," Winslow huffed. "I'm sorry that I moved Nora a tiny bit-even though she deserved it—"

"Winslow," Ketron cautioned.

"And I'm sorry that I was rude to Mrs. Paul."

"Apology accepted." Nora crossed her arms, held her head higher, and pursed her lips.

"I don't believe your heart was in it, but I'll accept your apology." Lisa put her hands on her hips and didn't break eye contact when he walked over the threshold.

Ketron pushed the children onto one area on the living room rug. It was colorfully woven, and Sonny and Nora took turns jumping from the red to blue in the pattern. "Children, stop!" Ketron quietly admonished.

"They ain't hurtin' nothin'. That rug was given to me by my aunt. She wove it herself, and it's a lot like her: too tough to give up the ghost."

"What's that mean?" Winslow asked.

"What? Give up the ghost?" Lisa laughed. "I reckon it comes from The Bible. King Herod fought an angel and gave up the ghost." She leaned in conspiratorially, waggled her eyebrows at the children, and added, "He died." They all gasped at the appropriate moment, and Lisa cackled.

Ketron told them to pick a spot to sit down, but Lisa waved her off. "Ya'll go in the back room. It used to be my boy's, and it should still have some toys."

The children filed down the hall, but Ketron held Amelia back. The baby was tired and chewing on the teething necklace around Ketron's neck. "Be sure to clean up anything you take out," Ketron called after them.

Lisa pulled open the refrigerator door and scanned the contents. "You said you don't like sweet tea," she remarked. "I have some half-and-half, ice water, and pickle juice. You'd be doin' me a favor if you drank the pickle juice." She winked at Ketron.

"I think I'll take the ice water," Ketron laughed.

After a few southern pleasantries, the reason for Ketron's visit still wasn't clear. Lisa stared solidly at her. "What's happened?"

The question took Ketron off guard, but she realized that it had been the perfect way to ask. She took a deep breath and decided to be honest. "I think the ghost of the little boy in the house possessed my son."

"You mean little Zeke?"

"Yes, it was Sonny." Ketron recounted the entire event. Lisa sat quietly though her description, alternating from staring at the door to looking at the floor. When Ketron was finished, she waited almost a full minute before Lisa spoke.

"It's him," she confirmed.

Those two words released a weight from Ketron that she hadn't known she'd been carrying. The short-lived feeling was replaced with a new set of worries. "What am I going to do? Should I buy some sage?"

A genuine laugh traveled from Lisa's belly and burst from her mouth. "Sure, that will work for some pranky spirits and negative energy that hasn't already laid its roots there."

"What can I do?" Ketron asked desperately. "What does he want?"

Lisa leaned back in her kitchen chair. "That's the million-dollar question, isn't it?"

"Should I ask him what he wants?"

Lisa's eyebrows almost met as she thought it over. "No, I don't think it would matter. He's surfaced for a reason, but I'll have to look into it a little more. I thought after he killed his father—"

"Whoa, what?"

The baby popped off Ketron's shoulder and looked around dreamily. She gave Lisa a drowsy smile and drifted back to sleep.

"It's just a theory I have," Lisa continued. Ketron stared at her expectantly. Amelia was asleep, and the children's stifled laughter trickled down the hallway. Ketron had the time to be patient. "Are you sure you want to know?" Ketron nodded, careful not to tickle her hair against the sleeping tot.

"Jeremy's father, Joseph, moved into the house after they found little Jeremy and his mother dead. Apparently, the parents hadn't officially divorced, and the house was his.

"He brought along a horrible little girlfriend, Steph. She had an obvious drug problem, and she talked too loud. I almost asked her if she had a hearin' problem, but I think she just grew up without getting attention from her parents, so it was her way to make sure she was heard. She would get mad at Joseph, and she'd screech. I could almost hear her up here with my windows closed. There was hardly a time I'd pass the place when I wouldn't see her yellin' with her hand on her hip. I don't know how they ever made up long enough for her to get pregnant."

Ketron's interest piqued when Lisa mentioned a pregnancy, but she didn't ask questions about it. Lisa would circle around to it again if it was important.

"Joseph had always been a drinker, but he must have doubled how much alcohol he drank when he started livin' there again. I'd see him out on his ridin' lawnmower, and his head would bob up and down with the bumps in the yard. He backed into the apple tree once, and he left the mower there for a week. That was around the time when someone in the neighborhood paid for a service to mow. They may have felt sorry for him, or they were tired of looking at the eyesore when they passed the house. I don't think Joseph even noticed."

Lisa stopped her story and took a long drink from her glass. She cleared her throat. "I'd ask you to join me outside while I smoked a cigarette if you wasn't holdin' your youngun'. I guess I better tell this last part and then go smoke. I'll need it by the time I finish the story.

"I was on my way to the store one morning, when Steph came runnin' into the road. Her black makeup was streaked down her face and her shirt was torn. I didn't want to get involved in a domestic dispute, but she was starting to show, and I thought of the little baby.

Steph told me that Joseph had been drinkin', and he'd come after her. He'd said some things about the baby not being as good as the son he'd lost because it was a girl, and he'd kicked her belly. She asked me to take her to the hospital, but I didn't really want any part of it. Cell phones hadn't made it to my neck of the woods yet, so I couldn't call an ambulance to pick her up. She was in a panic, though, so after I heard him yell for her from the house, I told her to get into the truck. He slung open the back door just as she was shuttin' her door, and he took off after us.

"I don't think I've ever run that truck so hard. We made it to the hospital in under ten minutes, and she told them I was her aunt. The nurses let me stay with her, and when I saw her shakin' like a leaf, I held her hand.

"The doctor checked her out and put one of those scopes to her belly. She didn't hear a heartbeat, so they took Steph for an ultrasound. I waited in the room, feelin' way outta place. When Steph came back, she couldn't talk. She'd cried until she was hoarse, and there was hair comin' outta her fists where she'd pulled it. She didn't have to tell me that the baby was dead."

Ketron had suffered her own loses, and she was uncomfortable with the turn the story had taken. She had agreed to hear it, though, so she tried not to focus on Steph's miscarriage.

"She was far enough along that she had to give birth to the baby." Lisa stopped her story to see if she would need to clarify, but Ketron nodded her head. She already knew about the procedure. "Steph didn't want to do it alone, so I held her hand while she delivered a beautiful little girl. It was silent and still when her little body entered the world."

It was Ketron's turn to take a long drink. The room was cool, but she was sweating.

"Are you okay?" Lisa asked, noticing the paleness of her complexion.

"I'm fine," Ketron assured her. "It just gets a little warm when they sleep on you." She inclined her head to Amelia who was breathing in tiny puffs on her neck.

"I remember those days!" Lisa caressed Amelia's arm. "It's hard to put 'em down, though, when they're resting so peaceful."

"What happened to Steph?" Ketron asked. Lisa hadn't painted a pretty picture of the woman, but Ketron couldn't help but feel emotionally invested in her.

"They kept her for a couple of days." Lisa busied herself with folding and refolding a napkin. "Joseph didn't visit her while she was in the hospital. By that point, he was too far gone in his drinking. When she got out of the hospital, she packed her bags and high-tailed it outta there."

"Good," Ketron said. "No one should be ignored by the ones they love in their time of need."

"Bless your heart, darlin'." Lisa found Ketron's hand and held it. "You must have been hurt mighty bad. Was it by that husband of yours?"

Ketron didn't meet Lisa's eyes, but she nodded. "It may not matter for long, though. I think the children and I are going to find another place to live."

"Now you be careful with a decision like that." Lisa didn't withdraw her touch, but she put slight pressure on Ketron's fingers to emphasize her point. "It doesn't only affect you."

Ketron dropped her head. "I didn't mean to say so much."

Lisa waited until she met her eyes. "Now, I don't blame you for being upset over his drinkin'."

"Is it that obvious?"

"He can't stand on his own two feet without swaying like a tree in the wind. Like I said, I understand that, but you have to fight for the people you love."

Ketron had been chastised, and she was uncomfortable sharing any more information about her relationship with Marvin. Lisa continued to prompt her.

"How long have you been married?"

"Almost eight years."

"Do you mean to tell me it's easy to give up on someone you've known for so long?"

"I've tried to help him," Ketron defended. "I can't make his decisions for him."

"Has he hit you or the young'uns?"

Ketron shook her head.

"So, he lets his temper get the best of him. Does he say mean things about you?'

Ketron nodded her head slightly. Lisa moved so close that Ketron could smell her last cigarette.

"I know it's hard. I remember that feelin' well. But has he always been that way?"

"No," Ketron squeaked out. She hadn't realized she was so close to tears.

"Have you given it your all?" the older woman asked.

Ketron's automatic response was going to be "yes," but something held her back. Had she done everything she could do to bring Marvin out of his downward spiral, or had she welcomed his decent? It had been easier to take care of the children without his conflicting views on parenting getting in the way.

Lisa sighed deeply. "I was married for thirty-seven years before the Lord took Amos home. We had fights, and we tussled a bit, but we were meant for each other. He got on my nerves worse than a brother, but it always felt nice to know he was by my side when times were tough.

"You made a vow to your husband to love him through sickness and health. The 'sickness' part of the vow is hittin' you hard right now, but you need to weather the storm. Spend the next month really tryin' to get him through this tough spot in his life. You may be surprised what happens when a disease is met with love."

"I'm glad it was able to work out for you." Ketron didn't want to commit to anything.

"I hope it works out for you, too," Lisa returned. "We're both strong women, and it's hard to live in the shadow of a strong woman."

Ketron chuckled and shook her head. "I don't know that I'm as strong as you say. I don't even work."

"There are homemakers who can run circles around working-class people, aren't there?" She slid her hand back onto the table and raised her eyebrows.

Ketron sighed. "There are probably a few, but no one will respect them unless they have a job."

Lisa's mouth drew into a thin line. "That's the view of the common masses. I'm here to tell you that you don't have to be a CEO in a big company to earn my respect."

Ketron was flattered, but she still felt uncomfortable. She had no intention of falling into Marvin's hole with him and trying to dig him out.

Ketron's phone vibrated, and she wiggled it out of her pocket. A line of drool leaked out of Amelia's mouth and ran down her arm. Shauna had texted Ketron, reminding her that she was on her way to her house for dinner.

"I have to go home," Ketron announced.

"I understand. I can tell you the rest of Joseph's tale some other time." Lisa pushed back in her chair and called for the children. "Maybe you can enlist some help from your little ones. Dinner guests are fun, but it takes a lot of work to feed them."

Ketron nodded her agreement, balancing herself out of the chair. Winslow grabbed her arm and steadied her. Amelia stayed in place, her mouth open and her arms dangling limply.

"Reminds me of when I was pregnant," Lisa laughed. "I guess we still carry our babies a lot like we did when they were in our bellies."

Ketron wanted to stay and learn more about Jeremy and his family, but she felt like hearing more of the story would take up the time she needed to prepare for Shauna, Matty, and Luke to spend the evening with them.

"Come back when you have a little more time, and we'll continue our conversation. And bring that pretty teenager. I have somethin' I'd like to give to her." Ketron promised to bring Bonnie the next time she visited.

The children had replaced everything they had played with in the back room, so Ketron felt confident that she wasn't leaving her hostess with a mess. Winslow, Nora, and Sonny lined up at the door and waited on their mother. Lisa bent down and caught Sonny's eyes. Something passed between them.

Ketron was half-way back to her house, calling to the children to watch for her neighbors' loose dogs, when a thought hit her so hard that it almost knocked the breath out of her. When Shauna had texted her, Ketron hadn't told Lisa the contents of the message. How had she known Ketron was having dinner guests?

Chapter Thirty-Two

Present

"She's clairvoyant," Shauna said, grabbing the last of the carrots on the serving tray.

"I don't know," Ketron replied. "It doesn't seem quite right, though."

"Well, it would explain how she knew that we were coming here." She spoke while crunching the carrot.

"Maybe."

"Look." Shauna took her hand. "You have enough to figure out without worrying about the crazy lady up the road."

"She's not crazy." Ketron narrowed her eyes. "I like her."

"Okay. I'm sure she's a great person and all, but you need to start thinking about what you're going to do and when."

"I may not be leaving anytime soon."

"I'd say you'll be leaving when Marvin sees the baby's new birth certificate."

Luke emerged from Marvin's room. He had tried for as long as he could to find common ground between Marvin and himself. It had been difficult, since Luke was a math professor who hadn't developed an interest for drinking beer and playing video games. Luke rubbed his eyes and blinked a couple of times. "It's dark in there."

"I'm sorry." Ketron looked up from tossing the salad. "I think it helps him see the graphics better."

Shauna huffed.

Luke tugged at the celery stalk in his wife's hand. "So, what are you ladies doing?"

"I was just talking to Ketron about when she's going to bring the children to stay at our guest house." Luke threw a nervous glace at Marvin's door, but Shauna waved off his concern. "I don't care if he hears me. He's had plenty of time to straighten up."

"His mother died last year," Luke pointed out.

"We've all been through things," Shauna countered, leaning into him so that he could wrap his arms around her.

Ketron loved to watch her friends stay enveloped in each other. They had never exited the honeymoon stage. Shauna had attributed their continued marital bliss to a healthy sexual relationship and had once suggested that Ketron employ the same tactic to bring life back to her marriage. Ketron hadn't been able to follow her friend's advice. She was too busy with her children. She couldn't sneak into her husband's room for a couple of hours at night when she fell asleep before her head hit the pillow. Besides, he would probably make her wait on the bed until he finished a game, and by then he may not even remember she was there.

Luke tried again. "He was" —he rolled around his thought before he finished it — "*different* before she died. They never had a good relationship, but he may be grieving the relationship he wishes they'd had."

"Good point," Shauna conceded. "But he needs to do it with less alcohol. And maybe he could grow up and be a father to his kids." Shauna shook her head. "Video games! Sonny would love to play catch with him in the yard. Nora would read him a book, and Winslow's been carrying around the same card game in his pocket for two months. How many times has he played it with him?"

"None," Ketron said before she realized she had spoken.

Shauna shook her head, aghast. "See?"

Luke seemed like he was either going to argue his point further or give up, but the sound of Marvin's rattling door interrupted them. "Hey, Luke!" His shiny red face peeked into the kitchen. "One of the guys picked up some new armor for their avatar. Come check it out!"

"Be right there, man!" Luke pecked Shauna's lips. "I know he's having a rough patch, but he's a good guy."

Once Luke had been sucked back into Marvin's world, Shauna sat down at the dining room table and talked to Ketron while she washed the dishes. "Luke knows that you and Marvin helped me when I was down," she explained. "He's giving him the benefit of the doubt because he reasons that anyone who helped me become the person I am today is a good person, too."

"That's convoluted logic."

Shauna shook her head and flicked a crumb off the counter in front of her. "Not really. Luke loves me, but I never would have been ready to receive his love if you guys hadn't taken me in and straightened me out."

"Shauna, you were ready." Ketron laid a dish too loudly on a plate and the sound startled Shauna.

She recovered quickly. "I wasn't ready. I thought about using all the time. It was part of my life. I woke up every morning, and all my thoughts focused on getting my first fix of the day. After that one wore off, it was all about the next fix. I didn't have a moment where drugs weren't in my life until you made me get off the floor of that church basement. You really made my life hard." She chuckled.

Ketron cringed when she remembered asking Marvin to screw Shauna's windows shut and their long walks to her addiction counseling sessions. "I'm sorry. I was kind of a warden when it came to your recovery."

"You think about it from your perspective, and, yeah, you went a little overboard sometimes, but I always felt like you cared. You were pregnant with Zeke, but you dragged me out of bed in the mornings. You had terrible morning sickness, and even though it made you sicker, you cooked steak and eggs so I would keep gaining weight." She stared at her hands and her voice was quieter. "That night Rocco came into town, you slept outside my bedroom door in case I tried to sneak out."

Rocco was Shauna's boyfriend when Ketron found her. She had dragged Shauna away while he was with his friend, presumably to find a lead on a score of drugs. Rocco and Shauna had shared a desire for heroine, so they thought they were in love. Shauna never confirmed it, but Ketron thought the two may have paired up and robbed a couple of out-of-the-way convenience stores. On the days they couldn't find drugs or money for drugs, Rocco would take it out on Shauna. When Ketron took her in, Shauna still wore the remnants of his last beating. "You knew about that?"

"Yeah," Shauna said sheepishly. "Because I tried to sneak out."

Ketron stared at her with wide-eyed shock. "I didn't hear or feel the door open. I wouldn't have known you had left."

"I know," Shauna said, meeting her eyes. "But when I saw you sleeping on the floor in the hallway, I couldn't go. Bonnie was there with her little head on your hip, and I knew she had school the next morning. I didn't want her to go to school and feel like she had failed to keep me safe from myself. It's too much for a kid to go through." As if inspired, she turned the subject to Ketron. "That's why you have to leave," she pleaded. "These children don't deserve to see their father drunk all the time. He won't do anything with them at home or go out as a family. If you're going to be alone, why don't you raise the children by yourself?"

Ketron took a deep breath. "Just like you, Marvin is worth saving." She relayed the conversation she and Lisa had discussed about Marvin. "I didn't like her reasoning, but I can't deny the truth behind it. I vowed to love him, so I owe it to him to give it one more try."

Shauna bit her cheek. "I disagree. I think you need to get out now before anything bad happens to you or the kids." Shauna's words were met with silence, so she added, "It might be a good topic for your next session with Dr. Richards."

Chapter Thirty-Three

Past

Ketron was too tired to move. Part of her welcomed the idea of resting in the dirt, away from her mother's deteriorating mind. The other part screamed at her to get away. Ketron thought about her spirit joining the frigid things that roamed Pale Woods and she bolted.

She ran to the house. Her "granddaddy" was having a hard time managing her mother's body, but he had guessed her direction and he was closing in. Ketron's feet turned, and she followed another path. She prayed that she was going in the right direction, but the forest offered little light. When she broke free on the other side, she ran into the clearing, and charged up the steps. She pounded on the door, desperate for Nora to save her. Bitter puffs of citrusy dill rained down with each knock of her fist. When she looked back her breath caught in her throat. Her mother's form was standing on the other side of Nora's herb garden. She blinked and the spiritual hijacker was revealed in his true form. His six-foot height could easily overpower her, even though he was sickly thin. Ketron could see pieces of her mother in his rounded chin and wide shoulders. He carried the shovel in one of his bony hands.

"Get over here, girl," he called in a voice that Ketron didn't recognize. He tried, but he couldn't pass the line of herbs. Ketron was drawn to him. She didn't want to follow his directions, but her legs moved without her permission. She was almost across the line before she was able to stop herself.

"No."

The word punched out of her and seemed to hit him. In an instant, his image cleared, and her mother returned. Gwynevieve Renfro's expression relaxed into a normal look, and her body moved into a different posture.

"Ketron? What are—" She looked at the shovel in her hand and dropped it.

In that moment, her mother was vulnerable and a little frightened. Gwynevieve brought her hands up to cover some of her emotions as she cried. The experience had scared her enough to return her to the person who had fought against the voices in her mind and took the medication that stifled their vile suggestions. She blubbered faithless promises to be a better mother as tears fell through her hands.

Ketron stepped over the remains of the herb garden and wrapped her arms around her mother's waist. Big heavy sobs echoed against the woods.

Nothing stirred as they walked back to the house. Animals didn't chatter their displeasure over the disturbance their feet made on the crackling leaves and snapping twigs, and the wind missed the trees in Pale Woods.

"We must get home before things begin moving."

Ketron was silent after her mother's cryptic words. She didn't want her voice stolen by the darkness.

They passed the fresh hole in the ground and her mother dropped the shovel into it. Ketron hoped it was her way of saying the shovel and the hole weren't needed anymore.

Chapter Thirty-Four

Present

"Do we get ice cream today?" Sonny asked her after they had left Shauna and Matty at the park.

"Maybe after we go pick up Bonnie," Ketron told him, buckling Amelia into her car seat.

Ketron had been thinking about the past, and old hurts were attempting to surface. She had hoped an outing with her friend would help her feel better, but Shauna had to finish typing out a paper for one of her classes, so Ketron was left to her thoughts as she watched the children play. Her mind took her back four and a half years ago, to a time she wanted to forget. It had been the worst day of her life.

"Are you going to buckle me?" Sonny asked, interrupting her thoughts. He held up the straps and shook his head. "I can't do everything around here."

Ketron laughed, but when Sonny looked offended, she straightened her features.

They drove ten minutes to Bonnie's father's house and waited ten more minutes for Bonnie to gather everything a teenager needed to transport between two houses.

"What did I miss this week?" Bonnie asked.

Glad that her teenager was in a happy mood, Ketron told her about the visit with Lisa and the woman's request to see Bonnie the next time they walked to her house.

"Uh. Do I have to go?"

Ketron smiled at Bonnie's unwillingness to leave her home. "Yes. She mentioned you specifically."

Ketron had poured dry pinto beans into a slow cooker and added water before they had met Shauna and Matty at the park, so dinner was ready to be dished out in bowls when they got home. Nora and Winslow had made cornbread while their father pretended to watch them. He had a new device that allowed him to use his phone like a game controller with a screen, so the only time the family had his attention was during dinner or his quick trips to the bathroom. Even then, he had a faraway look, as if his mind never left the digital world of guns, missions, and drop zones.

The family settled around the dining room table, and Ketron prayed over the meal. They hardly ever said a blessing, as people were usually already eating by the time everyone sat at the table, but Ketron had felt the need for God's influence over the otherworldly occurrences in her home.

Sonny poured ketchup onto his soup beans, and Ketron had to stop him before the beans were buried under a tomato-flavored layer. "That's enough ketchup."

"But I like it," he argued.

"Let him eat it," Marvin told her. "What's it gonna hurt?"

Ketron clenched her jaw but tried to keep an even temper. "Ketchup has a lot of sodium in it."

The dry sound of Marvin's laugh grated on her nerves. "When I was a kid, I poured ketchup on everything. Leave him alone."

"I don't raise my children the way your mother raised you and your brother."

He put his glass down a little too hard on the table, and the water threatened to spill over the sides. "Maybe you *should* raise these kids like my mom raised me. They might act better."

Nora cowered and Winslow pulled her into his arms. Sonny appeared vindicated and continued to squeeze ketchup into his bowl. Bonnie was unaffected by the change in atmosphere and fed small bites of cornbread to Amelia.

Ketron wanted to follow Lisa's advice and give her husband a chance to prove that he could do better, but it was hard to keep his comments from upsetting her. She was tired of keeping the peace and allowing her husband to diminish her attempts at discipline in front of their children. "If you would stop contradicting me in front of them, then they would listen to me better."

The bulb over them brightened and dimmed, and Bonnie watched it. The light sharpened images in the room and then lessened until it was comparable to the early evening daylight drifting through the windows.

"The kids are out of control, Ket. You need to take a firmer hand with them."

"And you need to spend time with them instead of with your video games!" She pointed to the modified cell phone next to Marvin's plate.

The light flickered and grew brighter.

Marvin grabbed his device and charged off to his room. "I'm always here," he called over his shoulder.

"There's a difference between being with your family and sitting in your room all night." Ketron yelled after him.

She was ready to let go of the argument, but before he slammed his door, Marvin delivered a low blow. "How would you know what a father should do? You never had one."

The light flashed in beats. Sending small pulses into a great vibration of light.

Ketron felt like a rug had been pulled out from under her. Her husband had always comforted her when she spoke about her childhood. He hadn't used her father's absence against her until after their recent move.

Ketron turned her attention to the children, but they were staring at the overhead light. Even Amelia was frozen with one hand in her mouth.

Ketron watched the light change in intensity. "It's just a surge or something," she explained to her children. "The dryer may be pulling too much power."

"Is the dryer on?" Bonnie questioned. She had her phone in her hand, looking from it to the light bulb.

Ketron listened for the familiar humming and clacking. "No, but it could be his game." She pointed to Marvin's room. "It may take a lot of power to play online."

"He wasn't playing his game when the light started flickering," Winslow reminded her.

"I think it's a message," Bonnie told her mother. "Watch the light." She pointed at the overhead bulb while staring at her phone. "You see? Di-di di-dah-di-di dah-dah-dah di-di-di-dah di dah-di-dah-dah dah-dah-dah di-di-dah." The rhythm tumbled out of her mouth naturally.

Ketron raised an eyebrow. "You can't be serious. You want me to believe a light bulb is trying to communicate with us." She pointed to the fixture above them. "At most, it's faulty wiring! A bulb has already broken over us once. We really need to call an electrician to look at it."

Bonnie pressed her phone into her mother's hand. "While you two were fighting, I downloaded an app that reads Morse code. Watch the screen. It's the same pattern every time."

Ketron looked between Bonnie's phone and the dining room light. She had to admit that the light was flashing out a sequence. Ketron lost count of the number of times she watched the order tap out in flickers of brightness. She could no longer blame it on natural glitches in the electrical current.

Bonnie slipped her phone out of Ketron's hand, but Ketron was still mesmerized by the structured arrangement. "What is it saying, Bonnie?"

Bonnie clicked a button on her phone to translate the code. She let out a slow breath, passing her phone back to her mother. "It says, *I love you.*"

After she spoke, the light went out.

Ketron jolted awake, almost rousing Amelia. Sonny didn't move. The soft sounds of his breathing sent puffs of air across her arm.

Had she been having a nightmare? She couldn't remember. Any dream she may have had in her head was growing as dark as the night.

The birds in the chimney rustled and clawed, as if they could sense her wakefulness. They settled, but the sounds they made were replaced by a repetitive hum. At first, she thought it was the refrigerator, but the humming grew louder, as if it were coming down the hall from Winslow's and Nora's room. It paused briefly when it was within range of Bonnie's room, but when it resumed, it was clearly in the living room with her.

Ketron had watched movies, and she'd seen actors dressed as priests rid houses of spirits. She gathered her courage and spoke, "I rebuke you in the name of—."

The buzzing vibrated over her head, and she turned. She saw nothing, but she could feel a tingling in her skin. It was almost as if the sound enveloped her. She was no longer frightened. She felt peaceful and almost complete.

The birds began scratching and screeching, and the feeling withdrew from her. She no longer heard a vibration in the air.

Truly alone in the night, Ketron wondered about the presence she had felt. What had sought to comfort her for those few small moments of time?

Chapter Thirty-Five

Present

"Could it have been your mother?" Shauna suggested.

They were sitting by her pool, soaking in the last few days of ninety-degree weather before the season changed. Ketron had recounted her experience. Surprisingly, instead of skepticism, Shauna embraced the idea of a spiritual interference in Ketron's house.

"No," Ketron said resolutely.

"Okay." Shauna threw her hands up defensively. "You said it felt like the energy was embracing you."

"I didn't say it embraced my neck." Ketron spoke before she caught herself.

Shauna reached out her hand and Ketron took it. "Can we finally talk about what she did to you?"

Ketron disentangled her fingers. "No."

"When are you going to tell me? We've been friends for five years."

Ketron scolded Winslow for splashing Nora in the face repetitively, and he sat with Shauna and his mother for five minutes before he was allowed to play again. Everyone was silent. Shauna expected her to return to their previous conversation as soon as Winslow rejoined the others. Ketron racked her brain for a suitable story to change the subject, and she didn't wait to launch into it when Winslow popped up and ran for the pool.

"I think the house is haunted."

Shauna was mildly irritated. "Okay, we can talk about that, but I had asked you about your mother."

"I know," Ketron acknowledged, "but I can't talk about it today."

Shauna nodded and her posture softened. If Ketron had said she *wouldn't talk about it* or she *didn't want to talk about it*, Shauna would have pounced on her for more information than she was willing to give. Ketron had said *can't*, though, and that word made all the difference. It signified an emotional component that could be unmanageable in the current environment. Shauna suspected Ketron's past experiences with her mother were traumatic, but she wouldn't push her to talk about them within range of the children.

"Why do you think the house is haunted?"

Ketron looked down at her hands. She had purposely avoided talking to her friend about the strange occurrences. She was worried that Shauna might think she was starting to show signs of her mother's disease.

Shauna yelled at Matty for running around the pool, and he burst into tears. Ketron would have consoled the child, or made herself available to him, but Shauna crossed her arms and raised her eyebrows. Matty looked over at his mother, and seeing her unmoved, he stopped crying and rejoined the other children.

Nora led Amelia around in her pool floatie. The swimsuit life jacket may have been a little much for the two feet of water in the pool, but Ketron didn't like to take chances around the water. Her eyes hardly left Amelia, even though she trusted Winslow and Nora with her.

Shauna turned her attention back to Ketron. Ketron sighed and shook her head. "Maybe I'm just being silly."

"I'll tell you if I think so," Shauna said, and Ketron believed her.

"First, Nora's tablet turned on by itself in the night," she began, even though she knew it wasn't the start of the spooky incidents. She waited for Shauna to say something. When it was clear she was waiting to speak until the conclusion of her story, Ketron continued. "I felt something watching me at night, Amelia's toy kept turning off and on, and—"

Shauna raised her eyebrows, but Ketron didn't want to tell her about Sonny. Talking about Sonny's possession may be too much to admit to her friend. Would Shauna compare her to Gwynevieve Renfro?

"And what?"

"I told you it was silly," Ketron answered, watching Amelia smile at Matty's silly faces. Nora's high-pitched laughter drifted up to them.

"I don't think it's silly."

Ketron chanced a look at her friend. Shauna settled back in her lounge chair and brought her evenly tanned legs to her chest. "I've gotten the heebie-jeebies a couple of times at your new house."

"Really?"

"Yeah. Especially around the fireplace and in the hallway."

Jeremy's mother had been found dead in the hallway, but Ketron hadn't felt ill at ease around the fireplace. The fireplace was in the dining room, though, and some mysterious things had happened in that room. She made a mental note to ask Lisa about it. "So, what do I do?"

Shauna laughed so loudly that the children glanced up at her, wondering what they had missed. "Burn some sage. I don't know."

"Lisa doesn't think sage will work."

Shauna grabbed a cola from the cooler. She offered a water to Ketron, and Ketron held up her almost full bottle.

"I'm not saying sage will work, but it might help clear up some bad juju." She took a sip. "What could it hurt?"

"Do you have some?"

Shauna smiled. "I used it when we moved in." She winked playfully, and Ketron was left wondering if her friend had actually cleansed her house of spirits.

Suddenly, Shauna started giggling. Ketron waited until her friend's merriment had subsided. Still smiling and coughing from her sudden outburst, Shauna said, "I was just thinking about Marvin going from one room to the next chanting, 'We don't want you here.' He's such a—" She paused, in search of a nicer word than the one she wanted to say. "—man's man."

"What do you mean?"

"My grandmother used to say that about closed-minded men. You know, men who thought it was too feminine to cry or say nice things about their wives."

"Marvin says nice things about me," Ketron defended.

"He used to."

"He still does." Ketron's eyebrows drew together.

Shauna humored her. "Okay. What was the last compliment he gave you?"

"He sends me a text every morning when he's at work. He tells me he loves me and to have a good day."

"Oh!" Shauna flapped her hand over her chest. "Be still my beating heart!" She dropped the act quickly. "How is that a compliment?"

Ketron understood her point. "He said that he really liked the beans I cooked last week."

Shauna sighed. "Luke grabbed my breasts this morning and told me how firm they felt. They're swollen because I'm about to start my period, but I didn't mind the compliment." Her mouth slid into a sly smile. "He was late to work."

Ketron smiled and distracted herself by watching the children.

Shauna playfully tagged her arm. "Oh, come on! I'm sorry. I forgot what a prude you are." Ketron opened her mouth to argue and closed it when no words came to mind. Shauna flicked her sunglasses from her head to her eyes as the sun lowered in the sky. "But really, you have five children, and we are adults."

"I'm just not as open about my sexuality as you."

"You don't talk about it at all, though," Shauna said. Her eyebrows peaked over her sunglasses as she was hit by a realization. "If you've been sleeping in the living room since before Amelia was born, how long has it been since you've had sex?"

Ketron pursed her lips. She knew the last day she had slept with her husband, but she didn't want to discuss it with her friend. She squirmed and bit her thumbnail.

Shauna let out a soft chuckle and leaned back against her chair, turning her face to the sun. "Okay, okay. I'll stop. But if Luke didn't sleep with me, it would drive me to drinking."

"Most of the time, he blames me," Ketron said. The words were out of her mouth before she realized she had said them. She wanted to stop them by putting her hands over her lips, but the damage was done.

"He's gaslighting you." All her friend's humor had evaporated. "Does he blame you for his drinking problem?"

Ketron couldn't think of a way to steer the conversation in another direction. She hoped one of the children would need her, so she didn't have to respond.

"I can't believe you let his drinking go on this long. It's really unlike you."

Ketron whipped her head around. "What do you mean? I can't control a grown man!"

"Sure ya can!" Shauna said, "Probably not without sex, but you can tell him what you will and will not tolerate. This could have all been solved if you would have spent a weekend with the kids at my house a month ago. He would have seen the error of his ways, and—"

"You're thinking about the last time I left him," Ketron said soberly.

"I—" Shauna couldn't argue the point.

"He's not in the right frame of mind this time. He wouldn't care."

Shauna hopped onto Ketron's lounge chair and put her arm around her. Ketron enjoyed the gentle squeeze. "I'm sorry. I didn't mean to make you think about that."

Ketron reached up and patted her hand. "I know. It just doesn't get any easier."

"We haven't talked about a support group in a while. Do you want to try one now that your health is better?"

Ketron shook her head. "It's been years. Besides, I already see Dr. Richards, and I don't think about it as much anymore."

"It might be easier to share your feelings with women who have had similar experiences." When Ketron was unmoved, Shauna took a long, deep breath. "I didn't mean to make our sunny day all doom and gloom." She picked up her phone and glanced at the time. "Do you want me to pick up Bonnie from soccer practice?"

Shauna's house was only a few minutes from the field, and it made more sense for Shauna to pick her up than for Ketron to load up all the children and struggle to get there on time. "They probably want more time in the pool," Ketron said. "And I'm sure Bonnie would like a nice swim after practice."

"It'll be good for her muscles," Shauna agreed, grabbing her keys. She didn't stop to put on clothes, leaving in only a hot pink two-piece bathing suit. Ketron admired her confidence.

Before long, Bonnie was bouncing around the pool as her siblings and Matty playfully splashed at her. She drew back, ready to jump into the pool in her clothes.

"Go shower off first." Shauna pointed to the bath house.

Bonnie rolled her eyes, and slumped her shoulders, stomping over to Ketron. Ketron held out her swimsuit. "I thought you might need this."

"How much longer will you keep the pool open?" Bonnie asked Shauna.

"Luke's going to drain it this weekend."

Ketron and Shauna talked while the children played. Ketron thought about leaving a couple of times, but she realized that it might be the last day they could use Shauna's pool this season, so she made excuses in her mind to stay longer. It wasn't until Luke came home from work and showered that she truly noticed the time. "Marvin's going to be so upset!"

After Shauna had picked up Bonnie from soccer practice, Ketron had silenced her phone. She pulled it out and there were two missed calls and three text messages from Marvin.

"Oh, crap! Your husband messaged me three times!" Shauna put her phone back on the glass table next to her. "What do you want me to tell him?"

"Wait until I leave and let him know I'm on my way back," Ketron replied. "We'll hurry and get the children in the car."

Bonnie was the only child whose skin wasn't pruned. She rushed her siblings into towels and ushered them to the van with their swimsuits on. Ketron buckled Amelia, and Bonnie fastened the straps on Sonny's seat.

"He hasn't had a nap," she told Bonnie, and when the teenager raised her eyebrows, Ketron added, "I'm going to regret that later."

Bonnie buckled quickly and pulled out her phone. "He had fun, though. It's not like there are that many days left before Luke drains the pool."

Shauna, Matty, and Luke had wandered to the driveway to see them off. Matty climbed his father, whining about dinner now that his friends were leaving.

"It'll be done in a few minutes," Luke promised.

He had already started a meal for his family, but Ketron wouldn't have dinner on the table for another hour. She had to fix large quantities of food to satisfy the appetites of every family member, and no one at the table agreed to share the same meal. Sometimes, Sonny ate whatever his father ate, and snuck bites off Ketron's plate. Amelia sampled food from all around the table, Nora ate almost anything she was offered, but Bonnie and Winslow were so picky that she had to feed them something entirely different from the meal she prepared Marvin.

"How was soccer practice?" Ketron asked Bonnie on their short drive home.

"Bella beat me in the mile run today." Bonnie pouted. "But then I scored the only goal against the new goalie."

"New goalie? You have a new team member in the middle of the season?"

"No. It's just Macy. The coach moved her from mid-field to goalie."

"That's a big change," Ketron commented.

"Yeah, but she's really tall." Bonnie moved her hand all the way up to the ceiling of the van where she envisioned Macy would reach. "They wanted me to try it."

Ketron glanced over at the full five feet of her daughter. "Did you do it?"

"For about five minutes." Bonnie laughed. "Delaney kept kicking it high."

"It went over your head every time, didn't it?"

Bonnie nodded. "What are you going to cook for dinner? I'm starving."

"You ate snacks at Shauna's, so you'll be okay. I'll have to see how mad Marvin is first." She had tried to call him, but he hadn't answered.

"Whatever. I'll be in my room."

"Take me with you!" Winslow called from the back. The room he shared with Nora didn't have a door, so they would hear every angry word Marvin spat at Ketron.

Ketron pulled in the driveway just as Marvin should have been getting out of the shower after work. To her surprise, he was clean and playing video games. She ran Nora, Winslow, and Sonny to the shower after she gathered their clothes. Amelia had learned to kiss, and she was trying to cover Ketron in saliva.

"Where'd you go?" Marvin slurred from his doorway. In her haste to move the children to the shower, she hadn't heard his door pop open.

"We were at Shauna's."

"Until almost six o'clock? Why didn't you answer my calls?"

"I put my phone on vibrate after Shauna picked up Bonnie from practice."

Marvin narrowed his eyes. "Why did Shauna pick her up?"

"It was easier for her to—"

He waved his hand and cut her off. "You know what? I don't care. It's just gonna to be a lie anyway."

"What? You don't think I was with Shauna?"

His eyelids drooped lazily over his eyes in a long blink. Her husband had drunk himself into his own conclusions. "I call it like I see it."

"What? What is that supposed to mean?"

"I call it like I see it," he repeated, retreating into his room like he had the moral high ground. Ketron had to talk herself out of bursting through his door and continuing the argument.

Amelia had stopped her kisses when she had seen her father. Most times, she was a little shy around Marvin, but she had grown a little scared of him lately. She laid her head on Ketron's shoulder and fell asleep. Ketron balanced Amelia while she prepared two different types of chicken nuggets and fries. She didn't want to use the stove top while the baby rested on her.

While she waited for the chicken and fries to cook, Ketron got the children out of the shower. Nora and Winslow helped Sonny dress and dry his hair.

Bonnie was going to take a shower, but she decided to wait until after she ate dinner. She took Amelia from her mother, so Ketron decided to add baked beans and a salad to their meal.

The children shuffled to the table. Ketron took Amelia back from Bonnie, and the baby settled against her shoulder. Sonny brought Buddy to the table, placing the stuffed dog where it could watch him eat.

Marvin didn't make an appearance until dinner. No one spoke, but Marvin made little grunts of dissatisfaction as he chewed the nuggets. "What kind of nuggets did you use?"

"I gave you the full meat ones," Ketron answered. The children had the dinosaur nuggets that had a full serving of vegetables in addition to their protein content.

"They're hard as rocks," he said, after he couldn't argue about their flavor. "Just like the fries," he added. Bonnie took her plate to the sink and went to her room.

"That one has no respect," he remarked. "My kids won't act like her."

The children looked at their plates and hoped their father wouldn't mention their sister again. They couldn't defend her, and they felt guilty for silently accepting their father's comments.

Ketron was more vocal when it came to Bonnie. "She took her plate to the sink. What more do you want from her? This isn't exactly a comfortable dinner."

"How could anything be comfortable around someone like you?"

"What are you getting at?" Ketron demanded. "Spit it out."

"Why don't you shut up?" He slung half a nugget onto his plate. "I can't eat this—"

Ketron held up her hand. "No language in front of the children."

Marvin mimicked her as he threw most of the dinner in the trash.

Ketron watched him, her anger rising. "What was wrong with the salad and beans?"

"You!" he accused. "You are what's wrong with everything! You stay gone all the time, and you don't lift a finger around here!"

Ketron looked around. Lots of toys, books, and blocks were scattered around the room, but the floors had been scrubbed and the dishes would be washed before she went to bed.

Both accusations were false, but Ketron decided to attack the first assertion. "I was with Shauna. Aside from today, I have only been out a handful of times."

supposed to be at that woman's house?" He jabbed a finger in the direction of Lisa Paul's house.

"I *was* at Lisa's!"

"Yeah, right."

"We went to Miss Lisa's house, Daddy," Nora squeaked. She lowered her head. "I played with her son's old robot."

"So that's why you're going!" he said, pointing at Ketron. "You're seeing her son!"

Nora and Winslow exchanged a glance. "We didn't see him," they said in unison.

"That's because your mother was busy *seeing* him in another room. Let me guess, she told you to go somewhere else in the house."

"No, Miss Lisa did," Nora spoke up.

She was only trying to defend her mother. She didn't realize that she had added fuel to her father's fire. Marvin jumped in place and a cruel grin spread across his sweaty face.

Ketron tried to keep her voice at an acceptable level. "Lisa and I talked in the kitchen. We let the children play in the back room so we could talk privately."

"Uh-huh. What do the two of you need to talk about *privately*?"

"Just stuff," Ketron answered.

"Where were you today then?"

"I was at Shauna's. I already told you. For goodness sake, the children came back in their swimsuits!"

"Maybe you were at Shauna's house, and the kids played in the pool, but Shauna didn't answer my messages. Was she even there?" His eyes widened. "Are you sleeping with Luke?"

"Mommy didn't sleep," Sonny said. "They sat in their chairs."

Ketron thought the word of his favorite child would settle the argument, but Mavin had ingested too much alcohol to fully comprehend his words. Marvin squatted in front of Sonny. "You don't have to repeat what Mommy *told* you to say. It's okay to tell Daddy the truth. Did you see Mommy take her clothes off around Luke?"

"Okay, that's it!" Ketron shouted, jumping up out of her seat. Amelia's head popped up. "You are not going to press the children for information when there's nothing to know. You are drunk! You can go lay down now, or we will leave." Ketron pointed to Marvin's room.

"Leave!" he shouted at her. "Go to your boyfriend's house. You better let him know I'll be down there to run my truck through his living room!" He called Luke a name that made the twins gasp.

Amelia started crying, and Ketron spoke to her husband while she tried to soothe her. "Go to bed, Marvin. Don't make me leave."

Marvin swept Sonny into his arms. Sonny didn't embrace his father. He reached for Buddy, but only managed to knock the dog onto the floor.

"*You* can leave," Marvin told Ketron. "But you won't take my son out of this house."

Winslow ran out of the room. Ketron heard him crying through the house. Her son wasn't crying real tears, but he was upset, and he wanted everyone to know it. She was thankful when she heard Bonnie's door inch open. *Maybe she can comfort him*, Ketron thought. They didn't usually get along, but Bonnie couldn't stand for someone to pick on her siblings.

"Why is he actin' like a crybaby?" Marvin asked about Winslow.

"Sonny isn't your only son," Ketron reminded him. "You have other children in the house."

Marvin brushed it off with a snort of derision. "The rest of 'em act like you. Sonny's the only one that really loves his daddy."

Nora blinked back her tears. She quickly took her plate to the sink and bolted to her room. Sensing a break in the yelling, Amelia stopped crying and tried to move herself into a nursing position.

Marvin kissed the top of Sonny's head. Sonny kept trying to wiggle away from his father to retrieve his stuffed dog. "Maybe I drank too much," he conceded, allowing Sonny to pick Buddy off the ground. Sonny hugged the stuff dog and leaned into his father's neck. Marvin held Sonny, and his face contorted. "We are so lucky he survived," he cried.

"Stop it!" Ketron warned. "Don't bring that up right now!"

"Why not?" He was still emotional. "Why have we never talked about it?"

Amelia started screaming again. Ketron was frustrated over her husband's accusations, and she was angry. "JUST STOP!" she yelled. "Not everyone is ready to talk about things at the same time as you. You may have had a six pack before we got here, but that doesn't mean—"

"You need help," he said. "You're acting crazy."

Ketron shut down. All Marvin had to do was hint about her mother's condition or call her mental health into question, and she stopped trying to assert herself.

Sensing he had won the argument, Marvin took Sonny into the living room and turned on a show for him. He grabbed a beer out of the refrigerator, and he didn't bother to conceal it. By then, Ketron had the baby calmed down.

After she washed the dishes, Ketron sat beside Sonny on the couch. He put his arm around her and rested his hand on Amelia. Ketron started to doze, but Sonny woke her up, speaking to someone.

"What was that, sweetie?" Ketron asked groggily.

"We love you," Sonny said.

Even though Amelia rested next to them, Sonny wasn't including his baby sister.

Chapter Thirty-Six

Past

"What the—" Big Red took a shaky breath and rephrased his question. "Is everything okay now? I'm across the country right now, but I'll head your way if you think she will try to put you in a grave."

Ketron cringed. She hadn't called it a grave, even though her "granddaddy" was clearly digging the hole with her death in mind. "I don't think she's going to put me there now." She paced her usual track from the kitchen through the living room and into her bedroom. "Besides, I really called to tell you what I found out about Gail."

Ketron enjoyed her weekly conversations with Big Red. For the past few months, he had listened to her and told her stories about his adventures on the road. He was usually jovial, but after she confessed that her grandfather had possessed her mother's body, Big Red was reluctant to begin a new subject.

"Are you sure you're okay?"

"Yeah," Ketron responded, barely registering the concern in his voice. "Ky, Ly, and I found this book in the attic. Ky said it was a family Bible, and it had the names and birthdays of everyone in the Renfro family."

She turned on her heel and directed her steps to the kitchen. Pansy and Marigold seemed to watch her steps as she passed them. She felt like they were listening to her, accumulating information to tell her mother, so she picked up the stuffed rabbits and put them outside as she spoke to Big Red.

"I checked the dates, and my great-grandfather, Able Thomas Renfro, had a wife before my great-grandmother. Her name was Gail Marie, and they had a baby they named Solomon Thomas."

"That's all interesting, Ketty-Kat, but how does that help you?"

"Now I know who's been pacing through the house at night!" She stopped, laughing. She took the same path when she was on the phone with Big Red as her ethereal sentinel. "It's Gail! She's looking out for me!"

"Are you feeling well?" he asked. "Have you had a fever?"

Ketron noticed the line of questioning. "My temperature is normal and I'm not crazy. There are spirits that live here. They're all over the mountain." She paused, and her voice dropped to a whisper. "Ky, Ly, and their Aunt Nora believe me."

"I believe you," he said carefully. "I've just never heard of spirits leadin' you on a scavenger hunt. What does Gail have to gain by showing herself to you?"

Ketron perked up. "Ky said it's because she wants me to know that she's protecting me."

Big Red was noticeably skeptical. "Anytime I've seen a spirit, it was tryin' to scare me."

"I *was* scared, at first." Ketron turned, picked up the Blue Ridge Pottery dish, and rattled her marbles in it. "But then I realized that she's always been there. It's just that she's stronger in this house."

"Why would Gail have traveled from her house to protect you?"

"Ky said she probably followed my mother and protected her after—"

"After what?"

"After her father killed her sister. You see, he may have had the same disease as my mother—"

"Hold on," Big Red interjected. "What disease? What's wrong with your mother?"

"My mother has a dissociative disorder." Ketron pronounced it the best she could, but it came out broken.

"I may have to look that one up. Is that why she's hidin' with you?"

Ketron hesitated. It was one thing to tell Big Red about her life and what she had found, but it was another to tell him about her mother's private business. She had already said too much when she told him about Gwynevieve's condition, but her response had been a knee-jerk reaction to his question.

"Are the police lookin' for your mother?"

That was a question that she could answer honestly. "I don't know."

"Has she hurt you? Did she hurt you before you went back to her homeplace?"

The conversation had taken a turn, and Ketron wasn't prepared to answer the questions Big Red asked. She decided to find a way to cut her call short. "I see my mother's car in the driveway. I gotta go." She spoke in a rush, but she waited for his response.

"Take care, Ketty-Kat. If you need me, you can call me collect." He paused, and she thought he was going to say "good-bye", but he whispered, "I love you, sweet girl."

Ketron ended the call. She was on her way to return the envelope with Big Red's number on it to the space under the linoleum floor when a loud banging sounded through the house.

She ran to the door, stuffing the envelope in her pocket. Ky and Ly bounced in and out of sight of the high widow on the door, their blond heads and blue eyes in view one moment and gone behind the door the next. Ketron opened it, and they almost knocked her over.

"Guess what we found out?" Ky said.

"Actually, I found it out," Ly added importantly.

"What is it?" Ketron jumped on her heels excitedly.

"Our nana knew Gail Renfro," they told her. She waited for them to continue. "They used to make apple butter together at the church pavilion when our nana was our age."

They stopped speaking together and Ky took the lead. "Nana told our mom that Gail was Able Renfro's first wife. He married Rebecca after her."

"I guess Rebecca was my great-grandmother," Ketron said. Her mother didn't talk about their extended family often, but she thought she had heard the name mentioned.

Ky waited until she paused to continue. "Gail visited our nana in her dreams after she died. She was upset because she couldn't find her baby."

"Didn't she die with her baby?"

"Yeah, but he must not have been there when she went into the spirit world."

The boys were excited, but Ketron felt like she had been punched in the stomach. "That's awful. She died with him, but she couldn't see him in the afterlife."

Ketron pondered why the information was so important until she heard a sound that turned her blood to ice.

Gwynevieve Renfro was pulling up the drive, and she wasn't alone.

Chapter Thirty-Seven

Present

"It's *my* dog!" Sonny screamed. "Tell her to put it down!"

Ketron flew into action. She had been replacing the batteries in Amelia's learning tree when she heard the fight erupt.

Amelia carried the stuffed animal into the kitchen, oblivious to her brother's cries. She squeezed it to her chest and kissed it.

Ketron bent down and said to her baby, "You like Mr. Dog, don't you?"

"Buddy," Sonny corrected. "He doesn't like baby slobber."

Buddy was already wet in a couple of places from Amelia's kisses. Ketron tried to pull him, but the toddler held onto the dog, smiling as if it were a game.

"Give him back!" Sonny yelled at his sister, attempting to force the toy out of her arms. For the first time, Amelia was concerned. She hugged it more tightly.

Bonnie appeared, and while Ketron tried to pry the stuffed dog out of Amelia's fingers, Bonnie consoled Sonny. He stared at the dog the whole time, though, and wouldn't respond to his older sister's reasoning.

Amelia wrenched free and toddled toward the living room. Ketron got to her feet as Amelia rounded the corner into Marvin's room.

"Stupid baby!" Sonny yelled.

Ketron was momentarily thrown off course. "No, sir," she scolded him. "We do not name-call in the house."

"Daddy does."

Before she could reply, a rolling thud sent Bonnie and Ketron running after Amelia. The baby was on the floor, her body shook, but her cries were held until they were released in one wailing sob. It was one of the saddest sounds Ketron had ever heard.

Amelia struggled into a sitting position, with her hands in fists at her chest. Her coloring was almost purple from holding her breath before letting out her cry. Buddy lay halfway across the room in an upright position.

Ketron picked her up and held her closely. At first, Amelia pushed against her mother's chest. The pain was so intense that it hurt to rest on her mother's shoulder.

Bonnie held up the white extension wire that ran from the internet router to Marvin's television. "Did she trip on this?"

Ketron hardly looked at the cord. She was trying to get Amelia to take a breath. Her nose was purple, and her bottom lip had already started swelling. "Do you think she broke her nose?"

"No," Bonnie said without looking at the baby.

Sonny wandered into the room. He scanned the area for his toy, found it, and swiped it up. He stared up at his sister. "Stupid baby." Ketron was too busy caring for Amelia to notice Sonny or his actions toward his sister.

"Who left this door open?" she called through the house. No one went into Marvin's room when he wasn't home except Sonny when he was looking for hidden snacks. "Sonny, did you leave your father's door open?"

The lack of a response told Ketron the answer to her question. "You caused your sister to have an accident."

"I didn't do nothin'," he defended.

"You may not have directly caused your sister's injury, but you left the door open. You know we can't have your little sister running in here."

Keys rattled in the door. Marvin held the screen door and kicked mud onto the porch.

"Why won't he take his shoes off?"

She hadn't realized that she had spoken aloud until Bonnie replied, "Because he's a Neanderthal."

Ketron stared at her. "Do you even know what a Neanderthal is?"

Bonnie rolled her eyes. "I've known since the third grade."

Marvin untied his boots in the doorway while Sonny told him everything that happened to him that afternoon in one long run-on sentence. "Let me get inside the door," he said, scooting past Sonny and dropping off his oversized lunchbox on the counter.

Sonny padded behind Marvin as he reached inside the refrigerator. He pulled out a bottle of beer and didn't bother to conceal it. "I'm taking a shower," he announced.

He stopped in his room for clothes, passing by Ketron with a sniffling Amelia in her arms. "Did you take money out of the account today?"

"No. I was here all day."

"Are you sure you didn't go to *Shauna's* house?"

Ketron didn't like his tone. "No, Shauna and Matty came here after I picked up the children from school."

"So, you did go somewhere."

"I dropped off and picked up the children from school. I thought that was implied."

"*Implied.* You and your college-educated words. No one talks like that around here. No wonder no one likes you."

Ketron was going to argue that Shauna and Lisa liked her, but she knew it would be useless. Her husband was upset, and he was taking it out on her.

"I won't dumb down my language."

He waved his hands in the air, imitating mock fright. "Whatever." Sweat ran down his temples, even though the room was chilly. "You can say whatever you want, but my boy won't talk like that."

"*Your* boy," Ketron echoed and sighed. Amelia had been in her arms sobbing through the whole conversation, and he hadn't even mentioned her swollen face. She walked out of the room, and Amelia rested her head on her mother's shoulder, worn out from her injury and the argument she had witnessed.

"I'm goin' by the bank tomorrow," Marvin called after her. "You need to come clean now if you took the money."

"Come clean about what?" she asked, charging back into his room. "Maybe you used it for your stupid video game obsession, or your even dumber drinking problem!"

He pointed to his console. "My video games are deducted directly from the account. I don't have to take out any money for them." He didn't address her second accusation.

Ketron stomped back into the kitchen and started banging pans on the counter. She decided french fries and chicken nuggets would go well with his unfounded accusations. If he wanted something better, then he could take the money in his account and buy it for himself.

A sharp tap at the back door startled her. The twins, who had been silent during their parents' argument, came running through the house. They stopped at the picture window that looked out onto the back porch, craning their necks to see who was on the back porch. "It's Miss Lisa," Nora shouted.

Ketron opened the door and Lisa's face fell. "What happened to that poor baby?"

Ketron related her baby's accident to Lisa. "Do you think she'll heal soon?"

"I'd imagine so." Amelia smiled when Lisa spoke, which made her injury just as sad.

She put a plastic bag in Ketron's hand. "Those are the rest of my cucs. You can pickle them, but I'd wait for a prettier day." She squinted at the overcast sky.

Ketron took the cucumbers and thanked her neighbor. "I don't know how to preserve pickles, but I can put them in salads."

Lisa sucked in a whistle. "Lord, girl! Didn't your mama teach you anything?"

The mention of her mother caused Ketron to pause. Ketron didn't notice the length of time before she spoke again, but Lisa did. "No, she didn't teach me how to cook or preserve fruits and vegetables. Cooking was a trial-and-error thing for me." Ketron held the door wider, beckoning Lisa inside.

Lisa shifted her weight. "Well, I see that your husband's here, so I won't keep you." She tossed her truck keys between her hands. "To be honest, I was at the door a few minutes before I knocked."

Ketron's face colored instantly. "You heard?"

Lisa nodded. "I didn't want to get in the middle of it, especially if he was drinkin'."

"That's the thing," Ketron told her. "He hasn't had anything to drink yet, but he's yelling and sweating like he's been drinking all afternoon."

"Could he be hitin' the sauce at work?"

"No," Ketron replied, balancing the bag of cucumbers and dodging Amelia's hands. The baby poked her mother's ear a couple of times before she started pulling the buttons on her shirt. "He wouldn't risk his job. Besides, one of the other guys would tell on him. Marvin has a really good job, and every worker there has a family member waiting for a spot to open up."

Sonny breezed into the room and pressed himself against his mother. Ketron watched as Lisa's faced drained. "Where did he get that dog?" Her voice was shaky, and Ketron wondered why the self-assured woman seem so scared.

"He found it," Ketron said carefully, not wanting to upset her friend more. She looked down at Sonny. "Where did you find it sweetheart?"

Sonny shrugged and hid his face behind his mother's thigh.

"I—I gotta go," Lisa stuttered, backing up the hill to the driveway. She turned around and almost jogged to her truck. Ketron worried that the activity might reawaken whatever injury had caused her limp.

Ketron closed the door and went back to preparing food. Sonny stayed close to her, hardly letting go of her leg. It was hard to manage her tasks with Sonny attached to her and Amelia grabbing handfuls of her hair. She put the baby down, but she couldn't stand to see Amelia so upset with her swollen nose, so she held her while she dragged Sonny through the kitchen.

Lisa had acted strangely about the stuffed dog. Ketron's curiosity was piqued, and she asked Sonny again, "Where did you find Buddy?"

Sonny buried his face deeper in her leg. He hugged the stuffed animal tighter, never revealing its secret.

Chapter Thirty-Eight

Past/Present

Ketron felt herself floating into a dream. She remembered who she was, but the body that directed her actions was not her own. It was like she was being carried around by someone else. She could see the world around her, but she couldn't affect it.

Ketron immediately recognized her house. The rooms were in the same places, but there was a partition between the living room and kitchen. The walls were covered in floral wallpaper and the furniture had cool blue tones.

The woman, for that's what she was, wore a blue and white checkered dress and the natural golden highlights in her chestnut hair reflected the afternoon sun streaming through the windows. It hung down over her shoulders, and when she moved into the kitchen, her hands reached up and tied her hair into a ponytail.

"What's for dinner, Mom?" a boy said as he bounced into the room. He had cerulean eyes, coal black hair, and a brush of freckles. His features were contrasted by his moon-kissed skin. A diamond-shaped birthmark was visible just above his left temple. He might have been seven or eight years old, and he was holding a graded paper in his hand.

"I think we're having tacos," Ketron's host replied. "What's that?" She pointed to the paper.

"It's my spelling test," he responded, showing off a mouth full of milk teeth and adult teeth in varying states of growth.

"Is this the one you studied so hard for?" the woman asked, taking the paper from him and smiling at the grade. "You did so well!"

"You helped me."

"But you did the work," she told him. "It was your beautiful brain that made this possible." She pulled him into a hug and bent down to smell his pine-scented hair.

"What kind of garbage are you feedin' that boy?" a male voice spoke. He sauntered out of a bedroom that would become Marvin's room. He was

prematurely balding and red splotches dotted his cheeks and neck. The man's belly extended beyond his pants and hung over spindly legs.

The woman didn't respond, but Ketron felt her anger. She patted the boy's shoulder and kept him close to her. "Why don't you set out the taco shells?" she suggested to her son.

"Tacos again?" the man whined. "Don't you know how to cook, woman?"

The boy stiffened. Ketron noticed the change in his posture, but his mother was focused on neutralizing the insult.

"What would you like me to make?" she asked calmly.

"Something with a little more imagination!" he yelled. "You cook the same things all the time!"

Ketron was amazed by the parallels between she and Marvin and this woman and her husband. The man seemed crueler than Marvin, but if Ketron were honest, their insults were the same.

"I try to cook the things you like," she said meekly, turning away from him. "But you don't seem to like many things."

"Are you tryin' to get smart with me?" he said. In a flash, he had crossed the distance between them and punched her in the back. Ketron braced herself for the blow, but she didn't feel it.

The boy pushed himself between them, taking a few of the punches. His mother pushed him away from his father, and he fell at the stove. The look on his face was reminiscent of the hate Ketron had seen on Sonny's face on the day he wasn't Sonny.

"Jeremy!" the woman screamed.

"That's the only thing you care about," the man yelled, rising to tower over her. A cruel smile spread across his splotchy face. "I think I know how to get you to do better around here."

The man stepped over to the stove and made a show of driving his fist back. Ketron tried to make it to the man before he delivered the first blow, but she was restrained by time and space.

"I'll do whatever you want," the woman cried. Ketron felt her frustration and hopelessness.

"Oh, I know," he chuckled, putting a meaty hand around her windpipe. "You're gonna quit talkin' back to me, and things are gonna change around here."

Ketron sucked in air like she had been holding her breath throughout her dream. It resonated with her and didn't fade like other nightmares.

Somehow, she had glimpsed a moment in time in the house, long before she and Marvin had signed the deed.

Cold pin pricks washed over her, covering her body in tiny pinches. She felt Jeremy in the hallway, looking at her. There was an interference in the air, as if it had to circulate around him.

Amelia's mouth hung open in her sleep, and Sonny was cuddled against her. Buddy sat on the console in the middle of the couch, watching them as they slept.

Ketron thought she understood the reason Jeremy's mother had stopped talking. She had heard that a person could develop selective mutism in response to trauma.

"I am so very sorry," she spoke into the air. "I don't know if you wanted me to know or not, but I saw it. Your father was a monster."

Ketron couldn't hear him or see him, and she could only guess about the reason Sonny had been able to interact with him over the past few months. The spirit's silence echoed years of pain, hurt, and, most of all, rage.

Now, in the dark, still house, Ketron wasn't afraid of him. His frustrations were focused on a long-dead time that he never forgave or forgot.

Chapter Thirty-Nine

Present

"WHO TOOK THE MONEY THEN?" Marvin boomed.

Ketron cowered. "I don't know, but it wasn't me."

"Where did you put it?" he shouted, pacing back and forth through the living room. "They had you on camera withdrawing a thousand dollars. You had Amelia with you! Are you gonna tell me that it wasn't you? Do you expect me to believe you?"

Ketron had no memory of the incident, and she was convinced that Marvin was lying to her. She demanded that she see the video, and they rode to the bank to validate Marvin's claim. A rather frazzled looking bank manager replayed it for her. The time and date stamp on the video matched the time and date in the bank's records. On the drive home, she was glad she and Marvin had taken separate vehicles.

"I was with Shauna last Tuesday," Ketron explained, pulling the keys out of the front door.

"Not at 10:28 AM," Marvin said, poking his finger at the bank receipt. "Where's the money, Ketron?"

He so seldom used her full first name that it got her attention. She stared at him, hoping that there was a reasonable explanation. Yes, she had been in the bank's video, but she couldn't remember parking in the parking lot and going inside. She had dropped off the children at school and taken a nap with Amelia. But that wasn't quite right, was it?

"Why would I need a thousand dollars?"

"You tell me!" He threw up his hands. The receipt parachuted to the floor. "Are you planning to leave me?"

"No," Ketron shot back, even though it wasn't entirely true.

"Did you buy something? Did you gamble it? Did you lend the money to Shauna?"

"No," Ketron repeated. "I don't spend that kind of money on anything, and Shauna never needs money."

"I forgot," Marvin huffed. "Luke came from a family with money. It must be nice. Other people have to struggle for everything."

"Luke inherited enough money to pay off his house and truck. He works at a decent job. I don't know why you think you're struggling when you're standing in a nice house with thousands of dollars in video games and equipment at your disposal."

Mavin paced between the dining room and the kitchen, running his hands through his hair. "You don't live in the real world. You think this money isn't a big deal, but they'll be some things that don't happen because it's gone." He stopped pacing and extended his index finger. "Number one: Winslow and Nora won't be able to join the basketball team this year."

Ketron wasn't surprised. Marvin hadn't enjoyed spending his Saturday mornings and Thursday nights at the YMCA gymnasium.

His middle finger shot up. "Number two: We're not buying Bonnie that bicycle you wanted her to have for Christmas. She can ride the one she has, or she can walk."

"But it's her year to have a special Christmas present!" With five children, it was hard to give every one of them a magical holiday, so Ketron and Marvin had decided to buy a couple of presents for each child and give one of them an extra special gift. Bonnie had chosen a bicycle so that she could ride with her family, and now Marvin was denying her choice because of money Ketron didn't remember taking.

"She has a dad. Tell him to get it for her." When Ketron stared at him in open-mouthed shock, he continued, abandoning the act of counting on his fingers. "You will not get the forty-dollar mascara you like, and Amelia can wear one of the other kids' old Halloween costumes this year."

"But I sold those to buy Sonny his shark costume last year. What will she wear for the pictures?"

"And no pictures!" When he saw her face fall, he added, "If you don't like it, give me back my money." He stormed into his room and slammed the door. The sound made Ketron jump and woke up Amelia.

Ketron rushed to the couch and found the baby rolling onto the floor. She was glad Amelia had picked up the skill of climbing off the furniture. It made it easier to lay her down when she napped, since Marvin hadn't bought her a crib.

Marvin had named every person in the house except for Sonny when he was dividing out his financial punishments. Ketron hoped she could find the money she had taken from their account when she had blacked out.

After Ketron had dropped Winslow, Nora, and Sonny off at school, she remembered lying down with Amelia. She had been a little nauseated, and she thought she could sleep away the feeling. When she woke, she had been parked outside Shauna's house. It was odd, but she had tried to cover the feeling of lost time by immersing herself in conversation with her friend.

Was she beginning to lose time on a regular basis? She couldn't be sure, since she stayed at home most of the time and repeated the same schedule. Where was her consciousness when she went to the bank? Was it an isolated incident, or would she start blinking out more often, using excuses for her missed time?

A reverberation sounded from the fireplace. Ketron almost dismissed it, but the noise seemed to rub up the side of the fireplace sending out a deeper echo. Ketron crept closer to investigate, hoping Amelia would stay in the living room. The baby played with blocks, oblivious to her mother.

The sound intensified as Ketron approached, and a musky odor almost gagged her.

At first, Ketron couldn't hear the birds, but then they started screeching. Her hand went to her mouth as she digested the suffering in the chimney. Claws tried to gain purchase against the stone before they were quieted.

Ketron was almost certain she knew what had caused their distress and subsequent death. She burst through Marvin's door, but he ignored her. When he finally took off his gaming headphones, Ketron relayed what she had heard.

Her husband stared at her without emotion. "Well, that ended our bird problem."

"Yeah, but now we have a snake problem."

He chuckled without mirth. "Who says it's a problem? Now I don't have to put anything over the chimney."

"Don't be glib. We need to get the snake out of the house."

"I think by saying *we* you mean *me*, and I am not crawling around the chimney looking for a snake."

"How did it get in anyway?"

"There's a drainpipe in the basement, and the snake could have crawled up that hole in the back of the fireplace. It leads to the basement.

She thought back to the snake she had seen in the basement weeks ago. "Do you think it's the same snake I saw?" When her husband ignored her, Ketron crossed her arms. "Well, I can't sleep in the house while a snake crawls around."

Marvin's avatar fell, shot by a member of the opposing team. He uttered a string of curses. "We live near the creek and the woods. Snakes are bound to find their way inside at some point or another." He turned in his chair and stared at her seriously. "I'm not goin' into the chimney after a snake, Ket."

Ketron raised her eyebrows, holding firmly to her point.

Marvin was equally stubborn. "The glass grate on the fireplace shuts tight, so the snake won't get through. Stack a couple of tubs in front of the fireplace if it makes you feel better."

Ketron doubted that storage containers would keep the snake out of the living area, but her husband was right. The grate shut tightly.

"Fine. I'll put something in front of the grate, but I better not wake up with a snake around my neck."

Marvin was already consumed by his game, and she thought he wasn't going to answer until he said, "You won't have to worry about the snake choking you if you get me killed again." He wore a smile, but Ketron believed he was only half-joking.

She grabbed two large plastic totes from the closet in the bathroom and placed them in front of the glass that covered the fireplace. Satisfied with her work, Ketron fell onto the couch next to Sonny. Amelia joined them, pulling at her mother's shirt.

"Why does that baby eat all the time?" Sonny asked her.

Ketron ruffled his hair. "You used to eat a lot, too. Amelia will grow up, like you, and she won't need so much food or attention."

Sonny stared at the stegosaurus in his hand. "Jeremy's wrong about you, Mommy. You still play with me, even when the baby's around."

Ketron tried to maintain a passive face. "I'm glad you're not letting Jeremy influence you." She felt like she had gained ground in whatever ghostly battle was going on in her house until her son spoke again.

"But we didn't like the birds. That's why he ate them."

Chapter Forty

Past

The man may have been attractive to middle-aged women, but Ketron thought he wore too much hair gel and smelled like he'd been hanging out in a public restroom. Maybe the thought of meeting his fiancé's daughter made him gassy.

Fiancé? When had her mother had time to become someone's fiancé? Ketron thought she was going out for groceries and toilet paper, not shopping for a new husband.

"Oh, Tom, you're positively droll!" she laughed, while Ketron stared.

Ketron had never heard the word *droll*, and she was unaccustomed to hearing her mother say it.

Ketron had been nervous when she opened the door for her mother and her male suitor. She was concerned that they had seen Ky and Ly in the doorway or had noticed them run out the backdoor, but the couple had missed them.

Ketron made them dinner and noted that Tom didn't question a preteen girl's presence in the kitchen while her able-bodied mother served him drinks. The beverages came from her mother's special glass bottles, and Tom was sweaty and red cheeked by the time dinner was served.

The only good thing about Tom's presence was that her mother was less cautious when she hid the phone. Ketron passed Tom as he swirled his drink, and she peeked into her mother's bedroom door. She watched her mother stuff the phone between her mattress and the box springs. She was unsure if it was the usual hiding place or a temporary one, but she marked the place in her mind and hurried back to the kitchen before her mother returned to her place beside Tom. Tom didn't look up as Ketron passed, and he tried to avoid her eyes, even though she thought she felt him looking at her when her back was turned.

Suddenly, he jumped and jerked up his shirt sleeve. "What was that?" He rubbed his arm where an angry red mark had already formed near his elbow.

Ketron smiled. "Thank you, Gail," she whispered.

Her mother practically pressed herself to Tom as they ate, and Ketron sat across from them. The steak was tough, and the biscuits were a little doughy, but Tom shoveled the food in his mouth without tasting it.

Ketron caught Tom staring at her strangely a couple of times, but she tried to dismiss it. It wasn't until he eyed her while rubbing her ankle with his foot that Ketron was truly uncomfortable.

As he sipped on his fourth drink, he jumped so hard that he rattled the table. He grabbed his leg, and her mother placed it in her lap. After she raised his pants and revealed the new bruise on his shin, she rounded on Ketron. "Did you do this?"

Ketron denied it, but her mother lifted her up by her arm and dragged her to the bathroom. It started out as a spanking, but her mother hit her back and legs as Ketron struggled to get away. "You will not ruin this for me," she whispered in her ear.

The light bulb overhead brightened until it lit almost every surface in the room. Her mother didn't notice or chose to ignore the intensity of the light, but Ketron was afraid it was going to burst.

She walked out of the room behind her mother and a breeze brushed the tears on her cheeks. It was the closest thing she'd had to a hug in months. "I'm okay," she said to her comforter.

"What did you say?" Her mother turned around and grabbed under her arm again. She smiled when she noticed Ketron's pinched expression.

"It was nothing."

Her mother dropped her arm and walked back to the kitchen.

Gwynevieve attempted light conversation when they rejoined Tom. Ketron hated the smug smile that laced his features when he saw her tears.

"Tom, how long will it take you to finish the project in Thailand?" Her mother batted her eyes at him. "I can't wait to honeymoon in England."

Tom put his arm around her. "That project will be done soon," he replied through a mouthful of mashed potatoes. "My flat in England should be ready next month."

"You'll have to teach me the culture there."

"You don't really have to worry about the culture in any country as long as you have money. They'll cater to you." They put their foreheads together and laughed.

Ketron felt her dinner roll uncomfortably in her stomach. Her mother had always wanted to travel, and it seemed that she had found a way to do it.

Ketron didn't want to leave her new friends, but it seemed that her mother had made other plans.

Tom had thrown back a half dozen of the drinks her mother brought to him, and he could hardly stand. He attempted to look around the house, but her mother carried him back to the living room after he missed his footing several times. "I can usually stay on my feet after a couple of drinks, but it feels like someone keeps tripping me."

Her mother laughed a little too loudly. Her expression wilted into contempt as she darted her eyes around the room, searching for the unseen culprit.

"This is a three-bedroom house, right?" he asked her.

Ketron had a flash of hope that he was going to bring a son or daughter to live with them, but when she asked, he laughed and responded, "No, I've dodged that bullet." Then he turned to her mother and asked, "Did you say this property stretched for twenty-five acres?"

The man was using her mother. It was obvious that he was interested in how much he could make from the sale of their house, but when Ketron dragged her mother away and told her what she believed, her mother slapped her across the cheek.

Ketron's hand went straight to her face. She couldn't believe that her mother had struck her. She didn't even seem worried that Tom would see the evidence of her abuse. "Tom is a nice man." She narrowed her eyes and grabbed Ketron's shoulder, squeezing it until Ketron squirmed. "I know you may not like the idea of sharing my attention, but I want a husband. Can't you tell that Tom is perfect for me?"

Ketron nodded. Her mother's words had hit the mark. She and Tom were perfect for each other. Her mother's grip tightened before she let her go.

Her mother didn't offer to give her the phone before she left. "Tom lives close by. I'll be right back after I take him home."

Ketron didn't bother to remind her mother that she had been drinking and shouldn't drive. For the sake of anyone else who passed her mother, she hoped the trip down the narrow mountain road was uneventful.

"I forgot my keys." Her mother pecked Tom's lips before she rushed to her room.

Tom put his thumb on Ketron's chin. "We didn't get to talk much tonight, but we'll become good friends soon." Ketron's stomach threatened to spill its contents, and Ketron couldn't hide her revulsion. Tom smiled and dropped his hand to her shoulder. He pulled his hand away quickly when they heard her mother's footsteps.

Ketron locked the door after they went out. The night was warm for the season, but there was still a chill in the air, and Ketron shivered when she felt it.

Ketron waited until the sounds of the car faded into the distance before she flew into action. Her mother's mattress was a little heavier than she anticipated, but she found the phone easily. She still had the envelope with Big Red's number on it in her back pocket.

Unexpectedly, her knees buckled, and she fell to the ground, sending the phone sliding across the floor. The pain in the back of her legs radiated as she picked up the phone and dialed Big Red's number. He answered on the second ring.

"Can you come get me?"

He chuckled, but it wasn't as full of his usual good nature. "I'm on the next flight outta here, Ketty-Kat. I booked it after you hung up on me."

"I'm sorry," Ketron started, and then she couldn't stop. "My mother's crazy. She's always been weird, but something about this place makes her worse. She brought back a man, and they're gonna get married, and he rubbed my ankle with his foot, and he says we're gonna be *good friends*, and—"

"Ketron," Big Red interjected, calling her by her name for the first time. "Can you go somewhere safe until I get there? My flight leaves soon, but it will still take some time for me to get there. Can you go somewhere until morning? Maybe you could stay with the twins or their Aunt Nora?"

Ketron was touched that Big Red had listened so closely during their conversations. She thought it was risky to visit Ky and Ly, but she might be able to slip out and go to Nora's house before her mother returned.

She was pushed and she fell onto the floor. Her head hit the hardwood, and the phone skittered under the dresser.

"Stop it, Gail!" She stood and came face-to-face with the specter of a girl about her age. Even though many years had put a distance between her mother and her sister, Ketron recognized the rounded chin, sharp nose, and cold eyes. "Gwynevere?"

The bruises on the apparition's cheeks and the dried blood on her nose were the only evidence of the beating that had extinguished her life. Her smile looked strange on her child-like features, and there was a coldness that extended from her ethereal body to the air around her. It blanketed Ketron, threatening to pull her into the darkness with her mother's long-dead twin. She was only visible for a moment before she blinked out of sight. Ketron felt under the dresser until she pulled out the phone, but it was plucked from her hand before she could stand. She thought Gwynevere had taken the phone until she realized that her mother was standing over her.

"I was right to leave Gywnnie here this time." Ketron hadn't suspected that her mother had made the excuse of searching for her keys when she had been conversing with her dead sister. Big Red was yelling through the phone, but her mother ended the call. "She certainly prevented a disaster."

Her mother cocked her head and listened to her ghostly sibling. "You asked him to come get you?" After another other-worldly consultation, her mother turned Ketron around and dug the envelope with Big Red's number on it out of Ketron's back pocket. "I don't think you'll need this anymore." She walked out of the room, ripping it.

Ketron followed her mother. She opened the front door and picked up Pansy and Marigold. "I can't imagine how my stuffed rabbits have offended you so much that you placed them on the porch." She shook her head and bolted the door. Ketron could have tried to run away, but she would have spent a considerable amount of time unfastening the bolts. With her mother awake and on alert, she'd easily pull Ketron away before she made her escape. Her mother had trapped her.

Gwynevieve scattered the pieces of the envelope on the floor flippantly. "I bought some new tea in town. Will you try it with me?"

She needed to placate her mother until she could find a way to get out or Big Red could get to her. She allowed herself to be led to the kitchen and she sat down. Her mother began a conversation that was directed at Ketron, but it seemed as though she were speaking to clear her own mind.

"I was young when my sister died," she reminded me, as if I hadn't just come face-to-face with her long-dead twin. "I was only a little older than you." She took down two yellow glasses from the top shelf of the cabinet. "I don't know if you can understand the type of loss I endured. I was scared, lonely, and" —she looked at one of the empty glasses in her hand and dropped it — "broken." The glass laid in shattered fragments at her feet. She picked up one of the shards. "This was me. I was part of a set that could never be whole, and her death made me only a fraction of my former self. Her death didn't just leave me alone, it left me destroyed." She pinched the glass between her finger and her thumb. Bright blood sprang from her skin, and she seemed satisfied to watch it coat the glass in her hand. "A week later, I was crying on a bunk in an emergency shelter when my sweet sister appeared to me." She smiled sadly and dropped the shard onto the pile with the other fragments. She reached into the cabinet and grabbed another yellow glass to replace the one she had broken. "Gwynnie told me that we would still be together, and it gave me strength. I struggled through foster homes and the abuse in them, but she held my hand when I stood up for myself and hugged me when I sobbed in the shower." She had her back turned to Ketron, but she noticed the reflective pause as her mother thought about that chapter of her life.

"I met Yancy when he picked up one of my foster brothers for school one day." She took a jar out of the refrigerator. It was a familiar tea, but Ketron didn't remind her that they had already sampled it. She wanted to keep her mother happy until Big Red's flight brought him closer to rescuing her. "My foster brother, Shaun, invited me to ride with them, so I hopped into the backseat." She placed her hands flat on the counter and looked up at the ceiling, remembering a time she hadn't shared with Ketron until that moment. "Yancy's bright blue eyes twinkled, and his dimples crinkled when he talked to my brother. Yancy didn't ignore me like my brother's other friends. When he looked at me, I felt my heart swell, and it wasn't long before he knocked on my bedroom window when the rest of my foster family was asleep."

She stopped in mid pour and hung her head. "I thought we didn't tell anyone about our relationship because he was eighteen and I was so much younger, but when I got pregnant, he said that he was getting married to another girl, Judy. He claimed the baby wasn't his, and his family wanted him to marry her anyway. I could see through his lies." She spat the words, but quickly regained her composure. "Judy had a baby around the same time you were born, so I guess he impregnated both of us."

She dug in her pocket for something that Ketron thought might be a tissue, as she was recounting an emotional memory. "I ran away from the foster home and started working at a diner. Everyone was nice to me, especially when my pregnancy started to show. I tried to keep up with my foster siblings for a little while, but Shaun talked about Yancy every time I called. He thought he was doing me a favor by telling me about your father, but it hurt me to hear that he had bought a new house and painted the nursery with Judy."

She stopped her story, and Ketron could see her mother's profile. A cruel smile played on her lips. "Yancy got what he deserved, though. Judy fell in love with the father of the little boys who keep coming to see you. She even befriended his wife to get closer to him."

Ketron didn't understand why that made her mother happy. Ketron just thought it was a whole lot of recycled hurt.

Gwynevieve took a spoon from the dish drainer and stirred the tea in one of the glasses. Ketron wondered if she had added sugar, but the sugar canister was on the refrigerator, and Ketron hadn't seen her mother get a spoonful from it.

The woman clinked the spoon merrily against the glass as she stirred. "So, I had you after only five hours of labor pains, and I did it alone. I didn't call anyone to tell them about your birth for a couple of weeks because no one cared about us. We were fine on our own. Shaun called me, but I ignored him until I went back to work. He wanted to see you, but I was on the run from the state, and he couldn't find a ride to my new place."

She walked over to the table with two glasses in her hand. The spoon still rested in one of the glasses. "I knew I was going to be a great mother. Yancy's lack of involvement meant nothing. I could do anything with my sister by my side." She looked to her left, and a benign smile stretched over her features. It was a warm expression, but it made Ketron feel like running away. Even though she had seen Gwynevere's ghost moments before, Ketron was certain that her mother had lost touch with reality. Maybe Gwynevieve's disturbed mind had not produced a vision of her dead twin, but there was still a sickness in her brain that worked its way to the surface more each day.

Her mother's features hardened. "I'm getting to it," she barked at the empty air. She handed Ketron the glass with the spoon and Ketron took two long drinks. Her mother nodded her head as if a task were complete. "Family is everything." The words were a whisper.

"You had a family, or at least a brother, that wanted you, but you didn't contact him." Ketron regretted her bravado almost immediately. Her mother's forced smile moved into a snarl. "A foster brother is not a blood sister. I have my real family with me."

Ketron apologized, but her mother wasn't finished with her diatribe. "I have done everything for you. I stopped my life for you. I didn't run around like other girls in their teens and twenties. I worked and stayed at home with you."

Ketron agreed with her mother, but secretly she remembered that her mother had only been physically present. She hadn't taught her to cook or read. Her mother hadn't kissed her goodnight since—

"When did you stop taking your medication?"

She was aware that her mother hadn't taken her prescription for a while, but she hadn't thought about the moment her mother's personality had shifted until she had recounted her experiences. She'd implied that she was a *great mother*, but Ketron hardly remembered a time when her mother did more than tolerate her. When she was younger, her mother took her to the circus and bought her ice cream once or twice, but her kindnesses were overshadowed by the years of hurt that had followed.

How had she missed it? The answer was simple: She was too young to process the gradual changes. Ketron had laughed when her mother had carried on conversations with thin air, or she had blamed it on alcohol. Her young mind had made excuses when her mother told her to hide from well-meaning visitors. Her mother's increased paranoia should have been a sign, but Ketron wrote it off. She had wanted to stay with her mother. She was the last blood link to her life. A realization struck Ketron, and it hurt her more than the stinging slap her mother had given her across her cheek: Her mother resented her.

Ketron took another drink and her mother seemed to relax, taking a seat at the table. "Look, we shouldn't squabble right now. That time of my life doesn't matter anymore. Tom says that it's time to move forward in our lives, and I plan to spend the rest of my life with him, traveling the world. I have devoted my life to you, but now it's time for me to live my life."

Ketron stared at her questioningly. Her mother seemed to double for a moment, but then Ketron's focus returned. "But I like it here. I have friends, and I want to go to school with them."

Ketron's mother laughed. "Oh, Ketron. How could I take you with me after the way you've behaved?" She clinked the ice in her glass. "Gwynnie told me that you were bad for us a long time ago. She tried to get me to give you up for adoption or to leave you at school every day after your first day of kindergarten." She stared at her glass like she was looking into the past. "I wouldn't do it, though. I kept thinking that Yancy would come back to me, and he'd be so happy that I raised his child well, that he'd marry me, and we'd be a family." She sighed heavily and extended her smile. "But that never happened, and at some point, I realized that he would never come back."

"Did he ever see me?"

Her mother was cold, but Ketron wasn't the focus of her hate. "No, he never laid eyes on you. He heard about you through Shaun, but Shaun couldn't tell him a lot after I quit calling him. By that time, Shaun had a new daughter and a drug problem. Perfect little Yancy couldn't be bothered to talk to his old friend when Shaun's reputation went downhill."

"I could call my father. We could see if he wants to meet me." Ketron slurred her words. She was getting tired, but she didn't want to sleep until her mother was ready to go to bed. She had to sneak away. She had lost Big Red's phone number, but she knew his name was John Winslow. Maybe the police could help her find him.

Gwynevieve drew her eyebrows together. "No. He made his decision, and it didn't include us." She slid her glass away from her and glared at Ketron. "Though, I have to see him every day when I look at you."

"I'm sorry." It was a knee-jerk reaction to apologize, but Ketron regretted it when her mother casually dismissed her effort.

"It's okay. It wasn't so bad when you were little, but the older you get, the bluer your eyes and the deeper your dimples are."

Ketron pursed her lips slightly to stretch out her cheeks. She hoped the indentions in her cheeks weren't visible.

Gwynevieve crossed her legs and pressed a piece of salt into her index finger before rubbing it off with her thumb. "It's going to be hard to leave you behind, but I have to have my own life now. I can't do that with constant reminders of Yancy."

"Where am I going to go?" Ketron asked the question carefully. She had already decided she was going to live with Big Red.

Her mother stood up, and when she did, Ketron's vision moved awkwardly. She could hardly keep her lids from closing over her eyes. It had been an emotionally charged day, but she hadn't expected to be so exhausted. "Gwynnie helped me with that dilemma. You're going to stay here." She threw her hands out in a grand gesture. "After all, our family is here."

Ketron held her head up with her hands. Her vision was dark around the edges, and she could only see something if she really focused on it. She trained her eyes on her mother and forced her words. "But they're all dead. How can I stay with them if they're dead?"

She didn't hear the answer to her question.

Chapter Forty-One

Marvin stared at the birth certificate in his hand. "What's this?"

Ketron plucked up her courage. "We both know that you bullied me into naming her after your mother. I changed her name, but I kept Amelia as her middle name."

"We've been calling her Amelia for a year. *You've* been calling her Amelia. Are you trying to confuse her?"

"No, I've been saying her real name when we're alone."

real name?" He crumbled up the birth certificate and threw it at Ketron's face. "You've lost your mind! Is this where my thousand dollars went?"

"The only cost was a thirty-five-dollar filing fee, and I paid it myself."

He stared at her, searching for something she couldn't give to him. He opened the refrigerator and grabbed a can of beer. He popped the tab and drank the entire contents in three long gulps. He opened another can and brought it to his lips.

"You need to slow down."

"Not until you stop stealing my money and changing my baby's name."

Ketron decided to argue another point. "Your mother was a terrible person. Don't you remember all the cruel things she did to you? I don't want you to be reminded of her every time you say our daughter's name."

He held the beer to his lips but brought it away before he took a drink. "She did the best she could. There were so many things stacked against her since she was such a young mother."

"And I wasn't?" Ketron pointed out. "I had just turned sixteen when I gave birth to Bonnie, but your mother was eighteen and married when she had you."

"You act like Kyle didn't marry you."

"He didn't marry me until after Bonnie was born. By then, it was only an unnecessary formality. We didn't work well together."

"Is that how you ended up with my brother?" He wanted her to think the alcohol was affecting his mood, but they both knew that it hadn't had enough time to change his perspective.

"Stop it." Ketron glanced in the direction of the children's rooms. "They don't need to hear your drunken revelations."

Marvin looked thoughtfully out into the dark night before he swallowed the rest of the second bottle of beer. "Do they ever wonder why they don't look like Sonny and Amelia?" He pointed at the twin's room and opened another can of beer. "Because her name *is* Amelia!"

Ketron didn't respond to his tirade. Instead, she scooped up the baby and headed outside. If he insisted on talking to her, then he would have to follow her outside, hopefully, out of earshot of her older children.

The air was much cooler that it had been that afternoon. The breeze chilled Amelia before Ketron was ready to go back inside and she wished that she had grabbed her keys before she went outside. They could have sat in the van, away from the elements, but she had started locking her vehicle after Mrs. Franks had mentioned the break ins at nearby homes. She opened the back door slowly, unsure what to expect.

Marvin cursed an online player on a video game. His buttons clicked as he shifted his position in the game chair. Bonnie had her earphones on at the dining room table, so she hadn't heard anything. Winslow, Nora, and Sonny were watching a unicorn series, its familiar theme song carried down the hall.

Ketron grabbed a baby blanket from the linen closet and wrapped Amelia in it. She hoped the baby would acclimate quickly, and she regretted taking her outside with her.

Ketron sat down on the couch, cuddling and feeding Amelia. Her body temperature helped warm the baby. Buddy looked on from the console beside them.

"Buddy, I don't know what I'm going to do," she said, more to herself than to the inanimate object beside her.

She never expected him to answer her.

Chapter Forty-Two

Present

"Why're you so jumpy?" Marvin asked.

Ketron took her hand off her chest, but her heart was still beating quickly. "I thought—" she reconsidered telling him who—or what—she thought had spoken to her. "Never mind. What do you need?"

"Can you fix me a banana split?"

"Sure," Ketron said flatly, pulling herself up from the couch while keeping the baby attached to her breast.

She prepared it quickly, almost slopping the ingredients into the long bowl Marvin's mother had given her for his favorite childhood treat. The senior Amelia had purchased a sundae bowl only for him; it wasn't a treat he was meant to share with his family. Ketron was certain he had requested the special snack since their argument had been about his mother and her relevance to his life. She plopped the sundae onto the bed beside him and shut his door.

Ketron prepared the children for bed. Sonny started falling asleep while she brushed his teeth, and Nora barely hugged her before she climbed onto her lower bunk. Winslow was the only one who seemed wide awake and preoccupied.

"Is there something wrong?" Ketron asked him, nervous about what he might tell her.

"No," he answered, but his eyes stayed distant.

She led Winslow into the living room and sat on the rug. Sonny and Amelia were already asleep on the chaise lounge, and Nora was less likely to hear her conversation with Winslow from where she slept.

She put her arm around her son and scooted him beside her. He claimed he was too big to sit on her lap, but Ketron wanted to pull him as close as possible and protect him from hard topics.

"Did you hear my argument with Daddy?"

"Yeah," he admitted.

Ketron took a deep breath. She had known her son was ready for the truth for a long time, but she had been scared that he would be bitter and hateful to her when he learned it. "Do you have any questions?"

Winslow wouldn't look at her. He put his head between his knees and asked, "Is he my real dad?" He pointed at Marvin's room.

"No," Ketron said quickly, before she lost her nerve.

Winslow raised his eyebrows and stared at his socked feet. "Who is it then?"

"Can I tell you the whole story?" Ketron tried to take his hand, but Winslow wouldn't allow the touch.

"I guess." He flicked a crumb off the rug. "Can I meet him?" He looked up at her hopefully.

"You should probably let me tell you the story first."

Ketron tried to keep her emotions in check, but they crept into her words. Winslow listened attentively throughout the story, wiser than his eight years.

"I was married to Kyle for a couple of years before he started making fun of me," she told him. Winslow was familiar with Bonnie's father, and he knew Ketron had been married twice. "Kyle said his insults with a smile, and Bonnie laughed at most of the things he said. She didn't understand that her father's words were meant to cut me." She chanced a look at Bonnie's room and was relieved that she was in it with the door closed. "For example, when I cleaned the floors on my hands and knees, my low-rise pants would slip down my back side a little, so Kyle would walk up behind me and say, 'I didn't know Ketron called a plumber.'"

As soon as the words were out of her mouth, she realized how silly they sounded. Kyle had made childish comments, and she should have overlooked them, but his words were meant to hurt her. Kyle had resented her, and she would never know the reason.

"We lived in an apartment that always needed repairs. The toilet would randomly fill up at night, the lights would turn off if I ran two appliances in the same room, and I think the building settled at an angle, because the doors of the cabinets would drift open until I closed them again. Anyway, one day I found a leak in the sink, and I called the landlord to fix it."

Winslow raised an eyebrow in a way that eerily reminded her of her mother. "What's a landlord?"

"It's a person that owns the property and rents it to people so they can have someplace to live. We had a good landlord, and he sent someone to fix it right away."

Ketron had promised herself that she would tell Winslow the truth when he asked her about his biological father, but it was harder than she had expected. "The guy that showed up was nice. He admitted that he hadn't been out of jail long, but he didn't make me nervous. We talked and laughed..." Ketron trailed off. "I hadn't laughed in so long."

"You don't really laugh now," Winslow pointed out.

"Maybe that's so," Ketron conceded, "but I'm older now, and I understand the world a little better. Everyone has good and bad times."

They sat together in silence while Ketron tried to find a way to tell him about her infidelity. She had always wanted the love and respect of her children, but how could anyone respect her after what she had done?

"The man's name was Oscar, but everyone called him Oz. He's your father." In an attempt to end the awkwardness between she and Winslow, Ketron had rushed through the explanation, and when she was finished speaking, she felt dread instead of relief. Should she have given her son more examples of Kyle's cruelty? Should she have mentioned that Oz had manipulated her into believing he loved her?

Winslow nodded. "Can I meet him?"

"No." Ketron's mouth dried up and her mind raced as she searched for the best way to communicate the reason for her refusal.

Winslow glared at her. "I get it." Bitterness dripped from his words. "You cheat on your husbands, and you keep kids away from their dads. Is that why you lock up Sonny's and Amelia's dad in that room?" His voice rose to a level that woke up his two youngest siblings. "I hate you, and I hope you die, so I can live with my real father!" He stomped out of the room. Each footfall echoed in Ketron's heart, and she regretted the way she had answered him.

Amelia climbed off the couch and picked up one of Nora's dolls. She chewed on its head while she inspected a toy bulldozer. Sonny sat up, blinked his eyes twice, and laid back down.

Marvin popped open his door a crack, but he moved it wider when he saw Ketron was sitting on the rug. His face was slack, and their argument was momentarily forgotten. "What was that about?"

"I had to tell Winslow about his father," she answered, standing up. "He heard what you said."

"I thought we were both going to tell them?"

Ketron surveyed his bloodshot eyes and sluggish movements. "You're in no state to answer his questions."

Marvin stood to his full height and puffed out his chest. "Oz was *my* brother."

"Yeah, and he died because of his addiction. Maybe you should think about that."

Marvin couldn't make a snarky response, so he quietly pushed his door closed. Amelia crawled up to her mother and tugged the leg of her pants. Ketron picked up the baby and felt her nestle into the crook of her neck.

She had invested her life in her children. Most of the people she knew had interests outside of their families, but Ketron's days were consumed with nursing, playdates, extracurricular schedules, and negotiating the gap between the Solo Dinosaur and Berry Batch Buddies so that most of her children could enjoy shows together. Shauna told her that she would have more time for her hobbies when the children were older, but Ketron imagined that she would focus primarily upon her children's wants and needs until they followed their dreams as self-sustaining adults.

Winslow's outburst was harder on her than she wanted to admit. She didn't require his approval, but some part of her sought validation for her actions. She understood that she was responsible for her decisions and their outcomes, but she had worn the repercussions for her actions like a badge of shame for years. The people who had known her before her affair with Oz had abandoned her to suffer the consequences alone. Oz had died in the early months of her pregnancy, and his brother had been the only person who had shown her any kindness. Marvin married her before the twins were born and he signed the birth certificate without hesitation. He protected Ketron from judgmental stares and harsh rumors, but his feelings for her had grown colder over the past year. Ketron wished she knew the reason for his change. She would do almost anything to connect with her husband the way they did when they were newlyweds.

Amelia breathed soft puffs of air on her neck, and her arms lost tension, slipping from Ketron's shoulders. She placed her baby on the couch next to her brother and watched her doze peacefully before she nudged between Amelia and Sonny.

Ketron's younger children had been the only ones who were unaware of the reason for her divorce from Kyle. She had treasured their innocent view of her, and now Winslow's perspective of her had changed. She wanted to go back in time and erase the act, but she couldn't alter it and keep Winslow and Nora. The only good thing that came out of her mistake was their birth.

Amelia whimpered in her sleep, and Ketron kissed the infant's soft, plump check.

"Maybe you won't hate me." Her voice broke on every word.

Chapter Forty-Three

Present

In the deepest part of the night, Ketron's eyes opened. She heard the air change as the spirit glided from Bonnie's room to the twins' room. She breathed carefully while the entity traveled back down the hallway and hovered behind her. She could feel the presence, but she couldn't see or hear it.

Sonny shifted in his sleep. "You're a good mommy." The words came from him, but it wasn't Sonny who spoke them. He was only the physical conduit. "Will you hug me?"

Ketron was unnerved by the request, but she was too scared to object. The last time she had angered a spirit, her son's hand had been badly burned. She turned her body, slipping Amelia safely between the arm rest and her back. Ketron tried to believe she was embracing Sonny as she put her arm around his midsection and pulled his body to her. She breathed his hair, filling her senses with its watermelon scent. A track of saliva had run down the cheek nearest to her and Ketron wiped the moisture away. Sonny's eyes were closed, but he smiled. Thankfully, it wasn't the cruel expression that had alerted her to his differentness the last time.

Ketron didn't sense the volcanic rage she usually noticed when Jeremy was near her. Instead, a serene comfort settled over her. It was familiar, though she hadn't experienced it for a long time. It was the peace a mother feels when she knows all her children are safe.

"I wish you could hug me all the time," he spoke, using his brother's voice.

Ketron jolted, pulling her arms away from her son. Sonny's body remained still, but the smile was gone. She couldn't feel the presence of anything ghostly in the room with her. He had retreated, separated from her by ethereal constraints.

Chapter Forty-Four

Present

"Let's do something different today," Dr. Richards suggested.

Ketron rubbed her hands together and traced the green line from Nora's marker that hadn't washed away. "Okay."

"I want to talk about your mental compartments. I think they may be too full, but you can remove things from them if you're ready."

Ketron understood his tactic, and she saw no harm in the exercise. "Like a mental spring cleaning."

He smiled without joy and pointed to her. "Bingo. Okay. You know the drill."

She laid back on the couch and closed her eyes. She had looked up at the same popcorn ceiling for years and tried to discern patterns in it, but after many failed attempts to see a face or an object in the uniform spackles, she preferred the lighted darkness behind her lids.

"I want you to imagine a large dresser."

Ketron folded her hands over her stomach and regulated her breathing. She pictured the dresser in Marvin's room.

"What does it look like?"

Ketron concentrated on the image before she spoke. "It's made of cherry wood, with two mirrors, and eight drawers."

"That's very specific. Why are there eight drawers?"

Ketron didn't have an answer. The dresser in Marvin's room only had four drawers, but the image in her mind doubled the number.

"Will you look into one of the mirrors and tell me what you see?"

Ketron could see herself next to Marvin's bed. She was wearing the same jeans and boat-necked shirt she had put on before her appointment. "It's just me. I'm in Marvin's room, but that's where we keep the dresser with my clothes." She didn't have to see her doctor to know he was nodding along to her explanation. It was the rustle of fabric against his neck when his head shifted that gave it away.

"Is there anything on the dresser?"

Ketron almost squinted before she realized that her eyes were closed. The dresser was far away from her, and she related the distance to Dr. Richards. "There are some family photographs on it."

"Good. Now walk over to the dresser."

That was difficult. The scene became a product of her imagination, instead of a natural exercise.

"You said there were photographs. Who is in the pictures?"

There were pictures of her family, but they weren't actual photos. "There's a five by seven picture of my baby and another eight by ten of Bonnie, Nora, Sonny, and me."

"Is Amelia in the family picture?"

"No, but neither is Winslow." She tried to stay focused on the scene in her mind, but she was distracted by Dr. Richards' pen scratching a note on his pad.

"Does he have his own picture?'

Ketron glanced across the dresser. "No."

"Interesting. Will you open a drawer?"

Ketron sat in front of the dresser. "Which one?"

"Any one. You select the first drawer you feel like opening."

Ketron grabbed the handle of the top right drawer. She couldn't feel the cool metal on her palm because Dr. Richards had not placed her under suggestion, but she tried to imagine the act of moving the drawer out to keep the vision fresh in her mind. "It's just a sock and underwear drawer."

"Whose socks and underwear are in the drawer?"

The obvious answer was that they were her underclothes, but when she thought about them, the underwear had superheroes dotting the fabric and the ankles of the socks sported the faces of meat-eating dinosaurs. "They're Sonny's."

"Is there anything else in the drawer?"

Ketron dug around. She didn't expect to find anything, so she was surprised by her discovery.

"It's a picture of Winslow." She glanced at the family picture. "I think it belongs in the picture on the dresser. It has the same background."

"Was it cut out of the picture?"

"The edges are ripped. Someone ripped it out of the photograph."

Dr. Richards scribbled something down. "Who do you think ripped it out?"

"I don't know." Her words came out a little harsher than she had intended.

He didn't respond to her tone. "Is there anything else in the drawer?"

Ketron had moved ahead of her therapist's request and had pulled out a stuffed dog. She put Buddy on the dresser facing away from her. "No."

Ketron had never lied to Dr. Richards, so the untruth prodded at her conscience. It would be easy to tell him she had made a mistake, but she didn't want to talk about the dog or its possible significance.

"Can you open another drawer?"

Ketron opened the second drawer. At home, her shirts were in the second drawer of the dresser, stacked neatly in compact rows. In her mind, she pulled out a faded blue flannel.

"It's my mother's drawer," she said hastily. "I found one of her flannel shirts. I'm not going through it today. I'll pick another drawer."

"That's up to you."

Ketron resented the judgement she heard in his voice. She banged the drawer closed in her mind, but a piece of the blue flannel shirt stuck out defiantly. She wanted to stuff it back inside the drawer, but she couldn't bring herself to open it again.

She chose the bottom left drawer. She bent down and pulled, but it was stuck, like it had been stuffed until the items inside prevented the drawer from moving. She finally freed it, and it slid down the track and onto the floor. She lost her breath, and tears pricked her eyes. One escaped, drawing a lazy track down her temple. Thankfully, Dr. Richards didn't see it.

"What's in the drawer, Ketron?" he prompted.

"I don't want to do this anymore."

He sighed through his nose. "I think it's important that you tell me what you found."

Ketron backed out of the image in her mind and opened her eyes. When she sat up, her therapist didn't seem concerned. She had just experienced something that had shaken her to the core, but he looked like he was sitting at a garden tea party, having pretty conversations that bored him. In all the years she had known him, Ketron had struggled to like him. His methods were useful and professional, but he lacked compassion. He knew most of her challenges, triggers, and traumas, but he had never expressed empathy or sympathy when she told him about the experiences that caused them. He was cold and clinical. The realization sent her overwhelmed emotions over the edge. "I'm done!" Ketron cried as she bolted off the couch and grabbed her purse off the table in front of her.

"We still have a few more minutes," the doctor responded indifferently. "I would like it if you stayed, but you are always free to go."

Ketron didn't like to upset anyone. She took a few seconds to breathe and reminded herself that her father was paying for her sessions. She didn't want him to think she was ungrateful. She reluctantly sat down on the sofa.

"Thank you, Ketron. I want to speak to you about the first drawers you opened."

"Okay." Ketron placed her purse back on the table.

Dr. Richards continued as if they had experienced a seamless session and Ketron had not threatened to leave. He crossed one leg over another and allowed his notes to rest on the inside of his calf. "The first drawer you opened didn't surprise me. Usually, the thoughts that are closest to the surface of a parent's mind involve their younger offspring. The picture of Amelia on the dresser and the contents of the first drawer point to your life as a mother." He tapped his pen on his shoe. "The picture of Winslow amid Sonny's underthings is confusing. It could be your mind's way of compensating for Winslow's absence in the family picture, or it could signify a ripple in their brotherly relationship. It may also be the way your mind connected them as your sons."

"Why was the drawer full of socks and underwear?"

Dr. Richards smiled. "That's a little easier to explain. This was an exercise. You weren't under hypnosis. I told you to look through the drawers of a dresser, and clothes are in dressers. Most people keep their socks and underwear in the top drawer of their chest of drawers."

He glanced at his notes and settled his elbow on the arm rest, bringing his pen just past his cheek. "Now, that brings us to the next drawer you pulled out. It was under the first one, was it not?"

"Yes."

"You discovered an article of clothing that had been your mother's. A faded blue flannel shirt?"

Ketron had forgotten that she had been so descriptive. "Yeah. I put it back inside the drawer, but when I closed it, a piece stuck out."

Without moving his shiny head, Dr. Richards glanced up. "Did you try to open it and put the shirt back up properly?"

Ketron shook her head.

"Interesting." He added to his notes, and Ketron thought she saw a large, black dot on his cheekbone. He had marked himself when he had brought the pen to his face. She opened her mouth to bring it to his attention, and he said, "Do you find it strange that you were comfortable with the shirt sticking out of the drawer?"

Ketron thought she could see his angle, and she attempted to dodge a line of more uncomfortable questions. "No." She forced a laugh. "I just hurried and shut the drawer so I could open a new one. As you can imagine, the dressers in our house look a lot like that. Children get out a shirt or a pair of socks and shut the drawer against some other piece of clothing." In truth, Ketron was meticulous about closing all the drawers properly, and she went behind the children and righted any drawer when it was shut against a shirt or a pair of pants.

"Are you sure you don't want to talk about your mother?" he asked her while he wrote on the notepad.

Ketron glanced at the clock. She still had fifteen minutes before he agreeably released her. If she didn't want to talk about her mother, then she'd have to talk about the last drawer she had pulled out. "Aren't you tired of hearing about her?"

Dr. Richards uncrossed his legs and placed the notepad on the table next to him. "I'm here to discuss whatever you need."

"Why do you think my mother has a drawer?"

Dr. Richards' mouth formed a thin line. "Your mother will always have a drawer in this activity. She was a large part of your life, and her actions when you were a child have caused you to make many of your decisions in your adult life." Ketron tilted her head to indicate that his statement stirred questions that she couldn't put into words. He tried to answer her unvoiced concerns. "From my observations, you have not been in a fully satisfying marital relationship and you have an insecure attachment to your children."

Ketron wondered if anyone else thought so poorly of her. "It's Marvin's decision to drink, and he can't do it around my children, so he stays in his room while I care for them."

"Your husband's alcoholism is an entirely different subject." He gestured while speaking, and he measured his impact on her by watching her reaction to his assessments. "What about Kyle? You said that he held similar beliefs and the two of you got along. Why didn't you remain in the marriage to see if your relationship was only in a valley?"

They had discussed peaks and valleys in relationships, where peaks were high points of happiness and valleys were low points with challenges. Ketron had explained to her therapist that the peak of her relationship with Kyle had been short-lived. "He was mentally and emotionally abusive," Ketron pointed out. "He loved to make fun of me."

"Could you have worked that out in marriage counseling?"

Ketron shook her head. "I don't think so. It was something he learned from his brother. They thought it was funny to put other people down."

"It sounds like a defense mechanism to me. Kyle and his brother may have made fun of other people to make themselves feel better about their own shortcomings."

"No." Ketron shook her head. "Kyle was just mean."

Dr. Richards turned in his seat and jotted something down in his notes. "Has Kyle ever remarried?"

"No."

"Has he had a serious girlfriend?"

"No."

Dr. Richards faced her again. "Why do you think that is?"

Ketron wanted to say, 'Because he's a jerk," but she gave the question some serious thought. "I always believed that he was a good person at his core. He has a lot of friends, and they all love him. I think his issues are deeper than the obvious."

"You've mentioned that before," Dr. Richards said. "You spoke about your sexual relationship with him and stated that it was missing something."

Ketron looked away from Dr. Richards's measuring stare. "I think he needed more than I could give him."

"Are you hinting that you believe your ex-husband is homosexual?"

Ketron breathed deeply. "I don't know. I felt like he needed more experiences with different people. I don't know if it would have been with women, men, or both."

"Do you think that he knows this about himself?"

"Maybe on some level, but he wouldn't want to disappoint his parents by being something they don't understand."

Dr. Richards moved his head within her peripheral vision. He wanted to reestablish eye contact, but Ketron wouldn't shift her focus back to him.

"Could his unfulfilled needs have caused him to create a defense?"

Ketron didn't want to talk about her ex-husband's sexuality and her unwillingness to explore it. She had been in therapy long enough to realize the revelation Dr. Richards wanted her to make, though. "Yes. Kyle may have put off marrying me for as long as possible because he really wanted to explore other sexual arenas. He may have resented me for my lack of vigor in the bedroom and he may have thought I guessed that he wanted other partners, so he put up a defense. It wasn't my job to rescue him from his feelings."

"It wasn't?"

"No."

"What about your vows?"

Dr. Richards didn't have to tell her to which vows he was referencing. She had broken them all.

She narrowed her eyes at her therapist and kept her hands clutched tightly in her lap. "What was I supposed to do? Should I have told him to tell his parents?"

"Maybe not, but you could have secured a safe environment for him to explore his sexuality. What could you have done differently?"

"I could have asked him to talk to me about the feelings he had for the friends I noticed him flirting with." She put her head in her hands. "I don't think they knew that he was flirting with them. He has a certain face he gets when he flirts—" She cut herself off.

"Go on."

"I could have told him that his heart was safe with me, and it was okay to explore his sexuality." She raised her eyebrows. "But not in our house. Bonnie didn't need to know about it, and I couldn't have been part of it."

"Those are reasonable boundaries."

"Do you think it would have helped?"

Dr. Richards glanced over at his notes, but it was only an excuse to look away. "We will never know, but I think it's important that you recognize that other people have faults, and you need to work through them before giving up."

"What does it have to do with my mother, though?"

"I think we can agree that your mother hurt you worse than any other person, but you cared for her and covered her illness. After the experience in the woods, where she—" Ketron turned away quickly, and Dr. Richards rephrased his explanation. "After the incident, you felt like you had been betrayed by the person who claimed to have loved you the most. Without an active father, your mind rationalized that anyone who loved you would eventually hurt you.

"Ketron, you deserve a good relationship. However, no one is perfect. You may have been too young to recognize that Kyle displayed certain sexual tendencies, but you were aware of Marvin's addictions when you met him. You seem surprised that he has developed a new habit, but I challenge you to find the reason for it."

Ketron looked at the clock. There were seven minutes left.

Dr. Richards noticed. "Sometimes sessions can be hard, but it's important to talk about big issues."

Ketron thought about a reason for Marvin's unhappiness. "His mother died. They didn't have the best relationship, but she was toxic, so he couldn't have improved it."

"Okay. Can you help him move through the stages of grief?"

Ketron shifted in her seat and picked at her jeans. She didn't think her husband deserved her help, but Dr. Richards wouldn't encourage that line of thinking. "We don't get along."

"Can you change that?"

Inwardly, Ketron rolled her eyes. "I could move back into the bedroom."

"That's a good start. You need to reestablish the sexual component of your relationship."

It felt awkward to talk to her therapist about sex, but he treated it the same as any other topic.

"I have the baby, and her molars are coming in."

Dr. Richards was pensive. "Did you stop having sex with Kyle when he began making fun of you?"

"You already know that I did."

"Can I offer my thoughts on it?"

Very seldom did Dr. Richards tell her anything outright. She usually had to arrive at her own conclusions. She was curious to hear thoughts he actually committed to, so she urged him to go on.

"It didn't escape my attention that Marvin wasn't in the family picture."

Ketron hoped he would say more, but it was her turn to make her own revelations. He was only her guide. "You think I'm ready to leave him."

"Whose clothes were in the last drawer?"

"They weren't Marvin's," she answered truthfully.

"I realize that. But were they clothes that belonged to another member of your family? Maybe someone you don't often talk about?"

"I'd love to talk about that more," she responded with a sly smile, "but we are out of time today." She pointed to her wrist where watches would have been worn if phones didn't provide more than a connection with other people.

"We can talk about it next time." He jotted another note down on the pad. She had almost gone through the door when he held up his hand to stop her. "I have one more thing to ask you about before we end today."

Ketron sighed. She wasn't going to talk about the contents of the last drawer, and she hastily planned an escape. "I have to pick up Nora and Winslow from dance class."

"It will only take a moment," he insisted. "It has to do with the financial side of our arrangement." He walked to a large mahogany desk in front of the window and typed on a small silver laptop. The afternoon light danced leaf shadows on his back. "The account that sends your payments every month was closed." He turned the laptop to face her. "I think we both know what it means."

"Okay," Ketron replied. "I can't afford to pay you."

"I know." He flipped the laptop back around. "Your father always paid a month in advance, so you have a couple of weeks to decide if you want to remain in my care. I'll offer you a better rate than the one I gave your father, and you'll probably have an inheritance that will help with the cost." He stopped talking until he had her full attention. "Ketron, you need these sessions. It's good to be certain that you don't show signs of a dissociative disorder, but you should also sort through your fear of intimacy."

"I have to go," Ketron told him. "I'll be in touch." She closed the door on their session, and part of her hoped she wouldn't be back for another one.

Chapter Forty-Five

Present

Shauna transferred a sleepy Amelia to Ketron. "How was it today?"

Ketron laid the baby over her shoulder. She smelled like Shauna's perfume, a whispery floral scent. "He thinks I have a fear of intimacy."

"You do." Shauna called Matty down for running up the slide.

"I think *our* relationship is pretty close."

Shauna shrugged. "It's okay. I mean, you disappeared for a month after Amelia was born."

"I was on a Baby Moon."

Ketron joined many new aged parents and took a "Baby Moon" when Amelia was born. It was like a honeymoon, but instead of spending time with a new spouse, parents took a leave from the public eye to get to know their newborn and learn to juggle the demands of their new life. She enjoyed the time she had spent with her family without interference from people outside her household, but there had been other reasons, besides bonding, that had led to her decision. She was overwhelmed by the demands of her mother-in-law, and she didn't want to share the special time with her.

Shauna shrugged. "It was an excuse. Everyone expected you to go into labor at any moment from the time you were eight months pregnant, and they looked at you like you were a ticking time bomb. You needed a little time to yourself. I knew you'd call me when you were ready."

Ketron put her hand on Shauna's arm. Her friend didn't acknowledge the gesture or pull away from the touch. "I'm sorry I upset you."

Shauna shrugged. "I wasn't upset. I was a little hurt—since you were the first person I called when I went into labor with Matty—but I realized that it had nothing to do with our friendship or me. You needed to decompress, and after that terrible baby shower, who could blame you."

Ketron shivered involuntarily. She hadn't wanted a baby shower, but Marvin had insisted on it. His mother was terminally ill, and she organized the entire event. The elder Amelia told Ketron not to worry about anything, and she took over. She had been upset when Ketron hadn't found out about the baby's sex, but she promised the party would be gender neutral.

The venue was beautiful. Purple and blue flowers hung from pergolas, and peaceful fountains dripped water. Marvin's mother, the senior Amelia, had told Ketron that her children were too young to attend the baby shower, but Ketron had taken them anyway.

When they had made their way to a table, Ketron noticed that everything was blue. "I thought I told you I wanted everything to be gender-neutral," she had told Amelia.

The older woman had laughed. "Marvin's already had one boy, so he'll probably have another one, unless a girl comes from your side of the family." Ketron had refrained from explaining the biology of gender determination to her mother-in-law.

Ketron had waited for Shauna while the guests arrived. The party was in full swing before she asked, "Didn't you invite Shauna?"

"It must have slipped my mind," Amelia had said. "It's probably not her crowd anyway. No one here has drugs."

Ketron had turned a bright shade of red. She didn't remind her mother-in-law that her son had been to jail for drug possession.

Amelia had led Marvin around the room, introducing him to each of her friends. People started to point at Ketron and whisper. They could have been talking about her growing pregnancy or complimenting her lacy yellow dress, but it made her uncomfortable, so Ketron took the children out of the garden. They hovered around the car and Ketron wished she hadn't given Marvin the keys when they arrived.

Forty-five minutes later, Marvin had found them playing a game under the shade of a tree. "Why are you out here? They want to play a baby game."

"Maybe they should play it with *you*." Ketron stomped to her feet, and one of her knees buckled. Winslow and Bonnie caught her before she fell.

"I don't have the belly for it," he laughed, missing the insinuation in her angry reply. He reached out to touch Ketron's stomach, but she moved away from him.

"You seem to be the star of the show," Ketron bit at him.

Marvin threw his hands up and started walking back to the garden. "Don't act so spoiled," he voiced as he stomped away. "My mom is about to die, and she wants to give me a nice party."

His words were not lost on Ketron. She finished the party, and she tried to be polite as women she didn't know touched her belly and measured it during one of the shower activities. The hardest game was guessing her weight. Ketron was sensitive about her weight, and Amelia knew it, but she started the game by telling the guests to guess a weight that was a little less than the size of a blue whale. Several activities later, all of Amelia's friends guessed that Ketron was having a boy, and by the end of the party, Ketron had silently prayed that they'd all be wrong.

A baby shower was meant to be fun and entertaining for the expectant mother, but Ketron felt emotionally exhausted and anguished after she was finally able to leave the venue. It seemed the party had been Amelia's way to silently roast her daughter-in-law. Ketron had no one there to defend her, and only her children saw the transgressions and comforted her.

Later that night, Ketron had made a bed for herself on the couch and had fallen asleep with Sonny wrapped in her arms. Marvin only loosely addressed the change.

"Zeke!" Shauna called, bringing Ketron back to the moment. He had wondered too far, but he ran back quickly. Ketron was surprised when he turned around at the sound of the nickname her friend had given to him.

"Anyway," Shauna continued. "A lesser friend would have kicked you to the curb, but I knew you needed mental rest, so I didn't freak out like everyone else."

"Thanks for that." Ketron put her arm around her friend and leaned in. She broke the contact after a few seconds.

"See there. Fear of intimacy." Shauna smiled playfully, but they both knew she was serious.

Shauna volunteered to walk a block away and pick up Winslow and Nora from dance class. When she returned, her eyebrows had climbed halfway up her forehead.

Nora and Winslow elbowed each other in the ribs. Their mouths were curved down in hateful frowns.

"What happened?" Ketron asked.

"He tripped me down the stairs and ripped my tights," Nora told her. Her eyes were moist, but she crossed her arms and stood to her full height.

"I did not!" Winslow defended, pointing his finger within inches of his twin's nose. "You tripped over your own clumsy feet!"

Ketron intervened before it turned into a full-scale argument. "That's enough. Winslow, go play with your bother and Matty. You will no longer lead down the stairs after dance class ends. Nora, come sit by me." Nora plopped onto the bench and circled her arms around her mother's waist. "I'm sorry about what happened to you. It looks like it hurts, and I know you're disappointed that your tights are ruined. Daddy and I will buy you a new pair."

"Thank you, Mama," she responded in her squeaky voice. "Can I go play?"

Ketron kissed the top of her head. "Of course."

When Nora joined the other children, Ketron commented, "See. No fear of intimacy."

Shauna rolled her eyes. "But only with your own children. You are a little stand-offish with Bonnie, though." She seemed to reflect on her statement. "It may be because she's getting older, or because she spends time with her dad."

Ketron had been through enough startling revelations for the day, so she didn't question her friend's analysis.

Nora fell off the swing and cried out. She wasn't bleeding, or in an immense amount of pain, so Ketron remained seated.

"I told you that you were clumsy!" Winslow yelled at her. He laughed and ran away before she could jump to her feet and chase him.

"Winslow looks just like you, but it's amazing how much Nora looks like him."

Ketron knew who Shauna meant when she said *him*. Shauna had known Oz for years before she came to live with Ketron and Marvin. When she was on drugs, Oz had been one of her best friends.

"She has his brown hair and eyes, but she has my mother's nose." Ketron waited for a moment before she added, "I had to talk to Winslow about Oz last night."

Shauna gave Ketron her full attention. "How did that go?"

"Pretty badly," Ketron admitted. "He told me that he wanted me to die so he could live with his father."

"Wow!" Shauna sucked in a whistle through her teeth. "That's pretty bad. You didn't tell him Oz was dead?"

"I didn't have a chance. He thinks I'm a temptress who keeps children away from their fathers."

"Didn't Marvin back you up?"

Ketron laughed without emotion. "He can't do that from the bottom of a beer bottle."

Shauna hung her head. "I'm sorry."

"It's not your fault."

Shauna lifted her head and stared out at the children. "You're right, but after I started battling my own addiction, it was my go-to response."

Ketron's heart fell into her stomach. "Oh, Shana. I shouldn't talk so much about Marvin's alcoholism. I don't want you to think that I thought that way about you."

"You didn't?" She picked at a spot on her chin. "I would have thought that way about me if I had been you."

She grabbed Shauna's hand. "You have overcome your addiction and stayed active in your family. Marvin has every opportunity to do better, but he chooses alcohol over involvement with us."

Shauna squeezed her hand once and let it go. Ketron had the feeling Shauna was going to move the focus of their conversation.

"It's just weird that he doesn't want to tell Winslow that Oz was his brother, but he wants him to know that he is not his son."

"He was just drunk. He wanted to hurt me."

Shauna watched Winslow help Matty onto a swing. "Yeah, but Winslow is really the one who suffers."

"Speaking of great fathers, I think mine is dead," Ketron told her.

"What?" Shauna jumped off the bench. "Maybe you should have led with that."

Ketron shrugged and noticed that Winslow was staring at them. He hadn't heard their conversation, but he had seen Shauna's reaction. He was still too mad at his mother to investigate the reason for Shauna's response, though. "It's no big deal."

"Ketron, I'm so sorry." Shauna sat back down and placed her hand on Ketron's shoulder.

"Really, I'm fine."

"Look, take it from me, my father sucks, but when he dies, part of me will mourn for him." She glanced away. "Or maybe I'll just mourn for missed opportunities."

"I never even met him. I have no feelings or missed opportunities. He made his decisions and he's gone." Ketron didn't mean everything she said, but it was the way she wanted to process her father's death. He was a stranger to her, so he deserved no more.

"What about siblings? Did he have other kids?"

"Yeah, but his wife was unfaithful. I don't think either one of her children were his." She laughed, but the sound was more like a dry cough. "His wife was the same woman he left my mother for."

"Are you going to the funeral?"

Ketron looked up in surprise. "No."

"Good."

Ketron's eyebrows met. "I thought you'd want me to go."

Shauna shook her head. "Nope. You don't need to go around a bunch of people you don't know and stare at your dead sperm donor. It's not good for your mental health."

Ketron relaxed a rigid posture she hadn't known she had been holding. "I'm glad we can agree on something."

Shauna was lost in her own thoughts for the next few minutes, pushing her chin up to pout her lip. When she spoke again, she said, "I think it might be a good idea to write him a letter, though."

"Dead people don't read."

Irritation flashed across Shauna's features. "I'm only saying it might help you to process some of your feelings about the way he treated you."

Ketron tried to transition their conversation to lighter notes before they rounded up the children to leave. "Sure. But for now, let's go to Bonnie's soccer game."

Shauna extended a warning finger. "I'm not letting this go."

Ketron smiled. "I'd never expect you to let me off that easily."

Chapter Forty-Six

Present

Bonnie skirted the defensive player in front of her and swung her foot in a perfect arc, sending the ball sailing over the goalie's head. The left side of the crowd erupted in celebration, but Kyle's shouts could be heard over them all.

"Does he have to do that?" Marvin asked. He rubbed his temples clockwise and then counterclockwise.

"I think we should all encourage Bonnie's abilities." Shauna cupped her hands over her mouth to project her cheers in Bonnie's direction. Behind her, the rest of the children echoed her shouts with loud whoops of their own.

Marvin snarled at her briefly, but he relaxed his face when Luke looked over at him. "It's your stepdaughter, man. She's really good."

"Imagine if it were Sonny out there," Ketron added, shifting Amelia's weight from one side to the other. "You could show a little support."

"I'm here, aren't I?" he spat. He leaned forward in his sports chair and placed his head in his hands.

Shauna shot Ketron a knowing look, and Ketron tried to distract her friend from her observations. "Is Matty going onto the field?"

Matty was excited about Bonnie's goal, and he rushed onto the field. Luckily, the referee didn't notice the boy until after Luke had swept him up with one hand. He kicked until his father sat him on the grass in front of his mother.

The siren inside the scoreboard called out the end of the game and everyone applauded and whistled. Kyle ran out onto the field and hoisted Bonnie into the air, running in little circles with her. Bonnie's teammates laughed and slapped hands with Kyle. The opposing team pointed at the spectacle, but it was clear that they enjoyed the show.

"Do you see that?" Marvin huffed.

"I see a man who is happy about his daughter's winning goal," Ketron told him. "The team they played tonight beat them pretty badly at the start of the season, so today's victory was a big deal."

"Maybe you should marry *him* then," Marvin quipped.

Shauna tensed. Luke asked Matty to go play with Sonny, and Matty ran onto the grassy hill behind them.

Kyle carried Bonnie to the team's bench and sat her down. He stood behind her, rubbing her shoulders while bottled waters were passed around. After a short talk with the coach, the girls were released, and Kyle walked Bonnie most of the way to the group of people waiting for her. Marvin eyed him, and Kyle stopped before he reached them, more out of the need to keep the peace than out of fear or respect.

"Goodnight, Kyle," Shauna called. He threw up a hand as he jogged in the other direction.

"Why does Shauna like your ex-husband now?" Marvin asked after they loaded the children into the van.

"Probably because she knows *he's* not a cheater," Winslow called up from the back seat.

Ketron said nothing about his outburst, but she caught Nora's confused brown eyes in the rearview mirror. What would her daughter think of her when she learned the truth?

Marvin was angry with Ketron, so he didn't defend her. He merely let Winslow's words sink in like they justified his own position in some way.

Marvin was pale and sweaty on the ride home, and he barely made it to the bathroom. Loud retching noises echoed down the hall.

"I hope he's not sick." Bonnie sat down on the mantle and unstrapped her cleats. "If he is, then I don't wanna catch it."

"I don't think you can catch what he has," Ketron commented. She opened the refrigerator. Marvin had shoved a twelve pack of beer in the crisper, and it had crushed her lettuce. She changed her dinner plans, thankful that he had waited until after Bonnie's game to start drinking.

At dinner, Marvin reeked of alcohol. He seemed to feel better, but he was still sullen. Everyone was relieved when he carried his plate to the sink after only a few bites.

Winslow popped up and ate while standing beside his chair. He moved his hips from side to side, dancing to a tune in his head.

Bonnie stared at him while her upper lip crawled over her gums. "What is he doing?"

It was the happiest Winslow had been since Ketron had talked to him about Oz. Usually, she asked the children to sit while they chewed their food, but part of her relaxed and savored her son's good mood. "It's okay," she told Bonnie.

Bonnie rolled her eyes. "He's getting on my nerves."

Winslow hummed more loudly and stared at Bonnie. He opened his mouth as he chewed.

"Stop," Ketron warned him.

"What are you going to do about it?" He mimicked the cautionary look she gave the children when they misbehaved.

Bonnie sucked in a breath. None of them had ever been so outwardly hostile toward their mother.

"Go to your room."

Winslow put a hand on his hip. "I'm eating."

Ketron picked up his plate and walked it to the microwave. She shut the microwave door a little harder than she intended.

"So now you're gonna deny your children their food?" Winslow spat.

"You can come back and eat when you have a better attitude."

His hand went to his hip. "I'll have a better attitude when I can live with my dad."

Ketron was fed up with Winslow's behavior, but she kept her temper in check. "I think we need to talk about that."

Winslow closed his mouth, but his bitter expression never softened. "So, can I go live with him now?"

"Not unless you're dead," Marvin said.

In all the commotion, Ketron hadn't heard his door open. He had taken a couple of beer cans to the room with him, and they were both empty. He swayed as he walked to the trash can.

Winslow stood there, trying to process Marvin's words. "Did my dad die?"

Ketron took a few steps toward her son. "Yes, honey. He died before you were born."

"Our dad's right here," Nora spoke up, pointing at Marvin. Bonnie motioned to her mother that she would take care of her sister, and Ketron was relieved when Nora obediently followed her older sister out of the room.

Winslow sat down in his chair. Heavy tears rolled off his cheeks and onto the table. "Now there's no one who can take me out of this family."

"You don't know how good you have it," Marvin slurred. "Oz was my brother. When I was little, he used to let his friends take turns punching me in the stomach to 'toughen me up.' When I was a teenager, he got me hooked on drugs. He told people he always protected me, but he threatened to kill me before he died."

"Maybe you deserved it," Winslow shot at him.

Marvin advanced on him, and Ketron stepped between them. "I think you need to go to your room," she told Marvin.

Marvin looked down at his clinched fists. "You're right." She watched him until his door closed.

Ketron sat down next to her son. They didn't speak for a long time.

Ketron put her arm around Winslow, and he didn't shake her off. She took it as a good sign.

"I never met my father," she told him.

Winslow looked up at her mistrustfully, and he keenly watched her expressions for a lie.

"Didn't you ever wonder about your grandparents on my side of the family?"

"Dad" —he stopped and shook his head— "or whatever he is, told us that your mom was sick in her head, but he didn't talk about your dad."

"I don't usually mention my father," Ketron admitted. "He left before I was born."

"Is that what my dad did?"

"In a way." Ketron wanted to answer him as honestly as possible. After his display over the past few days, she could see that it was best not to shelter him. "He had a drug problem."

"He took drugs?"

"Yes. He took a drug that caused him to get really aggressive. He lived with me for a little while, but he kept hitting me and pushing me while I was pregnant. I told him to leave after he sent me to the hospital with a broken wrist."

Winslow turned away and dug his nail into his plastic placemat. She hadn't won over his sympathy, but he clearly objected to the abuse.

"One day, he didn't have the drug he liked to take. He stole a gun and went to a place where people had the drug, and he demanded it from them. They shot him. He didn't even make it to the hospital."

Winslow put his head down on the table, surrounding it with his arms. He bawled and kicked his legs in his frustration, and his body shook with each sob.

Ketron held him and let him lie against her. Bonnie brought Amelia into the room, and she patted her brother's head. He raised his puffy eyes and bopped her nose.

After every good cry, Ketron enjoyed comfort foods. Since they had already eaten dinner, her mind settled on dessert. "Do you want to share some ice cream with me?" Ketron offered.

Winslow's mood darkened, and he narrowed his eyes at her. "I don't want to do anything from *you*."

Ketron was surprised by his outburst. She tried to search for something that would ease the tension, but commiserating words escaped her.

"You are nothing to me!" He rose from his chair, pointing at her. Bonnie opened her mouth, but Ketron held up a hand to stop her. "You made my dad leave, and you gave me that" —he pointed to Marvin's room— "as a replacement." Winslow stormed off just as Nora rounded the corner. He bumped into her, knocking her onto the floor.

Ketron called after him to apologize to his sister, but he ignored her.

There was nothing she could do. She had often felt unworthy of love and forgiveness, silently accepting the judgement of others instead of defending herself. She had carried her dirty laundry with her, and the stains of her past had only gotten darker with time.

A headache threatened her vision, bringing shadowy edges around her focus. Somewhere in the house, or deep in her mind, laughter echoed.

Ketron eased though the house, following the noise. She wondered if Winslow was crying after he had learned the truth about his father. She hoped she could comfort him and wondered why he hadn't remained in his bed.

The sounds were loudest in the dining room. Light from the outside streetlamp cast long shadows against the fireplace, causing blacks and grays to dance together in the stillness of the night.

The sobs were soft and close together, as if the crier's sadness was immediate and painful. A vibration rose from the fireplace, deep and guttural, as if a sleeping parent had issued a warning to a child that had wondered out of bed during the early morning hours.

The whimpering stopped, and before Ketron looked under the dining room table, a breeze shot up from under it. A voice spoke, and the words echoed in her mind instead of her ears.

Don't forget me.

The morning sun streamed through the windows, reminding her that the shadows of the night were far away, but her mind returned to the sound of the cries she'd heard when the crescent moon shined a Cheshire Cat smile.

She could no longer deny the possibility of another presence when Sonny and Nora shared tea with their "friend". Unlike Jeremy, the entity inspired laughter and harmony instead of gloominess and discord.

The pretend tea party event wouldn't have been mysterious if she hadn't noticed the difference in the contents of the cup after their tea party. She quickly dismissed the notion. *One of the kids drank it*, she told herself, but she knew that they hadn't touched the cup since they sat it in front of their invisible guest.

How many ghosts haunted their home?

Chapter Forty-Seven

Past

Ketron felt pebbles tickling her skin. As soon as they fell around her, others joined them. She could smell the earth, and the aroma was oddly fresh. She sneezed.

"She's awake," her mother said. Or was it Gwynevere?

Ketron carefully opened her eyes. Cold moisture soaked through her clothes, and wet leaves brushed her fingers. She pulled herself up, but her head didn't stick out of the hole.

Her mother, or whatever she was, bent down over her. "Lie back down and go to sleep," she said politely, as if Ketron had only awakened from a bad dream.

Ketron rocked on her feet and put her hands on the side of the non-symmetrical hole. It was the same one she had dug with her dead grandfather when he had invaded her mother's body, but her mother had taken the time to make it much deeper. She tried to climb out, but her bare feet couldn't dig into the hard earth. She reached for her mother's hand.

Her mother batted her away irritably. "Ketron, I told you to lie back down. I don't want to be here all night."

Ketron was groggy and disoriented, but when her mother knocked her lightly over the head with a shovel, a rush of adrenaline caused her to process the situation more clearly. "Let me out."

"Lie down, Ketron."

Ketron stepped on something, and it rattled. The dish of marbles was at her feet.

"Gail," she whispered, but she didn't feel her ghostly presence.

When her mother came into view with more dirt on her shovel, Ketron grabbed two handfuls of marbles and lunged them at her. They pelted her face and hands, but they only seemed to upset her and strengthen her resolve.

Her mother put her hand on her hip. "Now what am I going to do?" She shook her head and spoke to the air. "I can't. You told me the Belladonna would make her sleep until it was over." She moved out of sight. "Well, it's your fault. I poured the amount you told me to, so you take care of it."

One moment Ketron was listening to her mother argue with the silence, and the next moment she was defending herself from a snarling, vicious woman who had jumped into the hole with her. Ketron tried to push her away, but the woman was too strong. As Ketron fought her aunt inside her mother's body, she wondered if anyone would find her in the dark hole. Should she have pretended to stay asleep and let them pile the dirt over her body? Wouldn't she have eventually run out of air?

Her pre-teen body was no match for a full-grown woman. Ketron slipped on the wet earth and her mother/aunt pushed her onto her back. She rose, slapping dirt off her hands. "Now stay down." She spoke it in a voice that was unlike her mother's but still had the same crisp quality.

After some difficulty, she pulled herself out of the makeshift grave and stared down at Ketron. Ketron glared back in defiance, but she didn't challenge her again. It was best to stay there and try to think of another plan. Shovels of dirt landed on her. Most of it covered her feet, but it wasn't long before she was almost submerged.

Ketron wondered if Ky and Ly were camping in their fort. If she called for them, would they hear her?

Ketron's mind wanted her to accept her position. Her mother's narcissistic behavior had desensitized her to the situations that made most children cry, but big tears slid down her cheeks. Big Red wouldn't reach her in time, and Nora and the twins were too far away to hear her cries for help. Her own mother had betrayed her. She wanted to get rid of her daughter so that she could travel with Tom and her dead twin. Ketron started screaming, and tried to stand up, but she couldn't pull free of the dirt around her legs before her mother knocked her back down with the shovel.

"Lie back down or I'll cut your head off!"

Ketron hoped it was Gwynevere who had screamed at her, but she couldn't be sure.

She yelled until her voice was hoarse, but no one replied. She almost hoped the chilly spirits of Pale Woods would attack her mother, but they must have recognized Gwynevieve as one of their own and left her alone.

Ketron could hardly breath through the loose dirt that fell around her face. Soon, her mother would pack the earth over her, making it impossible to breathe fresh air. She tried one more time before the falling soil made it impossible to speak. "I loved you, Mother. Even when you were selfish. Even when you hurt me. I took care of you, and I loved you. No one will love you now."

The dirt stopped showering her for a moment, and Ketron could only hear her heart beating, but then damp earth rained down on her once more.

A hard thud echoed, and a weight was dropped over her body. Ketron had expected her mother to pack dirt over her, but it felt like a couple of sandbags had been thrown onto her. She coughed and grunted, unable to move under the heavy weight. She struggled, but the pressure was too much for her.

"She's in there!" a voice shouted.

"Help me get her out, Ky!"

Ketron recognized Nora's voice, and heard the boys call her name. She was too suffocated to respond to them. It took all her strength to expand her ribs enough to keep the load from crushing her completely.

"I got it. Now pull!"

The burden was lifted, but Ketron still couldn't move. The soil had been pushed against her.

"Ketron!" Ky yelled.

Three sets of fingers dug around her face and neck. She was so close to losing consciousness that she hadn't felt people jump into the hole. When her face was finally freed, she breathed deeply, and choked on lose dirt. It was a hard process, sucking in breath and coughing out wet earth.

They pulled her out, and she sputtered until she vomited. Ky held her hair and Ly rubbed her back.

Her mother lay at the base of a tree in an unconscious heap. Nora produced a bit of rope and tied her mother's hands behind her back, knotting the rope to a root that looked like a twisted hand. Dirt brushed her face and shirt. It had been her mother's body that had fallen on Ketron when she was in the grave.

"I should just bury *her* in that hole!" Nora snapped.

Ky read Ketron's fearful expression. "I'd say your mom'll be out for a while. We hit her on the head pretty hard."

"We?" His brother stopped rubbing Ketron's back to punch his brother in the arm playfully. "*You* hit a home run with her head."

"I'll bet Mama didn't think I'd be usin' my bat for that when she bought it for me." He and Ly chuckled weakly.

"Don't talk about Ketron's mama that way." Nora had looped the rope holding Gwynevieve's hands to the low branch of a nearby tree.

"But she was buryin' her!" Ly spoke incredulously.

"She's still her mother. Your father gets in a whole heap of trouble, but we won't hear strangers say bad things about him, right?"

The boys nodded and said, "We need to call the police, though."

Nora kicked Gwynevieve's foot. "Unless you want me to take care of this. No one would miss—"

Ly put a hand on his aunt's arm. It got her attention and cut her off. Ketron thought she was trying to lighten the situation, but her face never changed. The boys laughed nervously.

"We should probably call the police, Aunt Nora," Ky reasoned.

Nora spit on Gwynevieve and it ran down her unconscious face. She stomped further into the woods, but when the twins called for her, she came back immediately. Ly ran back to Nora's house to call the police. Ketron worried about him the entire time, and Ky's eyes darted around anxiously until his brother returned, covered in sweat and gasping for breaths.

"The police are on their way," he announced.

"Did you have any trouble?" Ky asked. His eyes searched the woods for the spirits that haunted them.

Ly doubled over and held his knees for balance. Once his breathing regulated, he answered his twin. "You know how it is. You always think they're followin' ya, just one step away from grabbin' ya by the neck and pullin' ya into one of their caves."

Ky nodded. "We're lucky that the night wasn't any colder."

The police found them in less than an hour. Nora cautioned the boys not to reveal their position until they were certain that the flashlights bouncing through the dark belonged to law enforcement officers.

Ketron's adrenaline was still rushing through her veins. At first, the police questioned Nora and put Ketron in the back of a police cruiser. Ky and Ly sat on either side of her, and she rested her head on Ly's shoulder. Ky held her hand and played with her fingers. It was an innocent touch to keep her awake.

She kept staring at the grave that her grandfather, aunt, and mother had intended for her. Ketron was amazed that she wasn't buried in it and floating around the Renfro property as a new ghost.

"How did you know?" The words were croaked, but the boys understood them. Her throat was raw from screaming and vomiting. Ly cautioned her to save the remains of her voice for the officer's questions.

Ky looked out the window. His words bounced off the glass, and when she raised her head from Ly's shoulder, she couldn't make out his expression in the reflection. "I heard you."

She knitted her eyebrows together. She had only started screaming moments before they arrived.

The twins shared a meaningful look. Ketron was about to chance her voice again when Ky elaborated. "I heard you in my mind."

Only weeks before, Ketron would have given him an awkward look and brushed off his admission as a joke. She had seen a measure of spirits in a short time, watched as her mother's dissociative personality disorder materialized into ghosts who wanted her dead, and had felt the evil influence of something sinister in the forest. She couldn't dismiss him so easily, especially now that she knew her mother's mind had been as haunted as the Renfro house. She stared at him silently, but she patted his hand. She hoped it would be enough to make him feel comfortable after revealing his secret.

"I think we get it from our father," Ly spoke up. Ky narrowed his eyes and his brother looked out the other window.

"Mom knows things, too."

"She gets her notions from the Farmer's Almanac and old wives' tales," Ly argued without facing Ky.

Ky stared at his brother, dropped his gaze to Ketron, and continued. "Ly and I used to think we could only hear each other. We were twins, and people seemed to accept it when we just sort of knew what the other one was thinking. But we started tellin' them what they were thinkin', and it scared them."

Ly twirled one finger around another in his lap. "Tell her about mom's miscarriage."

Ky sighed. "Our mom can't carry any more babies past a couple of months, but she can still get pregnant." He reached behind Ketron and shoved Ly. Ly's shoulder bounced off the door of the cruiser. "I don't want to tell her about hearin' the babies."

Ly rubbed his arm. "Fine. Tell her about hearin' your wife."

Ky's cheeks almost turned crimson in the muted light of the cab. "I'm not talkin' about that either. And she's not my wife yet." He shook his head. "Look, I can hear voices in my head. My brother can only hear my voice in his mind, but sometimes he can hear other thoughts because he can hear my mind."

Ketron nodded her understanding.

"We were in bed when I heard you wake up and yell in your head. You may not have known it, but you were afraid, and you pushed fear out in all directions." He stopped and attempted to clarify his point. "It was like you sent out radio waves when you were scared, and I heard them. I knew your mom's mind wasn't right, so I woke up Ly, grabbed my bat, and we high-tailed it over to Aunt Nora's house. She'd had gotten a call from some man who said you were in trouble, so she was already ready to go over to your house."

"Big Red?" Ketron croaked.

Both boys put a hand on her arm to keep her from speaking.

Ky was the first to withdraw his touch. "Maybe. I think she said his name was John, though. They've been talkin' on the phone about you for a couple of weeks."

Tears fell from Ketron's eyes without warning. Big Red had found a way to keep an eye on her.

Ky finished his explanation simply. "She followed us through the woods, and we ran toward the sound of your voice when we heard you cryin' for help. I guess you know the rest."

Ketron tested Ky's ability. *You found me by following my mind?*

Ky's eyes grew wide when he received her message. Glad that she had believed him, he said, "You went quiet for a while. I guess your mom gave you something to knock you out."

Yeah. She gave me something with Bella *in its name. But I was quiet because she was covering me with dirt, and I didn't think anyone could hear me when I was screaming.*

He nodded. "It makes it a little harder to pick up thoughts, even when the drug isn't at its strongest. If she had used a Belladonna plant from Pale Woods, then I wouldn't have heard you at all. I was worried when I couldn't hear you for a minute, but I knew you weren't dead, because—"

Ly threw him a daggered look that stopped his words.

"Anyway," Ky continued. "We found you, and you're going to be okay."

Ketron stared at her hands. Mud caked into her fingernails and the creases around her knuckles. *Thank you.*

The boys wrapped their arms around her, and they stayed that way, falling asleep together.

Chapter Forty-Eight

Present

The phone buzzed in her ear and the familiar melody of a call echoed through the room. Ketron tried to focus on the number, but her eyes would hardly open. She was finally able to slide the screen to answer the phone.

"Mom, where are you?" Bonnie asked. "I've been waiting for ten minutes."

"What?" Ketron bounced off the couch. Her stomach revolted, and Ketron held it, as if the palm resting on her midsection would prevent it from spewing its contents. Amelia wasn't beside her, so she hadn't woken her. Shauna had picked up Winslow, Nora, and Sonny from school so Ketron could take a nap. She must have dozed off while the baby was playing in one of her siblings' bedrooms. She ran from room to room searching for the baby while Bonnie spoke.

"The coach can't wait all day for you to pick me up. She has a life."

"I'll be there as soon as I get your sister in the van," she told her, and Bonnie hung up. Ketron would never get used to the abruptness of teenage phone calls.

Ketron called the baby's name, but there was no answer. She stood quietly and listened to see if she could pinpoint her child's location, but there were no gentle baby sounds or quiet rustlings.

She slung up the bed covers and looked under the table. She opened every kitchen cabinet and checked the front and back doors. The dead bolts were locked, but Amelia was gone. Ketron screamed for her baby. She ran outside and circled the house. Mrs. Franks noticed her and hurried over.

"What's wrong, Ketron?"

Ketron was suddenly aware that whatever she said would determine whether her children were ever left in her care again. She lied so fast that it surprised her.

"The man," she told her neighbor. "The man in the black car took Amelia." Ketron was already shaken and terrified for her daughter, so she didn't have to sell her story to Mrs. Franks.

"No!" Mrs. Franks sucked in air, and said, "I'll call 9-1-1."

Thirty minutes later, Mrs. Franks had brought Bonnie back home, and she stood with Ketron while she embellished on the story she had originally told her neighbor. "He had a black car," she repeated.

"Do you remember a make or model?" a kind police officer asked. The radio on his shoulder squawked with activity as he wrote down notes on a silver notebook.

"It may have been a Camry. I don't know. It happened so fast!"

"I understand, ma'am. How did he get the child?"

Ketron took a deep breath. "I was buckling her into the car seat, and he pushed me onto the ground, grabbed her, and ran to the car before I could get up."

"Had you buckled her into the seat yet?"

Ketron shook her head.

He turned to Mrs. Franks. "Did you witness any of this?"

"No, I just saw Ketron Gouge running through her yard screaming for her daughter." It sounded more like Mrs. Franks was giving a testimony in a court, instead of helping an officer file a report.

Marvin pulled into the driveway. Ketron had forgotten to call him, and he was livid with her when he learned that Amelia was missing.

After the police left, Ketron could only pace. Finally, she decided she needed to talk to someone who might not send her to a room with padded walls. Bonnie came along reluctantly.

Lisa's door fell open when she knocked, and they stepped inside. "Lisa?"

"I'm right here," Lisa yelled from the back of the house. She joined them in the living room and sat on the couch. "I heard. How're you holdin' up?"

"I don't know what to do," Ketron told her. "She was gone when I woke up. Do you think Jeremy took her?"

"I don't rightly know, but I wouldn't rule it out."

"Mama, you're scaring me," Bonnie cried, pulling on her mother's hand. "I thought you said a man in a black car took Amelia?"

Ketron didn't have time to fill Bonnie in on the truth about the ghostly occurrences in their home, so she dismissed her cries. "How can I get her back?"

The yorkie Ketron thought Lisa had referred to as Annie hopped onto Lisa's lap. "I'd imagine you gotta find her. Jeremy's most powerful inside the house, so she's probably somewhere close by."

Bonnie darted out the door, and Ketron was rattled by her rudeness. "I'm sorry. We barged into your house, and I didn't even introduce you to Bonnie." She glanced in the direction her oldest daughter had gone. "Do you think I upset her?"

Lisa just smiled. "There's no tellin' with teenagers." She pointed at a display of trinkets. "Look in the white dish with pink flowers."

Ketron obediently followed her command. She lifted two stones from the dish.

"It was a Cash Family Pottery piece that my mama passed down when she died," Lisa said, referencing the dish.

Ketron tried to put the stones in Lisa's hand, but she waved them away. "Those are for your daughter." She pointed to her porch, where, presumably, Bonnie was waiting for her mother. "Tell her to put them in her pocket. Make sure she keeps them there until you find a way to send Jeremy out of the house."

Ketron studied the two stones and wondered if they had crystal-like qualities. The black one was a smooth, palm-sized stone with no markings. Lisa confirmed that it was a black onyx and told her that Bonnie should keep it by her bed when she wasn't carrying it. The other stone was as dark as the onyx and semi-translucent when Ketron held it up to the afternoon sunlight pushing through the window.

"Apache tears obsidian." Lisa rubbed a hand down the length of Annie's back. "It's a pretty stone. Good for healin'. I picked it up after my husband died."

Ketron hoped Lisa wasn't waiting for her to have an epiphany just because she held the stones. Ketron didn't believe in the spiritual power of objects. She believed in people. People made decisions and they had to live with the consequences. Ketron had ignored the signs of a possible dissociative disorder affecting her life and now she was paying the price for it.

Lisa read her hesitation to comment on her gift. "I'm not givin' 'em to you. Your mind needs to be opened before it will receive what those stones have to offer. "Your child, though, she needs some protection, and she accepts more of the mystery in this world."

Ketron felt the urge to run back home and search every inch of the house for Amelia. At the very least, she needed to be there if the police called with an update, even though she knew they wouldn't have one.

Ketron closed her hand over the stones. "I'll have Bonnie thank you for your gifts the next time we see you. You never told me about Joseph, though. Could his story help me find Amelia?"

"I doubt it," Lisa said. "Joseph drank until he drowned in it."

"What do you mean?" Ketron thought she already knew the answer to her own question.

"One night he drank until he was too far gone to roll over when he vomited."

"He asphyxiated." Ketron's statement hung in the air until she asked, "Do you think Jeremy kept Joseph from rolling over?"

Lisa shrugged her shoulders. "I can't say for sure, but Jeremy certainly didn't help him."

Ketron's frustration bubbled over. "He's dead! How can he affect the world around him? Why can he move things, hold people down in their own vomit, or steal babies away from their mothers?"

She was close to tears when Lisa spoke. "I don't have all the answers, and there are things in this world that go past the reach of our minds. Best I can guess is that our souls have energy. Sometimes, that energy may get recycled when we die, but other times it lingers."

The need to go back home almost physically pushed her. Before she left, Ketron asked, "Is there anything else I can do?"

Lisa smiled sadly. "I think you know what you need to do, even though you may not want to." She winked. "You have everything you need to overpower that spirit's influence over your family, but you have to come to terms with who you are. You are a vessel, and spirits know it."

Ketron startled. "I'm a vessel?"

Lisa nodded. "I picked up on it the day I gave you the cucs. You absorb the energy around you, and it lets spirits in."

"Are you saying that you've seen me possessed by something?"

Lisa's face dropped into a grave expression. "I saw you at the bank a couple of weeks ago. You waved at me, but you didn't speak. It was like you had another person's smile on your face. And you held the baby different." She modeled the way she had seen Ketron carrying Amelia. "You held her out a bit, like you didn't really want her to touch you."

Ketron was struck by a possibility. "Do you think Marvin's been possessed? He acts differently, and he started drinking when we moved. Could Joseph's spirit have possessed him?"

Lisa held up her hand. "Now hold on. Not everyone can host a spirit, and I don't think your husband can do it." She softened her voice and looked at the wall. "I think he's sad. He may have started drinkin' because he feels somethin' in the house, but it's only touched him. It's not inside him."

Ketron thought she understood. Marvin's spirit wasn't soluble enough to accept a ghostly presence, but his actions could be influenced by the mood in the house.

"I still don't know what to do, Lisa. What if I can't find my baby?"

Lisa shook her head, "Pray, honey. Pray that she's not been pulled into the darkness."

Ketron ran to her house, still holding Bonnie's hand. The teen was horrified, but she allowed herself to be led. She accepted the stones her mother shoved into her hand and put them into her pocket.

"Why did you take something out of that lady's house?"

Ketron answered her between breaths. "She gave them to me. She wanted you to have them and keep them in your pocket or beside your bed."

Bonnie unleashed a string of other questions as their feet pounded down the hill. "What's going on, Mom? Who is Jeremy, and why would he have Amelia? Didn't you say a man in a black car took her? Did you know him? Was his name Jeremy?"

Ketron didn't want to answer her flood of questions, but she did her best to touch on a few of them. "I'm trying to find your sister and I'm exploring every possibility. Jeremy is the ghost in our house." She thought about her words and amended them. "Well, he's one of the ghosts in our house."

Bonnie stopped running. When she realized that her mother wasn't going to come back for her, she caught up to her. Her lips pressed together and every line on her forehead showed.

Ketron burst through the door. She ran through the house and Bonnie shut herself in her room.

Ketron looked in cabinets and under beds again. She slung everything out of the closets and plastic totes, but she couldn't find Amelia.

She collapsed on the floor in front of the twins' closet, screaming words she'd never remember and yelling prayers she hoped were answered. "Please, please, bring her back."

She didn't know when Marvin's arm surrounded her, but she welcomed the warmth when she felt it. "We'll find her," he promised, kissing the top of her head.

"It's all my fault!" she cried, squeezing a handful of her hair at the roots.

Marvin shushed her, pulling her hand away and covering it with his own. "No, it's not. You're a good mother, and you always look out for the children. No one blames you."

"Of course I'm to blame!" she yelled. Marvin tried to console her, but she weakly pushed him away. "My body failed my baby last time, and my mind failed my baby today!"

Marvin didn't ask why she thought her mind had failed her. "You're just upset, Ket. Any mother would be—"

"Mother?" Ketron questioned. "I'm a terrible mother! What mother can't even keep a baby alive in her womb or allows her to be taken from under her nose?"

Marvin put both his arms around her. "Listen. We'll get Amelia back." He paused, and his hold on her weakened. "As far as Solomon goes, he and Sonny were born early. His lungs just weren't—"

"But Sonny's were!" Ketron cried. "Sonny had a perfect set of lungs, and he was just as old as his brother when my labor started."

"I know. I know." He rocked her gently, massaging her arms. "It's not fair. I didn't want to say goodbye to Solomon so soon."

Ketron cringed when her husband said their son's name. Every time she heard it or said it, a wound opened and guilt and frustration washed fresh pain over her until she was buried in sorrow. "I didn't want to say goodbye at all!"

He held her closer. "Of course not. I know you loved him."

Ketron tried to stand up, but she fell in a heap in front of the twins' bunk beds, and Marvin dropped to his knees beside her.

"S-She's s-scared. I just know it." She didn't bother to wipe away the tears and snot that ran off her face. "What w-will she eat?" she wailed pitifully. As if in response to her question, Ketron's breasts swelled with milk, and it brought on a fresh wave of sobs. She looked up at the ceiling, hoping Jeremy or God would hear her and grant her request. "Please give me my baby back!"

Chapter Forty-Nine

Present

At some point, she fell asleep in Marvin's arms, but when she woke, he was in the kitchen pulling open the refrigerator. She hadn't felt him carry her to the couch and cover her with a blanket. She wrapped the blanket around her and walked into the kitchen.

She heard gurgling, and she was shocked. "What are you doing?"

He turned around with the empty beer can as the contents of it popped and sizzled down the drain. He unhooked the last beer from the ring that held the top and repeated the process. "It was time."

Ketron put her arms around him from behind and locked them around his waist. "It was *past* time."

He held her hand and finished pouring out the beer with his other hand. "I know."

Ketron breathed in the smell of hops and hoped it would be the last time she smelled it in their home. She was grateful for her husband's initiative to fight his addiction and she hoped that their family could start to heal once they had found Amelia.

"You know, I think about him sometimes," he said, continuing their conversation before Ketron's body had given out from emotional exhaustion. A touch of sentiment lined his words. "I think about what he would look like, what he'd play with—"

"Stop."

"No. I think we need to talk about it." His voice wasn't unkind, and he looked at her, searching for her eyes. When she was brave enough to meet his gaze, he spoke, "I loved him, too."

Ketron nodded slowly. "There are times when I think I see him and feel him."

The words came out before she realized she had spoken them. She hadn't rolled around the idea she had conveyed to her husband, but she realized it was true. The boy who was Sonny's size and had crawled under the table while she made doughnuts, the imaginary friend who played with Sonny, and the mysterious spectral embrace were all traces of Solomon.

To her surprise, Marvin didn't try to brush off her statement or use it to illustrate the similarities between Ketron and her mother. "I've felt the same way, especially lately."

"What do you mean?"

He stared out the dark window and blew a long puff of air out of his nose. "There were nights that I'd stumble in here, not needin' more alcohol, but wantin' it anyway. I'd try to open the refrigerator to get another beer, but the refrigerator wouldn't open. I told myself that I was too drunk to open it, but I could open the freezer. It felt like someone was pushin' against the refrigerator." He pulled her closer to him, wanting to hold her against his chest, but Ketron leaned back and watched his face. "I was layin' on my back one night, and I started to feel a little reflux. I breathed it in, and I was too drunk to move. The next thing I knew, I was on my side, coughin' and hackin'." He looked down at Ketron, and a tear dropped out of his eye, landing on her chin. She made no move to wipe it away. "I think Solomon saved me."

"He hugged me," she volunteered. "I'd had a hard day, and he found a way to let me know he loved me. At the time, I didn't know it was him, but I know it now. I think he stays close to Sonny." The admission caused her to dip her head. Since she and Marvin had started to break apart, she was used to feeling shame for making comments that hinted at anything unnatural.

He lifted her chin. "We *will* find our daughter, and we'll bring her home." He sighed, rubbing her arms, and looking around the silent house. "I think we should go get the children. It's too quiet around here, and I want them with us."

Ketron had called Shauna while she had waited for the police and Shauna had agreed that it was best for Winslow, Nora, and Sonny to stay with her. Ketron missed them, though, and she wanted them close to her. "Let me call Detective Lawson first and see if he's had any leads." She spoke the words with little hope in her heart and returned defeated within moments.

Marvin took her in his arms. "We'll find her."

"You can't be sure of that." Her voice was flat. She didn't have the energy to fight with him. Marvin had only been a father to Amelia in the sense that he sired her. He couldn't possibly know what Ketron was going through.

"Go get Bonnie. We'll go to Shauna's house together." He released her, and she shuffled away. "It will be good for you to see the children," he added. "They always make you feel better."

"Mommy, I drew a cat!"

Ketron took the paper Nora held out to her. "It's a pretty cat. You did a great job."

"Can we have a cat?"

Ketron smiled weakly. "Maybe one day, but" —she pointed to the color of the subject in the drawing — "probably not a purple one."

Sonny ran to Marvin and hugged him tightly. "I played with Matty all the time, but I missed you. Why didn't you pick me up after work?"

Marvin's voice caught when he spoke to his son. "Mommy and I had some things we needed to sort out."

Sonny reached out to Ketron and included her in the embrace. "I didn't like staying here so long without my mommy and my sister."

Ketron sobbed, and no matter how hard she tried, she couldn't keep the tears from rolling off her checks.

Winslow stood away from his siblings and parents with his arms crossed. "I like it here. Can I just stay with Shauna?"

Nora glanced up in alarm. She had never spent the night away from her twin.

Ketron couldn't look at him. One part of her wanted to grant his wish and the other part wanted to hug him until he hugged her back, no matter how long it took. The former would keep the peace during an already trying time, and the latter would make him struggle against her even more.

"I don't think so," Marvin told him.

Winslow narrowed his eyes at his parents. "Whatever. Where's the baby?"

"We'll talk to you about it at home." Ketron tried to keep it together, and Shauna rescued her from explaining further.

"Do you want to grab one of the sugar cookies to eat on the way home?" She brushed his hair to the side, and he allowed the touch. Ketron was secretly thankful. At least her son had someone who was a comfort to him.

Ketron had called Shauna on their way to pick up the children. Shauna argued that bringing the younger children home would be too much for Ketron, but she relented when she noted the exhaustion and despair in her friend's voice.

After Ketron loaded all the children into the van, forcing her eyes away from the baby's empty car seat, she climbed into the driver's seat. Her cell phone vibrated, but it was only a spammy text.

"Any news?" Shauna mouthed.

Ketron shook her head. Her friend hugged her, and they held each other for a long moment.

"Call me when you hear something."

Ketron nodded, but she wondered if they would ever hear anything. And if they found Amelia, would she be alive?

Chapter Fifty

Present

Ketron tried to get through the night. Bonnie played with her siblings, but all her jokes fell flat after the younger children learned about their sister's disappearance. Winslow was especially introspective. He hardly touched his late-night snack, and he was brisk with Nora whenever she spoke to him.

"Did you take her somewhere?" he asked Ketron suddenly. "Did you give her to another family?"

Ketron and Marvin had been passing around bowls of ice cream, and Winslow's words disrupted the quiet acceptance in the house. Ketron could only stare at her son.

Marvin took a firmer hand. "That's enough, son."

"Oh, I'm your son now." He stood up and shoved in his chair. His ice cream bowl slid off his placemat and onto the floor. "You act like I don't exist, unless I make you mad, and you're not even my *real* father!"

Nora's eyes were wide, but Ketron doubted that she understood her brother's accusations. Nora picked up her baby doll and held her close.

Ketron's thoughts shifted to cleaning up the ice cream before Amelia got into it, but then she remembered that her baby wouldn't see the mess. Who knew if she had even eaten? Ketron had expressed her milk twice since Amelia had been missing, and she tried to recall the last time she'd fed her. She could eat other food, but was she getting table food or even water?

"Just go to your room," he told Winslow. Marvin's fingers rubbed his temples.

Ketron noticed a grayness in his pallor. How long had it been since he'd had alcohol?

"Gladly," spat Winslow. "I don't need this family anyway."

Nora started crying, and Bonnie slung her spoon into her bowl. Little white drops of vanilla scattered across her arm. "You're such a drama king. Our little sister is missing, but you have to make this about you."

"Whatever." It seemed to be Winslow's new favorite word. He stomped off. Moments later, Ketron heard his favorite show echo down the hall. She caught bits of a conversation she assumed he was having with himself.

"Are you *my* father?" Sonny stared up at Marvin.

He swooped his son into his arms. "Yes! I am your daddy, and you are daddy's boy."

"Am I your daughter?" Nora asked.

Ketron stepped in for her husband. "What is a daddy?"

Nora scrunched up her face. "It's a *daddy*."

Ketron had expected her confused reply. "What does a daddy do?"

"They help you ride your bike and tell you about video games."

Ketron smiled. "Then this is your daddy." She motioned to Marvin.

When Ketron dragged out the blankets to take them to the chaise lounge, Marvin took them to his bed. Sonny had fallen asleep on the couch.

Ketron hesitantly followed him to their bed. They sought comfort in each other's arms, and after they dressed, Marvin carried Sonny from the couch to sleep with them. They each put an arm around their sleeping son and held hands as they fell asleep.

Chapter Fifty-One

Present

The moist earth gathered around her, filling the hole and erasing her from her mother's life. Ketron watched it fall and settle, blinking the dust away when it landed in her eyes. How could a mother bury her child alive?

Ketron woke with a start. Her heart pounded so loudly she was certain that everyone in the house could hear it. Her mother had tried to bury her in the hole outside the old Renfro home years ago. Would Ketron have done the same to her baby?

Ketron's hands had been free from dirt, but she could have washed them before she was conscious of her own actions again. The hole wouldn't have been large. She may have even used the same grave her mother had dug when she had tried to kill Ketron

She eased out of bed, slipping her fingers out of her husband's hand. After grabbing her keys and phone, she jumped in the van and drove to the Renfro property. Someone else owned it, but no one had lived in the house for years. The owners had tried to rent it out, but strange accidents that happened to the tenants kept the house empty.

Ketron wasted no time. She had a flashlight in her van's emergency kit, and she took it. She thought about bringing the road flare but left it in the van. She wished she had a shovel, but she would dig with her bare hands if necessary.

Thoughts of her sweet baby flashed through her mind. Amelia had just experienced a developmental spike. She even picked up blocks and threw them into a bucket. She liked to toddle to the edge of the couch and throw herself into Ketron's awaiting arms.

The old Renfro house blurred as she ran, tears distorting her vision, but she had been there many times in her nightmares, and her traumatized mind guided her. Ketron remembered where the grave had been dug for her, even though she hadn't returned to the spot in years. At least to her knowledge anyway. She ran alongside the creek and into Pale Woods.

Her phone rang in her pocket. She had forgotten to set it to vibrate before she went to sleep.

"Where are you?" Marvin sounded breathless and frightened.

"I'm at my mother's old house," she told him. She had shared her past with him years ago, so she didn't have to elaborate.

"Why are you there?" he yelled, his fear making him agitated. "What's going on? Did they call you about Amelia?"

Ketron was honest with her husband. "No one called. I had a dream, and I remembered something from my childhood. I'm going to look for Amelia where my mother tried to bury me."

"Wha— Why would you look for her there?" When Ketron wouldn't answer him, he said, "No, Ket. I'm on my way."

"You can't leave the children." Her argument sounded weak, even to her.

"Bonnie can stay here with them," he answered resolutely.

"But she's only thirteen." Ketron pushed through a clearing and made her way deeper into the woods.

"She'll be fourteen next month, and they're all asleep." She could hear his keys clinking. "I'll be there soon." He hung up before she could argue.

Memories whipped through her mind as fast as the branches whizzed by her face. She ran through the woods, following the same trails she had run with Ky and Ly years ago. They had mostly avoided that section of the woods after her mother was taken to the mental institution, though.

After John Winslow adopted her, he and Nora started talking frequently over the phone. Big Red and Ketron visited her every weekend, staying in a local motel at night and spending the days with Nora on her farm. She had just gotten used to the school in his town, when he announced that they were moving to Erwin to live with Nora. Big Red was an old-fashioned man, and he insisted that he and Nora were married before he and Ketron spent the night at her house.

Nora wanted a small wedding at the county courthouse, but Big Red told her that her first marriage should be more special, so they had a quiet ceremony at a nearby church. Nora was treated like a queen all day, and Ky's and Ly's mother was her matron of honor. Ketron was the flower girl, and Ky and Ly were ring bearers.

A couple of months after Ky had pinged her mother on the head with his baseball bat, Ketron had found Ly alone at the fort, and he had told her that Ky had taken a shovel to the hole and was going to fill it. Ketron didn't have to ask him what he meant. When Ky walked into the fort several hours later, with dirt on his hands and the knees of his jeans, Ketron knew that he had completed the job. They never spoke about it again.

She thought the hole had been closer to the house, and perhaps she was turned around from following the line of the property. The house could be closer than she realized, but the dark line of trees obscured a view of anything but their dead leaves and stark branches. Finally, she recognized the tree with the gnarled root, like a hand reaching out of the ground.

Her hands tore through the earth as echoes from her past ripped her apart. She threw clumps of dirt behind her as she snatched handfuls of soil from the same place where she had almost been buried alive and let the memories overwhelm her.

Chapter Fifty-Two

My baby lay motionless. No matter how much I willed the eyes to open, or to see a breath inflate the small, rounded body, my little darling stayed still. Tiny fingers wound into a palm, heavily indented with lifelines of unrealized lifetimes. Had the hand been reaching for me? How long did the fingers stretch before the attempt was futile?

I had so much hope for the future of my children. Each life held a promise and potential, golden and shining, but my baby would never hold a diploma high in celebration or call me with the news of a treasured partner.

Where had I been when my baby had needed me? What was I doing when my precious child had looked to me as a safeguard against the swirling abyss of death? Was I even aware, or was this just another consequence of the illness that had been genetically bequeathed to me? I was my mother's daughter. I knew that the occasional blackouts were a symptom of the same disease that had taken over my mother's mind. I had always condemned her for letting it possess her, but now I was guilty of the same inaction. I had heard the voices. I had seen the signs.

I hadn't wanted to be taken away from my children. I feared sitting passively in a numb room with medicated zombies as I was slowly erased from the memories of my children. The victim of my denial and subsequent neglect, was my own treasured child.

I was supposed to be the protector, but I hadn't even heard a cry. I was right there, and I never heard a sound. Had there been pain or screams for me while I was in that other state, that place my mind went when the disease invaded my consciousness? I was the one who was meant to keep the shadows away, but my child, my sweet baby, had been swallowed by the darkness.

I was there, and I didn't even remember how it happened.

Chapter Fifty-Three

Present

Marvin wrapped his arms around her the same way he had in the delivery room when they had shared a loss four years ago. "Did you think she was here?"

"Yes." Ketron's eyes had been locked on the familiar grave. She had lost track of time, even though she had stayed in her body, most of her consciousness had slid out so she didn't have to process the suffering she had felt on that terrible night.

"Did you think your mother put her here?"

Ketron stared at the dark earth on her hands and shook her head. "I know better than that. She's dead."

Marvin's voice took on an unfamiliar tone. "Did you think that you put her here?"

Ketron answered her husband honestly. "I didn't know. I had to see."

Marvin pulled her to him like he was trying to anchor her. "Ket, you are not like your mother. I may have said some things when we argued, but I trust you with the kids."

His words meant more to her than he would ever know. "But where is she?"

"You told the officer about the black car. Now we just have to let the police do their job." He studied her profile. "You did tell the police the truth, didn't you?"

"Yes," she replied. She still didn't trust her husband completely.

Chapter Fifty-Four

They pulled into the driveway. Ketron expected Marvin to get out of his truck, but he sat with it idling until she approached his driver's side window.

"I'm going to pick up some cigarettes," he told her.

"What?"

Marvin had given up smoking cigarettes when they met. It was the lesser of his addictions, but Ketron had been adamantly against having smoke around Bonnie.

"I'm dying for a beer," he admitted. "I think the cigarettes will take my mind off of it." He flipped the knobs on the radio as an excuse not to meet her eyes. "I won't smoke in the house."

Ketron felt completely drained. She didn't tell him that he was trading one habit for another. She turned around and walked into the house. His truck grumbled down the hill, possibly waking everyone in their neighborhood.

She opened the door and sat down at the dining room table. She felt completely defeated. She was trying to choose between crawling back in bed or taking a warm shower when she heard it.

It was a scratchy sound, much like the noises she'd heard when the birds had been in her chimney. The closer to the fireplace she drew, the louder it sounded. It was coming from the mantle as if it were buried beneath it. She tried to lift the stones, but they had been cemented into place decades before she had moved into the house.

She heard the noise again, and she was certain it was a whimper. Had Jeremy put the baby in the fireplace?

She slung open the glass grate. The hole in the back corner of the fireplace echoed her baby's cries.

The cries were constant, but distant.

She crawled through the jagged rocks that littered the basement's crawl space. She closed her eyes and let the sounds guide her.

It was almost like someone had been living in their basement, stealing the things they wanted. She could make out some objects, while others remained a mystery in the lack of light. String, denim pants, a ball, and a board game with rattling dice were in her path. She put her hand on a thick wad of crinkling paper, but she left it. She felt something she thought was a snake, but it turned out to be a cord.

Her hands landed on soft fabric. A blanket. She heard the cries more loudly, but they were just above a strained whisper. Ketron grabbed at the ground, cutting herself on something sharp. Finally, her hands touched soft skin, chilled from the lack of heat. She gathered the baby into her arms and blinked her eyes, but she was unable to see.

"Ket! What are you doing?" Crashing sounds followed her husband's attempt to climb into the hole in the wall.

Ketron cried over her daughter, reassured by the baby's movements. She pulled out her breast, and a weak mouth took hold. Amelia choked and coughed when Ketron's milk came down, and she wouldn't take the nipple again.

Marvin reached them with his hands. Ketron's eyes still couldn't adjust to the deep dark.

"What—?" He felt the baby and gasped. "Is that Amelia?"

Ketron couldn't answer him. She was too emotional.

Marvin took her hand. "Get her out of this place."

He had meant for Ketron to carry the baby out of the basement, but Ketron wanted to get her as far away from the house as possible.

Chapter Fifty-Five

Present

Most of Amelia's siblings rejoiced around her. Winslow was the only one who preferred sleeping over celebrating the return of his sister.

Marvin suggested calling an ambulance, but Ketron took Amelia to the emergency room herself. She rushed through the sliding double doors, but it wasn't like the scenes in the movies. The medical staff worked with the baby quickly, but they were unaware of Amelia's disappearance. Ketron filled them in on the circumstances, repeated her lie about the abduction, and relived the recent rescue.

Her nurse, a middle-aged man with golden flecks in his blue eyes, asked questions about Amelia. "How long ago did you find her?"

Ketron tried to be as specific as possible, but she couldn't remember the exact time. "About forty-five minutes ago."

"Where was she?"

"She was in the farthest corner of the basement, just under the fireplace."

Her answer caused him to pause with a stethoscope over Amelia's lungs. Ketron told herself that he was listening for the baby's breaths, but his eyebrows met, and his jaw clenched. His face was more relaxed when he removed the stethoscope. "Are you and the baby safe at home?"

She had been asked the same question by health professionals almost her entire life. It was part of the procedure, especially when there were injuries with dodgy circumstances, but Ketron was almost always caught off-guard by it. Her answer was complicated this time, though. Were they still in danger? Had Jeremy vanished, and would he leave them alone? She finally decided that the nurse needed a response about their immediate physical situation. "Yes."

He nodded as if he had expected her answer and rubbed Amelia's cheek. Her somber expression didn't change, but she followed his finger when he held it in front of her. Ketron wanted to cry over the change in Amelia, but she was determined to have her health evaluated first. She held her baby and thanked God that she'd heard her pitiful cries.

The nurse took Amelia's temperature and measured her oxygen saturation level. He informed Ketron that Amelia would be placed on IV fluids, and he would wait on the doctor to order tests. "Have you informed the police?" His voice was a little harder, and Ketron wondered if he had judged her as the person who had put Amelia in the basement or the individual who had allowed bad things to befall her baby due to her negligence.

She felt like she deserved his silent accusations, so Ketron kept her eyes on the floor or on Amelia. "No, I brought her straight here. You can call Detective Lawson. He's been working on her case."

"The doctor will be in soon." The nurse left quietly, closing the door behind him.

Ketron wondered how many people would believe her story when they found out where she had found Amelia. Would they think she had hidden her baby in the dark basement? She shook her head. Amelia was the main concern, so Ketron would stick to her story and feign ignorance over Amelia's reappearance. Even though she resolved to focus on Amelia's immediate circumstances, Ketron's mind kept wondering if she would be charged with reckless endangerment or neglect.

The nurse reappeared only to place a catheter in Amelia's vein and attach a bag of fluids to it. The infant didn't even flinch when her skin was broken.

Ketron held Amelia close and whispered to her. "What happened to you, sweet baby" She caressed her cheek, but Amelia's eyes didn't move. "You must have been so scared." Ketron lifted her shirt and offered Amelia her breast. When the infant finally took it, Ketron was relieved, until Amelia let go seconds later. She held the baby closely, and her eyes closed.

Ketron thought three short raps on the door signaled the doctor's arrival, but Detective Lawson entered the room. He was dressed in olive slacks and a white shirt with the county's emblem over his heart. He rubbed a hand across his hairless head before he wheeled the small round seat in front of Ketron and sat down.

"How is she?" he asked, motioning to Amelia.

Ketron put her hand over Amelia's back and rubbed it absentmindedly. "She's alive, but she's so scared that she won't even nurse."

He glanced at his notes. "She was missing for about thirteen hours, so she's likely traumatized by whatever happened during that time. Did you see any marks on her?"

"No."

"That's good." Ketron expected him to write down her answer in his notes, but he continued interviewing her. "Has she been checked by a doctor?"

"Not yet. I thought you were the doctor when you knocked."

He nodded. "They're going to check her thoroughly. Have you changed her diaper?"

His question was an attempt to see if Amelia had been sexually abused without outright asking it. "I changed her diaper a few minutes ago. Everything seemed the same, but the doctor can look more closely when he comes in."

"She," Detective Lawson corrected her. "I think Dr. Sing is visiting the ER rooms tonight. Both of the usual doctors are sick."

Detective Lawson asked her detailed questions about the way in which she found Amelia and the reason she thought she had been left there. Ketron answered all his questions with thoughts of maintaining her innocence. "I honestly don't know why someone would put her there. Maybe she cried too much, and they rethought their actions. Maybe they wanted to bring her back, but they didn't want to be seen doing it."

"Is your basement usually unlocked?"

Ketron thought about his question. "No, but I don't know if the door stays locked now. Before today, I haven't been down there since I almost stepped on a snake."

He wrote on an unlined piece of white paper. "Do you have any windows in the basement?" he asked without looking up.

"We have a couple. I think there are" —she paused while she counted them in her head — "six."

The artificial light bounced off his head when he bobbed it in response to her answer. "Are any of the windows broken?"

"One of the screens may be loose on one of them, but it'd be a really tight fit for someone."

"I sent an officer ahead of me to check it out," he informed her.

Ketron's mind went to the children. "Were the children upset when they saw him?"

He finished his notes and looked up at her. "I think they were all at school, except for the youngest one." He pointed his pen at Amelia. "The youngest one besides her."

Ketron smiled. "Sonny must have decided to stay behind with his dad."

"My deputy said your husband and son were sleeping." He rose from the swiveling chair. "You could use some sleep, too, I suspect. Try to get some rest while your little one is out."

"Okay," Ketron replied, doubting that she would sleep any time soon.

"Do you think it was someone in the family who did this?"

Ketron shook her head. "Aside from the people in my house, my husband and I don't have close family members."

"How sad." Upon noticing Ketron's bewildered look he added, "It's sad that you don't have other family. I don't know what I would do without my dad."

Ketron's thoughts brushed her late biological father, but they settled on John Winslow, her only true father. "Yes, my parents died in a fire almost ten years ago. I named my twins after them."

By the time she was ready to have Nora and Winslow, Marvin had proposed. She decided to take his last name, but she didn't want to lose the name Big Red had given her when he had adopted her.

"I'm sorry," the detective said, patting her knee. It was a sincere gesture of sympathy and Ketron appreciated it. "They were in one of the fires on the Miller properties, right?" He shook his head. "It was the strangest thing. It was almost like they started out of nowhere. And on the same night, too."

Ketron remembered that night very well. Kyle had woken her so she could answer her ringing phone. Ky, who, due to a traumatic event in his life, had changed his name to Johnny, cried hysterically over his mother and aunt. Somehow, his father had made it out of the house alive. Ketron could hardly process the loss. She and Johnny held each other during the funeral, flanked by their spouses and children. They both felt like orphans, even though some of their parents were technically alive.

Ketron expressed her appreciation over Detective Lawson's condolences and hoped it would end the conversation. She'd had enough involvement with ghosts. She didn't want to dig up any more.

The baby was dehydrated. She received fluids through an IV all morning. After the doctor examined her, she saw no need for other tests. She gave Ketron a choice: Amelia could stay at the hospital for another day, or she could go home. Due to the recent influx of flu patients and the hospital renovations, the hospital beds were full. If Ketron chose to stay at the hospital with Amelia, her daughter would be moved to the hallway and could wait most of the day for a room to become available. Ketron was confident that the baby was physically okay, so she opted to go home.

Dr. Sing prompted her to follow up with Amelia's pediatrician as soon as possible. The doctor wanted to be certain that Amelia would eat before she sent her home, so Ketron offered the baby her breast, and Amelia took it. She was still half-asleep, so it may have been to comfort herself more than for the sustenance, but Ketron was thankful for the nutrients the baby pulled from her body.

"David?" Dr. Sing called to the nurse. "Get her discharge papers ready, please."

He obliged, and his eyes bore into Ketron as he read off the instructions for the baby's at-home care. Ketron tried not to be offended by his obvious judgment. What would she think if she had heard a mother describe a similar incident with her child? She would be skeptical about her involvement in the situation, too.

Just after noon, she drove back home and thought about getting some lunch. She decided against it, opting instead to bathe Amelia as soon as possible. She remembered her appointment with Dr. Richards and wondered if she should keep it.

Marvin and Sonny were asleep on his bed when Ketron yanked her keys out of the back door. Sonny hopped off the bed first and put his arms around his sister. "Is the baby okay?"

"Yes, sweetheart," she told him, knowing that it was only half true. Amelia wasn't the happy little girl she had been before the incident.

Sonny hugged Ketron, and she squatted so he could plant a kiss on the baby's cheek. "Solomon protected her," he said. "He kept the darkness away."

An unexpected tear fell from Ketron's eye. Sonny wiped it away. "Don't worry, Mommy. He won't be strong for a while, but he'll be back. He won't leave without me."

Marvin walked into the den, but he had to grab a chair for support. He tried to sit down, and then he bolted to the bathroom. Loud retching sounds echoed down the hallway.

"Daddy's really sick." Sonny explained it to Amelia, but she stared past him.

"Daddy may be sick for a couple of days," Ketron told Sonny. "But he will be a better daddy now."

Marvin moved slowly into the room, doubled over and shaking. "I went through some of the stuff in the basement where we found the baby." He lowered himself into a chair with one hand on the back rest for support. "It looked like someone had been living in that crawl space for a long time."

Ketron stayed silent. She knew exactly who had been staying in their basement.

"I found the money," he said, nodding to a bank envelope on the counter. "I hope you had a reason to take out the money, and whoever was sleeping in our basement swiped it. Were you scared I'd be mad, so you lied to me?" The question came out in a whisper, and Marvin laid his head on the table before lifting it and wiping sweat from his brow.

Ketron didn't want to argue with her husband while he was withdrawing from alcohol. She waited for him to speak again, hopeful that he would change the subject.

"Do you think I could have one?" he asked Ketron. "It would take the edge off."

"No." Ketron stood with her hand on her hip. "I can drop off Sonny and Amelia at Shauna's house, but I'm going to keep my appointment with Dr. Richards. You need to be clear-headed when you pick up the children from school."

He nodded with his head in his hands and his mouth open. He understood that driving soberly was of upmost importance.

"Why didn't the children stay home from school?"

He swallowed hard and cringed from the aftertaste of his vomit. "Nora didn't want to go, but Bonnie and Winslow needed to be with their friends, so she decided she would go to school, too."

Ketron understood. Nora didn't like to be away from Winslow, and they were in the same class.

Ketron fixed Marvin a glass of clear soda and pulled the acetaminophen from the locked cabinet. She placed both on the table in front of him. "Will you be okay if I go?"

He waved her away. "It might be better this way. I'll sleep until it's time to pick up the kids."

She gave Amelia a bath and restocked her diaper bag. She was surprised by the silence in the house. She hadn't noticed the tension Jeremy had placed on their family, but she didn't feel his presence. The relief was almost tangible.

She called Shauna on the way to her house and her friend was waiting for her in the doorway with Matty when she arrived. Sonny and Matty spilled into the house and ran upstairs. Shauna was happy to watch over the children, but she worried that Marvin might not be able to pick up Bonnie, Winslow, and Nora from school.

"You can take my car to your appointment, and I'll drive your van to pick them up."

Ketron faltered. It shouldn't be hard to tell her friend that she trusted Marvin now. "Marvin poured out his beer last night. He's not going to drink anymore."

As expected, Shauna was skeptical. "Was that before or after you found the baby?" She put her hands on her hips and raised her eyebrows. Sonny knocked over something upstairs, and Matty's peels of laughter drifted down the steps. "You left him alone, didn't you? How easy is it for him to drive to the store to get a six pack?"

"He could hardly move!" Ketron objected.

"That's my point!" Shauna said a little too loudly. The noise upstairs stalled, and they waited until it resumed before they continued talking in lower tones. "You can't trust an addict. They may mean what they say at the time, but they will do anything to avoid the pain of withdrawals, or in Marvin's case DT's."

"Isn't it a little early for DT's?"

"How long has it been since his last drink?"

"It's only been about two days," Ketron told her, confident that she'd made her point.

"He's throwing up, isn't he?"

Ketron's silence answered her question.

"Has he started hallucinating?"

"No, but—"

"That might be next. What if he gets a drink to balance him out or he's too sick to focus on the road? Either way, do you really want him driving your kids in his condition?"

Ketron thought about how much she had begged for Amelia's life to be spared and how empty she had been without her. She'd feel the same way about any of her children.

She dropped the keys to her van into Shauna's outstretched hand.

Chapter Fifty-Six

Present

Ketron kept her appointment with Dr. Richards. She took Amelia with her, unwilling to be separated from the baby after the events of the previous day. Once she had filled him in, Dr. Richards was more understanding about the toddler seated on Ketron's lap.

"I want to be put on medicine."

Dr. Richards startled in his seat. It was more of a reaction than she had seen from him in years. "After an evaluation and diagnosis, I can certainly put you on antipsychotic medication, but I need to know if anything has spurred your sudden desire for that kind of treatment."

"Did you listen to what I told you?"

Dr. Richards uncrossed his legs and straightened in his chair. "I did. However, I did not hear anything about hallucinations or a psychotic break. You told the police that someone took Amelia." He studied her, and Ketron understood that she had to make a choice between the lie she had told and her mental health. "Did you misplace Amelia?"

She steadied herself and hoped that she wouldn't hurt her future with her children. "No, but I have been hearing and seeing things no one can see or hear."

His eyebrows elevated slightly. "What types of things?"

"I hear things in the fireplace, and I see dark shapes when everyone is asleep."

"Do the dark shapes speak to you? Do they tell you to hurt anyone?"

"No," Ketron replied honestly.

Dr. Richards relaxed. "Do you think you may be feeling anxiety?"

Ketron had never considered it, but she was certain that she was either haunted by a ghost or experiencing the onset of schizophrenia. She didn't want to stray too far from her actual fears, so she tried to move his mind away from his concerns about anxiety. "All mothers feel some nervousness, but

I'm either seeing a ghost, or I'm developing the same dissociative disorder my mother had."

Dr. Richards sighed. He rarely exhibited irritation during their sessions. "Maybe it's best to admit you into Strong Oaks for the weekend. We can observe you and determine whether you need further treatment."

Ketron was jarred. It was the first time he had mentioned institutionalization to her. She back pedaled quickly, offering excuses for her mind to play tricks on her. She thought the slightest smile touched the corners of his mouth.

She spent the rest of the hour talking about average stressors, like overcooking dinner and not getting enough sleep. She hoped it helped cover her earlier admissions. Dr. Richards nodded along, and even yawned while she spoke about Nora's last bedtime meltdown. When her session was complete, she hurried Amelia out of the office and almost ran to Shauna's car.

She was less distracted by her baby when she drove, as Amelia was safely buckled into her car seat, and Ketron's mind presented new possibilities to her. She reflected on her conversation with Dr. Richards. Why had he felt so removed from their conversation?

She was two blocks away from Shauna's house when it hit her. Her father had died, and his monthly checks only covered her sessions until the end of the month. It was doubtful that she would be mentioned in his will, since his wife was unaware of the brief conversations between Big Red and him.

When he was contacted by the state, her father chose not to welcome Ketron into his home, but he had agreed to pay for her weekly visits to a psychiatrist of his choosing. No other communication was established, but the checks showed up every month. Ketron visited Dr. Richards every week until her early twenties.

Her affair with Oz was shameful, and his decent into drugs made it difficult for her to get away. He became paranoid that she was meeting another man, and when she explained that she was going to therapy, he worried that she was revealing secrets about his drug abuse. Oz had pushed her up against the wall and yelled at her on the day she had decided to stop going to therapy.

After Solomon's death, when Ketron could hardly care for herself mentally or physically, Marvin contacted Dr. Richards, and they reestablished weekly sessions for Ketron. Dr. Richards had reached out to her father and negotiated the terms of his services. It was around that time that a mysterious stipend ended up in her bank account every month. Ketron thought her father had started funneling a small amount of money to help offset the expenses of a growing family. She was almost certain that the money wouldn't appear in her account next month.

Ketron had to pull the car over to catch her breath. She and Dr. Richards had shared a good patient-doctor relationship. After so many years of interactions, she had believed that there was a mutual liking between the two of them. On some level, she had thought he had cared about her. He wasn't like a part of her family, but he was a constant contact. He had watched her blossom into adulthood, and he had expressed concerns over her challenges and joys over her successes. In the end, their connection had been forced so that he could collect a check. His sorrow over the loss of her parents had been strained, and he had never acknowledged her when she waved at him at the market. She had thought it was only because of the nature of their relationship.

Tears cascaded down her face. Why hadn't she seen it before? She attributed her ignorance to her need to have friends. She had thought of Dr. Richards as a confidant, but he had viewed her as nothing but an inconvenient hour on his schedule. He had even tried to make a little more money off her condition by attempting to refer her to Strong Oaks for evaluation. He could have petitioned her insurance for the money to treat her in the facility. She was a compliant patient, and he could have retained her after observation with any excuse.

Ketron was devastated. When she finally made it back to Shauna's house, her friend could tell that she was more upset than she had been when she left. Winslow was playing upstairs, and Shauna instructed the older children to join him. Ketron sat Amelia on the floor, hoping she'd play with one of Matty's blocks that were scattered on the rug.

Ketron told Shauna about her dissolving relationship with her therapist. "I just feel so stupid. I told him everything." She glanced away, squeezing the wad of tissues Shauna had given her. "Well, almost everything."

"I don't want to kick you while you're down, but it's his job." Shauna held out a small waste basket for Ketron's used tissues and she dropped them inside it. "He was paid for a service, and he did his job. The only thing that upsets me is that he should have remained professional all the way through your last visit. If he managed it for this long, one more hour wasn't going to kill him."

"Do you think he wanted me to know how he really thought of me?"

Shauna shrugged "Maybe. Who knows what he actually thinks of you."

"But now, even if I can afford it, I'm not going back to him."

Shauna agreed, surprising Ketron. "He compromised your view of him today. You need a therapist you can trust."

Ketron shook her head. "I don't think I want to visit another psychologist. I can just talk to you."

Shauna smiled. "You know I love you, but I don't want to be your replacement therapist." Ketron opened her mouth to clarify her intentions, but Shauna waved her off. "I know what you meant, but I think you need a psychologist. You have a very real family history of mental health issues, and you need to work on them. Marvin's insurance will pay for a new counselor. The options may not be as qualified as Dr. Richards, but they can help you develop ways to cope with your daily stressors."

Ketron was reminded of how Dr. Richards was quick to suggest observation in a facility. "Do you think another therapist might send me to Strong Oaks?"

"I don't know. I guess they will if you need it." Shauna handed her another tissue and tossed the empty box on the floor. Amelia's eyes flicked to the box, but she made no move to grab it.

Ketron collected the tissue box and threw it into the waste basket. "I feel guilty about leaving Marvin this long. I should get home."

Shauna called for the children, and Ketron drove back in silence. The children were sleepy from the events of the previous day. Bonnie slumped in her seat and didn't try to turn on the radio.

The house was quiet when she walked in, and her husband was breathing gently on the bed in his room. She closed his door, debating on whether she should roll him from his back to his side in case he vomited in his sleep. She decided not to disturb him.

Ketron cooked breakfast for dinner, allowing Nora and Sonny to stir the eggs. Winslow didn't want to help them cook, so he stayed in his room.

Marvin stumbled into the kitchen, and Ketron wondered if it was because he was tired or if he had partaken of the beer he had mentioned before she'd left. Nora and Sonny retreated to the other end of the house.

He opened the refrigerator and glanced at the food on the stove. "Do you expect me to eat that?" He nudged the spatula in the pan and some of the scrambled eggs flipped onto the stove. "Eggs? That's just perfect for an upset stomach!"

Ketron had mentally prepared herself for some tension as her husband attempted to loosen the grip alcohol had on his mind and body. "I can fix toast for you, or you can have crackers and ginger—"

"Yeah, that's so filling." He drew out the o. "What's wrong with you anyway?" he asked, suddenly inches from her face. "Why can't you even cook a decent dinner?"

After what she had experienced in such a short time, Ketron should have cried. Instead, she was angry. "I don't have to put up with this."

She threw diapers into Amelia's bag and called for the children. Everyone, except Winslow met her at the door. "Go get your brother," she told Sonny.

"You're not taking my son!" Marvin yelled at her and tried to grab Sonny's arm before he slipped past him to get Winslow.

"You are in no condition to care for him," she shot back.

"I can take care of my son. I haven't had anything to drink for days."

"Two days," Ketron corrected. She thought back to the previous day's intimacy and swallowed a lump in her throat.

"He's not coming," Sonny announced. He sat down in the living room and smashed dinosaurs together.

Ketron marched into the twins' room and stared at her son. Winslow wasn't on his top bunk with his action figures. He was on the floor with his legs crossed. "Hello, Mother."

How had she missed it? She had been worried about Amelia, and she had been distracted by her emotions over her psychiatrist, so she hadn't noticed the sly smile and narrowed eyes. She tried to remember the last time she had known that Winslow was himself. "It was when I found the baby. You came up here and possessed Winslow."

He tapped his nose. "You're getting good at this. Now, you need to quit fighting with Father so I can eat. A growing boy needs his food."

She crossed the distance between them and grabbed his arm. "Get out of my son."

She was repulsed by the feel of his skin. It was Winslow's body, but he wasn't there.

When she let go of his arm, he grabbed the spot she had touched mocking a pained expression. "You're hurting me, Mommy."

Ketron didn't plan to touch him again. "I told you to get out of my son."

"I think I'm going to stay this time. He's a couple of years younger than me, but I can be very mature for my age."

Ketron's pulse quickened. "You're dead, but Winslow's alive." Fear and frustration formed a threat. "Don't make me get out the sage."

His mouth popped open in a laugh. "Sage is only an inconvenience. I'll be right back in no time. This is my house, and every corner of it protects me."

Ketron had an idea. It was a long shot, but she hoped it would work.

She backed out of the room slowly, while the thing that was not her son smiled at her. "Come play with me, Mommy," he mocked. "We're going to have so much fun. And once I get rid of the baby you're carrying, you'll have more time for me."

Ketron hugged Amelia more tightly to her. *I won't give you the chance to hurt her again,* she thought.

Marvin was back in his room playing video games. He sensed that she wasn't leaving.

Sonny had added a truck to his dinosaur fight. Ketron wondered if her eyes betrayed her when she saw it move on its own to attack Sonny's T-rex. Sonny noticed her reaction. "Solomon likes trucks."

Ketron's feet tripped. She almost dropped Amelia. "Who?"

Marvin peeked around the corner of his door. "Who did he say?"

"Solomon," Ketron told him. "He said, 'Solomon.'"

Chapter Fifty-Seven

Present

Ketron and Marvin spent the next hour watching him play, but Sonny never betrayed the presence of an entity. While she watched Sonny, Ketron went over her plan in her mind. She was almost afraid to think it too loudly for fear that Jeremy would hear her thoughts.

She hoped she was right about her spectral shadow. "I'm going to take a ride with Amelia. She needs a good nap. I'll cook a better dinner when I get back."

"Sonny might need a nap, too," Marvin suggested.

Ketron was surprised. Usually, he didn't want her to leave with Sonny.

Ketron asked Bonnie to go with her and she buckled Sonny into his seat while Ketron fastened a harness over a lethargic Amelia. The screen door flew open, and Nora ran to the van. "Can I go with you?"

"What about Winslow?" Ketron asked. "He's staying here."

"It's okay," Nora said without looking at her mother. "He's not being Winslow."

Ketron was happy to have most of her children away from Jeremy's influence. She had just started the van when Winslow, or Jeremy in Winslow's body, came to her window. He looked at the ground. "Can I go with you? I don't feel good."

It was a trick. Ketron dismissed him, and he hung his head all the way to the door. He turned around and his lip trembled. Ketron was compelled to go get him, but she told herself that Jeremy was trying to pull on her heart strings.

She drove to the old Renfro property and parked beside the mailbox. The blue paint had chipped away, leaving a rusted, unused metal box. Two stuffed rabbits, Pansy and Marigold, stared out at her from the dining room window.

"Stay with the children," she told Bonnie. "I'll be back soon."

Ketron climbed the old, dead steps, and pulled the door. It wouldn't give.

She hoped just standing on the porch would allow her to connect with Gail, and soon a puff of wind circled her hair.

"Gail," she breathed. "I don't know if you remember me, or if you check on me from time to time, but I need your help." The silence of the afternoon was the only response. She whispered her plan to the air around her and waited.

"What is that?" Bonnie scrunched up her nose. Ketron put the herb in the floorboard at her feet.

"Dill."

"Why did you come all the way up here for dill?"

Ketron didn't answer her, and Bonnie let the subject drop. There were more interesting things on social media.

"Nora got out to throw up while you were gone, so Winslow might not have been lying about not feeling good."

"I hope you don't get it." Ketron's voice was cold, but it was because she had one thing on her mind: executing her plan.

She pulled up to Shauna's house, and Shauna walked out onto her porch. Everyone got out except Nora.

"My belly hurts. Can I please go home?"

Ketron told Shauna that she didn't want the children to see Marvin as he went through a hard period of withdrawals.

"What about Nora and Winslow?"

"I think they might be sick," Ketron said, curious if Jeremy had possessed Winslow only to pick up a common stomach bug. Ketron was a little ill, too.

Ketron felt like a terrible mother for leaving her baby after a traumatic experience, but she couldn't risk further harm to Amelia by taking her back around Jeremy's influence again. She left her in Bonnie's arms, and Amelia hardly registered her goodbye.

Nora's face started to regain some color, but she wasn't feeling completely better when they got home. She ran inside, and her bedroom light turned on.

"Where are the kids?" Marvin stood in the doorway, swaying with his mouth open.

Ketron laid down the sage she had picked up from the store and the dill she had gathered at the old Renfro property. "Did you have a drink?"

His face contorted in rage. "I haven't had anything in days! Maybe I should have stopped a long time ago. It's obvious that you don't stay with the children. You just push them off on whoever will watch them."

"They're with Shauna, and I plan to get them as soon as I—"

He bumped her on his way out. "I'm going after Sonny, and we're getting away from you."

Ketron opened her mouth to protest, but she stopped when Marvin seemed unable to grab his truck keys. Ketron took in his changes and the sage next to his keys, and it was clear to her. Marvin may not have been a vessel for possession, but he was influenced by Jeremy. Jeremy may have targeted the children, but their father had been easily manipulated by his spirit, his past addictions making it almost effortless for the ghost to slip suggestions in his ear. Now that his hold was solidified, Jeremy was using his strength to control Marvin and Winslow. Ketron had to act fast.

"There's a beer in the cabinet."

He turned slowly. Why hadn't she noticed the lack of her husband's warmth and love? Had she assumed alcoholism had taken it all away?

"Which one?"

She pointed to the cabinet farthest from the door. "It's in there. I hid it from you months ago because I hated your drinking."

He cocked his head and Ketron could see shades of her husband, but he was shrouded by something else. It ran shadowy fingers over his outline, threatening to enter him and burst through, leaving nothing of the man she loved.

"What made you change your mind?"

Ketron prepared her lie quickly. "I fought against it, but I have to accept it." He nodded for her to continue. "It's just part of your life now. You need to drink to be happy."

Marvin made his way to the cabinet, but not before he stopped and wrapped Ketron in his arms. The embrace was lecherous, lacking warmth and sincerity. "Thank you, sweetheart." He moved his hand over her breast but stopped when voices echoed from the twins' room. "Later," he promised.

Ketron shuddered.

Ketron returned the affection, but she could feel the cold indifference in his arms. And Marvin had never called her *sweetheart*.

Once his back was to her, Ketron pulled out the lighter and grabbed a handful of sage. She lit it. At first, it seemed like it wouldn't catch, but then the plant began burning.

Marvin threw everything out of the cabinet. "You lying— Hey! What are you doing? You're gonna catch the house on fire."

Ketron fought with her memory for Jeremy's father's name. After a brief internal struggle, it came to her. "He is not Joseph! Let go of him!" She thrust the burning sage at him and repeated herself.

The smoke reached her husband and he blinked. The dark leech on his body let go, and Marvin's face crumbled. He stared at the fireplace and back to Ketron. He passed her with tears rolling down his cheeks, picked up his keys, and walked out the door. She wasn't sure if he understood his drive to leave the house or if Jeremy had hinted it before he detached his hold.

Ketron didn't have any more time to waste. She had given away her element of surprise to try to rid Marvin of his spiritual hitchhiker. Jeremy would be ready to defend himself.

She gathered all the sage and carried it under her arm. She held the burning herb in front of her.

When she got to the twins' room, they were sitting on the bed holding hands. Nora had Sonny's dog in her lap. "Sonny forgot Buddy," she said.

"Are you guys feeling better?"

"Yeah," Winslow replied. Jeremy was doing a good job of acting like him in front of his sister. "I just have a headache. Could I have some children's medicine?"

Ketron nodded. "I think this will help, too." She moved the burning plant toward Winslow. Nora jerked away from it.

Nora scrunched up her nose. "What is that? Will it burn down the house?"

"No," Ketron told her daughter while keeping her eyes on Winslow. "It should help Winslow feel better, though."

Winslow didn't back away until the burning sage was inches from his nose. "Get it away from me. It stinks, Mom."

There was something about his tone that jolted Ketron. It held the same notes as the boy that had screamed at her and confided his dreams to her for the past eight years.

Ketron registered Winslow's wide-eyed shock just before her world went black.

Chapter Fifty-Eight

Past

"Does she know she's related to you?" Johnny asked.

It had taken time to adapt to calling him "Johnny" instead of Ky, but Ketron was used to it now. After the terrible accident that had caused him to begin using his middle name, Ketron had slipped many times. He allowed a few of her mistakes, but when she'd shouted after him and used his first name at school, he had turned around and told her, "*My name is John.*" He'd said it through gritted teeth, and Ketron had felt chastised. He had apologized for losing his temper with her, but Ketron had nursed her hurt feelings for a week. She decided to address him as Johnny, and she felt like it was her pet name for him until his girlfriend started calling him *Johnny*, too.

Ketron leaned back onto Johnny's arm and breathed in the mossy smell left behind after a short rain. A gentle breeze flicked the Star Wars curtains in the fort's window. "No, but her friend agreed to let me know about her without letting her know, so I'll keep up with her. She was my mother's foster brother's daughter, so I don't think I count as a relation." She felt silly after she explained her connection to the girl she had tracked down.

Johnny chuckled, the blonder parts of his bristly facial hair catching the light. "It reminds me of a song about being your own grandfather." He slid his arm away and hopped up quickly, putting distance between he and Ketron.

Ketron tried to make her face unreadable. Over the years, there had been a few times when she and Johnny had gotten close. One night, not long after he had changed his name from Ky to John, he had snuck out and appeared under her bedroom window. They talked for hours at the window's sill, and almost kissed, but Big Red woke up and went to the bathroom, scaring Johnny away. However, a hayride at the fall festival with a girl from his biology class had cooled his flirtations with Ketron.

Awkwardness flittered through the fort. They rarely came to the fort together anymore, but Ketron had failed a chemistry test and Johnny wanted to cheer her up.

"Shauna's pretty lucky, though," he said. "Not many people have someone watching over them with good intentions."

They reflected on his words solemnly. They both wished they'd had more people watching out for them when they were younger.

He sat back down next to her, drawing her attention to his excited blue eyes. "Hey, I forgot to tell you. I had a dream about Gail the other night."

Ketron raised an eyebrow.

"She told me to go back to the attic." He spoke the words carefully, waiting for her reaction.

Any other person could have dismissed the dream, but Ketron had witnessed Johnny's connection with the supernatural. Her only objection was a feeble one. "I haven't been back there in years."

Johnny put his hand over hers, but quickly retracted it when she looked up at him. He cleared his throat. "I know it might be hard to go back there, but I thought it might be easier if you had a friend with you." Ketron thought he put a lot of emphasis on the word *friend*.

"It's okay," she assured him. She sighed and stood up, hardly able to stretch under the low ceilings in the fort. "It's not like she's going to be there waiting for me."

Johnny knew who Ketron was referencing. "Have you answered her letters yet?"

"No, and I'm not going to!" Her voice was angrier than she had intended.

"I'm sorry, Johnny. She just doesn't deserve forgiveness." Tears threatened, but Ketron blinked them away. "She tried to bury me! I overlooked everything until that night. She didn't want me anymore, and she and her dead sister were willing to bury me so that they could run away with Tom. I hate her, and that will never change."

Johnny's eyes never left the ground as Ketron spoke about her mother. "I know what it's like to hate someone." Ketron reminded herself that Johnny was still grieving.

"Johnny, I'm sorry. I shouldn't have said anything."

He looked up with a forced smile. His eyes were rimmed in red, but no tears were in them. "I'm the one who brought it up. You have every right to feel the way you feel."

Ketron seldom got these stolen moments with Johnny. He had been wrapped up with his new girlfriend, so they hadn't spoken a lot. It had been hard for him to bring up the subject and going to the fort may have triggered more emotions.

Ketron put aside her own misgivings to spend more time with Johnny. "Let's go. Let's see what she wants."

Johnny and Ketron took the familiar trail to the Renfro property. He held Ketron's hand when he helped her down steep parts of embankment, and she wished he wouldn't let it go.

Halfway to the house, Johnny picked up on her growing affection for him. "You know I want you to be happy, right?"

Ketron's heart sank. He really liked his new girlfriend, but she hoped that he would tire of her after a couple of months.

"I know this guy you might like," he went on. He forced a chuckle. "His name is Kyle." Ketron heard little past their shared first names. She knew the guy he was talking about, and she wasn't impressed by him. "Anyway, I could introduce him to you, and you guys could go on a double-date with Miranda and me."

"Oh, that'd be great!" Ketron caught her own sarcasm, but Johnny chose the tone he wanted to hear.

"Great! I'll talk to Kyle tomorrow."

The covered grave was visible through a line of knotted trees. Ketron still considered it a grave because any hope of saving her mother had died in it that night. Johnny put his arm around her and guided her the rest of the way.

The house had been sold to another family, even though her mother had claimed it as her own. Ketron had learned that her mother's weekly trips to town included dropping off a small amount of money to the family who owned it for rent and utilities. Her mother had collected a check each month for her mental health disability, and she had a small jar of savings. As far as Ketron knew, the money was still in the jar under the sink.

They tried the door, but it was locked. Ketron was willing to give up on their impromptu adventure, but Johnny flew around the house, and he opened it for her within seconds. He bowed and stretched his hand in the form of a greeting. "After you, my lady."

Ketron walked into the house with her head held high. The scent of moss and untouched dust rushed up to meet her. Everything was in order, and it looked the same as it had when she and her mother moved in. Pansy and Marigold sat on a shelf, their beady eyes blaming her for their abandonment.

She must have lost her balance, but Johnny steadied her before she fell. "Are you sure you can do this?"

Ketron stared into his deep blue eyes and willed him to kiss her. She put every ounce of energy into her desire, but he stayed inches away from her face, only looking at her with friendly concern. "I'm okay." She directed her steps to the dining room, and Johnny followed her.

The attic door was closed but when her feet touched the boards in the room, the movement seemed to pop the door open, like something on the other side had unlatched it for them. They climbed the stairs warily, but nothing impeded their ascent. Ketron knew where Gail had wanted her to go, and she went straight to the storage container. As if an X on a treasure map was on display for her, the dish of marbles sat on it. She picked up a blue and white marble and studied it. The swirls were delicate and intentional.

Johnny took the dish from her and sat it on a nearby dresser. Ketron stuck the marble in her pocket. "I wondered what had happened to the marbles after the—" She didn't know how to finish the sentence. *Intended burial* was what came to mind, but she didn't want to say it out loud. "I guess they go wherever Gail goes."

Ketron opened the lid on the plastic tote, and a molded yellow scent drifted up to meet her. She reached down the side of the container, and when her hand closed over the cold metal, she blacked out.

When she opened her eyes, Johnny was pacing and running a hand through his hair. He looked down at her, as if suddenly seeing her in the room. "You're back!"

"Where did I go?" Her voice sounded groggy to her.

"You were her," he told Ketron. "You told me—" He stopped and shook his head. He resumed pacing. "She was inside you, and she told me about her death."

"Gail was *inside* me?"

He waved his hand dismissively as if possession was a common occurrence. "She told me she lived here before the woods were cold."

"That's cryptic."

He stared at her and sighed. "She told me about the fire."

Ketron's stomach rolled. She suddenly felt fevered and weak.

"She said that she was asleep in the house when the fire started. She tried to get out, but the fire was everywhere. She died listening to her son's cries."

"That's terrible," Ketron commented. "Is that all she wanted to say to us?"

Johnny's face took on an unfamiliar expression. Ketron knew beyond a shadow of a doubt that he was about to lie to her.

He unconsciously ran a hand over the right pocket of his jeans. "Yeah, that was about all. She just described her death to me."

Ketron's head throbbed. "Why did she need to possess me to talk to you?"

"I don't—" He put his arms around her, but instead of comforting her, it made her temperature skyrocket. "Hey, are you okay?"

Ketron tried to run into the woods, but the best she could manage were some stumbling steps while Johnny held her upright. She made it to the porch before she gave into her quivering stomach and hurled its contents over the railing. Johnny held her hair back and wiped her forehead with the sleeve of his shirt.

When her retching stopped, she fell against the porch, happy for the way the cold boards felt against her face and arms. A fine layer of sweat coated her body, and it cooled her quickly. Johnny wrapped her in his arms before she realized she was shivering. "You lied to me."

Johnny didn't try to deny it. "She said I couldn't tell you."

"Look at me," Ketron demanded in a voice she hoped sounded more furious than the trembling one she heard. "She used me to communicate with you. Don't I deserve to know what she said?"

Johnny seemed to contemplate telling her, but he shook his head. "All I can tell you is that she's here for you if you need her."

Ketron was feeling better, but she was still a little woozy. She shot up out of Johnny's arms and hobbled down the steps. "That's just great! My great-grandfather's first wife used me to tell the boy I love a secret, but I can't know about it." She stared back at the house and called to the attic window. *"But she'll always be there for me!"*

She stalked into the woods with Johnny close behind her. The air was much colder, and part of her dared the spirits of Pale Woods to show themselves.

"You love me?" Johnny was keeping up with her, but his breaths were labored. "I thought you were supposed to end up with my—"

Ketron rounded on him. "For someone with special abilities, you'd think you would have known that I've always liked you."

He was stricken, but he kept pace with her when she started walking again. "I knew you liked me, but I've always been honest with you. Miranda's going to be my wife."

She glared at him. "How do you know? Is it something you heard in your head? Doesn't she have a say? What if she doesn't want you?" Ketron gestured to the woods around them. "What if she can't take all the stuff that happens to people like us?"

Johnny hung his head. "She's my escape from all this."

Ketron laughed. "Great! Just great! Well, at least the universe decided that you could have a break from—" She stopped. If she kept going, she was going to cry, and she did not want to break down in front of Johnny.

She stalked to the fort where they would have to go in separate directions, him to the south and her to the north. By the time she got there, she had simmered down, but she wasn't completely cool.

"Hey!" Johnny called after her when she started up the path to the home she shared with Big Red and Nora.

Ketron stopped and crossed her arms, unwilling to face him.

Johnny put his hand on her shoulder. His touch was warm, but it lacked the heat she wanted to feel from him. "I don't want you to be mad at me."

Sincerity dripped from his words, and Ketron decided that it was more than enough to soften her attitude toward him. "Well, you are technically my cousin, so it would have been weird for us to be together anyway."

He laughed and wrapped her in a hug. She took in his smell. It reminded her of pine needles, even when he hadn't been in the woods.

"Do you want to go back to the fort for a little while?"

Ketron shook her head. "I want to get home before your aunt's cornbread gets cold."

Johnny raised his eyebrows. "You know she's your mother now."

"It's just that the word *mother* feels tainted to me now. I don't want to put Nora in the same category as that woman."

He ran his thumb and forefinger down his chin thoughtfully. "You could always think of— What was her name? Gwynevieve? You could think of Gwynevieve as just a person. Nothing more."

Ketron understood his meaning, and she planned to think about what he had said, but it was hard to erase the years that she had suffered under her mother's diseased mind. "Maybe I'll think of it differently when I'm a mother."

"I hope so," he said.

They locked eyes, and Johnny dropped his gaze. He waved goodbye before the awkwardness stirred between them again.

Ketron regretted taking the metal object she had swiped from his pocket, but when she saw him with Miranda at school the next day, it was easy to deny that she had lifted it. She let him believe that he had dropped it on the trail and Pale Woods Forest had swallowed it up.

Chapter Fifty-Nine

Present

Her head thumped down the stairs, the pain from each step making her a little more aware of her surroundings. She didn't know how many she hit before she could lift her head. Nora and Winslow each had one of her legs, and they were pulling her down the basement steps.

Ketron tried to look around, but her vision was still blurry. She blinked several times, but the haze didn't clear.

She touched the knot forming just above the nape of her neck. She had been standing in front of Nora and Winslow? Who had hit her?

Once she'd regained consciousness, the twins stopped dragging her. Nora was shaking so hard that Ketron thought she would fall. She usually clutched a baby doll when she was scared or upset, and Ketron felt the urge to find her favorite doll to ease some of her daughter's fear.

The imposter inside Winslow's body handed his twin a rope. "Tie her hands."

Nora understood that her brother was not in control of his actions. She looked at the rope and continued to tremble. "I don't want to."

Jeremy sighed and picked up a hammer from Marvin's open toolbox. He angled it over his head and Nora cried out. "Do you want me to bash your brother's brains in?"

Nora could only shake uncontrollably and scream. She finally lost her battle with fear and collapsed. Ketron inched her body to her daughter. "You're a monster!" she said to him.

Jeremy cocked his head and feigned innocence. "You wouldn't say that about your oldest son, would you?"

"You're not Winslow."

Jeremy chuckled. "Try to tell that to anybody. They'd have you thrown into the asylum with your mother." He bent down to tie her hands.

"How do you know anything about my mother?"

A chuckle escaped him. It was a dry, hoarse sound. "I've been inside your mind." He pointed up, in the direction of Marvin's room. "And I listen to how that man talks to you. I can hear everything through the fireplace."

Ketron was unwilling to cause harm to Winslow, so she didn't want to lash out at Jeremy. She had to do something, though. "Gail," she spoke into the cold basement air. A breeze lifted around her, circling her skin, and raising the hair on her arms.

Ketron thought she would black out when she allowed Gail to enter her body, but she only took a backseat in her mind. She could hear and see everything that transpired, but she couldn't control the movements she made or the words she said.

Gail stared straight into Jeremy's smirking face, unflinching.

"So, you're Gail," he commented. "I wondered if you found a way to follow us here."

Us? Ketron wondered, and then it hit her. She tried to say it out loud, but Gail's influence over her actions prevented it. A small look of shock must have passed through, though, because a self-satisfied grin stretched across Jeremy's face.

"You have so many children, Mom." He almost spat out *mom*. "You didn't notice that your little girl was acting differently."

Ketron thought back to when Nora had asked to go with her. She didn't have her baby doll, and she would never have left the house without it. Ketron had thought that Nora had been upset about her twin's change and wanted to get away from him, but it was really Jeremy, looking for a way to see what she was doing. That meant that she'd missed the opportunity to get Winslow away from the house before Jeremy could take him over again.

"What do you want, Jeremy?"

Ketron had often wondered the same thing. Lisa had counseled her to ask him, but he never made it easy for her to pose the question.

Ketron had studied the faces of each one of her children from birth. She recognized Winslow's broad shoulders, blue eyes, and slash of a mouth. The look his features made when Jeremy inhabited his body was much different. Jeremy held an aloof posture and cut his eyes often. One side of his mouth was always lifted, as if he were amused at getting his own way. Gail's words startled him and Ketron glimpsed a scared boy.

"Isn't it obvious?"

"You want a family," Gail replied.

Jeremy looked at Winslow's feet. Ketron desperately wanted the boy who wore those shoes back.

"I want a mother." He dropped the rope. "Mom was good to me. We played games and she listened to me. But she left without me. I died at the bottom of those steps." He pointed to Ketron's left. "I climbed out of my body, and I saw my mom in the hallway. She tried to crawl to my dead body, but she was too weak. I waited on her. After she died, though, she didn't stay with me."

"I lost my baby in a fire," Gail told him. "Solomon was King David's most prized child, and after two of my other babies had died before I held them, I felt the same way about my boy, so I gave him the name of the wisest king in the Bible. His laugh was like the sweetest notes of a melody, and his words, however limited, touched my heart. I was so involved with my baby. Instead of tending to my housework or my husband's needs, I tickled him or rolled little marbles across the floor with him. I started telling people that he learned to run before he could walk. He was never still." She shifted Ketron's weight so that she could sit up. "We lived in a beautiful Victorian home, and we lit a candle in every window. One night, one of the curtains in my room fell from the hook and ignited. I was asleep on my bed and my baby, Solomon, was with me. By the time I woke, we were surrounded by fire, and I put him on the ground where there was less smoke so I could get wet rags to cover our noses. I opened a window and decided that it was our best chance to escape. I found rags and dabbed them in the water from the dressing table, but when I went back to where I'd placed my baby, I couldn't find him. I heard him running and crying" —she swallowed hard— "and then shrieking in agony, but I couldn't find him. The last thing I remember is running into the flames in response to his cries. I died listening to Solomon's tears."

Ketron wanted to hold Gail and comfort her. She had never realized just how deep her link to Gail was until that moment. After all, she had named her dead child Solomon. Perhaps a part of her subconscious had made the connection for her. No wonder Gail had sought to protect Ketron's mother, her aunt, and her. Ketron felt close to Gail as they shared something intimate. Both of them had lost babies and had been looking for them. Unlike Gail's child, though, the baby Ketron had named Solomon had not moved on. His spirit still lingered, growing in spectral form alongside his twin.

"Do you like to play marbles?" Gail pointed to the stairs where a Blue Ridge Pottery dish had appeared.

"I don't know how to play."

"I could teach you," Gail offered.

Jeremy hesitated. "Don't you want to go back to your house. What if your little boy is still there?"

"I think we both know he left this world, like your mother. I should have passed through, too, but I was consumed with guilt for putting him down instead of keeping him with me. He died in fear, thinking that I'd left him."

"I don't want to be dead." Jeremy's voice cracked, and Ketron finally saw a different side of him. Had he only been malicious because he'd been jealous?

Gail stood up and clasped Ketron's hands in front of her waist. "I didn't want to die either, but life is for the living, and you're keeping poor little Winslow from growing up."

Jeremy furrowed Winslow's brow. "But he hates his life! He says he wants to be dead, or he wants to go meet his real dad. Why can't I trade places with him?"

Ketron's body shuddered, and she retched onto the concrete floor. Gail wiped her mouth. "Twins may have more energy, but your hold weakens the longer you stay inside them. You may have had some success hopping from Winslow to Nora" —she pointed to Nora— "and back again, but eventually that wears out." She reached for his hand, and Ketron's hopes lifted when he gave it to her. "Winslow is sad and confused. He feels betrayed. He won't die if you take him over. He'll live in a haze, unable to make his own decisions. It's a fate worse than death."

"Won't you be weaker if you stay here?"

"I will be weaker, but I'll still have plenty of energy to play with you." She embraced Jeremy. "We won't lose each other."

Jeremy pulled away from her and searched her eyes. "What if I want to live in your house?"

"I think that would be wonderful."

Chapter Sixty

Present

Gail carried Nora and buckled her into her booster seat. Nora was still unconscious, but she breathed in regular motions. Winslow held onto a bowl and dry heaved into it repeatedly in the fifteen minutes it took them to get to the old Renfro property.

Gail parked the car close to the house and opened the door. It had been locked when Ketron had twisted the knob, but it swung open easily to receive them.

In the dining room, Ketron felt a pull, like a hook in her midsection dragging her along until it broke free. She almost fell, but she grabbed the wall for support. Winslow had a similar experience, but he sat in one of the oak dining room chairs.

The attic door popped open, and footsteps pounded up the stairs. Almost immediately, Ketron heard marbles dropping and rolling across the attic floor.

"What happened, Mom?" Winslow stared at her with drooping eyelids and a pale face.

"I think you're sick, honey," Ketron told him, wrapping him in a solid embrace. He leaned against her, and she tried to keep her actions neutral. She wanted to hug him and carry him out of the house, but she didn't want to scare him. "Let's get you home."

Ketron stayed at Shauna's door while her friend collected Bonnie, Sonny, and Amelia. Marvin had tried to pick up Sonny, but Shauna had sent him away.

"See you later, Zeke," Shauna called to Sonny as he pulled open the sliding van door.

Bonnie waved Amelia's arm up and down. "Say goodbye to Aunt Na Na."

"Na Na," Amelia obeyed.

Ketron was relieved that the baby was acclimating to her surroundings again. She exchanged a smile with Shauna but refrained from excessive celebration.

Bonnie pointed at Ketron. "Are Winslow and Nora still sick? We're not going to get the plague, are we?"

"No," Ketron assured her.

When Bonnie took Amelia to the van, Shauna put her arms around Ketron. Ketron hugged her back, thankful for a true friend. "I think we need to talk."

Shauna pulled away. "You're not breaking up with me, are you?" she joked.

"Never. But I need to tell you something I should have told you a long time ago."

Shauna raised her eyebrows. "What is it?"

Ketron glanced at the van. Bonnie was yelling at one of her siblings. "Can I come over tomorrow?"

"Yeah. Are you okay?"

Ketron nodded. "Just like any other family, we have a lot to sort out, but I think everything is going to be fine."

Chapter Sixty-One

Present

Ketron climbed the steps to Lisa's house for the last time. She had read about her friend's death in an online obituary, and Marvin told her that he'd stay with the children so she could take a walk.

Bonnie had opted to go with her mother. She and Marvin hadn't fully repaired their relationship.

Ketron placed a purple flower in front of the door. "I didn't know her that well, but she was so good to us."

Bonnie put her hand on her shoulder. "I wish I could have met her."

Ketron's eyebrows drew together. "You did."

Bonnie retracted her hand. "No, Mama. I never met her. You gave me those rocks from her, but—"

A rusty red Toyota rumbled into view, pulling into the driveway. A man hopped out, his snakeskin boots crunching the gravel. He walked up the steps with his head down. He took off his Stetson and looked at the door.

Lisa had only spoken about one living relative, so Ketron guessed the name of the other visitor. "Dusty?"

"Yes, ma'am," he responded. "You musta known my mama, 'cause she's the only one who called me that. Most people call me Dustin."

Ketron extended her hand and lowered her eyes to cover her embarrassment. "I'm sorry, Dustin."

He accepted her hand and shook it firmly. "That's alright, ma'am. Seemed appropriate since I was at my mama's house when you said it."

Dustin had gotten his bright red hair from his mother, and he was a little shorter than most of the men Ketron knew. His skin was brown and rough, as if overexposure to the sun had turned it to leather.

Dustin sat in one of the black metal chairs, smiling when it creaked. Ketron let Bonnie sit in the other chair and she remained standing. "We just came up here for a minute. We understand if you need some time to be alone."

"I've had plenty of that." He rubbed his eyes with his thumb and forefinger. "Time to be alone," he clarified. "I suspect that I'll have plenty more."

"I'm so sorry," Ketron said. "Your mom was so sweet to my children and me." She was glad Bonnie didn't contradict her. "She was a good friend."

"Mom talked about you a lot." He smiled sheepishly. "She said you have a whole football team of kids."

Ketron chucked. "It seems like we're working on it."

"Can I get you ladies somethin' to drink? Mom probably had some soda in the refrigerator." His eyes unfocused from a memory. "She used to call a refrigerator an icebox." He jumped up from his seat, massaging his eyes again. "I think her mom called it that."

Ketron nodded. She doubted an icebox was part of Lisa's childhood, but the word could have been used when Lisa's mother was a young girl.

Dustin had rubbed his eyes until they were red, or maybe they were red because he had tried to rub the tears out of them. Either way, the pink rims reawakened with grief.

"It's okay," Ketron said, placing a hand on his arm. "We need to go anyway."

"How did your mom die?" Bonnie asked.

Ketron could have cried from embarrassment, but Dustin didn't miss a beat. "She fell in the house. She broke her hip and her wrist. I don't think she feared dying from her accident. She seemed to be more concerned about losing her independence. Anyway, she was gettin' better, but a nurse called me around two o'clock one mornin' and told me that my mom had developed pneumonia, and she wasn't responding to their treatment for it. She was breathin' in what they call the 'death rattle' when I got there, and she was gone before three o'clock that mornin'."

"It was that fast?" Ketron touched his shoulder. "I'm so sorry."

Dustin sat for a long moment before he spoke again. "Thank you for being a friend to my mom."

"She was a lovely person, and she was good to me."

"Not a lot of people could look past" —he motioned to the neighborhood — "the gossip that went around about her."

Ketron raised an eyebrow.

"I got into a lot of fights because of it." He paused and waited for a bird to finish its boisterous song. "I wasn't about to let people call her a witch."

"Why did they call her a witch?" Bonnie interjected before Ketron could stop her.

He gave Bonnie a brief once-over and chuckled. "You're at that age where you want to live your own horror story."

Bonnie stared at him with wide eyes, ready to take in his account of his mother's odd behavior.

"Well, Mom used to make money by tellin' people about their dead relatives. I couldn't see 'em, but she acted like they came in and sat on our couch."

Bonnie gasped. "Did you ever see her talk to a ghost?"

"That's enough, Bonnie. It's not appropriate."

Dustin threw up his hand. "Don't worry about it. She's only curious." He rocked in the chair but stopped when the squeaking metal shrieked. "And I don't mind talkin' about my mom. Seems memories are all I have now."

He turned his attention to Bonnie. "I saw her talk to ghosts, laugh with them, and yell at them to get out of the house." He smiled at a memory. "One time this ghost thought he was callin' on my mom. She told him that he was dead, but that didn't phase him none. She said he sat and watched her all day, but he stayed in the living room, so she had privacy anywhere else in the house."

Dustin and Bonnie traded a few more stories, but Bonnie never mentioned the spirits that had been in their house.

"I think we should get back," Ketron told Bonnie.

"It is gettin' late," Dustin conceded. "Are you sure you don't want to come inside? I'm goin' through Mom's stuff. I'm sure she'd want you to have a trinket or somethin' to remember her by."

Ketron felt conflicted. On one hand, she didn't want to take anything because she had hardly known Lisa. On the other hand, she felt obligated to follow Dustin inside after the tone of his offer. After a brief internal battle, Bonnie made her decision for her when she followed Dustin into the house.

A thought hit her when she walked into the quiet house. "Did you take the dog?"

Dustin was baffled. "What dog?"

"The little yorkie," Ketron clarified. "I think your mother called her Annie."

"Annie's been gone seven years now," Dustin replied soberly. "It broke Mom's heart to let the vet put her down, but she was sufferin'."

Ketron recalled her visits to Lisa's house. She had seen the dog each time. She shook the image from her thoughts. Lisa had probably gotten another dog, but if that were the case, where had it gone?

Dustin rustled through papers and scanned old mail. He pointed to a wooden shelf and indicated that they could choose one of Lisa's porcelain or glass sunflowers or hot air balloons. Finally, Ketron grabbed a green and orange balloon, and turned to say farewell.

Dustin had been watching them. He handed Bonnie an envelope. "My mom had somethin' else for you."

Bonnie opened it, and an obsidian necklace rolled out. She pulled the slip of paper in the envelope out and read it aloud: "You may need this if you're going into haunted houses."

Ketron's hand went to her hip. "Are you going into haunted houses?"

Bonnie wouldn't look at her. "They're not exactly haunted. Nothing's happened."

Dustin interrupted a possible mother-daughter face off. "Wherever you're goin', my mom thought you needed that for protection." He pointed at the necklace.

As he was helping Bonnie fasten the clasp, Ketron's eyes fell on Lisa's obituary. Dustin told her the paper had been delivered up until the previous week, as, in his grief, he had forgotten to cancel the subscription.

Lisa's biography spoke of her devotion to her husband and son, and it touched on her time with certain community organizations. Ketron let out a small gasp when she reread the memorial. "I think they misprinted the date of death on your mom's obituary." She had been afraid to voice her observation. She wasn't related to Lisa, and she didn't know how Dustin would respond to her remark.

Dustin put his finger on the paper and flipped it toward him. "No, it's right," he confirmed. "You don't forget the day your mom dies."

"But I just saw her last week." Ketron felt the world swim around her. She controlled her breathing and hoped she wouldn't pass out.

Dustin stared at her. "You saw her." He grinned, and his smile reminded Ketron of his mother. "I wondered if she'd find a way to come back. What'd she say?"

Ketron opened her mouth, but she couldn't respond. She grabbed Bonnie's hand and flew out the door, offering apologies as she left.

Chapter Sixty-Two

Present

Surrounded by her family, the baby opened her eyes.

Marvin had held her during her short nap while playing a board game with Winslow and Bonnie. Ketron had heard the dice rattling from the kitchen.

A truck rolled up to her feet, and she placed it beside Sonny. She thought she saw it move across a pile of stuffed animals, but she couldn't be certain. She had started to recognize Solomon's spirit in the house with her. His touch was almost tangible at times, like when he wrapped his arms around her waist when Sonny hugged her, or he put a hand on her back when she cried. If she had gained nothing else from her experience with Jeremy, at least she could recognize Solomon's presence.

Nora ran into the kitchen with Marvin and Winslow trailing behind her.

"Will Shauna be here soon?" Marvin asked. Amelia reached for Ketron, and Marvin handed her over.

"She just parked on the other end of the driveway. I think she's having trouble getting Matty out of the car."

"I'll go help," he volunteered.

Ketron watched out the window as Marvin knelt and extended his hand to Matty. After they exchanged a few words, Matty allowed Marvin to pick him up and bring him inside.

"What magic did you work?" she asked her husband.

"I may have told him that he could play Super Baby Smash on my game console." He winked at her. "But it worked."

Matty ran up to Sonny and tackled him. They rolled away from each other, pretending to be dinosaurs as they snarled and fought with their invisible tails.

Shauna breezed into the back door, dragging Luke with her. "Okay, okay. We're here. Now let's hear that baby's name."

Marvin didn't know that Shauna had known the baby's new name since she had placed it on the online form. When Ketron came home after leaving Gail and Jeremy at the old Renfro property, Marvin had been waiting for her. He had tearfully begged her to stay with him, and he had promised to be a better husband and father. He told Ketron that he would accept Amelia's name change, and if she wanted, he would start referring to Sonny as *Zeke* or *Ezekiel*.

Ketron had embraced her husband's apology. "I think we should start calling Amelia the name on her new birth certificate, but I don't think you should change how you address Sonny," she had told him.

He seemed grateful for her forgiveness, and he had been a good husband and father. He still played video games, but he did it after the children had fallen asleep at night. During the evening, he kicked the soccer ball with Bonnie, had dinosaur battles with Sonny, watched the Berry Batch Buddies with Nora and Winslow, and even changed Amelia's diaper when Ketron was busy.

Ketron and Marvin exchanged a glance. He shrugged. "All the family's here."

"Now that I know I'm family." Shauna put an arm around Ketron and brought her close. "You should have told me sooner."

Shauna released her and leaned into Luke's chest. Luke pointed at his wife and then at Ketron. "I would never have guessed that you two were cousins."

Nora, tired of listening to grownup chit-chat, jumped up and down and chanted. "What's the baby's new name?"

Ketron glanced at Marvin and was happy to see him beaming down at their growing group. He placed one hand on Amelia, and the other hand on Ketron's waist. They had more than one announcement, but they could share their other news after dinner. He met his wife's eyes and nodded, giving her his consent. Ketron was consumed with the love of her children, and the fresh start between her husband and their group. His red-rimmed lids had been replaced with a healthy attitude and a new mantra that embodied family togetherness. She could almost feel Solomon's hand on her back, giving her support with his ethereal touch.

On the day Ketron had decided to rename her, the baby's new name had flashed in front of her eyes. It was almost supernatural. The name seemed even more fitting now, as it represented something they all needed. She stared down at her baby and announced, "Her name is Grace."

Chapter Sixty-Three

Present

Seven months later, Marvin paced beside the hospital bed. Bonnie stood beside her mother, reminding her to breathe between contractions. "I thought you'd done this before," she teased her stepfather.

"It's never easy to see the person you love in pain," Marvin told her, taking Ketron's other hand.

Two quick pushes later, cries filled the air, and both parents breathed a sigh of relief. Bonnie took out her phone to message Shauna about the baby's birth.

"It's a girl!" the doctor announced, handing the slippery infant to Ketron.

Marvin begged to hold her, but Ketron couldn't stop looking at her baby's perfect features. Every part of the infant was beautifully symmetrical, from her arched eyebrows to her dimpled chin.

"What should we call her?" Ketron asked her husband.

"Oh, no!" He held up his hands. "You did all the work, so you should name her."

Ketron appreciated the sentiment. During her pregnancy, she had been diagnosed with a condition called hyperemesis gravidarum, and she had vomited at least once a day throughout the pregnancy. Marvin had been attentive and empathetic, respecting her decision to keep the baby's gender a secret until her birth. They had tossed around a few names but never settled on one.

Ketron considered a couple of the choices as she passed the baby to Marvin. He only held her for a few minutes before she was whisked away by the assigned nurse to spend some time under the radiant warmer. Bonnie followed the nurse, snapping pictures with the camera on her phone as the infant was weighed, measured, and given a brief exam.

A team of three nurses worked as the baby cried. At first, she released little lamb-like sounds, but then she began shrieking.

Ketron asked her husband for her overnight bag, and she dug out a new pacifier. "Please give this to her," she begged, holding it out to the nurses.

The labor and delivery nurse replied to her kindly without looking up. "You can give it to her in just a minute."

Ketron started to get anxious about her baby's screams. Maybe she was overstimulated by the experience, or part of her remembered a labor and delivery experience that had ended with the death of one of her sons. She looked at Marvin, pleading with him with her eyes.

He picked up on her silent cue. "Can I just give it to her?"

He reached for the pacifier, but when Ketron tried to hand it to him, it wasn't in her hand. She pulled at the sheet beneath her and felt around her body, but it was gone. The screams subsided, bringing peace to the room.

The nurse had just checked the baby's spine, and she flipped her over. "That was pretty slick," she commented, staring at Bonnie. "How did you get it in her mouth without me seeing you?"

Bonnie stared at the nurse, shaking her head. The nurse gave her a knowing smile and returned to caring for the baby.

Gooseflesh lifted across Ketron's arm. She looked at Marvin, and he stared back before directing his gaze back to the newest addition to their family.

Once swaddled, a nurse gave the baby back to Ketron. She sucked on the pacifier contentedly.

The nurse stood over Ketron for a moment, admiring the newborn. "That's a very strong sucking reflex."

Ketron studied her baby in wonder. *How had she gotten the pacifier?*

Ketron didn't want to think about Grace's trances and the pictures she drew after one of them. At times, she was physically in the house with her family, but her mind was somewhere else. She hadn't been the same since Ketron found her in the basement. Ketron thought she had been traumatized and had sought help from a play therapist, but Grace appeared happy and well-adjusted to everyone outside of their home. No one else saw the far-away looks that haunted Ketron.

"So, what's her name, Mom?" Bonnie asked.

There would be plenty of time to talk herself out of what had happened. Ketron reminded herself that the Winslow, Nora, Sonny, and Grace had developed their gifts over time, and a newborn couldn't possibly exhibit powers of apportation. Could she?

Ketron pushed thoughts of other-worldly abilities away and returned to the moment. She looked at her infant and decided on a name that paid tribute to someone who had played a much larger role in her life than she had realized until a few months ago. The newborn continued to rest and give intermittent sucks to her pacifier as Ketron told Marvin and Bonnie, "I've decided to call her Gail."

The Man Who Chose Not to be My Father

Yancy Williams II,

I threw away three pages of notebook paper before I settled on what I should call you. I decided it didn't matter. After all, how many times did my name pass your lips? My guess is that you only spoke about me to my therapist.

By the way, thanks for that. He may have helped me work through some hard times in my life, but I feel worse now that he's shown his true colors. I guess people like the two of you are cut from the same cloth. He wanted money from you, and you wanted your wife's money.

How did that work out? Did you enjoy raising children that may or may not have been yours? Yeah, I know. It's a low blow. But you abandoned me, so a verbal sucker punch is the least I can do.

Did you even know how to pronounce my name? The e is short, and my name is derived from a Viking-Scottish word that means true victory. I plan to live up to my name, especially where you are concerned. After this letter, I will send my thoughts about you into the darkness, where, more than likely, you wonder alone.

How many times did I enter your mind? I think Shaun forced you to remember I existed. My mother may have been upset that he brought you into their conversations, but I bet he didn't let you escape thoughts about the girl you impregnated and the child you abandoned either. I'd say that the real reason you cut ties with him was because you didn't want to be reminded that you'd left a child behind with a mentally unstable person.

In fact, you never contributed a dime of your precious money until the state demanded a blood test from you. You signed your parental rights away so fast that the ink was still wet when you left the office.

I used to wonder if you ever secretly watched me. I used to leave little notes under rocks in hopes that you would find them. I was a good child, and in my mind, I thought you could take me home with you. I believed your wife would grow to love me, and her children and I could play together. As Winslow says, though, "Whatever."

Oh, yeah. I'm a mother, but that doesn't make you a grandfather. You don't deserve the title. That tiny bit of money you sent was simply child support in arrears.

I'm a parent, and I just can't understand why you never wanted to meet me. My mother wasn't a good person, but what was so bad about me that you couldn't call me and wish me a happy birthday, a merry Christmas, or ask me if I was okay after my mother tried to kill me?

Yeah, about that. My mother tried to bury me alive before I was as old as she was when you got her pregnant. You knew about her disease, and you didn't even bother to check on me. You may be roasting in the fires of Hell for that one, and if you are, then turn over and get crispy on the other side. You can probably high-five my mother when you do it. Most likely, she's sandwiched between Genghis Kahn and Charles Manson.

Did you ever wonder why I never tried to reach out to you? I didn't even try to look you up on social media. I used to think it was because I didn't want to see how much I looked like you. My mother told me we had dimples and blue eyes in common. But now I think I avoided you because you didn't want me. It was clear. I got the message, and you didn't even have to say it.

I'm supposed to say that I forgive you, but I can't find a reason to do that. I think I'll be mad at you a little longer. If anyone asks me why I can't let it go, I'll just blame my anger on raging postpartum hormones.

So, rest in peace. I hope you don't feel like I'm part of your unfinished business or anything. I don't want to see your ghost in the wee hours of the morning.

This letter is my farewell. I hope you had a good life. Thanks for leaving me with a crazy mother, and I appreciate the sessions you allowed me to have with the psychiatrist you paid. I'm sure he reported all my private thoughts to you. I hope you enjoyed them.

I'm going to go hug my children now. They'll hug me back, and when they tell me they love me, I won't be sad anymore. They are the light of my life, and I will never leave them.

Goodbye, Yancy Williams II. Go into the darkness.

Sincerely,

Ketron Renfro Gouge

Did You Like This Book?

If you enjoyed this story, would you please write a review on Amazon, Goodreads, and/or BookBub? Something as simple as "I liked it!" helps the author so much! Your feedback can make the book more visible to other readers, and it gives the author a reason to dance a jig when she sees your review!

You can sign up for Courtnee's newsletter, and you will receive exclusive bonus content, like cover reveals, sales, and news about upcoming releases.

Thank you for reading Solomon's Tears!

About the Author

Courtnee Turner Hoyle is the author of the award-winning My Brother's Keeper. She also penned the Pale Woods Mystery Series, It's About Time Series, and the Rasputin's Dynasty Trilogy. Courtnee lives in Northeast Tennessee with her children. She graduated with two undergraduate degrees and a Master of Arts in Teaching from East Tennessee State University. Courtnee enjoys reading, writing, and any reasonable music. She spends her days in comfortable chaos, avoiding sweet tea, chocolate, and unannounced visitors. Follow her on Instagram @pale_woods_mysteries and visit her website: www.courtneeturnerhoyle.com

Deleted Chapter

"Kill your darlings, kill your darlings, even when it breaks your egocentric little scribbler's heart, kill your darlings." **- Stephen King, On Writing: A Memoir of the Craft**

"Your gills?'

"Yeah," Sonny replied, rubbing his sides.

The older kids roared with laughter. "Those are your *ribs*," the meanest one of them lectured. "You're just a dumb baby."

Ketron listened without reacting. She hoped Sonny would handle the situation on his own, but she worried that the other kids might get rough with him. She turned slowly under the guise of reaching for a wipe out of the diaper bag. Two boys Winslow's age lightly pushed around Sonny on a platform before the swinging bridge.

"I—I am not a baby," Sonny asserted, stepping onto the swinging bridge. When his foot fell against the moving wood, his knees buckled. He lunged forward, grabbing for support, and he bumped his nose on a wooden post. Immediately, he began to wail, and Ketron jumped up, ready to help her injured son.

"See," the oldest boy jeered. "I told you he was a baby! Cry baby!"

"Cry baby!" the other boy echoed.

Winslow and Nora made it to Sonny before Ketron. Nora comforted her brother, and Winslow faced the bullies. "He's four years old, Tony!" he yelled at the oldest one.

"Look! It's another cry baby!" the boy beside Tony laughed.

"You should talk," Winslow addressed the boy. "You used to cry all the time when people made fun of your name, *Kelly*."

Kelly pushed Winslow into Sonny, and Sonny sobbed. Nora tried to drag her younger brother away, and Tony joined the fight by pushing Winslow again.

"Enough!" They turned their wide-eyed stares to Ketron. "Where are your mothers?"

They pointed to a bench on the far side of the playground. The older boys were the only other children on the playground, and Ketron wondered why their mothers had chosen to sit on a bench so far away. Ketron assessed Sonny's and Winslow's injuries, daring the other boys to move. When Sonny's cries turned to intermittent sobs, she grabbed his hand and led the group over to the other side of the playground.

Ketron second-guessed her plan when she saw Tony's and Kelly's mothers huddled together, passing a cigarette between themselves. They were chatting loudly, cracking their gum between sentences. Their bottle blonde heads bobbed, and they clacked long acrylic nails against the bench. One of them was older and louder than the other one, and her tanned face showcased more lines around her lips than her eyes. Her big brown eyes matched Tony's, so Ketron assumed she was his mother.

"Hello."

They dropped their smiles when they turned to her, simultaneously leery and apathetic. "What do you want?" the older one asked.

Ketron was surprised by their reactions, especially since she had their children in tow. "I'm sorry to interrupt your conversation, but I had to break up a fight just now."

"So?" the younger one said. She flipped her hair over her shoulder and turned her attention to her purse. She fished out another cigarette. "What do you want us to do about it?"

Ketron was going to walk away until she saw Kelly smirk. "Your boys were terrorizing my four-year-old."

"Oh, yeah," the older one said. "Tony harasses his little brother all the time. It just toughens him up."

"Well, he hurt Sonny pretty badly."

"What?" Tony chuckled. "Your name is *Sonny*?" The boys guffawed and their mothers forced a laugh to show solidarity.

Ketron realized she was fighting a losing battle. "Look. Just keep your boys away from mine."

"It's a free playground," Tony's mother said, shrugging her shoulders. "My boy can do whatever he wants."

"Mine too," the younger mother echoed.

"Well, I'm sure they'll make fine inmates one day," Ketron commented before she turned on her heel, dragging Sonny with her and expecting Nora and Winslow to follow her.

"So they just get away with it?" Winslow called after her. "Stand up for us, Mom!"

Ketron rounded on him. "That may be okay for children, but in the real world, adults who fight get put in jail."

"But they didn't care!" Winslow pointed to where Tony and Kelly stood. Ketron noted that their mothers were yelling at them to leave them alone and go play. "Sonny was so scared."

Ketron softened her voice. All Winslow wanted was justice for the harm he'd witnessed. "Honey, those women weren't going to listen to us. They live in a different environment, and that's how they deal with problems."

"But they got away with it," Winslow insisted.

Ketron glanced at the cars in the parking lot and made a reflexive decision. Her minivan was parked next to a truck. The man who owned it had unloaded his mountain bike and pedaled away when they had arrived. The other vehicle in the lot was an older model black Honda with racing stickers on the back window. Ketron was pretty sure it belonged to one of the women.

She stopped at her van. "Wait here with your siblings," Ketron instructed Winslow, wishing Bonnie was with her instead of at her father's house. She took the baby with her, unlocking the doors to her van with the key fob while walking to the Honda. She positioned her house key in her fist between her first and second fingers and angled it to scratch the side of the car.

"Please don't," said a small voice.

Ketron jumped at the sound and noticed a boy around Sonny's age peeking around the side of the car. When they locked eyes, he moved into full view. He had the same eyes and build as Tony, so Ketron assumed he was his younger brother.

"It's all we have left," he continued, nodding to the car. "My dad sold all our other stuff."

Ketron closed her eyes and sighed. She shouldn't have been so quick to pass judgement on the women, especially since she had told her son that they came from a different situation. "I'm not going to damage the car," she told the worried child.

"What's your name?"

The boy looked at his feet and drew a circle with one of his worn sneakers. Ketron noticed bruises along his arms and circling his wrists. "Christian."

"Hey, Christian. I have an idea." The boy looked up hopefully. "Do you see that little blonde boy over there?" She pointed at Sonny and Christian nodded. "Could you be his friend?"

"But I don't know him."

"Are you starting school soon?" Ketron asked. Christian nodded again. "Then you could talk to him on the first day of school. His nickname is Sonny, so the teacher might say Ezekiel when she calls his name. He's a little shy, but I have a feeling that you would be the perfect friend for him."

Christian smiled. "It can be our secret?"

"Yes," Ketron answered. "Now, I'm going to back my van up soon, and I don't want to hit you by mistake, so can you go play by your mother?"

Christian bolted for the playground, but his smile lingered on her heart. She wished that she could take him with her and give him the life he deserved.

"What did you do, Mom?" Winslow asked when she got to the van.

She buckled Amelia and shook her head. "I was going to do something wrong, but Christian stopped me."

"Who's Christian?" Nora asked.

"A very nice boy," she answered, looking at Sonny.

Acknowledgements

It takes a village to raise a writer, especially an introverted one!

I appreciate the continued support of my eldest children. Tosha maintains my website and claims that I'm her favorite author, Stereling pretends to be excited over my small accomplishments, and Legacee will look at amazing cover designs-as long as she's the first person to see them!

My younger children inspired the interactions between the siblings, but they don't mirror the children in this book. Although, Journee claims she can see her actions reflected in Winslow.

My mama introduced me to some of my best friends: books! Thank you, Mama!

When I was a young adult, I had a good friend. There are many reasons for a relationship to end, but I'm so glad I knew her. Some of the things that altered the course of our friendship can be found in the pages of this book. There's a story in every experience, and I'm glad I had such a wonderful friend.

Thank you, Stephen King, for writing the novels that shaped me into a young writer. You can reach out anytime!

Did you see the cover? It's absolutely fantastic! Thank you, Taylor Dawn, for your amazing graphic design!

My ARC readers are wonderful! They help me so much with reassuring words and insightful reviews. I appreciate them so much!

Thank you, Tina Hogan Grant and TATTERED PAGES Facebook page. I truly appreciate the mentorship I have received from Tina and the support the members of TATTERED PAGES have shown me.

I appreciate all libraries and the people who work in them. Go find your next adventure in your local library!

Readers, you are the reason I can continue writing. Thank you for reading my story!

Ketron's Cheesy Butter Noodle Recipe

Total Time: 20-25 minutes

Ingredients

- Spaghetti noodles or angel hair pasta (you should be able to stand the proper amount in the center of the palm of your hand)

- 8 slices of cheese*

- 1/4 stick of butter**

Procedure

1. Boil the noodles in a pot of water until desired texture

2. Drain the water from the pasta into a colander

3. Dump the pasta back into the pot and place on the stove

4. Immediately add the butter, stirring until melted throughout pasta

5. Add the cheese, turning up the heat on the stove as you do so

6. Continue to stir until the cheese is melted but not burnt

7. Allow to cool and enjoy!

*American cheese seems to work best for this recipe, but you may use any cheese you desire. Vegan cheese may also be substituted.
**Ketron uses vegan butter, but most butters will satisfy the recipe.

More of Courtnee's Titles

Available Now!

Pale Woods Mystery Series, Book One

My Brother's Keeper
Courtnee Turner Hoyle

Seventeen-year-old Jerrod Miller has struggled with the guilt of his actions for an event that took place almost a year ago. His friends have abandoned him, his family ignores him, and he lost his best friend. To make matters worse, he was unable to access records that may have revealed his father's whereabouts. His sister, Ella, guides Jerrod as he tries to learn and accept secrets his family has tried to hide. However, a sinister spirit may be influencing Ella's actions, and it has an agenda of its own.

Sold on Amazon or on the author's website.

More of Courtnee's Titles

Coming October 2022!

Hollis's Hobby

Can you trust your lover?

After an abusive childhood and soul-splitting heartbreak, Hollis hovers around her hometown, secretly killing the men who are unfortunate enough to fall for her charms, until her lonely friend, Josie, asks Hollis to move in with her. Hollis attempts to drop "Holli", the alter ego who dispatches her unsuspecting lovers, but she finds it difficult to function as a teacher when she sees the evidence of abuse on the people she values. In an effort to veer away from her murderous path, Hollis forms a relationship with the father of one of her students, Quillen, but he's running from a secret Hollis may not understand.

Hollis's sad and twisted past has never been unearthed, but will Quillen's influence cause her to dig up details that could risk her capture? When all Hollis's secrets threaten to come to the surface, will she continue to live under the guise she's created, or will Hollis's hobby be revealed?

Coming October 2022!